Dark Storm

Titles by Christine Feehan

SAMURAI GAME
RUTHLESS GAME
STREET GAME
MURDER GAME
PREDATORY GAME
DEADLY GAME
CONSPIRACY GAME
NIGHT GAME
MIND GAME
SHADOW GAME

HIDDEN CURRENTS
TURBULENT SEA
SAFE HARBOR
DANGEROUS TIDES
OCEANS OF FIRE

SAVAGE NATURE
WILD FIRE
BURNING WILD
WILD RAIN

SPIRIT BOUND
WATER BOUND

DARK STORM
DARK PREDATOR
DARK PERIL
DARK SLAYER
DARK CURSE
DARK HUNGER
DARK POSSESSION
DARK CELEBRATION
DARK DEMON
DARK SECRET
DARK DESTINY
DARK MELODY
DARK SYMPHONY
DARK GUARDIAN
DARK LEGEND
DARK FIRE
DARK CHALLENGE
DARK MAGIC
DARK GOLD
DARK DESIRE
DARK PRINCE

Anthologies

DARKEST AT DAWN
(includes Dark Hunger *and* Dark Secret*)*

SEA STORM
(includes Magic in the Wind *and* Oceans of Fire*)*

FEVER
(includes The Awakening *and* Wild Rain*)*

FANTASY
(with Emma Holly, Sabrina Jeffries, and Elda Minger)

LOVER BEWARE
(with Fiona Brand, Katherine Sutcliffe, and Eileen Wilks)

HOT BLOODED
(with Maggie Shayne, Emma Holly, and Angela Knight)

eSpecials

"DARK HUNGER" from HOT BLOODED
"THE AWAKENING" from FEVER

DARK STORM

A CARPATHIAN NOVEL

CHRISTINE FEEHAN

BERKLEY BOOKS, NEW YORK

THE BERKLEY PUBLISHING GROUP
Published by the Penguin Group
Penguin Group (USA) Inc.
375 Hudson Street, New York, New York 10014, USA
Penguin Group (Canada), 90 Eglinton Avenue East, Suite 700, Toronto, Ontario M4P 2Y3, Canada (a division of Pearson Penguin Canada Inc.) • Penguin Books Ltd., 80 Strand, London WC2R 0RL, England • Penguin Group Ireland, 25 St. Stephen's Green, Dublin 2, Ireland (a division of Penguin Books Ltd.) • Penguin Group (Australia), 250 Camberwell Road, Camberwell, Victoria 3124, Australia (a division of Pearson Australia Group Pty. Ltd.) • Penguin Books India Pvt. Ltd., 11 Community Centre, Panchsheel Park, New Delhi—110 017, India • Penguin Group (NZ), 67 Apollo Drive, Rosedale, Auckland 0632, New Zealand (a division of Pearson New Zealand Ltd.) • Penguin Books (South Africa) (Pty.) Ltd., 24 Sturdee Avenue, Rosebank, Johannesburg 2196, South Africa

Penguin Books Ltd., Registered Offices: 80 Strand, London WC2R 0RL, England

This book is an original publication of The Berkley Publishing Group.

Cover design by George Long.
Cover handlettering by Ron Zinn.
Cover photographs by Thinkstock and Shutterstock.
Endpaper design by Diana Kolsky; images by Shutterstock.

FIRST EDITION: October 2012

Library of Congress Cataloging-in-Publication Data

Feehan, Christine.
Dark storm : a Carpathian novel / Christine Feehan.—1st ed.
p. cm.
ISBN 978-0-425-25580-3 (alk. paper)
1. Vampires—Fiction. 2. South America—Fiction. 3. Romantic suspense fiction. I. Title.
PS3606.E36D3898 2013
813'.6—dc23
2012028952

PRINTED IN THE UNITED STATES OF AMERICA

10 9 8 7 6 5 4 3 2 1

For three amazing people
who came through when I needed them most:
Brian Feehan, Domini Stottsberry
and Cheryl Wilson—
with much love and many thanks.

For My Readers

Be sure to go to http://www.christinefeehan.com/members/ to sign up for my private book announcement list and download the free eBook of *Dark Desserts*. Join my community and get firsthand news, enter the book discussions, ask your questions and chat with me. Please feel free to email me at Christine@christinefeehan.com. I would love to hear from you.

Acknowledgments

There would be no *Dark Storm* without Brian Feehan, Cheryl Wilson or Domini Stottsberry. They worked long hours to help me with everything from brainstorming ideas and scenes to doing research and edits. There are no words to describe my gratitude or love for them. My sister, Anita Toste, always answers my call for aid in strange rituals. I just have to include Dr. Christopher Tong, who always finds the time in his crazy busy schedule to come to my aid whenever I ask. And a special thanks to Dr. Newell for all of his support. Thank you all so very much!

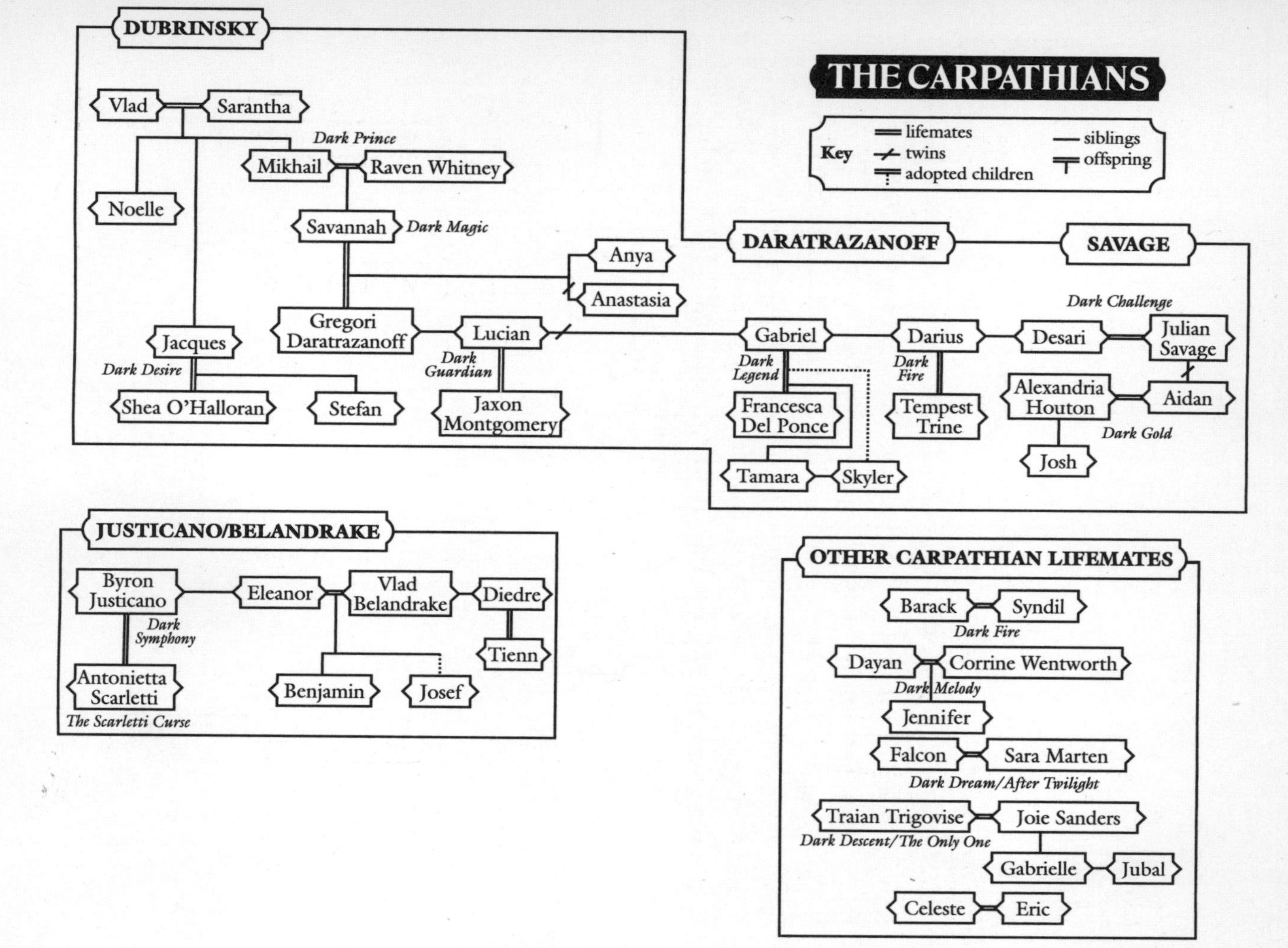
THE CARPATHIANS
Key
lifemates
twins
adopted children
siblings
offspring
DUBRINSKY
Vlad
Sarantha
Noelle
Mikhail
Raven Whitney
Dark Prince
Savannah
Dark Magic
Jacques
Dark Desire
Shea O'Halloran
Stefan
Gregori Daratrazanoff
Anya
Anastasia
Lucian
Dark Guardian
Jaxon Montgomery
DARATRAZANOFF
SAVAGE
Gabriel
Dark Legend
Francesca Del Ponce
Tamara
Skyler
Darius
Dark Fire
Tempest Trine
Desari
Julian Savage
Dark Challenge
Alexandria Houton
Aidan
Dark Gold
Josh
JUSTICANO/BELANDRAKE
Byron Justicano
Dark Symphony
Antonietta Scarletti
The Scarletti Curse
Eleanor
Vlad Belandrake
Diedre
Tienn
Benjamin
Josef
OTHER CARPATHIAN LIFEMATES
Barack
Syndil
Dark Fire
Dayan
Corrine Wentworth
Dark Melody
Jennifer
Falcon
Sara Marten
Dark Dream/After Twilight
Traian Trigovise
Joie Sanders
Dark Descent/The Only One
Gabrielle
Jubal
Celeste
Eric

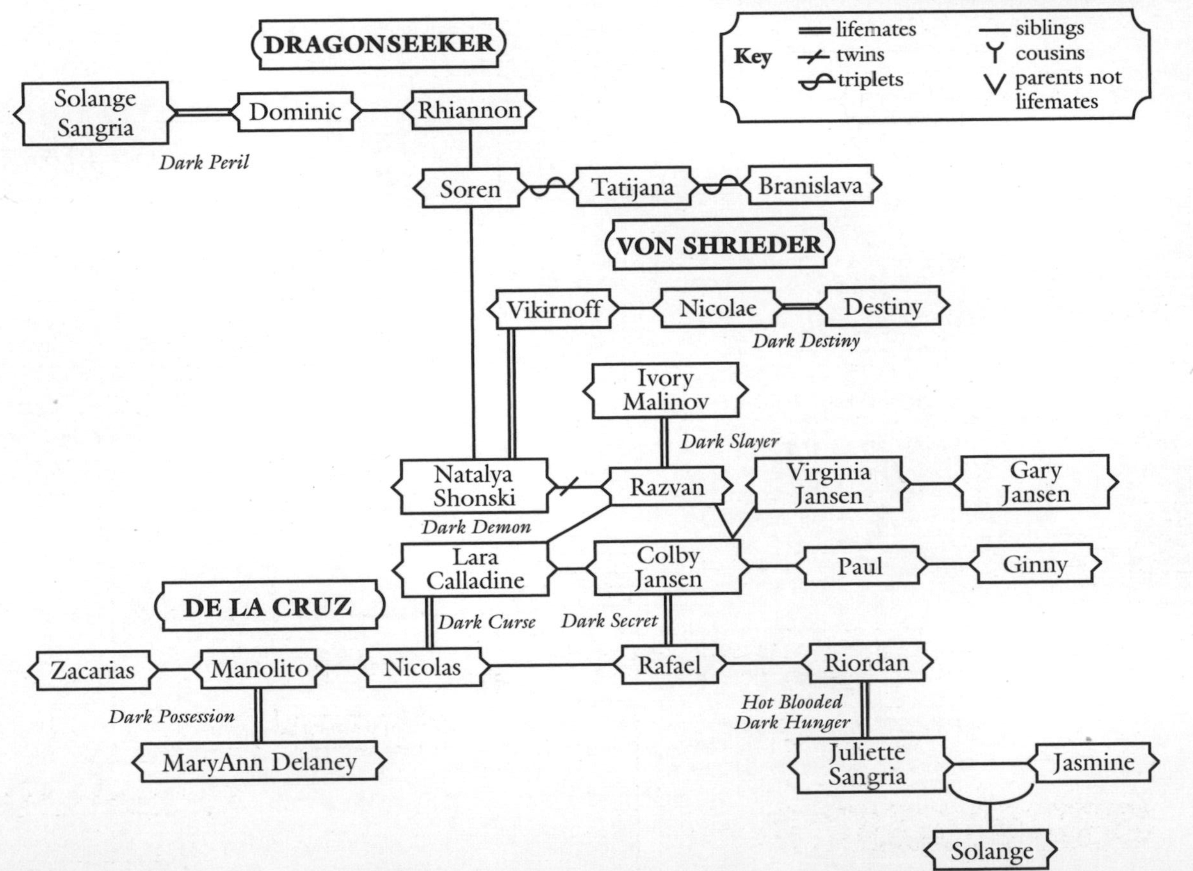
THE CARPATHIANS
Key
lifemates
twins
triplets
siblings
cousins
parents not lifemates
DRAGONSEEKER
Solange Sangria
Dominic
Rhiannon
Dark Peril
Soren
Tatijana
Branislava
VON SHRIEDER
Vikirnoff
Nicolae
Destiny
Dark Destiny
Ivory Malinov
Dark Slayer
Natalya Shonski
Razvan
Virginia Jansen
Gary Jansen
Dark Demon
Lara Calladine
Colby Jansen
Paul
Ginny
DE LA CRUZ
Dark Curse
Dark Secret
Zacarias
Manolito
Nicolas
Rafael
Riordan
Dark Possession
Hot Blooded
Dark Hunger
MaryAnn Delaney
Juliette Sangria
Jasmine
Solange

DARK STORM

I

"I can live with being on a small boat with no privacy for seven long days, the sun turning me into lobster girl, and mosquitoes feasting on me, I really can," Riley Parker informed her mother. "But I swear to you, if I hear one more complaint or disgusting sexual innuendo from Mr. I'm-So-Hot-Every-Woman-Should-Bow-Down-To-Me, I'm just going to shove the idiot overboard. His constant licking his lips and saying he likes the idea of mother and daughter gives me the creeps."

Riley cast a glance of pure loathing at Don Weston, the annoying idiot in question. She'd met a lot of narcissistic pigs while earning her doctorate in linguistics, and a few more among the faculty at University of California, Berkeley, where she now taught, but he took the cake. He was a great brute of a man, with wide shoulders, a barrel chest and an attitude of superiority that irked Riley. Even if she wasn't already so much on edge, the presence of that awful man would have made her so. Worse, her mother was very fragile right now, making Riley extremely protective of her, and his constant sexual innuendos and filthy jokes around her mother made her want to just shove him overboard.

Annabel Parker, a renowned horticulturalist famous for her efforts to reestablish thousands of acres of Brazilian rain forest lost to deforestation, looked at her daughter, dark brown eyes twinkling and mouth twitching, obviously itching to smile. "Unfortunately, honey, we're in piranha territory."

"That's the point, Mom." Riley cast another pointed glare in Weston's direction.

The only benefit of the horrible man's presence was that plotting his demise gave her something to focus on other than chills slowly spreading through her body and making the hair on the back of her neck stand up.

She and her mother made this same trip up the Amazon once every five years, but this year from the moment they had arrived in the village to find their usual guide ill, Riley felt as if a dark cloud hung over the trip. Even now, a strange heaviness, an aura of danger, seemed to be following them up the river. She'd tried hard to shrug it off, but the ominous feeling remained, a weight pressing down on her, chills creeping down her spine and ugly suspicions keeping her awake at night.

"Perhaps if I could accidentally cut his hand as he goes overboard . . ." she continued with a dark smile. Her students could have warned the man to beware when she smiled like that. It never boded well. The smile faded a little, though, as she glanced down at the murky water and saw the silver fish churning around the boat. Were her eyes playing tricks on her? It almost looked as if piranha were following the boat. But, piranha didn't follow boats. They went about their business.

She stole a glance at the guide who muttered to the two porters, Raul and Capa, ignoring their charges—a far cry from the familiar villager who usually took them upriver. The three looked very uneasy as they continually studied the water. They, too, seemed a little more alarmed than usual about being surrounded by a swarm of flesh-eating fish. She was being silly. She'd been on this same trip many times before without freaking out over the local wildlife. Her imagination was working overtime. Still . . . piranha seemed to be all around their boat, but she couldn't see a single flash of silver in the waters surrounding the boat chugging ahead of them.

"Ruthless child," Annabel scolded with a small laugh, drawing Riley's attention back to the aggravating presence of Don Weston.

"It's the way he looks at us," Riley griped. The humidity was so high that every shirt Riley wore clung to her like a second skin. She had full curves, and there was no hiding them. She didn't dare raise her hands to lift her thick, braided hair off the back of her neck or he would think she was deliberately enticing him. "I really, *really*, want to smack that oaf. He stares at my breasts like he's never seen a pair, which is bad enough, but when he stares at yours . . ."

"Maybe he hasn't ever seen breasts, dear," Annabel said softly.

Riley tried to smother a laugh. Her mother could ruin a perfectly good mad with her sense of humor. "Well if he hasn't, it's for good reason. He's disgusting."

Behind them, Don Weston slapped his neck and hissed out a slow, angry breath. "Damn insects. Mack, where the hell is the bug spray?"

Riley suppressed an eye roll. As far as she was concerned, Don Weston and the other two engineers with him were liars—well at least two of the three were. They claimed to know what they were doing in the forest, but it was clear neither Weston nor Mack Shelton, his constant companion, had a clue. She and her mother had both tried to tell Weston and his friends that their precious bug spray would do no good. The men were sweating profusely, which washed off the insect repellent as fast as they could apply it and left them feeling sticky and itchy. Scratching only aggravated the itching and invited infection. The smallest wound could quickly become infected in the rain forest.

Shelton, a compact man with burnt mahogany skin and rippling muscles, swatted at his own neck and then his chest, murmuring obscenities. "You threw it overboard, you big bastard, after you used the last of it."

Shelton was a little friendlier than the other two engineers and not quite as obnoxious as Weston, but instead of making Riley feel safer, his proximity actually made her skin prickle. Maybe that was because his smile never reached his eyes. And because he watched everything and everyone on board. Riley had the feeling Weston vastly underestimated the other man. Clearly Weston thought himself in charge of their mining expedition, but no one was bossing Shelton.

"We should never have thrown in with them," Riley murmured to her mother, keeping her voice low. Normally, Riley and her mother made the trip to the volcano alone, but when they'd arrived at the village, they found their regular guide too sick to travel. Alone in the middle of the Amazon, without a guide to accompany them to their destination, she and her mother decided to team up with three other groups traveling upriver.

Weston and his two fellow mining engineers had been in the village prepping a trip to the edge of the Andes in Peru, in search of potential new mines for the corporation they worked for. Two men researching a supposedly extinct plant had arrived from Europe seeking a guide to go up a mountain in the Andes as well. An archaeologist and his two grad students were heading to the Andes looking for a rumored lost city of the Cloud People—the Chachapoyas. All of them had decided to pool their resources and travel upriver together. The idea seemed logical at the time, but now, a week into the journey, Riley heartily regretted the decision.

Two of the guides, the archaeologist and his students and three porters were in the lead boat just ahead of them with a good deal of the supplies. Annabel, Riley, the researchers and the three mining engineers were in the second boat with one of their guides, Pedro, and two porters, Capa and Raul.

Trapped on the boat with eight strangers, Riley didn't feel safe. She wished they were already halfway up the mountain, where the plan was to go their separate ways, each with their own guide.

Annabel shrugged. "It's a little too late for second thoughts. We made the decision to travel together and we're stuck with these people. We'll make the best of it."

That was her mother, always calm in the face of a brewing storm. Riley was no psychic, but it didn't take one to predict trouble was coming. That feeling was growing with every passing hour. She glanced at her mother. As usual, she appeared serene. Riley felt a little silly saying she was worried when Annabel had so many other things on her mind.

Still bickering about the discarded bug spray, Weston flipped Shelton the finger. "The can was empty. There must be more."

"It wasn't empty," Shelton corrected, disgust in his voice. "You just wanted to chuck something at that caiman."

"And your aim was as bad as your mouth," the third engineer, Ben Charger, chimed in.

Ben was the quietest of the bunch. He never stopped looking around with restless eyes. Riley hadn't quite made up her mind about him. He was the most ordinary looking of the three engineers. He was average height, average weight, a face no one would notice. He blended, and maybe that made her uncomfortable. Nothing about him stood out. He moved quietly and seemed to simply appear out of nowhere, and he watched everything and everyone as if he were expecting trouble. She didn't believe he was a partner with Weston and Shelton. The other two stuck together and obviously had known one another for some time. Charger appeared to be a loner. Riley wasn't even certain he liked either of the other two men.

Off to the left shore, her eye picked up a white cloud, moving fast, sometimes iridescent, sometimes a pearly color as the cloud twisted together, forming a blanket of living insects.

"Fuck you, Charger," Weston snapped.

"Watch your mouth," Charger advised, his voice very low.

Weston actually stepped back, his face paling a little. He glanced around the boat, his gaze settling on Riley, whom he caught looking at him. "Why don't you come over here, or better yet, Mommy come here and lick the sweat off me? Maybe that will help." He extended his tongue toward her, probably hoping to look sexy, but he got a mouthful of bugs and ended up coughing and swearing.

For one terrible moment, when he called her mother "Mommy" and made his gross suggestion, Riley thought she might hurl herself at him and really push him overboard. But then, with her mother's little snicker, her anger was gone, her unfortunate sense of humor kicking in. She burst out laughing. "Seriously? Are you really so arrogant you don't know I'd rather lick the sweat off a monkey? You are just *so* gross."

Out of the corner of her eye, she caught sight of the pearly cloud of insects growing closer, widening as they moved in formation over the water. Her stomach gave a little flip of fear. She forced air through her lungs. She wasn't one to scare easily, not even when she'd been a child.

Weston leered at her. "I can see when a woman wants me, and baby, you can't take your eyes off of me. Look at your clothes! You're showing off for me." He flicked his tongue at her again, looking for all the world like a snake.

"Leave her the hell alone, Weston," Jubal Sanders snapped, impatience edging his voice. "Don't you ever get tired of the sound of your voice?"

One of the two men researching plants, Jubal didn't appear to be a man who spent a lot of time in a lab. He looked extremely fit and there was no doubt that he was a man used to a rugged, outdoor life. He carried himself with absolute confidence and moved like a man who could handle himself.

His traveling companion, Gary Jansen, looked more the part of the lab rat, shorter and slender, although very well muscled from what Riley had observed. He was very strong. He wore black-rimmed reading glasses, but he seemed every bit as adept outdoors as Jubal. The two kept strictly to themselves at the beginning of the journey, but somewhere around the fourth day, Jubal became a little protective of the women, staying close whenever the engineers were around. He said little, but he didn't miss anything.

Although some other woman might be flattered by his protectiveness, Riley wasn't about to trust a man who supposedly lived his life in a lab, but moved with the fluid grace of a fighter. Both he and Gary clearly carried weapons. They were up to something, and whatever it was, Riley and her mother had enough trouble of their own without needing to get involved in anyone else's.

"Don't be a hero," Weston snapped at Jubal, "it won't get you the girl." He winked at Riley. "She's lookin' for a real man."

Riley felt another small surge of anger wash over her and she whipped around to glare at Weston, but her mother laid a gentle, restraining hand on her wrist and put her head close to whisper. "Don't bother, honey. He's feeling like a fish out of water out here."

Riley took a breath. At this late date, she wasn't going to resort to violence over sexual harassment no matter how much of an ass the man was. She could ignore Don Weston until they went their separate ways.

"I thought he was supposed to be so experienced," Riley answered her mother, her voice equally as soft. "They claim to be mining engineers who've traveled to the Andes countless times, but I'm betting they flew over the peaks and called that going into the rain forest. They probably don't have anything at all to do with mining."

Her mother gave a quick nod of agreement, warmth lighting her eyes all the same. "If they think this is bad, wait until we get into the jungle. They'll be falling out of their hammocks and forgetting to check each morning for venomous bugs crawling into their boots."

Riley couldn't help but smile at the thought. The three engineers were supposedly from a private company seeking prospective mines in the mineral-rich Andes. She couldn't see that any of them were very well versed in the ways of the rain forest, and they sure didn't give much respect to their guides.

All three complained, but Weston was the worst and most offensive with his constant sexual innuendoes. He spent a great deal of time snapping at the guides and porters as if they were servants when he wasn't complaining or leering at her and her mother.

"I raised you away from here, Riley. The men in some countries have a different philosophy toward women. We aren't considered their equal. Clearly he's been raised to believe women are objects, and because we've come out here alone, unescorted by a dozen family members, we're easy." Annabel shrugged, but the faint humor faded and her dark eyes went very somber. "Keep that dagger close, honey, just to be on the safe side. You know how to handle yourself."

Riley shivered. It was the first time Annabel had indicated she thought something was amiss as well. That moved Riley's fanciful notions from ridiculous right back into the realm of reality. Her mother was always calm, always practical. If she thought something was wrong, then it was.

A bird sounded in the forest on the riverbank, the noise traveling clearly across the open water. To lighten her mother's suddenly troubled mood, Riley cupped her hands around her mouth and repeated the call. She didn't get the delighted laughter she'd hoped for but her mother did smile and pat her hand.

"That's totally freaky how you can do that." Don Weston had left off slapping at bugs and was now staring at her like she was some carnival sideshow. "Can you imitate anything?"

Despite her dislike of the man, Riley shrugged. "Most things. Some people have photographic memories that let them remember anything they see or read. I call what I have 'phonographic' memory. I can remember and repeat virtually any sound I hear. That's one of the reasons I went into linguistics."

"That's quite a talent," Gary Jansen remarked.

"Isn't it?" Annabel slid an arm around Riley's waist. "When she was little, she used to imitate crickets chirping inside the house just to watch me go crazy trying to find them. And heaven help her father if he slipped up and used language he shouldn't in front of her. She could repeat it perfectly, right down to the pitch of his voice."

Riley's heart dropped at the sorrow and love in her mother's tone. She forced a little laugh. "I was also good at mimicking my teachers, the ones I wasn't particularly fond of," she volunteered with a small, mischievous grin. "I could call from school and tell Mom just what a wonderful student I was." Now her mother did laugh, and the sound filled Riley with relief.

To Riley, Annabel was beautiful. She was of medium height, slender, with dark wavy hair and darker eyes, flawless Spanish skin and a smile that made everyone around her want to smile. Riley was much taller, with bone-straight blue-black hair that grew almost overnight no matter how many times she cut it. She was very curvy, with high cheekbones and pale, nearly translucent skin. Her eyes were large and the color was nearly impossible to define—green, brown, Florentine gold. Her mother always said she was a throwback to a long-dead ancestor.

To her knowledge, her mother had never been sick a day in her life. She had no wrinkles, and Riley had never seen a single gray hair on her head. But now, for the first time, Riley saw vulnerability in her mother's eyes, and that was as unsettling as the crackling in the air signaling a coming storm. Riley's father had died only two weeks ago, and in their family, husband and wife rarely lived for very long without one another. Riley was determined to stick close to her mother. She could already sense Annabel pulling away, becoming more despondent by the day, but Riley was determined not to lose her. Not to grief, and not to whatever was hunting them on this trip.

Early morning had seen the last of the main river; the two boats were now traveling up a tributary toward their destination. In the reed-choked waters, the ever-present insects were getting worse by the moment. Clouds of bugs continually assaulted them. More rushed toward the boat as if scenting fresh blood. Weston and Shelton both went into a frenzy of cursing and slapping at exposed skin, although they both remembered to keep their mouths firmly closed after eating a mouthful of bugs. Ben Charger and the two researchers endured the insects stoically, following the example set by their guide and the porters.

The locals in their party didn't bother to even slap at the bugs as the pearly cloud descended en masse. Riley could see the boat ahead and they were even closer to the shore, yet as far as she could tell, the bugs hadn't attacked anyone aboard. Behind her, Annabel let out a soft startled cry. Riley spun around to find her mother completely enveloped in the cloud of insects.

They'd abandoned everyone else and every inch of Annabel's body was covered with what appeared to be tiny flakes of moving snow.

La Manta Blanca. Tiny midges. Some said tiny mosquitoes. Riley had never researched them, but she'd certainly felt their bites. They blazed like fire and afterward, the itch drove one crazy. Once scratched and open, the little bites became an invitation for infection. She dragged a blanket off the flat board seat and threw it over her mother, trying to smash the little bugs as she took her mother to the floor of the boat, rolling her as if she was putting out a fire.

"Get it off of her," Gary Jansen called. "You won't get them all that way."

He crouched down beside Annabel and yanked at the blanket. Annabel rolled back and forth, her hands covering her face, the insects attached to every bit of exposed skin, clinging to her hair and clothes. Many were smashed from Riley's efforts. She continued to slap at them, trying to save her mother from further bites.

Jubal snatched up a bucket of water and threw it over Annabel, brushing at the insects to get them off of her. The porters immediately added buckets of water, dousing her again and again, while Gary, Jubal and Riley scraped the soaked insects from her with the blanket. Ben eventually crouched down beside her and helped to pick the bugs from her skin.

Annabel shuddered violently, but she didn't make a sound. Her skin turned bright red, as a thousand tiny bites swelled into fiery blisters. Gary rummaged through a satchel he carried and drew out a small vial. He began smearing the clear liquid over the bites. It wasn't a small job as there were so many. Jubal held Annabel's arms pinned so that she couldn't scratch at the maddening itch spreading like waves across her body.

Riley clutched her mother's hand tightly, murmuring nonsense. Her previous suspicions came roaring back to life. The tiny little midges had gone straight for her mother. There was no one more attuned to the rain forest than Annabel. Plants grew abundant and lush around her. She whispered to them and they seemed to whisper back, embracing her as if she were Mother Earth. When her mother walked through the backyard at their home in California, Riley was fairly certain she could see the plants growing right in front of her. For the forest to begin attacking her, something was terribly wrong.

Annabel gripped Riley's hand tightly as the two researchers lifted her to her feet and helped her stumble back to their sleeping area made private by the sheets and netting hung across thin ropes.

"Thank you," Riley said to the two men. She was all too aware of the stunned silence out on deck. She wasn't the only one to notice that the white bugs had attacked her mother and no one else after their initial swarm. Even those knocked from her body had struggled to their feet and crawled toward her as if programmed to do so.

"Use this on the bites," Gary Jansen said. "I can make up some more once we're in the forest if she runs out. It will take the edge off."

Riley took the vial from him. The two men exchanged a look above her head and her heart jumped. They knew something. That look had been meaningful. Profound. She tasted fear in her mouth and quickly looked away, nodding her head.

Annabel attempted a halfhearted smile and murmured her thanks as the two men turned to go, giving the women privacy to find bites beneath clothing.

"Mom, are you all right?" Riley asked, the moment they were alone.

Annabel gripped her hand tightly. "Listen to me, Riley. Don't ask questions. No matter what happens, even if something happens to me, you must get to the mountain and complete the ritual. You know every word, every move. Perform the ritual *exactly* as you've been taught. You'll feel the earth moving through you and . . ."

"Nothing's going to happen to you, Mom," Riley protested. Fear was giving way to sheer terror. Her mother's eyes reflected some inner turmoil, some innate knowledge of a danger she knew of that Riley was missing—more a terrible vulnerability that had never been there before. None of the married couples in their family ever long-survived the loss of a spouse, but Riley was determined her mother would be the exception. She'd been watching her mother like a hawk since her father, Daniel Parker, died in the hospital following a major heart attack. Annabel had been grieving, but she hadn't seemed despondent or fatalistic until now. "Stop talking like this, you're scaring me."

Annabel struggled into a sitting position. "I'm giving you necessary information, Riley. Just as my mother gave it to me. And her mother before her. If I can't get to the mountain, the burden falls on you. You are part of an ancient lineage, and we've been given a duty that has passed from mother to daughter for centuries. My mother took me to this mountain, just as her mother took her. I've taken you. You are a child of the cloud forest, Riley, born there as I was. You drew your first breath on that mountain. You took it into your lungs and with it, the forest and all that comes with living, growing things."

Annabel shuddered again and reached for the vial Riley held. With shaking hands she drew up her shirt to reveal the tiny midges clinging to her stomach, brushing with trembling fingers to get them off. Riley took the vial and began smearing the soothing gel onto the bites.

"When my mother told me these things, I thought she was being dramatic and I scoffed at her," Annabel continued. "Oh, not to her face of course, but I thought her so old and superstitious. I'd heard the stories of the mountains. We lived in Peru and some of the older people in our village still whispered about the great evil that came before the Incas and could not be driven away, not even by their most fierce warriors. Stories. Dreadful, frightening stories handed down for generations. I thought the stories had been passed down mostly to scare the children and keep them from roaming too far from the protection of the village, but I learned better after my mother died. Something is there, Riley, in the mountain. Something evil, and it's our job to contain it."

Riley wanted to believe her mother was delirious with pain, but her eyes were steady—even more, afraid. Annabel believed every word she was saying and her mother wasn't given to flights of fancy. More to reassure her mother than because she actually believed the nonsense about some evil being trapped inside a mountain, Riley nodded.

"You're going to be fine," she assured. "We've been bitten by Manta Blanca on previous trips. They aren't poisonous. Nothing's going to happen to you, Mom." She had to say the words aloud, needing them to be true. "This was only a bizarre event. We know anything can happen in the rain forest . . ."

"No, Riley." Annabel caught her daughter's hand and held it tight. "All the delays . . . all the problems since we arrived . . . something is happening. The evil in the mountain is deliberately trying to slow me down. It is close to the surface and is orchestrating accidents and illness. We have to be realistic, Riley." Her body shuddered again.

Riley hunted through her pack and came up with a packet of pills. "Antihistamines, Mom, take a couple of these. You'll probably go to sleep but at least the itching will stop for a while."

Annabel nodded and swallowed the pills, chasing them with water. "Don't trust anyone, Riley. Any one of these people can be our enemy. We must go our own way as soon as possible."

Riley bit her lip, refraining from saying anything at all. She needed time to think. She was twenty-five years old and had been to the Andes four times, not including when she was born in the cloud forest. This was the fifth trip that she remembered. The hike through the rain forest had been grueling, but she'd never felt terrified as she was now. It was too late to turn back and from what her mother said, it wasn't an option. She needed to let her mother rest, and then they had to talk. She had to learn much more about the *why* of the trip to the Andes.

She dropped the sheet in place as soon as her mother appeared to be drifting off and went out onto the deck. Raul, the porter, glanced at her and looked quickly away, clearly uncomfortable with the presence of both women. Goose bumps rose on her arms. She rubbed them away, turning to walk along the railing to try to put some distance between her and the rest of the passengers. She just needed a little space.

There wasn't enough room aboard the boat to find a quiet corner. Jubal and Gary, the two researchers, sat together in one of the few secluded spots, and judging from the expressions on their faces, they weren't very happy. She gave them a wide berth, but in doing so ended up beside Ben Charger, the third engineer, the one she couldn't quite make up her mind about. He was always courteous to both women and, like Jubal and Gary, seemed to be developing a protective streak toward them.

Ben nodded at her. "Is your mother all right?"

Riley flashed him a tentative smile. "I think so. I gave her an antihistamine. Hopefully, between that and the gel Gary gave us, the itch won't make her crazy. Those are nasty little bugs."

"She must have been wearing something that attracted them," Ben ventured, half stating, half asking. "Maybe a perfume?"

Riley knew her mother never wore perfume, but it was a good explanation. She nodded slowly. "I didn't think of that. The attack was so bizarre."

Ben studied her face intently, his eyes so watchful, she found his gaze disturbing. "I've heard you and your mother have come here before. Has anything like that ever happened?"

Riley shook her head, grateful she could tell the truth. "Never."

"Why do you and your mother come to such a dangerous place?" Ben asked curiously. Again he didn't blink, or take his eyes from her face. He stared at her with the eyes of an interrogator. "It's my understanding that even the guides haven't traveled to this mountain. They had to get the information from a couple of others in the village. It seems such a strange destination for two women. There aren't any villages on the mountain, so you're not here for the linguistics."

Riley gave him a vague smile. "Mother's work as a horticulturist and advocate for the protection of rain forests takes us many places. But we come here also because we're descendents of the Cloud People and my mother wants us to learn as much as possible so the people aren't forgotten." She pressed her lips together and put a defensive hand on her throat. "That sounded mean. I love the rain forest, and I enjoy the trips with my mother. I was actually born in the cloud forest, so I think my mother thought it would be a good tradition to carry on, coming every few years." She glanced toward the guide and lowered her voice. "We weren't certain these men actually knew the way, that's why we thought it would be safer traveling with all of you."

"I've never been," Ben admitted. "I've traveled around many rain forests, but not to this particular mountain. I don't know why Don said we all had been here before. He likes to think he knows everything about everything. Is the forest as dangerous as everyone says?"

Riley nodded. "Very few people have ever traveled to this peak. It's a volcano and, although it hasn't erupted in well over five hundred years, I'm suspicious sometimes that it's waking up, although mostly because of the way the locals talk about it. There's some story handed down through the various local tribes about that mountain, so most avoid it. It's difficult to actually find a guide willing to travel to it." She frowned. "Truly, it has an off-putting feeling. You find yourself growing uneasy the higher you climb."

Ben ran both hands through his hair, almost as if he was agitated. "This entire side of the rain forest seems infested with legends and myths. No one wants to talk about them to outsiders, and all of them seem to involve some creature that preys on the lives and blood of the living."

Riley shrugged. "That's understandable. Practically everything in the rain forest is out for your blood. I've heard the rumors, of course, and our guide told us that it wasn't the Incas who destroyed the Cloud People, or the Spanish. The locals and descendents whisper of a great evil who murdered in the night, sucking the life from them and turning families against one another. The Cloud People were fierce in battle and gentle in their home life, but they supposedly succumbed one by one or fled the village to the Incas. When the Incas came to conquer the forest people, apparently most of the warriors were already dead. It's rumored that the Incas living here suffered the same fate as the ones killed by the marauding evil. Their bravest warriors died first."

"That's not in the history books," Ben said.

Still, she had the feeling he wasn't surprised, that he'd heard that whispered version. There were many more stories, of course, each more frightening than the other. Tales of bloodless victims and the tortures and horrors they'd endured before being murdered.

"Are you talking vampires?"

She blinked. He'd slipped that question in so casually. Too casually. Ben Charger had a deeper agenda than mining for traveling to the barely explored region. Old legends? Could he want to write? Whatever his reasons, Riley was certain they had nothing to do with mining. She frowned, thinking it over. Could the evil entity whispered about be a vampire? The myth of the vampire seemed to have existed in every ancient culture.

"I honestly have no idea. I've never heard whatever the entity is called a vampire, but the languages have changed so much over the years, quite a bit is lost in translation. I suppose it's possible. Vampire bats play an important part in Inca culture and among the Chachapoyas as well. At least based on what little my mom's told me and what I've managed to learn on my own. There isn't a lot to go on."

"Fascinating," Ben said. "If we get a chance, I'd like to hear more. I find cultures interesting, and here, in this part of the rain forest, the tribes and stories seemed to be shrouded in mystery, which intrigues me all the more. I'm a bit of an amateur writer and I take every opportunity when exploring a new region to learn as much as I can about old myths. I find that no matter where I go, certain legendary creatures have infiltrated the cultures all over the world. It's intriguing."

At a soft sound, Riley turned to find her mother standing close. Annabel was unguarded for a moment, her face swollen with bites, her eyes watchful and very suspicious of Ben. Riley stared at her in surprise. Her mother was the most open, gentle woman Riley had ever been around. She didn't have a mean, suspicious bone in her body. As a rule she shared information, was at ease with everyone, and most people gravitated toward her. Riley always felt protective toward her mother because she was so trusting where Riley wasn't.

Annabel blinked and the look of suspicion was gone, leaving her mother simply looking at Ben. Riley felt a little as if her world was spinning. Nothing, no one—not even her mother—seemed familiar. "You should be resting, Mom. So many bites can make you sick."

Annabel shook her head. "I'm okay. The gel Gary gave me is very soothing. It took the itch away, and you know the bites aren't poisonous. Gary and his friend must be very good at studying the properties of plants, because the gel really works."

Ben glanced over at the two men. Although both were clearly American, Gary and Jubal had journeyed from somewhere in Europe to search for a mythical plant with extraordinary healing properties that supposedly grew high in the Andes. By the expression on his face, he thought both men were slightly insane.

Annabel took Riley's hand and they nodded at Ben and moved toward the railing of the boat, in the center where they were alone.

The river narrowed more so that in places the huge root systems of the trees along the bank nearly scraped the boat. Lines of bats swayed high in the trees, an eerie sight. They were large, hanging upside down up in the thick canopy. Riley had seen the sight before, even as a child, but for some strange reason, this time it was disturbing, as if the bats were lying in wait, motionless, waiting for dark to begin the hunt—this time for human prey. She gave a little shudder at her own dramatic fantasy.

She was allowing the edginess of close confinement to get to her. She knew better. The bats were large and definitely vampire bats—feeding on warm blood—but she doubted if their hunger was personal and certainly they weren't just waiting for an unsuspecting boatload of humans to come along.

She felt eyes on her and turned to see Don Weston staring at her. He grinned and pretended to shoot an imaginary rifle at the motionless creatures. Riley turned away. Weston's need to be the center of attention every moment disgusted her. But his reaction to the bats was just a little too close to the way she was feeling—and she didn't want to feel anything at all in common with the man.

She turned her attention back to her mother, taking her hand and gripping it tightly. This morning they'd left the main river and begun the journey up the tributary toward one of the most remote parts of Peru. The jungle had closed around them, at times nearly scraping the sides of the two boats chugging upriver. The forest was in constant motion, almost as if the very animals were following them. Monkeys stared with great round eyes. Colorful macaws fluttered above their heads, darting in and out of the tree canopy.

They were definitely entering the world of the rain forest, the lush jungle of mystery that only deepened and became more dangerous with each passing second. The river narrowed, and the air grew still with the dark pungent scents of the deep rain forest. She recognized the signs. Soon, the river would be impossible to navigate. They would be forced to abandon the boats and tramp through the forest on foot. Unlike many places in the rain forest where it was easy to walk because very little could live on the forest floor without too much light, this area was dense. She'd traveled extensively, but the smells and the stillness of this place was a thing she'd found nowhere else on earth. Unlike any of her previous visits, this time Riley felt a little claustrophobic.

"Hey, Mack," Don called to the other engineer. "What the hell is going on now? I swear the jungle is alive." He gave a nervous laugh as he pointed out the strange way the branches dipped down and reached toward them as the boat passed.

Everyone turned to watch the bank closest to them as a great green wave built, following them. Every branch shivered, leaves unfolding and stretching out across the water as if seeking to stop their progress upriver. The first boat had passed unscathed, but the moment the second boat came close to the bank, the leaves reached for them. The stirring was eerie, as if the jungle had really come alive like Don said.

Riley's heart dropped. She'd seen the phenomenon many times before. Her mother attracted plants everywhere she went. There was no getting around it. The force of the magnet in her had never been quite this strong, but the thick foliage along both banks welcomed her with opened arms, even grew inches in an attempt to try to touch her. It never was good to draw too much attention to oneself in the rain forest around the superstitious guides and porters. Riley felt a deep need to protect her mother. She stepped between her mother and the bank, gripping the railing with both hands and staring out at the unfolding plants with wide, shocked eyes.

"Wow," she added to the sudden murmur of conversation. "This is amazing."

"It's creepy," Mack said, stepping back away from the rail.

The porters and the guide stared at the reaching plants and trees and then turned to look directly at Annabel. They whispered to each other. Riley felt other eyes on them. Both Gary and Jubal were looking at her mother as well. Only the three engineers stared into the rain forest as it closed in around them.

The two boats continued upstream, drawing closer to the mountain. Black caimans, giant dinosaurs of the past, sunned themselves on the banks, keeping a hungry eye on the small boats invading their space. Great clouds of black insects bit every inch of exposed skin and got caught in hair and even teeth, this time mosquitoes and other bloodsucking bugs. There was nothing to do but endure it. Below them, the dark waters grew shallow, slowing progress, and twice, the boat ground to a halt and had to be cut free of the tangled reeds reaching out greedily to wrap about the underside of the motor and propeller. Each time the unexpected lurch sent everyone aboard sprawling across the deck.

Weston picked himself up with an oath and staggered to the side of the boat to spit into the water. "This is ridiculous. Couldn't you have found another way?" he demanded of their guide, Pedro.

The guide shot him a tense look. "There is no easy way to this place you want to go."

Weston rested his butt on the railing as he gave the guide the finger. "I think you're just trying for more money and it's not going to happen, pal."

Pedro muttered something in his language to the two porters.

This one the jungle can eat, Riley interpreted. She didn't blame them.

The guide and porters snickered.

Weston lit a cigarette and glared out over the dark water. The boat staggered again and then, as they were all desperately trying to gain their footing, it gave a huge lurch. Weston fell forward, hanging up for one heart-stopping moment on the railing. Everyone leapt to help him as he hung precariously, arms down, closer to the water.

Riley caught his belt buckle while Annabel reached over the side to grasp at his arms. The moment Annabel leaned down, arms covering Weston's, the water came to life, boiling like a cauldron, flashing silver with muddy patches of red.

"Mom!" Riley cried, reaching for her mother, still holding Weston. His weight was pulling them all forward.

The others rushed to help as Annabel slipped farther toward the dark, reed-choked water, now boiling with frenzied piranha. There was no blood in the water so the turmoil made no sense. To Riley's horror the fish began to leap out of the water, hundreds of them, narrow bodies and blunt heads shooting from the river like rockets, the triangular-shaped jaws with razor-sharp teeth snapping open and shut with terrible clacking sounds.

Although the stories of piranha frenzies abounded, Riley knew attacks on people were quite rare. She'd swum in the water with them on several occasions. This bizarre behavior was extraordinary, as unnatural and unsettling as the La Manta Blanca attack. And just like with the Manta Blancas, it seemed clear the piranha were bent on reaching her mother, not Don Weston.

It was Jubal who caught Annabel and yanked her back away from the rail, practically throwing her into Gary. Then he caught Weston and hauled him back on deck, too. Instead of being grateful, the engineer slapped at Jubal's hands, cursing and sliding down to sit on the deck, his breath coming in great gasps. He glared at Pedro and the two porters as if the three men had deliberately tried to murder him.

The guide and porters both stared at Annabel with a look that made Riley wish she had a concealed gun close at hand. Before anyone could speak, the boat nearly ran aground, and the two natives turned back to their work. A low branch overhead dipped down, and a snake dropped onto the deck with a thud right at Don Weston's boots.

"No one move," Jubal hissed as the snake stared at the engineer. "That viper's extremely poisonous."

Pedro, the guide, turned back, catching up the machete that was always close. Before he could take a step, the viper did an abrupt spin and launched itself at Riley. She stumbled back into her mother. The snake flashed between her legs heading straight toward her mother. Gary Jansen yanked Annabel off her feet and twisted around, holding her in the air while Jubal shoved Riley aside, yelling at the guide, hand up in the air.

Pedro tossed the machete and in one smooth movement, Jubal slammed the sharpened blade across the neck of the viper, severing the head. There was a moment of silence as Gary lowered Annabel to the deck, holding her steady so that she didn't fall.

"Thank you," Riley breathed softly to both researchers. She didn't try to hide the fact that she was very shaken.

Her mother stared at her with stricken eyes. Riley's world crumbled. Capa, Raul and Pedro looked at her mother with the same look they had on their faces when they'd first seen the viper. They were in real trouble if the guides and porters became hostile toward them. She reached for her mother's hand and held on tightly.

2

Nights were hell in the jungle. Right at sunset, the buzzing started. It wasn't as if the insects were silent—they were producing a constant steady drone—but Riley could push the sound away. This was something altogether different—a soft, persistent noise, a low frequency that jangled every nerve in the body. She'd awakened to the strange noise the very first night they entered the rain forest.

Strangely, Riley couldn't identify the low, irritating buzz, nor could she tell if it was outside or inside her head. She'd observed several others—including her mother—rubbing their temples as if their heads ached, and she feared that same low frequency of whispers one couldn't quite catch was invading insidiously, adding to the danger of their travel. During the day the whispers were gone, but the effects lingered.

Her senses, since entering the rain forest, seemed to have blazed to life and were working overtime. She noticed every little suspicious glance toward her mother. Jubal Sanders and Gary Jansen were armed to the teeth and she was very envious of their weapons. The two moved in silence, kept to themselves and watched everyone. She came to the conclusion that they knew a lot more about what was going on than they let on.

Don Weston and his friend Mack Shelton were a pair of idiots as far as she could see. Neither had ever made the trek into a rain forest, and clearly they were afraid of everything. They blustered, complained and bullied the porters and guides when they weren't leering at Riley or feeding the rampant distrust among the travelers.

Ben Charger seemed much more knowledgeable about the rain forest and the tribes occupying it. He'd done extensive research and had come prepared. He didn't like either Weston or Shelton, but had to work with them and clearly wasn't happy about it. He spent a lot of time talking to the guides and porters, asking questions and trying to learn from them. Riley couldn't really fault him for anything. Perhaps she was just nervous about everyone at this point.

The archaeologist and his students were very excited and seemed completely oblivious to the tension running through the camp, although she noticed they were uneasy at night, sitting close to the fire. They seemed driven, amicable and very focused on their mission. Dr. Henry Patton and his two students, Todd Dillon and Marty Shepherd, were more excited about the ruins they'd heard about than interested in whether or not a woman in their company was bringing bad luck to the travelers. They seemed young and naïve, even the professor, who was in his late fifties. His entire world revolved around academia.

Riley felt a little sorry for all three archaeologists, that they were so clueless, and more grateful than ever that she'd chosen to concentrate her studies on modern languages rather than dead ones. She enjoyed traveling, talking with people and living life too much to be locked in an ivory tower, poring over dusty tomes. Of course, she'd studied ancient languages as well, but primarily as a window to the evolution of languages and their impact on various cultures.

Riley glanced toward Raul and Capa, the two porters who had shared the boat with them coming upriver. She didn't like the way they whispered and sent surreptitious glances toward Annabel's sleeping hammock. Maybe that terrible buzzing in her head was making her as paranoid as everyone else, but in any case, there was no sleeping. She didn't just have to worry about the men in her camp; the insects and bats and every other night creature seemed to stalk her mother as well.

She'd gone four nights without sleep, watching over her mother, and it was beginning to show, fraying her nerves so that she found it nearly impossible to tolerate Weston's snide, leering presence. She didn't want to add to the problems by being ugly to him, but she was definitely at that point. The fire blazed bright. Just outside the ring of fire, a jaguar coughed. He seemed to follow them, yet when the guides went out to check in the morning, they couldn't find tracks. It was impossible not to be affected by that sawing, grunting cough.

She could hear the slow fluttering of wings over Annabel's head. Vampire bats landed in the trees, brushing the leaves and filling the branches until the tree groaned, trying to support the weight of so many. Riley swallowed hard and slowly turned her head toward the leaping fire. The porters and guides stared at the tree filled with hanging bats. The creatures had gone from interesting to sinister in a matter of seconds for the fourth night in a row.

Pedro, the guide, and Raul and Capa, the two porters from her boat, moved a little into the shadows. All three gripped their machetes. The looks on their faces as the flickering flames revealed their expressions frightened her. For one heart-stopping moment, the men seemed every bit as threatening as the bats. Riley sat up slowly. She'd left her boots on, knowing she'd be protecting her mother.

Annabel slept restlessly, groaning at times. Her mother had always had acute hearing, even in her sleep. A cat walking across the floor would wake her, but since entering the rain forest, she seemed exhausted and weak. At night she twisted and turned in her hammock, sometimes weeping softly, pressing her hands to her head. Even when the bats dropped to earth and surrounded her, using their wings to propel them through the thick vegetation, Annabel never opened her eyes.

Riley had prepared her defenses carefully, using torches she could easily light, even going so far as to build a small circular fire wall around her mother's sleeping area. As she unhooked her netting, she caught sight of Raul creeping toward her. He was staying low and to the shadows, but she could make him out, sliding from one dark place to another, stalking prey. Riley glanced over at her sleeping mother. She feared Annabel was the porter's intended prey.

Heart pounding, tasting fear in her mouth, Riley slipped from her hammock and drew her knife. Going up against a machete, especially one wielded by a man who used one on a regular basis, was insane, but he was going to have to go through her to get to her mother, just as the vampire bats would have to do. And it wouldn't just be her knife, if he came at her mother. Riley picked up a torch and held it to the low fire she'd prepared earlier as a defense against the bats.

She would kill him if she had to. The idea made her sick, but she steeled herself, going through each move in her head. Practicing. Bile rose, but she was determined. No one—*nothing*—would harm her mother. She'd made up her mind, and nothing would stop her, not even the idea that what she was about to do might be considered premeditated murder.

Raul inched closer. Riley could smell his sweat. His scent was all "wrong" to her. She took a deep breath and let it out, easing toward her mother's hammock, putting her feet carefully in position. She could feel the ground under her, almost rising to meet each footfall. She'd never been so aware of the heartbeat of the Earth. Not a leaf rustled. No twig snapped. Her feet seemed to know exactly where to step to keep from making a sound, to keep from twisting an ankle or falling on the uneven ground.

She positioned herself in front of her mother's hammock, picking a spot she could easily move in to try to keep any attack from her. Movement close to her sent her pulse pounding. A man's shadow loomed over the hammock, thrown by the flames in the fire pit suddenly leaping toward the sky. She never would have seen him otherwise. Jubal Sanders was that quiet. She twisted fast to face him, but he'd gone past her to take up a position at the head of Annabel's hammock. Had he wanted to kill her mother, she would already be dead—he'd been that close without Riley's knowledge.

She knew, almost without the confirmation of turning her head, that Gary Jansen was at the foot of her mother's hammock. She'd spent the last four days trekking through the hardest jungle possible and she knew the way he moved—silent and easy through the rough terrain—but it still surprised her. He just seemed as if he'd be more at home in a lab coat, the absentminded professor. Clearly he was brilliant. You couldn't talk to him and not realize he was extremely intelligent, but he moved every bit as easily through the jungle as Jubal and he was equally as well armed and probably just as proficient with weapons. She was glad they had chosen to help her protect Annabel.

The terrible buzzing in her head increased so that for a moment her head felt as if it might explode. She pressed her fingers tightly against her temple. She was looking directly at Gary when the pain exploded through her skull and rattled her teeth. He gripped his head at the same moment, shaking it. His lips moved, but no sound emerged. She looked at Jubal. He, too, was feeling the head pain.

The words were foreign. Jumbled together, almost like a chant, but definitely words. She had excelled in studying ancient and dead languages as well as modern ones, but she didn't recognize even the rhythm of the words—but both Jubal and Gary clearly did. She saw the expressions on their faces, the alarm exchanged in their eyes.

Ben Charger staggered up to the other side of Annabel's hammock, pressing his hands to his ears. "Something's wrong," he hissed. "This is about her. Something evil wants her dead."

Jubal and Gary nodded their agreement. The bats overhead stirred. Riley's heart pounded hard enough that she feared the others could hear. She took a better grip on her knife and torch and waited in the darkness while Annabel moaned and writhed, as if evading something terrible chasing her, haunting her dreams.

Raul came out of the shadows, machete clutched in his hands, muttering the same phrase over and over. *"Hän kalma, emni hän ku köd alte. Tappatak ŋamaŋ. Tappatak ŋamaŋ."*

Riley heard the words clearly as the porter repeated them over and over. She knew most of the dialects of the tribes spoken in this part of the rain forest. She knew Spanish and Portuguese. She knew European languages and even Russian and Latin, but this was nothing like she'd ever heard before. Not Latin in origin. Not any of the dead languages she was familiar with, but the words meant something to the porter and—she glanced at Jubal and Gary—to the two researchers.

Raul chanted the sentences over and over in a guttural, hypnotic voice. His eyes glazed over. She'd seen ceremonies that had placed recipients into trances and the porter definitely appeared to be in one, which made him doubly dangerous. Sweat poured from his body, dripping from him to splatter darkly across the leaves that were now crawling with thousands of ants. He shook his head continually, as if fighting the sound in his head, stumbling backward a few feet and then relentlessly moving forward again.

Her mouth went dry as the bats overhead began to descend, dropping to the ground like menacing raptors, creeping through the vegetation. Beady eyes stared at Annabel as they used their wings like legs, propelling themselves toward their prey. Raul shuffled closer, his movements awkward, very unlike his normal easy movement, the murmured chant growing in volume and intensity with each step forward. Closer now, the jaguar gave another haunting, grunting cough. Riley could not believe what was happening. It was as if everything hostile in the rain forest was out to kill her mother.

Riley lit her torch, holding it away from her body, and quickly began lighting the torches she'd placed around her mother. The torches flared, forming a low wall of light and fire around Annabel.

Raul kept coming in spite of the fact that he tried desperately to stop himself. Each time he succeeded in moving backward, away from Annabel, his body would begin a forward motion again. Not fast. Not slow. A programmed robot, chanting louder, that same phrase over and over. A command now. A demand. *"Hän kalma, emni hän ku köd alte. Tappatak ŋamaŋ. Tappatak ŋamaŋ."*

The porter appeared not to see the macabre bats with their disturbing wing crawl. His glazed eyes remained fixed on Annabel, the machete in a two-handed grip as he approached.

"Riley," Jubal said. "Get inside the circle of light and keep the bats off with your torch. Let me handle Raul."

She tried not to be relieved. It was her duty to protect her mother, but the porter's diabolical mask, filled with some insane, fanatical zealous purpose, was truly horrifying. She slipped back into the circle of fire closer to her mother.

Jubal Sanders lifted a gun as he raised his voice. "Pedro, Miguel, Alejandro," he called to the three guides. "Stop him before I shoot him. And I will shoot. If you don't want Raul to die, you'd better restrain him. He's got about seven more seconds and then I pull the trigger."

There was no doubt Jubal was fully prepared to shoot the porter. His voice resonated with command, although delivered in a low, firm tone. Time slowed down. Tunneled. Riley saw everything as if in a distant dream. The inevitable turn of heads, the expressions of fear and shock. The shuffling forward of the bats. The porter one step closer. Jubal, calm, gun in hand.

Miguel, Pedro and Alejandro, all brothers, rushed toward Raul while the others stood undecided, apparently in shock at the porter's clear intention of murdering a woman. Dr. Patton and his two students seemed to notice for the first time that something was wrong. All three stood up quickly, staring in horror at the scene unfolding. Flames rose eerily from the main fire pit and streamed from the torches placed in the ground as if a wind had suddenly gusted, but the air was still.

"Hän kalma, emni hän ku köd alte. Tappatak ŋamaŋ. Tappatak ŋamaŋ." Raul continued to chant the foreign phrase over and over.

Riley could hear the words distinctly now. She recognized the strange cadence buzzing in her ear, as if that same refrain, although distant for her, was being fed into her mind—into all of their minds. There were dozens of hallucinogens in the rain forest that the guides and porters, probably the researchers and anyone in the group could know about. Anyone could be responsible for these attacks on her mother. Weston fed the superstition, although both he and Shelton appeared to be sleeping restlessly in their hammocks, unaware of the unfolding drama.

Time ticked by in slow seconds. Raul continued doggedly forward. Jubal didn't blink. He could have been carved from stone. The bats shuffled toward Riley, closing in on the flaming torches and the circle of light around Annabel.

"Hän kalma, emni hän ku köd alte. Tappatak ŋamaŋ. Tappatak ŋamaŋ."

Her heart slammed hard, beat after beat, that same menacing rhythm of the porter's diabolical chanting. She realized immediately that even the bats were dragging themselves toward Annabel at that same exact pace. Everything around her, from the bizarre swaying of the trees to the dancing of the flames in spite of the stillness of the wind, leapt to the porter's chant. That chant was emanating from *inside* their heads. Someone in the camp had to be targeting Annabel, using hallucinogens and casting suspicion on her. The fact that the plants and trees responded to her only fed superstition. It made no sense at all.

Miguel and Pedro closed in on one side of Raul. Their brother, Alejandro, came in fast from the other side. All three frowned in concentration, shaking heads to get that wicked chant out of their minds while they tried to save the porter from Jubal's gun. He was related to them in some way, Riley remembered, but many of the villagers were related. Their affection for him thankfully overcame the terrible hallucination Raul seemed trapped in.

As they closed around him, grabbing his hand to keep the machete out of play, the porter continued to try to walk forward, ignoring the three guides hanging on to him. He kept up his macabre chant. Riley swept her torch across the ground as the first line of bats came too close to her mother, even as she tried to puzzle out the meaning of those strange, guttural sounds emerging from Raul's mouth.

The scent of burned flesh permeated the air. Bats scrambled back as she swung her torch again in a circle, low to the ground, driving the creatures back and away from her mother's hammock. Two were already starting up the tree trunk. She jabbed at them both with the business end of the torch and then, when they caught on fire, knocked them to the ground, kicking at the fireballs to get them away from Annabel.

She heard the scuttle of the wings dragging through vegetation behind her and she whirled around to find the bats had circled to the other side of the hammock. Ben Charger caught up a torch, the flames throwing his face into sharp relief. Deep lines cut into his face, making him look maniacal. His eyes blazed with a kind of fury. For a moment she was afraid for her mother, but he took the torch and swept it over the approaching vampire bats, driving them back, setting the persistent ones on fire.

Gary battled more on his side of the hammock. She raced around behind Jubal and swept her torch across the line of bats sneaking their way beneath the hammock from that direction. The smell was horrible, and she couldn't stop coughing as black smoke rose around them. Annabel never woke, but twisted and fought in her hammock as the three men helped Riley protect her.

Miguel and Pedro dragged Raul away, through the thick vegetation, as he refused to stand, refused to retreat, trying desperately to continue forward in spite of the threat of the gun. The porter continued to repeat the same phrase over and over. The others growled commands at him, but he didn't hear, so far gone into his hallucination. Alejandro retrieved the machete, keeping it well clear of Raul's seeking hands.

They dragged him to the far side of the camp and held him prisoner there. The archaeologist and his students hesitantly came across the ground to study the mess of dead and dying bats and to watch the others retreat from the flames ringing the hammock.

"Are you all right?" Dr. Patton asked. "This is bizarre. Did that man seriously try to kill one of you with a machete?"

He seemed as if he was waking from a daze. He looked so shocked Riley had an unexpected urge to laugh. He'd been tramping through the rain forest with them for four long days. He'd heard the stories of snake and piranha attacks over and over thanks to Weston, who didn't seem to be able to talk about anything else, and yet, for the first time, the archaeologist seemed to realize something was wrong.

He blinked, noticing the gun Jubal still held in his hand. "Something's going on here."

A sound escaped her throat before she could stop it. Hysterical laughter, maybe. "Was it the machete that tipped you off, the diabolical chant from hell or the horde of crawling vampire bats?" Riley clapped her hand over her mouth. There was no doubt she was hysterical to answer like that. But really? Something was *going on*? What was his first clue? He was taking the absent-minded professor bit just a little too far.

"Easy," Jubal whispered. "She's safe now. I think it's over for the night."

Riley bit her lip to keep from retorting. The rain forest was filled with predators of every shape and size, all of them seemingly intent on attacking Annabel. How was her mother going to be safe from that? The sense of welcome, of homecoming they'd always experienced on their previous visits was utterly absent. This time, the rain forest felt savage and dangerous, even malevolent.

She forced her attention back to the remaining bats. Thankfully they were retreating from the light and the stench of their roasted companions. That knot in her stomach eased a little as she inspected the tree trunk and the branches above her mother. The insects were retreating, too.

"I should have helped you," Dr. Henry Patton said. "I don't know why I didn't."

His two students had followed him at a much slower pace, looking as dazed and confused as their teacher.

Riley bit back an angry accusation. None of this was the archaeologist's fault. Maybe he had the means and knowledge to understand the properties of a hallucinogenic plant and the entire expedition, but what would be his motives? What could possibly be any of their motives?

She swept a weary hand through her hair, exhausted. She hadn't dared to sleep in the last four nights, not since entering the rain forest. Not since that terrible whispering had begun. The endless buzz was enough to drive any sane man crazy, and clearly she was the least affected of their group.

The three guides and the rest of the porters circled Raul, restraining him with ties of some kind. He continued to chant that guttural, unfamiliar language, sometimes murmuring, sometimes shouting, and kept trying to move toward Annabel's hammock. His cousins were forced to tie him to one of the trees to keep him from attacking her again. His hand was clenched in a fist as though he still gripped the machete handle. He swung his arm back and forth through the air in a disturbing pantomime.

"What is Raul saying?" Riley asked Jubal, once the excitement died down and everyone returned to their hammocks. She nodded at the porter tied to the tree and watched Gary's expression. "I can see that both of you recognize the language." She looked Jubal right in the eyes. "Don't deny it. I see the looks you two give one another. There's no doubt that you know what he's saying."

Jubal and Gary turned almost simultaneously to glance over their shoulders at Ben Charger. It was obvious they didn't want to talk in front of anyone else.

"Let me give you a hand clearing away these bats," Gary said.

Riley deliberately began to make a sweep of the dead and dying bats surrounding her mother. It was ugly, sickening work. Both Jubal and Gary pitched in, which was a good thing because she would have followed them back to their hammocks for an explanation.

Ben worked with them for a few minutes, kicking the roasted bodies away from Annabel's hammock, but when Gary began digging in the vegetation to dispose of them all in a mass grave, the engineer called it quits.

"I don't think you'll need me any more tonight. Things seem to be settling down."

Only then did Riley realize the terrible buzzing in her head had faded away. Although she couldn't hear it anymore, she could tell by the red eyes and the frowns on the faces of the others that it hadn't stopped altogether. "Thank you so much for your help. I wouldn't have gotten them all without you. You acted fast."

Ben shrugged. "They went right for her. I wasn't going to stand by and let her get hurt. I'm a light sleeper. If anything happens again, give a shout and I'll come running."

Riley forced a brief smile. "Thank you again."

Ben rubbed his temples, scowling as he turned away from her. Riley helped push the remains of the bats into the hole Gary had dug, waiting until Ben was out of earshot before she turned to Jubal.

"All right," she said, "he's gone. Now tell me what Raul was chanting. And what language was he speaking? It's certainly not native to this country or any tribe here in the Amazon."

Jubal slipped his gun into some kind of harness beneath his loose jacket. Riley found it interesting that he hadn't put it away until Ben had left.

"The language is an ancient one," Jubal said. "It originated in the Carpathian Mountains, but there are very few who still speak or even understand it today."

She frowned at him. "The Carpathian Mountains? How in the world could a poorly educated porter from a remote village in the Amazon come to know and speak an ancient European language that even I've never heard of? Never mind. We can talk about that later. For now, I want to know what he was saying."

Jubal looked over her head at Gary.

"*Don't* do that. Look at me, not him. I know you understand what he said," Riley insisted. "That man was trying to kill my mother. And the whole time he kept saying '*Hän kalma, emni hän ku köd alte. Tappatak ŋamaŋ. Tappatak ŋamaŋ.*'" She repeated the phrase with perfect pitch, intonation, sounding exactly like Raul. "I want to know what it means."

Jubal shook his head. "I don't know the answer to that. I really don't,

Riley. I'm not as good at the language as Gary is, and I don't want to make a mistake. I think I got the gist of what he was trying to say, but if I mistranslate and alarm you . . ."

"The man came after my mother with a machete. I don't think it's going to be more alarming than that," Riley snapped and was immediately ashamed of herself. She needed this man's help. Gary, Ben and Jubal had no doubt not only saved her mother's life, but probably her own as well. "I'm sorry. You helped defend my mother, and I appreciate that. But I'm afraid for her and I need to know what I'm dealing with."

Gary moved around Annabel's hammock to stand in front of Riley. "I'm sorry this is happening to both of you. You must be very frightened. It sounded to me, and this is a loose translation, that he was chanting 'Death to the cursed woman. Kill her. Kill her.' That's as near as I could make out." He looked at Jubal. "Did you get the same thing?"

Riley knew he'd switched his attention to Jubal in order to give her time to recover. She'd suspected the translation would be something threatening—but still, she felt as if someone had punched her in the gut and driven every bit of air from her lungs. She forced herself to breathe as she looked up at the night sky through the canopy, a film of hazy leaves. Who would target Annabel? She was an amazing, kind woman. Everyone she met loved her. The attack didn't make sense at all.

"Raul has definitely spent his entire life here in the rain forest. He truly doesn't have that much contact with outsiders, none of the villagers do. How would he ever pick up such a nearly extinct, clearly foreign language?" Riley struggled to keep the challenge out of her voice.

Without a doubt this man had saved her life, *but* Jubal Sanders and Gary Jansen researched plants. They both admitted they'd come to the Andes in search of a plant that was supposed to be extinct everywhere else and that the plant was native to the Carpathian Mountain range in Europe. If this language had originated in that same area, what were the plant and language doing in South America? And what a coincidence that everyone in their traveling party was experiencing the same hallucination all wrapped around this ancient language both men understood?

Jubal shook his head. "I have no explanation."

He was lying. He looked her straight in the eye. His expression didn't change, his handsome face carved with worry lines, his jaw and mouth firm, but he was lying.

"Oh, yes, you do," she retorted. "And you're going to tell me what it is, right now."

Gary sighed. "Just tell her, Jubal. Worst case, she'll just think we're as crazy as the porter."

"Honestly, we don't know for certain what's going on, but we have our suspicions. We've seen things like this happen before in other parts of the world." Jubal hesitated. "Do you believe in the existence of evil?"

"You mean like Satan, the devil?"

"Sort of, but I'm not talking about God and the angels."

Riley forced down her first reaction. Strange things happened in the Amazon. And her mother certainly had gifts that couldn't be explained. There was the trip to the Andes every five years and the ritual performed on the mountain. There were also rumors, the legends and myths handed down of a great evil having destroyed the Cloud People and then the Incas. Of course, no one believed it, but what if it was the truth?

"Yes," she admitted, "I believe in evil."

Jubal hesitated again. "I—we—suspect that something ancient is out here, an evil being that has the power to command the insects and to prey on our minds, to trick us into believing things that aren't true."

Riley instantly recalled her mother's agitated rambling about the evil trapped in the mountain. The two of them were traveling to the mountain to reseal it, to keep the volcano from exploding, and Annabel was worried about being late. Riley knew generations of women had come to this mountain, and the trip had been even more rigorous and dangerous in the past, yet they'd continued to travel to that same spot and perform the same ritual.

So could it possibly be true? Was there really something evil trapped in that mountain? Something the women of her family had been keeping contained for hundreds—possibly even thousands—of years? Riley shivered, pressing a hand to her knotted stomach.

"Why would this evil thing target my mother?"

"Clearly it considers your mother a threat to it in some way," Gary said. *"Something is happening. The evil in the mountain is deliberately trying to slow me down. It is close to the surface and is orchestrating accidents and illness."* Riley shivered, remembering her mother's fearful warnings. She'd brushed them off as shock-induced ramblings, but now Riley wasn't so sure. Could it possibly be true?

Jubal shifted closer to her mother's hammock. Riley nearly leapt at him, but his body language exuded protection. He faced the forest, his body alert. She became aware of the silence then. The constant, never-ending drone of the insects had disappeared, leaving behind an eerie silence.

Instinctively Riley stepped close to her mother. Annabel writhed. Moaned. Sweat beaded on her body. Her hands rose and she began a complicated pattern of movement, a mesmerizing twisting of her fingers and hands, a conductor of a symphony, yet each flowing motion was precise and beautiful. Riley had seen those movements several times. Her own hands automatically followed the pattern, as if the memory was pressed into her bones rather than her mind. She made the effort to keep her arms down, but she couldn't stop her fingers and wrists from twisting with her mother's, or the flutter of graceful motion.

Her mother's body turned toward the east and Riley found herself facing the same direction. She could feel the flow of earth rising from beneath the soles of her feet, moving through her like the sap through the trees. A heart hammered, deep beneath the soil. She could feel her pulse syncing to that steady drumming beat. She felt grounded, roots spreading beneath her to find that beckoning life force deep in the earth.

She felt the individual plants, each of them with their own character and personality. Some poison, some antidotes. She recognized them as sisters and brothers. She felt them take root inside of her, spreading through her veins, into her internal organs, and wrapping around her very bones until her veins sang with the lifeblood of the rain forest.

Awareness of every living tree, shrub and plant nearby rose until it was absolutely acute. Heart and soul reached out to them and they reached back, feeding her courage and resilience, the earth her mother, willing to aid her at any turn. She felt a stain of evil spreading through the ground itself, seeking a target. But something else was there as well—something strong and brave. Predatory. Protective. *Hers.* Abruptly she pulled herself back.

Apparently, Jubal and Gary weren't far off with their assessment of the situation after all. This was no mass hallucination, but a carefully orchestrated plot to attack her mother, to delay her trip to the mountain and prevent her from carrying out the centuries-old ritual. Riley couldn't tell why, or what was in the mountain. She could only discern that it was desperate to get out, to survive, and it would use any means available to do so—including killing her mother.

So this was why her mother was so in tune with plants. She felt them, was connected to them, and not in some small way. Riley had never felt that connection before, and it occurred to her that some form of awareness and power was being transferred to her. That possibility only alarmed her all the more. Was her mother inadvertently doing something in her sleep to pass her knowledge on to her daughter, as she'd said each generation of their ancestors did before their deaths?

"What is she doing?" Jubal asked, curiosity in his voice. Curiosity and something else. Recognition, maybe?

Riley actually started, so caught up and absorbed by the myriad plants around her and the feeling of being almost transformed, mesmerized by the existence of such intense life all around her that she'd nearly forgotten there were witnesses to the ritual movements her mother performed up on the mountain. Both Jubal and Gary looked at her with far too much knowledge.

Riley shrugged, reluctant to explain her mother to anyone, although she felt as if the two men had earned an explanation—she just didn't have an adequate one.

"Have you seen these movements before?" Jubal asked. "The way she's moving her hands is almost ritualistic."

"Yes." Riley had been as honest as possible and felt they had been as well. Both were skirting around each other, reluctant to say something they couldn't take back.

"I've seen similar gestures in the Carpathian Mountains," Jubal admitted. "When we've worked in the remote parts of the mountains. Has your mother been there before? Does she have any ties to Romania or any of the countries the range goes through?"

Riley shook her head adamantly. "We've traveled to Europe once, but nowhere near the Carpathian Mountains. We mostly stay in South America. Mom's come here many times. Most of the women in my family were born here, my mother included. We're descendents of both the Cloud

People as well as the Incas so my family has always had a huge interest in this part of the world. My mother was raised here and only went to the States when she met and married my father. He was from there."

"Are you adopted?" Jubal asked. "You don't look anything like your mother."

Riley pressed her lips together. She'd heard that all of her life. She was tall and curvy with translucent skin and large, very different oval eyes. Her hair was as straight as a board and as black as midnight. Her mother was slender, of medium height, with wonderful olive skin and curly hair.

"I'm not adopted. I look like one of my great-great-grandmothers. She was taller with dark hair, at least if the drawings of her can be believed. Mom showed them to me once when I was all upset because I towered over everyone in middle school."

She was talking too fast, too much, as she sometimes did when she was upset. They were asking a lot of personal questions. What did it matter if she didn't look like her mother? Why were they so interested? She just wanted to grab her mother and make a run for it. If not for the fact that the forest itself seemed intent on attacking them, she might have done just that. Her mother had an amazing sense of direction when it came to the mountain. Twice when they'd made the journey and the guides were lost, it had been her mother who had found the way.

But now, with Annabel sick and the attacks on her growing more violent, Riley didn't dare separate from the group. Jubal and Gary offered a level of protection she couldn't afford to dismiss.

"Thank you both so much for your help. I have to get some sleep tonight. I don't know why the forest has gone silent, but I don't feel any immediate threat. I don't want my mother to know about this right away. I want to tell her myself and see if she has any ideas why these attacks on her are happening."

She needed time alone with her mother, and that was nearly impossible surrounded as they were by the various travelers. The guides and porters regarded them with suspicion now, and that would make privacy even more difficult.

"Go ahead and sleep," Gary said. "We'll keep an eye on things."

3

Far beneath the surface, buried deep in the hot, rich, volcanic soil of the Andes, Danutdaxton woke to a steady pounding in his head and heat rising all around him. His eyes opened to the familiar darkness, the sting of sulfur in his nose and the stabbing hunger for blood beating at him with stony fists.

Dax's hands flexed as he checked his safeguards throughout the chamber. He was not alone. Another pounding wave of pressure slammed into him. Despite the pain, the attack made him smile with grim admiration.

"Manners, my old friend," he murmured.

To his credit, Mitro Daratrazanoff was as relentless a foe as Dax was a hunter. They had pursued one another for countless centuries before being trapped in this volcano, and in the countless centuries since their entombment, they had continued their battle, never giving up, each constantly searching for a moment of weakness to exploit. The fight had become their entire existence. Hunter and hunted, predator and prey: their roles switched continually, but they were so well matched neither ever had the upper hand for long.

Dax drew a breath and let the heat and pain and darkness wash over him. His body calmed. The ravenous hunger subsided as the heat and power of the volcano sank into his flesh, feeding him its energy, its strength. He drew sustenance from the earth, much the way a Carpathian drew sustenance from the veins of his human prey.

Once, only blood could have assuaged his hunger. Once, only blood could have given him strength. But the last five hundred years of being locked in the heat and pressure at the heart of a volcano had changed him. He was no longer "just" Carpathian. He had become something different, something . . . more.

Flesh and bone had grown denser, harder, less susceptible to injury. He had a much higher tolerance for heat and fire. He could probably stand in the heart of a bonfire without raising the slightest blister. His hair, once long and thick as most Carpathians wore it, had been singed close to his scalp, leaving a short, thick pelt, and his eyes could amplify the slightest light, enabling him to see clearly in nearly pitch-black conditions. And in caverns where not the smallest hint of light shone, he had developed the ability to see through other means. Heat signatures were clearly visible to him, and even in the coldest, darkest caves and tunnels, he could differentiate between the vibrations of energy in the rock and air and thus "see" his surroundings.

Those vibrations whispered across his skin, as he woke fully from his healing slumber, his body shifting and stretching in the heated soil. Parting the soil with a wave of his hand, he rose from his resting place into the empty magma chamber above. Cracks in the hardened black rock revealed glowing orange lava bubbling restlessly in pools below that lit the chamber with a dim orange light.

The earth rumbled beneath his feet, and the ground gave a sudden lurch that nearly knocked him off balance. Steam vented from the glowing orange cracks in the chamber floor, and with it came the familiar, decaying stench of evil.

Dax's muscles clenched. He'd grown used to the rumblings and movement of the volcano over the years, but this was different. The volcano was awakening. And Mitro was the one waking it.

Another wave of pressure slammed into him, throwing him to his knees. The ground shifted and rolled. Dax steadied himself and sent feelers stabbing into the soil, trying to locate his ancient enemy. But the clinging, oily miasma of the vampire's decay had saturated everything inside the volcano, making it impossible for Dax to track the evil back to its source. Mitro was here, working to break free of his bonds and use the explosive force of the volcano to free himself.

For too many years, Mitro Daratrazanoff had fought to escape his prison. Dax had pursued him through the caverns and tunnels of the volcano, hunting, tracking, fighting to destroy him. And for the same amount of years, first Mitro spurned his lifemate Arabejila and then her descendents, who had come to the volcano once every five years to strengthen the bonds of Mitro's prison and keep him contained until Dax could finally kill him. Without Dax constantly hunting him, fighting him, and without Arabejila and her descendents continually renewing the strength of Mitro's prison bonds, the vampire would long ago have escaped to wreak his unimaginable evil on the world.

Unfortunately, over the last few decades, the power woven by Arabejila's descendents had been growing weaker. Their renewal rites no longer imparted the same adamantine strength to the bonds as before. And with the weakening bonds, Mitro's attempts to escape had come increasingly closer to succeeding. The last three times, Arabejila's descendent had arrived just in the nick of time, renewing the bonds only scant days—even hours—before Mitro broke through.

Worry crept down Dax's spine. Judging by the volcano's increasing turbulence, Mitro had already found enough of a chink in his prison walls to work his influence on the outer world. It did not bode well. Mitro must have woken much earlier than Dax this time. He'd grown stronger—too strong.

Concerned, Dax sent his senses out, searching for that frisson of awareness that alerted him to the presence of another Carpathian. He'd been able to use that awareness over the years to track the progress of Arabejila and her descendents when they came to the mountain. His senses soared out, passing through rock, soil, into the sky above the volcano, then across the dense, tropical jungle.

After several long minutes of searching, he found her. Arabejila's descendent. She was approaching the mountain as she had once every five years for the last who-only-knew how many centuries, but she was still hours away. She was not going to get here in time. The woman was too far out and Mitro had grown too strong.

Dax had been considered the greatest hunter of the entire Carpathian race, yet still, fight after fight, Mitro had eluded him. Being locked in the earth for so long without blood to sustain them should have weakened them both, possibly even killed them. But just like Dax, Mitro had found a way to survive and grow stronger. The intense pressure, heat and harsh environment of the volcano had changed them both. If Mitro escaped now, there would be nothing, no one strong enough to stop him.

Dax couldn't let him escape.

The whispers grew stronger, demanding, incessant. For months now, even as he slept, the voices had whispered in his ears, a never-ending chorus. Urging him to visit the cavern near the heart of the volcano. The heat and pressure there was intense, so close to the volcano's main magma chamber that Dax had never been able to stay more than a few seconds at a time. But *something* was there. Something powerful and fierce. Something that normally did not like to be disturbed.

Something the earth believed Dax needed, because it had been driving him back to that chamber again and again and again over the centuries.

The push was stronger now than it had ever been. Every part of him felt both driven and pulled toward that chamber deep in the heart of the volcano. What lay there was waiting for him, and he could delay no longer. The strength he needed was there, offered up to him if only he had the will to claim it.

He dispatched the wards surrounding his resting place and shifted into a clear mist, traveling swiftly through the lava tubes and fissures in the rock, descending deep into the earth until he reached the superheated chamber. A small section of the floor on the far side of the chamber had cracked, and molten rock from the adjacent magma chamber was spilling into the room, thick and glowing orange. The pool was rising rapidly. It wouldn't be long before the entire chamber was completely filled.

In the center of the room, its hindquarters half submerged in the deepening magma, lay the petrified remains of a dragon. Immense and breathtaking, the creature lay curled tightly, wings tucked against his back, tail curled around his body, head resting on diamond-clawed forepaws. The entire dragon had crystallized, its body turning to ruby and diamond in the intense heat and pressure of the volcano. The dragon's chest was destroyed, crushed. Huge chunks of faceted crystal spilled around the petrified carcass.

The heat rising from the magma made the air around the dragon ripple, distorting Dax's vision until the entire crystallized carcass seemed to tremble and move.

Take it. Take what remains. Take what is offered.

The whispers filled Dax's head, making him dizzy. Before him, the heat waves rising from the magma pool seemed to shimmer and take on a translucent fire-red hue, but the shimmer was . . . dragon-shaped?

Dax shook his head, rubbed his eyes, and looked again. The image was still there . . . hazy, translucent, a dragon formed of insubstantial red mist. He stretched out his senses, but could detect no concentrated stench of evil.

The Old One offers you his strength. You were not ready before, but we have made you so. Take what is offered. Without it, you cannot defeat your enemy. Take it. Quickly, before it is lost to the volcano. The earth continued to whisper to him, pushing at him to take a chance that could result in his death.

Dax moved closer. The heat from the magma was so intense, he half expected to burst into flame at any moment, yet his burnished skin didn't even blister. Another step brought him close to the dragon's head and a mere five feet from the widening magma pool. Now, he could sense the power radiating from the crystallized dragon. Where had it come from? He'd been here in this chamber before. He'd found the crystallized dragon, half-crushed but still an awesome discovery, but he'd never sensed this pulsating energy. It almost felt alive.

Stepping closer still, Dax reached for the shimmering veil of energy. The instant he touched it, a raw, savage wildness roared in response. Power slammed into him like an iron fist, plowing into him with enough force to knock him off his feet. He landed hard and pain streaked across his back and jaw, which had taken the brunt of the strike.

Take the power. Take what is offered.

"That was an offer?" Dax got up, dusted himself off and rubbed his aching jaw. "No offense, dear friend, but whatever that is clearly doesn't want to be taken."

Without the Old One's strength, you cannot win. You must take it. But first, you must prove yourself worthy.

"Wonderful." Dax moved his head, stretching the tendons and cracking the joints in his neck. He regarded the translucent image of the dragon shimmering in the hot air. "So be it, Old One. Let us roll the bones."

This time, as he approached the crystallized dragon carcass and the veil of energy hovering above it, he braced himself for attack. The blow, when it came, struck twice as hard as before. Power tore into him with diamond-hard claws. The sheer intensity of it threatened to rip him to pieces, but he set his jaw and leaned into it, firing back a blast of his own, meeting power with power, force with force. The shimmering dragon roared and flexed its wings.

And the fight was on.

Waves of energy swirled around the room. A powerful force built underneath and around him. The walls of the chamber began to tremble. Tiny particles of rock and sand fell from the ceiling. Dax thrust calming waves into the ground, stilling the rupturing earth.

The flow of magma into the chamber increased, forcing Dax to step back. Gases bubbled and spat in the magma pool. The heat increased. The air sparked. The gases caught fire in a flash of boiling orange flame. Dax closed his eyes and flung up a shield. Heat poured over him like an ocean wave.

A voice that sounded like thunder growled and rumbled in his brain. *Only the strongest may hope to hold a dragon's soul. How strong are you, Danutdaxton of the Carpathians?* The dragon spoke in his ancient language, Carpathian, allowing Dax to understand him.

Each word boomed and burned inside his mind as if a hammer made of flaming lead were pounding against his skull. Dax fought the urge to cover his ears, knowing it was useless.

"As strong as I must be to defeat my enemy," Dax replied. A dragon's soul. Was that what fought him now? Or had Mitro found a way to trick him after all? "Do you think me your enemy?"

Does a lion name the flea his enemy?

"A flea, am I?" Dax was mildly insulted at the thought. He reached for the heat rising from the magma, drawing it to him, shaping it between his hands into a ball of fire, which he flung at the center of the insubstantial creature. But rather than punching a hole through the shimmering red mist, the fireball exploded against the surface, spreading out in tongues of flame that were swiftly absorbed. The red-mist dragon seemed to grow larger, as if the flames only made it stronger.

The enemy of heat was cold. Dax tried to drain the heat from around the veil of mist, but the heat was too intense for him to do more than cool the room a few degrees.

"If you mean to help, Old One, then help," Dax said. "There is a great evil locked inside this volcano. While I fight you, it is trying to escape."

What should I care of this evil thing? You have awakened me from my resting place and I care nothing for your troubles.

Dax puzzled over that for a moment. The dragon had no reason to care. His time was long past. All that he knew and loved was gone from the earth. Even his body was gone.

Perhaps there is no reason other than you are a dragon, and a great warrior, or so I have been led to believe.

There was a moment of silence. *A dragon's soul is a mighty power. Only the strongest of vessels could hope to contain it. All others would shatter.*

Power slammed toward Dax again, but this time he tried a different tack. In his years of training with the ancients of his race, he'd learned when to stand firm and when to bend like a tree in the wind. He ducked the dragon's main blast and rolled forward beneath it, coming up close to the beast's shimmering presence.

His feet sank into the edge of the magma pool. Fiery pain streaked up his legs as flesh scorched and burned. Dax shuttered his mind against the agony and tried to absorb and use the heat as the dragon's soul had absorbed and used his fireball earlier. His hands shot out, tracing wards in the air, spinning and twisting energy and the molecules of air in the room into a shining web that he cast around the insubstantial mist of the dragon's soul. A rainbow of light reflected through the room as the energy swirled around his opponent.

Determination and calm rolled through him as the net settled over the dragon. He could feel the spirit gather itself, like any creature would before it strikes. He spread his fingers wide and held them, palms out, between himself and the dragon. Gently, he touched thumb to thumb, then forefinger to forefinger, completing a circle of power, and through that circle, he drew his net of energy tight.

The beast thrashed and roared in outrage, but the bonds of his net held fast. Slowly, relentlessly, Dax pulled the net tighter and tighter. He inched his way backward, dragging the protesting weight of the dragon with him.

Heat jetted out, splashing over him like a geyser. His skin burned. His hair singed. He did not release the net. He kept pulling it through his circle of power, drawing the dragon's soul in tight, folding it in upon itself, pulling it away from the magma pool that he suspected was feeding its strength.

As he pulled, he began to weave new, cooler threads of power over the others. And with each precisely woven thread, his connection to the dragon's spirit increased. He could feel its consciousness pressing up against his own. Each writhing fight, each blast of heat and power, was as much instinctive self-protection as it was a test of Dax's own strength. As the last bit of Dax's net passed through his circle of power, a great force snapped out, but this time the power didn't strike him; it raced up the flows binding it, following them back to Dax.

"No." Realizing its intent, Dax straightened abruptly and tried to weave protective wards. But his efforts were too late, and in speaking he had left an opening, a second circle of power, only this one led into him. The soul rushed forward, a blazing pulse of light and heat that shot into his mouth and down his throat. Energy, heat, power flooded him, burning him from the inside out. He staggered back, releasing his now empty web of power.

The dragon's soul was inside him, searing him. An immense fiery presence that threatened to burst his body asunder. Dax spun a new web, only this time around himself, drawing the threads tight around his own body, adding even more strength to the skin and bone made dense by his centuries locked inside the volcano.

His skin turned dark and began to shudder. Red scales rippled down his arms. Dax held up his hands in surprise as his nails grew crystal clear and lengthened like claws . . . like the dragon's own diamond talons. The change didn't feel like a normal Carpathian shapeshifting. It felt elemental, as if the transformation was happening at more than a cellular level.

Dax fought back, unwilling to relinquish his own body to the soul that had leapt into him. He willed his hand to change back, his nails to soften and shorten. Inch by inch, he fought back the change sweeping over his body, fought to keep his own form.

Inside his body, a second, similar battle raged, only this was not a battle of flesh, but a battle of minds. The dragon's soul surrounded his own and tried to absorb him into itself. It tried to dominate him. But Carpathians were predators, not prey, and Dax was a hunter of immense skill and drive and determination. He did not surrender. Not when fighting the most powerful and heinous vampire the world had ever seen, and not while fighting a powerful, ancient soul for control of his own body.

The dragon rifled through Dax's memories, tearing into his brain, past his substantial inner barriers, ripping through the outer hunter into the depths of Dax's soul. The life of aloneness. The friends and fellow hunters who had turned to evil. The other hunters who had feared and avoided him once they realized he could tell which of them was about to turn vampire. He'd known before they did. Known, and waited close by to kill them before they could harm others.

The Old One found his memories of the friends loved and lost to Mitro Daratrazanoff's evil. The family who had taken him in after his own parents were killed by yet another friend turned vampire. The wish, long forgotten now, for a lifemate of his own. The beautiful Arabejila, companion and friend for more years of life than any unmated Carpathian warrior should ever have to endure. And yet with her, all things had become bearable. The years had not weighed so heavily. The emotions lost to him as he aged had always seemed close at hand when she was near. He had always admired her. Honored her gentleness. Respected her quiet strength. And she had been strong. As strong as he was in her own way. She'd had to be to endure the ruined life Mitro had left to her.

Never once had Dax heard her complain. Oh, he'd seen her eyes grow dark with sorrow. Heard her weep softly in the day when she thought he was asleep. But she'd never complained. Just as she'd never blamed him for not killing Mitro when he had the chance.

Dax had always known Mitro was not right. He'd always stayed close by, waiting for the darkness growing in Mitro's soul to spill over. But when Mitro's soul recognized Arabejila as his lifemate, Dax had thought them safe, thought the power of that bond would keep Mitro from the brink, would heal what was broken inside him.

Instead, it had unleashed the monster. And Dax, who had been lured into a false sense of security, had not been watching as he should—as he would have had Arabejila not been Mitro's lifemate. He'd thought her strong enough to heal him, as she so effortlessly healed all things and all people with just her presence.

She was of the earth. The dragon's voice thundered in Dax's head again, pounding at the edges of his skull.

"Yes," he confirmed. "Stronger in her gifts than any I ever knew."

She sent you to me.

"No, Old One. She is dead. She died long ago."

She is of the earth. She and her daughters. She sent you to me. She sends a daughter to you now.

It surprised him that the dragon knew about the approach of Arabejila's descendent, but perhaps it should not. The dragon, after all, had been buried in this mountain much longer than Dax. It had *become* the mountain; its flesh had become the mountain's stone; its fire had become the mountain's fire.

"That daughter will not arrive in time. That is why, if you have strength to give, I ask that you give it to me now. If I cannot stop the vampire, he will destroy this world. So tell me, Old One, will you help or hinder me? There is no time left. Decide now." Dax drew a breath and dropped his defenses, baring his mind to the dragon's consciousness, everything he and Arabejila had fought for all these years, everything he had loved and lost, everything he believed in, everything he fought for.

As the dragon's mind had pillaged his mind, its power had tested his power, its strength, his strength, now its soul invaded his, peeling him down to the barest essence of his being and examining him with ruthless thoroughness.

Dax felt like he was drowning in the fires of hell. Before, when the lava had burned him, he'd managed to compartmentalize the pain, push it from the forefront of his mind and ignore it, but now there was nowhere that was not wide open and raw and throbbing with agony. Sweat poured down his body, turning to steam against his superheated skin. Dax hardly noticed. An inferno raged inside him.

Hoping to escape the indescribable agony, Dax transitioned into pure energy, a skill normally used to heal someone else, but even as his body became a white glow of light, he could not escape. The vast, fiery redness of the dragon's soul was there, searing him. Body, mind and soul were invaded with burning heat and energy. A latticework of magic and energy led back to every particle of his being, connecting them. That latticework grew tighter, pulling Dax's light form and the dragon's shimmering red soul together, closer and closer until they touched.

In that instant, for a brief flash of time that seemed to stretch to eternity, the dragon's memories sped through Dax's mind. Eons of existence. Soaring flights. Fiery battles fought between winged behemoths dominating the skies. Dense, savagely beautiful jungles, a world that had existed long before the first footsteps of man. A mate, sleek and beautiful, with wide, wind-filled wings and sharp, curling talons. Then man with his steely spears, hunting the creatures he feared. The beautiful mate fallen to the spears of men. Rage. Fire. Blood and destruction raining from the sky. And finally, age and weariness . . . a wound draining ancient strength. A choice to sleep in the heart of the volcano until the world passed away.

The Old One was ancient indeed. A vast, primordial power. An ancient intelligence birthed when the world was still young. Red dragon. Fire dragon. No wonder it had chosen a volcano's heart for its final resting place. The wonder was that it even considered sharing any part of itself with Dax at all.

And share it did. The dragon's long life, each moment of thought or feeling, instinct and craving before this one became part of Dax's memories, part of him. The two became one. Not two beings merged together, but two souls connected by a single body. They could feel each other, move with one another.

The magma pool rose to fill the chamber, and the crystallized remains of the dragon melted back into the liquid earth's blood that had spawned him.

Centuries of living deep in the labyrinth of caves meant Dax had explored every inch possible. He knew the river of lava flowing beneath the earth, a long ribbon of bright orange and red magma and the long tubes that formed the underground subway. He knew every chamber, some with walls of crystalline beauty and others under steaming water. Mud pools bubbled and spat while pools of hot mineral water sent steam rising like fog through caverns.

The problem was that Mitro had had the same time to explore his environment as well. Dax could no longer separate the evil scent from the living abomination; the stench of the undead was everywhere, making it impossible to track him—unless you were a dragon.

Dax felt the Old One stretch, testing senses. Suddenly, like a stick puppet, Dax's body whipped around awkwardly and began moving toward the lava tube on his left. He staggered, his body impossible to control, falling sideways into the wall. The sharp edges of rock scraped at his skin, peeling off the top layer. In the glare of the magma pool, his burnished arm appeared covered in overlapping ovals of red gold. He blinked down at the strange patterning and then touched them. The ovals felt hard, like armor. With his strange diamond-hard nails he tapped them tentatively.

Scales? Like a lizard?

At least it kept him from bleeding. That could come in handy in battle. He'd evolved there in the volcano, and clearly now there would be more changes. The enticing whispers of the earth hadn't disclosed that his body would be altered on an elemental level if he allowed the Old One's soul to share his physical form.

Before he could make a move, his body jerked again toward the lava tube, a large round tunnel he knew went for miles beneath the peaks. He felt like a marionette being jerked around by a drunken puppet master. He sensed the dragon's impatience and realized that being without emotions was a double-edged sword. Carpathian males lived for so long that not feeling was a terrible burden, yet with that came an advantage when hunting.

The dragon was eager for the chase, believing Mitro to be no more than an irritation. He wanted to slumber, didn't want to remain awakened, and once Mitro was disposed of, he planned on doing just that. Dax's body jerked again, his foot lifting awkwardly and then setting down a large stride away, nearly throwing him off balance.

Exasperated, he scowled. *Just give me direction. Don't try to control the movements of my body.*

How was he going to fight Mitro when he could barely take a step without falling? The dragon hadn't had a body in centuries and Dax's body was far too small for him to comprehend how to move it around.

The dragon gave a snort of derision. *It is no wonder this great evil has prevailed. You are a puny one, Carpathian.*

Perhaps that is so, Dax soothed. After all, in relation to size, it was true. *But I can maneuver this body much more easily than you. If we fight one another how will we succeed in our mission?* If pandering to the dragon's ego would result in destroying Mitro, Dax could manage it with no problem.

Power pulsed deep inside, pushing against the restraints of his physical frame. His entire body vibrated, his brain crashing hard against his skull. His body hit the side of the tube hard, this time flinging him to the floor. He couldn't imagine how frustrating it had to be for a massive dragon to find himself confined in a human frame, but Dax was finished reasoning.

And I was told your kind was so intelligent.

Fiercely he pushed back, slamming a wave of massive force straight at the Old One's soul. The internal explosion sent his body reeling. For a moment his head felt as if every bone in his body would shatter. He set his jaw and accepted the pain.

We can do this all night, or work together to destroy the vampire.

Amusement filled his mind. The dragon had a rusty sense of humor. *For a puny lizard, you have a hard punch. How do we do this? I cannot work this strange body.*

If you can find him, point me in the direction. I'm Carpathian. I know you are aware of the things we can do. I'll shift into whatever we need to hunt him. If we need your form, you take over, otherwise we work as a unit, with you guiding me where we go and me getting us there. Is that acceptable?

There was a long moment of silence. *So be it.*

Dax didn't give the Old One time to change his mind. He moved into the lava tube at the dragon's urging. As Dax shifted into mist and sped away through the vents and fissures in the black volcanic rock, the dragon was there with him, part of him, a separate soul and consciousness sharing his body, his gifts. Together, yet still separate. More powerful together than either had been apart. Neither of them would ever be alone again. And both of them streaked through the volcano with one purpose foremost in their minds: to stop Mitro Daratrazanoff or die trying.

The tube was miles long, an old subterranean flow that had long since shifted, leaving a wide tunnel extending under the mountain. Dax had been in it often, following Mitro, knowing the vampire was up to something within the tube, but he'd never managed to catch him at anything. As mist, he could travel without giving away his presence if Mitro had set a trap for him, which he did habitually.

Wait. Here. He has not gone beyond this point.

Dax stopped moving instantly, the mist stretching out along with his senses, trying to reason out where Mitro could have gone. The stench of the undead permeated the tube, and he couldn't feel or smell a difference, but he trusted the dragon's instincts. The creature was a fierce hunter and well adapted to stalking in caves.

The tube didn't have any tributaries, not any that Dax could see, or that he'd ever found, yet the dragon sensed that the vampire hadn't continued along the tube, which meant he'd found another way through the mountain—or was disguised and lying in wait for his enemy.

Dax went still, reaching for his dragon senses. The undead was a repulsive, loathsome stench in the home of the Old One. The creature of myth and legend found the presence of a creature so against nature to be abhorrent. The fact that Mitro was in his home had the dragon outraged.

The stench was strongest to his right. Dax studied the rock outcropping. The wall was dark reds, yellow and deep brown. He could detect no hint of Mitro tampering with the wall itself. He experimented with moving slowly, inch by inch, his patience at odds with the dragon's growing emotions of hostility toward the unwelcome abomination in his home.

The hunt took patience, something the dragon had never had to really develop. Dax skimmed along the rock wall, allowing the mist to touch the various colors and settle into the cracks, examining them to see if there was an opening too small to see. Nothing. He moved lower, taking in every inch of the wall. The tube sloped downward, coming to the floor in a relatively smooth overlap. Again there was no sign of Mitro, but he was beginning to feel a sense of urgency.

Dax knew from centuries of experience that when a hunter felt that sudden push, it meant his prey was close and up to no good. He waited a few heartbeats, going still again, getting a feel for the tube and anything that might be out of place. The overhead ceiling was mottled with grays, blues and deep rust colors. The floor was yellow and brown, chunks of rocks scattered everywhere. Small flecks of gray, blue and rust dusted the top of three of the rocks directly below him.

Dax turned his attention to the ceiling, the mist moving in close, pressing against the mottled rock. The surface was much smoother here, the tiny cracks and crevices harder to discern. As mist, he could seep into the little spaces, going as deep as possible before they dead-ended, and he could examine large portions of the ceiling at the same time.

Clever, clever Mitro. There was a pinhole, so small only a tiny bore worm would be able to insert itself into that dot, but the moment the mist touched it, Dax felt the familiar pull that told him he was not only on the trail, but was very close. He moved deeper inside that small opening and almost immediately it widened in circumference. The worm had grown to enormous proportions, burrowing through the rock and then pushing any flakes to the side. A few had escaped through that little pinhole and landed on the rocks below.

Many times over the centuries, Mitro had worked at finding his way out, burrowing close to the shield set in place by Arabejila so many years earlier. The vampire at times had managed to weaken the barrier when the women had become less powerful, but once the ritual was performed, that safeguard held. Clearly, now that the volcano was close to exploding, and the woman was late, Mitro was making another try.

With great stealth, Dax seeped through the ever-widening hole. The larger the bore worm, the more efficient and faster he could go through the rock. Mitro expanded his worm the moment he thought it safe to do so. It was a brilliant and cunning plan. Dax would never have found that tiny pinhole on his own. The stench of the vampire was too strong everywhere, especially in the lava tube. Mitro had made certain his presence was known in every corner and chamber underground. He knew it was his best defense.

Dax wasn't in the least surprised that Mitro had managed to bore a great distance through, up to the barrier itself. He was finding it hard going once he hit the shield. It may have weakened without the necessary reinforcement Arabejila's kin would bring, but the safeguards were still powerful.

Dax crept up behind the great worm. The creature spun fast, turning over and over, a living drill, its head equipped with a diamond-hard bite while the tail acted like a rudder. Dax timed his moment, a hand reaching out of the mist, grasping the spinning tail, shackling it in a grip impossible to break. Immediately he reversed direction, backing up and dragging the worm with him.

Mitro thrashed and fought, but the hole was tight, preventing him from turning and sinking his teeth into Dax. He tried shifting, but Dax refused to relinquish his hold. Mitro couldn't go forward or shift into insubstantial mist. As the hole began to narrow, he shifted just enough to use his diamond-hard nails on his feet like the claws of a dragon, cutting through the rock as if it didn't exist. He widened the hole, maintaining his grip on the worm's tail as he moved backward toward the lava tube.

The moment he felt the air sliding over him, he shifted again, back into his human form, dropping to the floor of the lava tube, dragging Mitro with him. The worm swung his head around, the massive drill bit driving at Dax's body. Without letting go of the tail, Dax pulled his chest out of the way of that whirling diamond point.

The ground lurched, sending him sprawling against the tube. The worm went wild, slamming itself into the wall, trying to bank off the rocks to get at Dax. Deep inside the dragon roused, a blast of warning reverberating through Dax's skull. Temperatures soared in the lava tube, and steam vented through several places in the floor. The ground shook a second time and molten rock burst through the openings. The floor crumbled and melted, dropping down into the lava flowing beneath the tube.

Dax gripped the struggling worm's tail with both hands, determined they would both be destroyed in the magma rocketing into the tube. More and more geysers slung the melted rock high into the air so that it hit the ceiling and splattered in all directions. Desperate, Mitro reversed direction and slashed at Dax's wrist, driving through flesh. The ground gave another lurch, and Dax sprawled onto the floor.

Beneath him the floor opened and magma shot through. He heard his own scream as the flesh of his legs burned away. He lost his grip on Mitro. For a moment it looked as if the molten rock had engulfed the vampire, but with the orange and red stream of magma rose a suspicious steam. Shrieks of pain and rage filled the tube.

Dax had no choice but to survive. Cutting off the excruciating pain was impossible, but he shifted, knowing it was the dragon's scales that saved him. His flesh was burned away and he needed the healing earth immediately. Once again, fate had favored Mitro. The timing of the blast through the tube's floor hadn't been the vampire, but the volcano preparing for a major eruption. The body of the worm had saved Mitro, but he, too, would have to seek the healing soil. Neither had much time; the volcano wasn't going to wait for them.

4

"Damn, I missed the entire thing," Don Weston whispered overly loud to Dr. Henry Patton. "All those bats going up in flames and Raul losing his mind and wanting to machete someone. I slept right through it. Next time, wake me up!"

Deliberately, he glanced over his shoulder at Annabel and Riley, pretending to be covert, as if his booming voice was so low in his pretend whisper that they couldn't possibly overhear him or know he was talking about them as they trekked in single file through the narrow opening of brush on the small game trail.

Ahead of her, Annabel stiffened, but she didn't turn around.

Riley pressed her lips together tightly. Weston was only making things worse. He wanted to stir up trouble because neither Riley nor her mother would give him the time of day and his ego was bruised. She sighed and wiped the sweat from her forehead. She couldn't wait to make it to the base of the mountain and part company with the engineers, although Ben Charger had stayed true to his word and kept a close watch, along with Jubal Sanders and Gary Jansen.

Annabel reached her hand back and brushed Riley's arm. The touch was featherlight, but Riley could feel her trembling. Her mother had gone very quiet, rarely speaking, her face pale and for the first time, lined a little with age. Riley tried not to feel panic, but she honestly felt as if her mother was retreating from her, slowing slipping away. Everyone had talked nonstop of the incidents in the middle of the night.

Half the camp regarded Raul as if he suddenly had become a serial killer. He didn't seem to remember much, just kept repeating it was a nightmare he'd been caught up in and how sorry he was. To be strictly honest, Riley felt terrible for him. She was still afraid of him, but she couldn't help but see the misery in his eyes—and he had tried to resist that continual pressure and command in his mind. She'd seen him two or three times trying to go back to the fire, to stop moving forward toward her mother's hammock.

Annabel hadn't made a single comment, not even when Riley had explained she'd been the intended target. She'd just looked at Riley with hopeless eyes—almost with that same defeated look Raul had—and shook her head. She'd hardly eaten anything before they'd started out again. The guides were hoping to get to the base of the mountain by nightfall. From there, each group would go their own way. Riley had to admit, she wasn't as eager to part company with Gary and Jubal as much as she'd thought she'd be. There was something very reassuring about both of them.

"I wish he'd stop talking," Annabel said suddenly. She rubbed her temples as if she had a headache.

Riley realized Weston was still going on about the snake attack days earlier in the boat and how he wanted to barbecue vampire bats. His voice droned on and on, almost as endless as the drone of insects.

"He's a moron, Mom," Riley said, trying to keep humor in her voice. "He likes to hear himself talk."

"He's afraid," Annabel replied, her voice low. "And he should be."

Her voice was low and ominous, sending a shiver down Riley's spine. Walking through the jungle wasn't easy. They weren't in the area where the trees grew so high that light couldn't filter through, negating ground cover. This was hard going—miles of thick, dense foliage that covered every possible trail almost as fast as it was hacked out. This was the type of terrain that was extremely dangerous. One wrong turn, one loss of sight of the person in front of you and a person could be lost completely.

Riley knew to watch her hands and feet, to try not to brush up against plants and trees. Most were benign, but the hostile ones were extremely hazardous. She found it difficult to identify a tree that was safe to touch versus one that was poisonous and would cause an instant skin reaction. Most appeared the same to her, and yet her mother knew almost instinctively.

Plants, for Riley, were equally difficult to distinguish no matter how many times the guide pointed them out to her. She knew by looking at the bright colors of the frogs and lizards which were hazardous to her health, and tarantulas the size of dinner plates could be obvious, along with every snake she encountered, but insects were too plentiful for her to remember which were extremely venomous.

Her mother stumbled and Riley caught her to keep her from falling. In the rain forest, her mother *never* tripped over roots. She'd always been surefooted and moved easily among the plants and foliage.

Annabel tightened her hand around Riley's arm, glanced over her shoulder at the porter, Raul's brother, Capa, following close behind. "The moment we get to the base of the mountain, even if it's already night, we have to keep moving with our guide and a couple of porters. No matter how much they protest, we have to get up the mountain tonight," Annabel insisted, her voice so low Riley could barely catch the sound. "Something is really wrong, and I fear we're too late. This is my fault, honey. I should have set out earlier on this journey."

"Dad had a heart attack, Mom," Riley defended, but her sinking heart knew her mother was right. Something was wrong, but rushing up the mountain in the middle of the night wasn't going to solve the problem. "What were you supposed to do? Dash off and leave him there alone in the hospital? We came the moment we could."

Annabel swallowed hard, blinking back tears. She had slept in the hospital bed with her husband and held him in her arms when he died. He'd lingered two weeks before his heart succumbed to the disease he'd fought most of his life. Riley knew her parents were inseparable and that her mother mourned her husband every single moment of every day. Annabel had always been alive and vibrant but since her husband's death, she seemed far more subdued and distant. The truth was, Riley stuck to her side, afraid of losing her mother to pure sorrow.

Dressed in boots, with jeans tucked in to prevent insect bites and scratches from hostile foliage, both women knew what it took for a prolonged trek through the jungle, but the going was difficult. As a rule, Annabel seemed to have an innate sense of direction, where Riley was completely turned around within moments of stepping off the boat and into the dimly lit interior.

Her mother had always had such an affinity with the land, especially here in the rain forest, almost as if she had a built-in compass. Right now, she showed signs of distraction and anxiety, so rare in Annabel that Riley's alarm for her increased. That along with the occasional stumble told Riley her mother was pulling even further away.

She let her breath out slowly as she dropped back to step closely in her mother's footsteps. She'd learned, even as a young child, the safest place in the jungle was directly behind her mother. The plants protected her rather than attacked her. Everywhere her mother stepped, plants grew as she passed over the thin trail. Fronds unfolded and vines untangled. Flowers sometimes dropped around her. As long as she walked in her mother's footprints no thorn or spiny-leafed plant would harm her.

They walked for what seemed like hours. The heat was oppressing in the stillness beneath the thick canopy. At times the ground beneath their feet was open and it became easy to walk, and then suddenly they would once again be in thick foliage, nearly impossible to penetrate. Riley kept a very close eye on her mother as they trekked, noting she began to lag behind more and more.

Both Jubal and Gary slowed their pace, obviously keeping an eye on Annabel. Riley took her pack. It was significant that Annabel made no protest when Riley shouldered her mother's pack with her own. After half an hour, Ben Charger dropped back and took the pack. The three men took turns carrying it. Annabel never looked up. Her shoulders became slumped, weighed down, the closer they got to the base of the mountain. Her footsteps dragged, as if she waded through quicksand and every step was a terrible effort. Even her breathing became labored.

It was clear the guides were rushing the sun, trying to make the base of the mountain before nightfall, which suited Riley, but her mother wasn't going to make it. She'd fallen silent, watching Jubal's back to stay in line, but she swayed with weariness and her clothes and hair were damp with sweat. They had to stop and rest.

Fortunately, Weston complained bitterly. "Are we in some kind of race?" he demanded. His voice rose with every step.

"Miguel." Jubal's voice carried authority as he spoke to the guide in Miguel's native language. "We have to stop and rest. Half an hour. No more and we'll start out again. Let them rest and get a drink. They'll move faster for you."

Miguel glanced up at the sky, looking very apprehensive, but he nodded abruptly and found a tiny clearing with a few rocks for them to sit on. Riley nodded to Jubal in thanks as she took her mother's pack from him and moved to the edge of the trees to give her mother some privacy. She was grateful more attention hadn't been drawn to her.

"We can't stop," Annabel whispered the moment they were alone. "We have to hurry."

"You need rest, Mom," Riley protested. "Here, drink this." She handed her water pack to her mother.

Annabel shook her head. "You'll have to leave me if I can't make it."

"Mom." Riley forced herself to be firm. Annabel looked so exhausted and pale she just wanted to wrap her in her arms and hold her protectively. "You have to tell me what's going on. What are we facing up there on that mountain? I can't be kept in the dark anymore."

Annabel looked around for a place to sit, found a small boulder nestled between two trees and sank down onto it. Her hands trembled as she folded them carefully into her lap. "All those stories you were told as a little girl about the mountain and the Cloud Warriors, those weren't scary stories, Riley. They were the truth. The history of our people."

Riley swallowed hard. Those "stories" were the thing of nightmares. A terrible evil preying on the greatest warriors, tearing out their throats, drinking blood, demanding human sacrifices, children, young women, yet nothing appeased the demon. "Mom, the Incas conquered the Cloud People . . ."

"They were able to because," Annabel interrupted, "their best warriors had already been killed. The people were living in fear." Her eyes met Riley's. "The Incas were strong, with fierce warriors as well. They took some of the Cloud women as wives. Including your ancestor, a woman named Arabejila. She was the one who handed down the truth—as well as her gifts—to her daughter. The evil continued for years and years, killing the warriors of the

Incas just as it had those of the Cloud People. No one seemed able to defeat such a bloodthirsty demon."

Riley wanted to scoff at such ridiculous lore. She'd heard the stories, but she'd also read history, as much as had been compiled about the Cloud People and the Incas. There were a few obscure references to human sacrifice and warriors dying, but very little, certainly not enough to support the story her mother was telling her . . . But, the feeling of evil was growing beneath her feet as they grew closer to the mountain. She felt the earth tremble every now and then, and with all the strange events, the attacks on her mother, how could she just dismiss what her mother was telling her?

"Keep going." Riley wanted to put her hands over her ears. Her heart beat too fast—in time to the heartbeat of the earth. She felt the shiver beneath her feet, as if the ground itself was listening and trying to warn her, whatever that evil was, that it was about to escape.

"There was one man who had come with your ancestor from a strange land. He fought battle after battle but could not defeat this evil. In the end, Arabejila lured the evil into the volcano with the warrior, a tremendous sacrifice. She locked them there, but every so many years, to keep the volcano from erupting, which would allow him freedom . . ."

"No one could live in a volcano for hundreds of years, Mom, and still be alive." Riley made it a firm statement. It was the truth . . . wasn't it? The fear she tasted in her mouth said something altogether different.

"I know they're locked in there, at least that evil creature is still there. I've *felt* him, and right now, every single person here is feeling him. I'm late, and if he escapes, everyone he kills—and he will kill over and over—will be on me."

Riley scowled at her mother. "That's ridiculous. You had no choice but to stay with Dad. We've been delayed here over and over . . ." She trailed off. If that evil entity was in some way influencing those traveling with them, was it so far off to think that he could be delaying them? "How could this thing still be alive after all this time? You're talking five hundred years more or less."

"He is. I feel him. You feel him. Evil lives and walks this earth, Riley, and it's your job—and mine—to help stop it. That's the legacy we were given and we have no choice. If the thing gets out into the world and kills, we've failed."

"What do we do when we get up the mountain, Mom?" Riley made up her mind. No matter what, Annabel was determined to go up that mountain and perform the ritual taught to her by her mother before her. There would be no stopping her, no matter how worn she looked, so Riley was getting her up that mountain and getting the job done as quickly as possible. Her mother wasn't living in a fantasy. She meant every word she said. Riley heard the ring of truth in her voice.

"You know what needs to be done," Annabel said. "I've taught you since you were a child. If we succeed, you have to come to this mountain when you're pregnant and have your daughter here. She must be a part of the earth. The gifts are strong in you, much stronger than they ever have been in me, or even my mother. I could feel the earth accept you as her child the moment I put you down into the cradle crevice." She wiped sweat from her face. "The sun will be down soon. That's the most dangerous time, Riley. He's quiet during the day, but at night, he can take command. Never underestimate him. From what I was told, he can appear beautiful and charming but he's wholly evil. If something happens to me . . ."

"Mom," Riley protested. "Don't say that. Don't think it. I won't let anything happen to you. I won't."

Annabel held up her hand. "We can't pretend. There's every possibility. And then he'll go after you. We're a threat to him and he will do everything in his power to eliminate us."

Riley scrubbed her hand over her face, as if that could remove the clawing fear. The energy running beneath her feet thrummed of urgency. She had become so aware of the surrounding rain forest, of the vegetation she walked on, and now, the dirt itself, reaching out to her with veins of information, silently screaming to hurry—hurry.

Riley forced herself to nod. Her mother needed reassurance that she could handle whatever was thrown at them. "I think the two researchers, Gary and Jubal, know about the stories. I asked them what was happening last night and both used the word *evil*, as if it was spreading across the land and influencing all of us. They've been keeping a watch over us and I don't think I could have saved you last night without them. Ben Charger has been sticking close as well, helping to guard us. He seems to realize something beyond the normal is influencing everyone as well, but I haven't discussed anything with him."

Annabel shook her head. "You can't really trust anyone, Riley. This thing—this evil creature—is capable of turning anyone against us."

"We still need allies, Mom," Riley said. "Those men have helped us so far, and they're armed to the teeth. Both carry all kinds of weapons on them, some I've never seen before. They didn't seem to care, when they strapped them all on this morning, that the guides and porters could see them. In fact, they *wanted* them to see—I think to help protect us."

Annabel frowned and rubbed sweat from her forehead. She pushed back the damp curls corkscrewing around her face. "How would they get any weapons through customs? Through the airport? Don't you think it's strange they even have weapons on them? As if they already knew something would be wrong and they came prepared?"

Riley leaned in close to her mother. "I honestly don't care how they got them, or why they brought them. They saved your life last night and we need them. Something bad is going to happen soon. We both know that. We need these men and their weapons. In fact, I'm going to see if they'll lend me one." She infused determination into her voice, daring her mother to disagree with her. Clearly Annabel wasn't thinking straight, or she would see they couldn't do this task alone.

Annabel simply shrugged, wiping her face again, hanging her head, shoulders slumped. Riley bit down hard on her lip. Her mother was definitely giving up and she couldn't have that. She had to find a way to make her feel as if they were empowered—as if whatever this evil entity was they had a chance against him.

"Mom, if this Arabejila is our ancestor and she was able to lure this evil killing machine into a volcano and hold him there, and keep the volcano from erupting for years, and then my great-great-grandmother, all the way to you have done it, then together, we can do it, too." She infused confidence into her voice. "We aren't less than they are. We have the same blood. The forest reacts to you, and now to me. I feel the earth's heartbeat . . ."

Annabel rocked gently and shook her head. "I don't. I can't anymore. Before, her heart beat with mine. My blood ran with the sap in the trees and underground rivers. She's lost to me. I could feel her fading after your father died."

Riley leaned close to her mother. "Stop it, Mom. I mean it. Pull yourself together. You're giving up because Dad is dead. I saw Grandma do the same thing. You can't leave me here in Peru, surrounded by danger. I need you to be strong. You're the one pulling away from the gifts you have, pulling away from me. I'm your daughter. Your only child. What do I do if you just give up?"

She put her hand on her mother's knee and softened her voice. "You taught me to be a fighter, to never give up. Now, whatever this is, no matter how bad, you say we *have* to succeed, that innocent lives depend on us. So let's get the job done, no matter the cost to us. We do this thing all the way, and we succeed."

Annabel looked up, her eyes meeting Riley's. For a moment there was that spark of absolute determination Riley recognized in her mother. And then she blinked back tears. "I know I haven't been myself, honey. It's just that your father and I were so close. I can't breathe right without him. We just fit together more like one person and without him, I'm having a hard time functioning."

"Mom." Riley leaned close. "Of course you feel that way. Dad's only been gone a short time. You haven't had time to come to terms with his death. Neither have I. We just lost him and we're supposed to be home grieving, not out here in the rain forest, climbing a mountain surrounded by strangers and dealing with something profoundly evil."

Annabel swallowed hard and shoved at the damp curls springing around her face. The humidity and heat had sent her hair into a frenzy of brown frizz and corkscrews all over her head.

Annabel reached out to touch Riley's thick, long hair, straight as a bone, not a frizz in sight in spite of the humidity. She wore it in a long braid to keep it off her neck and away from her face. "You're so beautiful, Riley, and so different. You belong here. Your soul is here whether you know it or not and the land is calling to you. I can feel it. I'm certain you can as well. Listen to what it says to you. Trust your instincts."

Riley's heart jumped. Her mother sounded like she was saying good-bye all over again. Her hands trembled as she smoothed Riley's hair. She looked so fragile Riley's heart ached. Clearly, Annabel wanted to help Riley, but in her defeated state she felt incapable. That small surge of determination faded far too fast.

Riley let her breath out slowly. "You need to drink more water, Mom," she advised, giving up on trying to rally Annabel's defenses. The best she could do was get her mother up the mountain and keep anyone from killing her. And that required a better weapon than the one she had.

Jubal was off to her left, not far from them. Gary was on their other side, a discreet distance away, and Ben had found a resting place in front of them, as if guarding them from the others. Riley couldn't count on her mother, and she needed these men to help keep her mother safe. She needed to plan every step carefully and prepare for any emergencies. That meant her pack as well as her mother's needed extra supplies.

She always carried rations and her own water filtration system. She'd been backpacking for years and knew how to survive, but she needed weapons. "Mom, rest here. I want you to eat this." She held out a high protein bar to her mother. "You need to keep up your strength. I'm just going to go over there"—she indicated Jubal—"to talk to him for a minute."

"You can't trust them," Annabel hissed, her eyebrows coming together. "You really can't. Evil looks beautiful and good can look quite rough and terrible. You can't know who is on our side."

"Maybe not, Mom," Riley said, forcing the protein bar into her mother's hand. "But at the moment, I need a weapon and he's got one. Eat this and just wait for me to come back. Don't move."

Suspicion slipped into Annabel's eyes. Her hand closed around the protein bar gingerly, as if her own daughter might be trying to poison her.

Riley's heart sank as her mother turned away from her, hunching her back and rounding her shoulders. She actually felt Annabel pulling away from her, distancing herself. The look in her eyes was both defeated and accusing.

Riley shook her head and squared her shoulders. Her mother was obviously ill, her grief overcoming her ability to function. Riley set her teeth and marched over to Jubal. She couldn't help glancing over her shoulder often to make certain no one dared approach her mother while she was away.

"Riley," Jubal greeted with a slight nod. His gaze was restless, moving over the camp, up into the trees and along the ground. "Is your mother all right?"

Riley shook her head. "She's exhausted, but she wants to get up the mountain. Maybe if we make it to the site, she'll feel better. That's my hope."

"How far up the mountain?" Jubal asked. "The tremors are getting worse. The mountain hasn't blown in hundreds of years, but that doesn't mean it won't. I'm not certain we're going to be entirely safe on that mountain. Gary's trying to get us some data. He's got to wait for the satellite, but we should be able to find out if there are any changes to the shape of the mountain. Photographs of all these volcanos are regularly taken from space."

Riley sighed. It wasn't as if the tremors hadn't gone unnoticed. "One more thing to worry about. Do you really think the volcano will explode?"

Jubal frowned thoughtfully. "It feels like it to me. I'm not certain it's such a great idea to go up, although the plants we're looking for are supposed to be close to the ruins. If those plants are really there, we need them."

"Look." Riley made up her mind to lay her cards on the table if she had to. She didn't have much of a hand, but she was going to get the job done and protect her mother no matter what. The determination grew in her that she had to go and stop whatever was inside that mountain from getting out. "I know you and Gary are armed to the teeth. You're not exactly hiding the fact from anyone."

"I thought it might help deter anyone thinking they could use a machete to hack up members of our party," Jubal pointed out.

She winced, feeling she deserved the slight reprimand. She shrugged it off. "I don't like anyone prying into our business so the last thing I want to do is pry into yours . . ."

Jubal smiled at her, although there was no humor in his eyes. Maybe understanding. "But?" he encouraged.

"How did you get all those weapons and your equipment into this country? I've never even seen some of those weapons. You couldn't possibly have gotten them onto a plane."

"We have a few friends in this country with private planes and ships. They had everything we asked for waiting for us when we arrived. These plants are as important to them as they are to us. The plants have never grown anywhere but the Carpathian Mountains, and they're extinct there. If these are truly the same ones, you have no idea what an important find it would be for us."

She heard the underlying animation in his voice. He was telling her the truth—or at least part of it. There was an urgency about his need to go up the mountain and, God help her, she was grateful for it. She wouldn't have to go alone.

"I need a gun."

Jubal's eyes met hers. She refused to look away. She *needed* that weapon and she wasn't going to back down or be intimidated into backtracking. He was not going to get to look at her as a hysterical woman, because she wasn't hysterical. She was absolutely serious.

Jubal's eyebrow shot up. "Have you ever fired a gun?"

"Yes. I'm quite a good shot. My father's best friend was a police officer, and he took me to the shooting range when I was ten and I've been shooting ever since."

"Shooting a human being isn't so easy, Riley. If you hesitate . . ."

"I would have tried to kill Raul with my knife last night," she said, meaning it. "And I wouldn't have hesitated, not with my mother's life at stake. I won't hesitate if I need to protect her," she assured.

"What if you need to protect yourself?"

Her chin went up. She refused to look away, holding her gaze steady on his. "I'm not a shrinking violet, Jubal. If I need to defend my life, I'll do it vigorously. And no one is going to harm my mother, not if I can help it. Will you lend me a gun?"

Jubal frowned and pulled a pistol from inside his light jacket. "Tell me what this is."

She knew he thought she'd lied to him about knowing how to fire a gun. She sent him a sweet smile. "You're holding a Glock 30 SF, 45 auto, a powerful, excellent weapon. My godfather gave one to me on my sixteenth birthday. It has a smaller grip, and I have small hands so it suits me quite well."

Jubal sighed. "Whatever is up there, Riley, this isn't going to stop it."

"It will stop anyone traveling with us from trying to kill my mother."

Jubal handed her the Glock. Her hand closed around the grip, taking it slowly. She checked the magazine to make certain it was full. He handed her a second magazine, which she slipped into her pocket and zipped the flap closed.

"Riley!"

Riley spun around to see her mother rushing toward her. Annabel's face was white, her eyes wide with terror. Behind her, the ground had come to life—large, almost dinner-plate-sized tarantulas scuttling in the vegetation, coming down from the trees and looking very focused as they shuffled relentlessly forward.

Riley rushed to intercept Annabel before she could flee into the rain forest. "A tarantula bite isn't fatal, Mom. Calm down. Irritation from their hair is sometimes worse than the bite."

"They're chasing me," Annabel gasped, gripping Riley hard. She lowered her voice, hissing between her teeth, her eyes wild, hair disheveled. She looked nearly demonic. "They're *chasing* me, Riley, can't you see that? They want to kill me."

Riley didn't know what multiple bites from the large tarantulas could actually do, nor did she want to take any chances. She caught her mother's wrist and pulled her toward Gary Sanders, who was closest to the small ribbon of a stream. Surely the spiders wouldn't follow them into the water.

Annabel choked back a sob. "I can't do this anymore, Riley. You have to go on without me. I just can't . . ."

"Stop it," Riley snapped as she pulled her mother over a series of stones and ferns to get to the stream. "We can do anything we have to do. You were the one who taught me that."

She glanced behind her. Jubal, Gary and Ben formed a line of defense against the crawling spiders. She stopped her mother's forward momentum before she could step into the stream.

"Let me take a look, Mom," she cautioned. Piranha wouldn't be in that tiny stream, but with all the strange attacks from insects and animals, she didn't want to chance missing anything. "We'll step in only if they get past everyone."

Gary pulled a hose over his shoulder and stepped forward. The moment a spout of fire gushed from the flamethrower, the rest of the camp became aware something was wrong. Heads turned, one by one. Riley was glad she and Annabel were in the shadow of the trees. It looked as if the three men were being attacked, not the women. They were a good distance away. She added to the illusion by sitting on a rock beside the stream and drawing her mother down to sit beside her as if they'd been resting there in the shade.

Weston and Shelton predictably made a huge fuss, Weston actually running away from the spiders. Not only were they not close to him, but the migration was moving away from him. It didn't matter. He berated the guides.

"You chose a rest stop right in the middle of killer spider territory. Are you trying to do us all in? I'm reporting you, and you'll never get another guide job again," he snapped.

Riley rolled her eyes. The guides ignored him, rushing to help the three men. The porters grouped together in a tight circle, watching. The archaeologist and his students stared at one another with shocked, almost comical expressions, as if they couldn't quite understand what was happening. The three just stood there, openmouthed, while the ground came to life with large hairy spiders crawling through the vegetation. Her idea of archaeologists admittedly had been formed by the action-hero Indiana Jones movies, but Dr. Patton and his students were fast putting that fantasy to rest.

She could actually hear the spiders scuttling through the debris as they advanced, but the smell and sound of Gary's flamethrower began to quickly drown out every other noise. Annabel covered her face with her hands and rocked back and forth. Riley put her arm around her mother to comfort her.

Annabel moaned softly. "It's so late, Riley. In a couple of hours the sun will go down."

"We'll leave in a few minutes," she assured. "The guides will take us up the mountain and this will be over. We're so close now."

Annabel continued to rock back and forth, Riley's arm around her shoulders for comfort, but all the while, Riley studied the members of their traveling group, trying to discern who she might be able to count on if things went wrong. The shivering in the ground told her bad things were bound to happen. All three guides had rushed to help the three men with the spiders. They didn't appear to be afraid of them at all. In fact, they picked some of them up very gently and turned them around.

She found the way the three natives handled the tarantulas fascinating. They clearly wanted to save them, not destroy them. The tarantulas seemed confused, turning in circles, avoiding the hot flames. Gary switched off the very efficient flamethrower and, like Riley, watched the guides gently managing the spiders away from everyone and back into the rain forest.

Not one of the porters had helped, Riley noted. They huddled close together, whispering. Her heart sank. They would need a couple of porters going up the mountain and at least two would accompany Gary and Jubal with their guide.

"Come on, Mom," she said. "We're heading out again. Drama's over. The guides dealt with the spiders, and we're back on track."

The ground shivered again. "We have to hurry," Annabel whispered. "Hurry, Riley." She glanced up toward the sky. The sun would be down in a short time.

Riley positioned herself directly behind her mother on the narrow trail the guides had chosen to make the last miles to the base of the mountain. She would argue with her guide later to keep going up the mountain. Right now, it was imperative that they just get moving. Annabel's agitation grew with every passing minute.

Ben and Jubal went in front of Annabel, and Gary chose to bring up the rear behind the last porter. Riley was grateful she was a good distance from Weston and Shelton with several people between them. Once they actually got started, the guides and porters hacking out the dense trail, Annabel ceased muttering and just walked, her gaze on the back of Jubal's shirt.

The whispers in their head started up an hour before the sun set. The sun had faded, bringing shadows into the rain forest, changing the appearance of plants to monstrous shapes. Riley could see the effects of the incessant buzzing in everyone's head. For her, the sound was faded and far into the background, but even her mother began to mumble a protest.

Perhaps because of the danger to someone she loved, Riley's senses seemed to increase with every step she took, along with awareness of her surroundings. She found herself seeing things she'd never noticed before. Individual leaves. The way the moss and fern grew and the flowers wound their way up trunks to the skies. For the first time in her life, she was wholly fascinated by the growth of the plants. She could hear the life force of the earth, a pounding beat that nearly drove out those soft meaningless whispers trying to invade her mind. For a few moments, as darkness began to drop its shroud, the surrounding plant life had seemed frightening; now it was exquisitely beautiful and even comforting.

The colors in the rain forest seemed far more vivid, even as night began to fall, flowers creeping up trunks and bursting across the ground. Moisture dripped, the sound musical rather than annoying. Riley felt as if the land she walked on recognized her for the very first time and was signaling acceptance of her presence. The hostility she felt was from an outside source, some subtle force she couldn't yet identify, but felt weaving through the forest like a disease.

Behind her, the porter Capa muttered in his own language under his breath, hacking at the tangle of vines and flowers springing up as Annabel walked. Riley was careful to step close to her mother, covering her tracks, so the porter couldn't tell the plants pushing through the thick vegetation hadn't already been there.

Her mother glanced over her shoulder, back at Riley, looking exhausted. She sent her daughter a small smile and mouthed, "I love you."

Riley felt a flood of love for her mother, streaming strong. She blew her a kiss.

Overhead, monkeys suddenly shrieked, so that the rain forest erupted into a cacophony of noise. The monkeys followed their every movement, running along the tree branches overhead throwing twigs and leaves. Some brandished branches threateningly and displayed teeth—another new phenomenon for Riley. In her experience, the monkeys and wildlife kept their distance.

Without warning, something landed on her back, driving her straight to the ground. Sharp claws gripped her shoulders, raking at her pack. She was hit again and again as more monkeys sprang from the trees, their combined weight knocking her backward. She heard Annabel scream and Jubal curse. The sound of Capa's chanting grew loud above the shrieking of the monkeys.

"Hän kalma, emni hän ku köd alte. Tappatak ŋamaŋ. Tappatak ŋamaŋ."

Frantic, screaming for Gary and Jubal, Riley fought to throw off the monkeys and pull out the Glock at the same time.

5

Riley twisted out from beneath the pile of woolly monkeys, coming up on one knee, using a two-fisted grip to steady the gun. She couldn't see anything. There were dozens of gray and olive, red-brown and black monkeys between her and Annabel. The ones leaping on her mother had driven her back into the dense brush, and all Riley could see were the furry bodies in some kind of shrieking frenzy. She didn't dare shoot at them for fear of hitting Annabel.

Her mother screamed again, the sound terrified, reverberating through Riley's head. She scrambled to her feet, only to have another wave of primates slam her back to the ground. Each woolly monkey weighed close to seventeen pounds, and they dropped hard from the branches overhead, using their weight and sheer numbers to crush the humans under them.

The buzzing in her head, that awful chant, swelled in volume—in command. *Hän kalma, emni hän ku köd alte. Tappatak ŋamaŋ. Tappatak ŋamaŋ.*

She could hear the words echoing through her mind, over and over, a guttural, deep-throated chant, almost like the monks she'd heard in Tibet when throat-chanting. The sound disturbed on the most elemental level, raising the hair on her body, making her skull ache, flashing through her nervous system until she wanted to shriek like the monkeys.

Riley tried to roll away from the attacking creatures, but they stuck like glue, attaching themselves to her hair and clothing and pack, holding on as if their lives depended on it. As a rule, woolly monkeys lived in the higher elevations, farther up in the cloud forest, and they weren't threatening to anyone. They lived in social groups of up to forty, but the numbers dropping from the trees and attacking all members in their party were far more than forty.

Sobbing, Riley threw monkeys off of her, uncaring that they were using teeth and claws to drive her to the earth, and every time she hurled one away, they shredded skin. She rose to her feet fast, whirling in a circle trying to orient herself. The woolly monkeys were everywhere, an army of them, and the men were trying to fight them off, just as she was.

She kicked at them, and one sank his teeth into her leg, trying to drag her down just as she spotted the dense foliage where her mother fought off the crazed primates. The entire scene was surreal, unreal, a nightmare of violence and blood and screams. A gun barked behind her, and somewhere in front of her, another answered. She ran forward, kicking and swearing, sweeping a path clear to get to her mother. Twice she shot one of the monkeys in midair as they flung themselves at her face.

She ran toward the spot where she was certain her mother had been dragged. Annabel's screams were loud and shocked and horrible, an animal in pain, pierced through with utter terror. Riley couldn't see her through the screen of bodies. She had no idea where the porter, Capa, or Gary was, so there was no way to fire into the thrashing bodies of the primates safely even though every cell in her body commanded her to do so.

Woolly monkeys arrived in masses, far more than one troop of forty, dropping through the trees faster than the humans could get on their feet. The battle was something out of a horror movie, vicious and unreal. Her mother's screams abruptly stopped. Riley's heart jumped and more adrenaline flooded her body. The lack of sound was far worse.

Cursing, sobbing, Riley fought her way through the solid barriers of maddened primates to get to the place where Annabel had been driven off the trail. There was blood everywhere, dark pools of it. As she kicked away an aggressive monkey, a crimson arch sprayed into the air, splashing across the leaves of nearby brush, across tree trunks and the monkeys. For a moment she thought the monkeys were bleeding, but then she saw him. The porter. Not Raul, but his brother, Capa, chopping down over and over with a bloody machete.

Her heart stopped. She couldn't see if it was her mother or the monkeys he was attacking, but there was so much blood. Far too much. With another vicious kick, she sent another monkey sprawling on the ground, giving her a glimpse of her mother's body. She squeezed the trigger over and over, emptying the magazine into Capa, running forward as she shot him, knowing it was already too late. She slapped the second magazine into place.

Simultaneously, Gary shot, his bullets entering the porter from the side, spinning him around. Uncaring that she was running into a blaze of gunfire, Riley rushed forward, kicking and punching and even shooting the monkeys to get to her mother. Capa went down hard, the machete flying from his hand. Gary continued to shoot the primates surrounding her mother.

Riley pushed aside the brush and stopped abruptly, her mouth wide open, an agonized scream nearly shredding her vocal cords. She stared into the brush with absolute horror and shock filling her. She wasn't even certain what she was seeing, comprehension impossible. For one moment, it looked as if she'd stumbled on a massacre. Her mind tried to tell her that everything soaking into the ground and brush was from monkeys, but her body had gone into some kind of shock, almost numb, frozen and somewhere deep inside she knew, she just couldn't accept the truth. There was so much blood. She couldn't see flesh, only strips of cloth and hair. She forced her body to move forward, bile rising.

"No, Riley." Arms came around her, preventing her from moving. Hands covered hers, removing the Glock. "Come away from here. There's nothing you can do and there's no need to see this." Gary's voice was extremely gentle, coming from a long distance away.

The world faded in and out. Her stomach lurched and she tried to turn her head, to look away from the mangled body, but it was impossible. The blood was so dark. Curly hair lay on the ground, strands and tufts across fronds of fern, matted and muddy red. She saw fingers and part of a hand. Strips of clothing covered in blood. There wasn't a place in a five-foot radius that wasn't soaked red. It was impossible to tell what lay in that dark dense foliage.

She was aware of the sudden silence in the rain forest. No sound at all. No drone of insects. No gunfire. No shouting. The buzzing in her head was gone, to be replaced by her silent screams of protest. The world around her receded and then sharply focused, only to recede again.

"Riley," Gary spoke in her ear, his voice calm and firm. "You have to come with me now. Looking at her isn't going to help."

His hands urged her frozen body to move, to take steps, but she had no control, the shaking, the anger, the grief welling up like a volcano, from deep beneath the shivering ground, straight through her body, until her heart wanted to stop beating and her lungs refused to work.

She tried to tell Gary she couldn't breathe, couldn't draw in air. The scent of blood was too heavy, permeating the entire area. He simply lifted her off her feet and began to stride away. She caught a glimpse of Capa, the porter, lying in his own pool of blood, the machete a few inches from his hand. His body was intact, although all life had run out of him onto the ground.

A sob escaped and she gripped Gary's arm hard, her only reality in a world gone mad. Annabel murdered in such a savage way was unthinkable. Her mind just refused to process, but her body was wholly aware and reacting with shutting down. She wasn't certain she could have stood on her own if her life depended on it. Gary allowed her to sink into the carpet of vegetation, a short distance away from the site of her mother's murder.

She was aware of her traveling companions on some level, actors in a play. Their slow reactions. Turning heads. Mouths open with shock. The bodies of dead monkeys were scattered like litter across the ground, adding to the macabre scene. Everything around her blurred, and it took a moment to realize her eyes were swimming with tears.

The monkeys that hadn't suddenly taken to the trees appeared as confused as she felt, wandering in circles, as if they'd lost all direction. On the edge of her vision, she saw the three guides picking themselves off the ground, all disheveled and streaked with blood from the attacks of the woolly monkeys. The three brothers ignored the scattered primates and looked uneasily toward the rain forest and the two bodies that lay just out of their sight. They whispered to one another in low, hushed voices, before making up their minds to see what had transpired.

Jubal moved out into the open to face them, his clothes torn from the vicious, concentrated attack, showing evidence he'd tried to get back to Annabel and was stopped just as Riley had been. The three guides hesitated, but continued slowly forward, craning their necks, hands gripping weapons.

Dr. Henry Patton picked himself up gingerly from the ground and hurried over to help one of his students, Marty Shepherd, up. The man appeared to be in tears, almost hysterical, slapping at Patton and fighting when Todd Dillon rushed over to aid him as well. Marty was pulled to his feet, but instantly sank back to the ground with the other two men bending solicitously over him.

Riley rocked herself back and forth, trying to take in that her mother had been murdered just feet from her. She looked down at the rich dirt, thick from hundreds—thousands—of years of vegetation, of death and rebirth. Above her head, the sky darkened subtly. She glanced up as she dropped her hands and buried them deep in the layers of black dirt. Clouds swirled ominously overhead, forming towers rising high. The wind stirred her hair, even there, under the stillness of the canopy, while the branches of the trees emerging from the canopy whipped back and forth in a frenzy of activity.

She took a breath and let it out. A long keening moan escaped from her throat. At the sound, the remaining monkeys took to the trees, the mourning notes following them through the rain forest. Instead of moving up the mountain, the troop of woolly monkeys moved *away* from their natural home high up in the cloud forest.

Don Weston and Mack Shelton stumbled back into sight. Both had run when the monkeys had descended. Neither appeared to have a scratch. They'd made it far enough away from the battle to evade the onslaught of the primates. They both appeared shaken.

"What the hell happened here?" Don demanded, surveying his scratched and bloody companions as well as the furry bodies on the ground. "I thought monkeys were the least of our worries."

Miguel turned to look at him over his shoulder. "Monkeys do not attack men."

"I got news for you, genius," Don responded with a shuddering snort. "They just did. Do they have rabies?" He actually stepped back away from the others and swept his arm across Mack's body to prevent him from getting any closer to the others.

Jubal sighed. "They don't have rabies, Don, but we have to disinfect every single scratch before anyone gets an infection. Marty, I need you and Todd to get busy doing that. Start with yourselves. The medical kits are in the packs. Once you make certain both of you have covered every scratch, use the antibiotics and then split up and help the others."

Riley heard him from a distance. She even knew what he was doing, taking charge, bolstering the two shaken students, giving them something active to do in order to help them recover. She couldn't move a muscle. There was no recovering. She felt numb, beyond comprehension. Her mind struggled to understand, and on some level she knew she was in shock, but she couldn't pull herself together.

She dug her fingers into the soil, the only thing real she could hold on to. Dragging two fistfuls out of the earth, she closed her fingers tight around the dirt and just let herself cry. Tears ran down her face, obscuring her vision, falling into the soil, but she could hear the others coming out of their shock, moving around, doing as Jubal instructed.

Jorge, Fernando and Hector, three of the four remaining porters, all cousins, approached Jubal hesitantly from the left side, careful to keep an even pace with the guides who were confronting Jubal straight on.

Ben Charger moved in behind them, deliberately making noise so they were very aware of his presence. Across from the porters, closing in on Jubal, was the fourth porter, Raul. Gary followed him at an easy pace, but, like Ben, making it known he was right behind the porter. He carried his weapon openly.

Miguel stopped in front of Jubal. "Who is hurt?"

"Not hurt, dead," Jubal corrected. "Your porter murdered Annabel. What's left of her is in those bushes over there." He nodded toward the dense foliage but didn't take his eyes from Miguel or step back.

Miguel's gaze followed the direction of Jubal's nod. He swallowed hard and took a step toward the darkened brush. "What about Capa? Where is he?"

"He's dead, too," Jubal answered, his voice grim, a warning inflection in his voice. "We were too late to stop him."

Silence once again descended, the news clearly shocking everyone. The men looked at one another. Miguel nodded and led the way to the bloody brush. His brothers followed him silently. The porters skirted around Jubal, who turned to face them all. Ben and Gary flanked them from either side, clearly not trusting what their reaction to the death of their cousin would be.

Don and Mack followed a little behind them, craning their necks, trying to see. Riley held her breath as the men approached the dense foliage. She didn't want any of them seeing her mother that way. She wanted to scream at them to get away from the body, especially the two engineers. She knew the moment they all spotted the body.

The porters stepped back, backs and shoulders stiffening. They looked from Capa's body to what was left of Annabel. There could be no doubt what had transpired.

Don leaned over and was sick again and again. Mack gagged and turned away, pressing his hand to his mouth. Riley felt the exact moment they both turned their horrified gazes on her. She refused to look at them. If she held herself very still, her mind wouldn't fly apart and her shattered heart would remain inside her body. The screams in her head would stay there, locked away forever.

Don stood up slowly, glanced once more into the brush and hastily turned his head away. He made his way slowly over to Riley. He stood there for a moment in silence before clearing his throat.

"I'm sorry about your mother, Riley."

She couldn't look at him. She nodded her head, pressing her hands deeper into the dirt. She was so numb that the only thing she could feel on her skin was the sensation of the earth.

Mack shuffled over, just as awkward, but well meaning. "I'm so sorry, Riley. There are no words. This is terrible."

Again she nodded, unable to answer them. Life was pulling her back from the brink of disaster. She couldn't completely lose control. She had to find a way for her brain to function, to think of what to do next.

The four porters picked up the body of their cousin and carried it off into deeper brush.

"What are they doing?" Jubal asked Miguel.

"They will bury him properly," Miguel said. "In our way. We will take care of . . ."

As the three guides stepped closer to Annabel, Riley's entire body rebelled. Even the earth beneath her seemed to violently protest, shuddering in a wave of protest. The ground shivered, rose up in two-inch waves and sent vibrations through her body. She "felt" the instant protest and with it came a need to act, to move quickly, to *do* something—she just wasn't quite certain what.

"Don't let them touch her," Riley pleaded. "Jubal, they can't touch her."

Miguel turned to her, his eyes filled with sorrow. "We didn't wish for this to happen, Riley. We would never want your mother dead. Capa was not himself. He was a gentle man with a wife and son. He would never harm someone if he wasn't out of his mind. We need to give your mother a proper burial in the way of your people."

She knew the guide was sincere. She heard it in his voice and saw it on his face, but a deeper force drove her. Her mother's body could not be touched. Riley forced herself to her feet, shaking her head. Her body felt weak, her legs rubbery, but she *had* to get up. Beneath her feet, the earth pushed at her, driving her out of her shock.

"Don't let anyone touch her," she repeated, looking past Miguel to Jubal. She forced herself to meet the guide's eyes. "We have our own ways, Miguel, and I must attend to her."

She found it a little terrifying to approach that horrible site of blood and death in front of all of them, but it had to be done, even if she had a complete breakdown. She had no idea what she needed to do, but the drive was powerful in her now, pushing her to move.

Weston and Shelton stepped back silently to allow her to walk slowly toward her mother's body. Riley was aware of the hush descending once more on the group. The two students, busy disinfecting the wounds on themselves and their professor, halted to watch her approach the brush, marred with bloodstains.

"Tell us what you need, Riley," Gary said, coming up beside her. "We'll help you."

She wasn't altogether certain what she needed, but she nodded slightly, waiting a moment before she looked at her mother. She approached cautiously, steeling herself for the sight of Annabel's mangled body. It wasn't her mother, she reminded herself, only the shell left behind. Her mother was long gone and once again with the man she loved so much for so many years.

The wind touched her face as she neared the dense underbrush, fingers of comfort tugging the tears from her eyes. She held her head high, chin up, took a deep breath and then allowed her gaze to move very slowly, one inch at a time, into the darkened brush. Her stomach lurched, and she caught her breath, a lump in her throat threatening to choke her. The ground moved again, gently urging her forward.

Deep beneath the thick vegetation, Riley felt the thrum of the earth's heartbeat. Her pulse jumped—matched that steady, comforting rhythm. She felt her veins tingle, a network running through her body, connected to the very planet she lived on. The flora and fauna around her breathed life into the air, and she took it into her lungs. Inside, she felt something stir, awaken, become aware. With each tentative step she took toward that place of murder and death, she became more certain of what she needed to do.

Her veins throbbed and burned, an electrical current flashing through her body until she felt her blood ran with the very sap in the leaves of the trees, connecting her to all of nature. Like a sleeping dragon awakening for the first time, the energy arced and spread until it consumed every cell in its wake. Her mind filled with images from a life not lived or previously known, but so familiar she recognized everything as if the knowledge had always been there, imprinted in her brain just waiting for this moment when she woke.

Riley paused, everything in her going still, the better to absorb the monumental changes happening so fast in her body and mind. Around her, the others faded far into the background as her every sense seemed to heighten. Moisture hung heavy in the air. She could feel the individual droplets on her skin, breathe them into her lungs. Beneath her feet, the earth moved again, urging her forward. She knew exactly what she had to do—cleanse her mother's body and consecrate her, preparing for her return to Mother Earth. Annabel was a daughter of the earth, lent for a short time and she needed to be returned with reverence and thanks.

She would have to set the four corners and call in the elements and directions that would bind the energies, but first she would honor her mother by purifying and cleansing her body. The blood seeping into the ground no longer sickened her. Everywhere that dark liquid of life touched, the soil reached for the richness, her mother's life, refueling and enriching in the cycle of rebirth.

Riley raised her hands to the sky, calling to the moisture, drawing all those heavy drops to her. Rain answered, a fine shower, falling across the remains of her mother's body, mixing with her blood so that it seemed to come alive, moving in droplets off the leaves and branches to roll to the ground and slowly begin to seep deep into the earth. When the last of the blood had disappeared into the ground, Riley called to the currents of air swirling in the canopy, waiting all along for her to utilize the element. The rain ceased as the wind circled the body, acting as a fan, drying Annabel's remains.

Deep inside, Riley felt a burning through her body, that electrical current leaping to light, and her hands stretched toward her mother, weaving an intricate pattern in the air. She was absolutely certain of every movement, no hesitation, the weave leaping to life until a low blue ethereal flame burned over the remains and was instantly gone.

She reached down and took soil into her hands. "Mother Earth, I'm returning your daughter to you. I thank you for the gift of life. The years of happiness. The service to humanity." As she murmured the words, she allowed the rich soil to drift over Annabel's remains.

Riley looked to the north and called in the power of Air. As the currents once again began to swirl around her, she faced south, calling on the power of Earth. The ground answered, trembling, coming alive. She turned toward the east and called Fire, until the area around her mother's body was etched in low-burning flame. She faced west and called to the power of Water to purify and renew.

Riley's hands again began to weave a pattern, a conductor of an orchestra, as she murmured soft, powerful words. "Air, Earth, Fire, Water, hear my prayer. See your daughter look upon her child this night. Aid her healing through this plight. Let fire fuel a savage cleansing. Let air sweep away negative endings. Water clears the cleansing pyre as Earth brings forth renewed desire. Air, Earth, Fire, Water, design a ring of natural power. Circle round and thrice be bound, take your daughter into the ground. Accept your daughter back this night and always hold her close and tight. Let none disturb this place of peace and within this circle may my mother find peace. As above, so below."

Earth took a long breath. Riley felt it. Heard it. The answer to her prayerful ritual. The ground trembled. Rippled. Came alive. Everywhere the pools and spattered droplets of Annabel's blood had sunk deep, flowers and green plants shot up, pushing through rich soil toward the sky. Again the land shivered. Beneath the torn body, the rain forest floor cracked and sank, pulling Annabel's remains into those deep crevices. Black loam bubbled up, rich with minerals, and with it, shoots of green burst through the dirt to reach for the sky.

There was no trace of Annabel, or the gore that had been. Plants were so thick the entire terrain had become a grotto of beauty. Lying in the middle of a sea of starry night flowers was Mother Earth's offering—her mother's necklace. The piece had been handed down through generations, and Annabel had never taken it off once her mother had died.

Riley placed one foot carefully in front of the other, circling her mother's resting place, allowing the peace to seep into her bones. She sank into that field of white flowers, and placed her hands on either side of the gift remaining from her mother. The stalks and petals reached for her. The soil moved over her, rushing around her, welcoming her.

The connection hit her like a fireball, storming through her body, unfurling in her brain, the earth reaching out to her, welcoming her daughter, sharing her gifts. Knowledge grew fast, spread through her veins, into her bones, pressed into every cell. From the core of the planet, she felt the heartbeat, heard the whispers of truth, of creation. The plants close to her reached to wrap tendrils around her, to touch her. Trees bent without wind, dipping low to honor her. The wind touched her face, breathing cool air across her warm face.

The soil poured over her bare fingers, and as it did, she felt the easing of her terrible grief. The lump burning in her throat lessened, giving her relief. As her fingers dug deep, searching for that last connection with her mother, she felt a ripple in the ground, a subtle echo of evil. Her mother's consecrated resting place pushed that whisper, that last gasp of evil away, but Riley's stomach lurched. Everything her mother had told her about her past and the volcano was true. Triumph permeated the soil, harsh glee that her mother had been brutally murdered, leaving evil to once again emerge and roam free, feeding on innocents.

Her heart stuttered. The evil faded back in the direction of the volcano. A sense of urgency assailed her. She *had* to get to the mountain and seal it before whatever monstrous thing was held prisoner could escape. Quickly she pulled her hands from the soil, and turned her head to look toward the smoldering mountain.

Riley reached down into the bed of white star flowers and lifted the heirloom from the blossoms, a gift given by Mother Earth to her long-dead ancestor. Her fingers trembled as she ran the pad of her thumb over the fine silver in the shape of a large dragon with eyes of fiery agate. The claws held an orb of obsidian. She stared down at the piece, remembering all the times her mother had shown it to her, hidden there like treasure around her neck, guarded beneath her clothing. The thin chain was gone, so Riley slipped the gift into her pocket and zipped the pocket closed.

Gary held out his hand to her and Riley allowed him to help her up. For the first time she looked around at her fellow travelers. They all wore sympathetic expressions and were watching her closely. She realized that the forest had obscured their vision of her and what she was doing, branches reaching out, both brush and trees, to hide the purification ritual from interested eyes.

"We need to tend to those wounds," Gary said.

"I have to go," Riley said. "There's no time."

Gary shook his head. "You know you can't take chances. Disinfect the bites and scratches and we'll gather everything and get going."

The others one by one filed past Annabel's resting place, touching Riley's shoulder, nodding at her, some murmuring a prayer. The three guides performed their own ritual. Riley, as Gary turned her battle wounds into streaks of fire, looked around for the porters.

"It wasn't his fault," she said. "Capa. It wasn't his fault."

Miguel turned to look at her. "Thank you for that."

"Don't you feel the difference? That awful droning buzz is gone," Riley pointed out. "Ouch." She pushed at Gary's hand. He ignored her and continued dabbing on some fiery liquid. "Don't you feel lighter? The dread is gone. All the tension. Two people just died and we should all be very tense, but instead, that horrible feeling of impending doom has disappeared."

Ben, standing close, answered her. “I noticed that, too. The professor and his students want to turn back. And the volcano is definitely waking up. I don’t know how much time we’ll have before it blows, and we won’t want to be anywhere near it when it goes off.”

Riley shook her head. “They can turn back, all of you can, but I have to keep going and I have to get there fast. There’s no time to lose.”

Ben frowned. “The volcano is a real problem we can’t just overlook, Riley.”

“I can’t explain it, but I have no choice. If I have to, I’ll go alone. I’ve been to this particular mountain several times and I can find my way if need be.” She was no longer surprised that it was the truth. She glanced up at the swirling clouds. “Night is falling fast. We have about an hour, and we’re going to have to hurry through some very dense jungle.”

Gary and Jubal exchanged a long, knowing look. Riley wasn’t going to ask. They knew, just as she did, that whatever evil was trapped in the mountain would get out if she didn’t stop it. They accepted the truth, just as she did. If they had prior knowledge and weren’t saying, she didn’t care. She was going up that mountain and nothing was going to stop her.

“Weston and Shelton want to turn back as well,” Ben said.

“The porters don’t want to go, either,” Weston defended, a little belligerently. “A couple of them may have bailed on us already. Two didn’t come back after burying the other one.”

“The ground is shaking constantly.” Mack pointed out the obvious. “There’s no doubt an explosion is imminent. We have to get as far from that mountain as possible.”

Riley nodded. “I’m in complete agreement. You all should head out of here as fast as possible. I have no choice. I’m heading up the mountain.” She pushed past Gary, strength and determination pouring into her. “I’m leaving now. I don’t have time to argue with everyone.”

Miguel let his breath out. “I’ll take you. My brothers can take the others back.”

Both of his brothers shook their heads in protest.

Miguel swept his hand toward Annabel’s resting place. “I failed her. I will not fail her daughter.”

Jubal lifted his pack and swung it onto his back. “I’ll go with you.”

Gary silently donned his pack as well. Ben Charger did the same.

Weston swore under his breath and not only caught up his backpack, but reached down and took Riley's as well. "I'll carry this for a little while."

Shelton shook his head. "Are you crazy? Damn it, Don, we're going to get killed if that mountain blows. We need to hightail it out of here as fast as we can in the opposite direction."

Don shrugged. "Let's just get it done, and then we can run like hell."

"Pick up the pace, Miguel," Jubal ordered. "We want to make the base of the mountain before nightfall if possible."

Miguel lifted a hand toward his brothers and set off without another word. The professor and his two students remained with the other two guides and two of the porters, who argued heatedly among themselves. At the last moment, Hector caught up a pack of supplies and hurried after Miguel, leaving his cousin shaking his head. Weston and Shelton followed the porter and guide.

Jubal fell in behind them, nodding toward the archaeologist and his students.

Riley caught up her mother's pack and eased it over her shoulders. She hadn't realized how battered and bruised her body was from the monkeys' knocking her around. She followed Jubal.

"Good luck," Gary called to the others as he paced behind Riley, clearly prepared to protect her.

Riley didn't look back. The sense of urgency grew in her even as she realized everything around her had changed. Her focus. Her awareness. Her feet seemed to find the right path of their own volition, avoiding every hazard. The forest breathed for her, providing oxygen to enhance her ability to move quickly through the narrow trails. She knew before she rounded a turn just what was ahead. She felt the forest living in her, whispering comfort, sharing information, advising her.

The pace was fast as the ground tremors increased in frequency and strength and night began to descend. Still, there was a calm and rhythm to the group that had never been before. Riley felt as if she was a part of each of the travelers as they made their way through the tangled jungle.

Behind her in the rear position, she felt Gary, calm and steady, watchful, always alert, ready for anything, just as Jubal, ahead of her, appeared to be.

Ben Charger moved well in the forest, his strides sure and his manner confident. Don and Mack were far less so, both nervous and fighting the rugged terrain, although both tried. They were just out of their element.

Miguel, however, familiar with the way and danger of the entire area, radiated fear. Each vine, every branch, the brush blocking their trail was met with a clean stroke of his giant black blade as he removed obstacles from their path. She felt the separation of the long vines, so real she could almost feel the air rush past as each separate piece fell to the forest floor. The foliage tried to retreat from the blade, subtle vibrations warning plants ahead of them.

She began to whisper softly under her breath, asking forgiveness for cutting a trail. They had to rush. There was no time for avoidance, or even the rain forest itself might be lost. Open the trail to them, let them through.

Riley drew in a swift breath. How many times had she heard her mother whispering in a soft, singsong voice as they backpacked through heavy jungle? With every step connecting her to the earth, she felt more connected to her mother, closer to her, more aware of memories.

She touched the end of a severed branch in a kind of reverence. Already there was a light-colored liquid oozing out to meet her fingertips. The plant's lifeblood was cool and sticky, and a calm descended into her mind, helping her to focus on what she needed to do. She placed one foot in front of the next, allowing her hand to linger, keeping contact with the plants until the last possible moment. She felt the shift inside of her, her tight lungs easing, drawing a full breath of fresh air, letting the plants take much of the burden of her sorrow and fear of what was to come.

The tremors continued, giving her a feeling of extreme urgency, a need to hurry faster, and with that came an awareness of the growing fear in their guide. Miguel knew what those tremors meant—an impending eruption. He was responsible for the travelers and he already felt as if he'd failed Annabel. Little by little he was changing the direction, a subtle shift so that it was barely noticeable, but Riley's sense of their objective was acute now, as was the map in her head, leading her to the precise location she needed to be.

She didn't blame Miguel. How could she? He felt weighed down with responsibility and guilt. A memory surfaced of Riley as a child, during one of their trips, a storm raging, pounding the shelter the guide had hastily set up for them. She'd been wrapped in the strength of her mother's embrace as her mother sang softly to take away her tears.

The long-forgotten memory sparked the knowledge of what she had to do. The song came out soft and low, barely a whisper, but she remembered the words and melody from that long-forgotten trip. Her mother had sung the song while they hurried along muddy trails with the rain pouring down. The words formed in her mind and grew in strength.

It wasn't long before the others began to slow their pace, to be closer, to hear more. Riley picked up the pace, moving past Jubal, touching him on the shoulder. Her nodded to her, obviously aware of the soothing quality to her voice and approving of what she was doing.

She continued to walk forward, quickening her pace, softly singing, passing each traveler, touching them gently as she did so, easing their burdens and growing in confidence and power with every step. She reached Miguel. It was clear how far his efforts had taken them off course. The guilt was tangible, but she felt only sadness for him. She understood his need to protect them all, and he'd braved her anger to try to get them away a safe distance from the volcano.

She moved in front of him even as her song drifted to a low hum. Her hands came up and she wove a pattern as she sang to the jungle. The path opened, leaves and branches pulling back to let them move through quickly. Beneath her feet, the ground urged her to hurry. The sense of need grew and spread until it was all-consuming. She became aware of the silence, as if the insects held their breath waiting for her arrival. She felt pressure building beneath her feet.

As if the others all caught that sense of urgency she was feeling, they double-timed it, their feet pounding out the rhythm of her song. The ground shook harder, longer, throwing them all to the forest floor just as they reached the base of the mountain. Riley dug her hands into the soil and felt the enormous force and the tremendous heat in the ground. Instantly she was aware of the triumph of malicious evil rising like the tide, rising with the gases.

She looked up at Jubal with stricken eyes. "I'm too late. It's too late."

6

The ground wept drops of blood like honey dripping from a comb—a dark sorrow invading and spreading through the earth. She was dead! At long last, Arabejila was dead. If he could have done so without attracting the hunter, Mitro would have danced. He'd done it! He'd destroyed the one woman who could bring him down! He could barely contain his glee. He'd expected a bigger impact, the ground rolling and swaying in protest—or even trying to retaliate against him—but none had come. He had grown strong while she had grown weak. He'd sensed that over the centuries, that slow decline without her lifemate—without him. She hadn't been able to hold on as he had.

She had needed him to live, but she'd chosen to side with the arrogant Carpathian hunter, thinking they could defeat him. She'd chosen poorly. Once again he'd proven he was stronger, better, far more intelligent and cunning than the rest of them. The hunter and his whore had lost the game to Mitro's superior skills. He had known all along he'd outsmart them. He proved time and again he deserved the position as right-hand man to the prince, yet he'd been cast aside because the prince had feared him—feared others would recognize that Mitro was a born leader and turn against the prince.

Even as injured as he'd been from their last encounter, he'd managed to rise first—or maybe the hunter had been burned in the magma. He knew better, but it was a nice thought. No one could defeat him. Not the famous Danutdaxton and not Arabejila.

Now, with Arabejila dead at last, his victory almost made him giddy. He had to focus. He had everything he needed at long last. His quest had been successful, and he was invulnerable now. Nothing would stop him. With Arabejila dead and his newfound treasure in his possession, once he was out, there was no hunter who could ever destroy him. The world and all its riches would belong to him.

Mitro kept his movements slow and deliberate in spite of the urge to rush toward the thinning crust and push hard to get out. He had succeeded where so many others failed because he was patient and tenacious. They had made a terrible mistake, trapping him inside the volcano. They thought it a prison, a torture chamber, but he had grown into something else, something more. He found a treasure beyond price, and he had all the time in the world to plan his revenge—and his vengeance knew no bounds.

He still had to evade the hunter and get through the barrier Arabejila and her assassin had erected to keep him close to the center of the volcano. Over time he had tested that barrier, and over the past years he had thinned it in one place without the hunter noticing. He had been stealthy, staying away from the area for long periods of time and careful never to leave a trace behind. He had even worked at the safeguards in other places, determined this spot would be his true escape hatch should the others fail. This was his chance and he wouldn't risk losing it by giving away his position too soon.

Mitro couldn't chance another battle with the hunter. Just as he'd grown into something more, so had Danutdaxton—a relentless hunter he'd known since childhood. "The Judge," they called him. Even as a boy he'd been a serious warrior and everyone, including the prince, had made a big deal over him. Mitro had done his best to pretend to be his friend, but watching everyone grovel around him was truly sickening.

Mitro was intelligent—far smarter than Danutdaxton would ever be—and the prince should have seen that. *All* of them should have seen it. Mitro had been wronged so many times. They'd all been jealous of him—especially his brothers. They had said he was ill, that his heart was black, just because he didn't make clean emotionless kills as the Judge did. Mitro *enjoyed* watching the damned suffer. They deserved it. They'd been condemned, so why shouldn't he have a little fun after he took the time and effort to hunt them down? What business was it of anyone how he dispatched an enemy?

And humans were fodder. Food. Their women were fair game. He *felt* when he stared into their eyes and took their bodies without their permission while their men watched in horror. So helpless. Like children. Like the animals he ran across and spent hours torturing. The suffering, watching the life leave their eyes, it was all exhilarating. The prince and his brothers didn't want to admit they had the same nature. They weren't supposed to be civilized. The prince wanted to "tame" them, to subdue their natural predatory instincts.

Mitro had tried hard to make the prince understand the harm he was doing to their people. The men lost emotion because their true natures were suppressed. If he could feel without his lifemate, the woman who would cripple him, force him into a mold, take away the very essence of who he was, then so could the other hunters. The women hobbled them—turned them into rabbits when they were meant to be at the top of the food chain.

His brothers tried to stop him from advising the prince, cowards every one of them. They knew he was right, but they feared banishment and loss of status if the sniveling prince disagreed with him. Mitro had been unafraid. He knew he was right. He had the brains and the strength to do what had to be done. He could have anything he wanted, not live restrained by the dictates of a man without any vision.

But now—at last—things would be different. Arabejila was dead, and he would soon be free to rule the earth, as he should have done from the beginning. He floated, rising slowly, careful to exert no energy, knowing any disturbance would draw the hunter to him. He reminded himself how close he was, he just needed to do this right, move so slow, drift with rising gases toward the barrier and reach that very thin wall. He had to time it perfectly. Already he could feel the hunter on the move. He hadn't died then, but Mitro had known all along it wouldn't be that easy.

His heart jolted hard, sending an electrical charge through his body. The current robbed him of breath but gave him a deep satisfaction. He could feel what others could not. He had changed—evolved—to a higher purpose.

His imprisonment had only made him stronger and more determined. He would escape and elude Danutdaxton. Without Arabejila to track him, the hunter had lost his edge.

Mitro's veins throbbed and burned; after all these years of suppressing his need for blood, the craving was more powerful than ever, and with it, the yearning to see that horror and revulsion, that terrible fear as he held life or death over his victim. He always chose the strongest of the warriors to kill, deliberately torturing them so the others would see how useless fighting him was. He could turn whole villages against one another. They would sacrifice their children to him when he demanded it. Their young daughters. Their firstborn sons.

He fed on terror. Fear was every bit as important as blood to him. He needed it the way he needed sustenance—delicious, delicious terror. The more he thought of people trembling before him, begging for their lives, the stronger the compulsion became. He'd been too long without food and he craved the fear-inspired adrenaline in his victim's blood when he drank.

He flexed his muscles as he continued to rise toward the barrier keeping him from the top of the volcano where he needed to be when it finally blew. Without Arabejila calming it, the explosion would be catastrophic, flattening and killing everything for miles. His plan was in place, and nothing would stop him now. Not some silly woman and not the Carpathian hunter. He would be free, and he would reign supreme!

The wind rushed down the mountain while towering black clouds chased to the top of the atmosphere, churning and boiling with a dark, ominous anger. Lightning forked across the sky, whips of sizzling electrical currents, snapping and crackling with a kind of rage. Beneath her hands, Riley felt the rising volcanic gases and with those noxious fumes, something else—something horrifyingly evil. These men had come with her and she led them into certain danger. If they remained where they were, and she couldn't slow the blast or redirect it, all of them would die.

"Miguel, you have to take the others and get out of here now," she ordered, already grabbing her mother's pack. "The volcano is going to blow. I can feel the pressure building in the earth."

More than that, she could feel the spreading triumph of evil running below the surface. If she hadn't fully believed the things her mother had told her before, she certainly did now. The malevolence was so acute, her stomach lurched. This was the source that had focused on murdering her mother. The porters were pawns, just as the insects and monkeys had been. Glee and triumph poured from the ground.

Tremors continued, the rain forest shivering constantly. Riley didn't wait to see if Miguel took her at her word—they all had to know an eruption was imminent. She began to run up the narrow trail leading up the mountain. She wouldn't make the entry to the cloud forest, but she'd get close enough. She glanced over her shoulder to see the men hesitating.

"Go now," she urged. "Run."

"Riley, it's too late," Gary called after her. He reached down and caught up her pack and raced after her. "You can't be on the mountain when it goes."

Riley didn't slow down or acknowledge his concern. If she couldn't ease the pressure in the volcano or redirect the blast, not even the archaeologist and his students would be safe. The explosion would be similar to a nuclear bomb going off, devastating everything for miles. She could hear Gary's boots pounding up the trail after her, and then those of a second man and a third. It didn't matter. She couldn't stop them. Each one had to make their choice at this point, and hers was to try to save everyone and make a last effort to keep whatever evil thing dwelled in the volcano trapped.

With every step she took she judged the shivering, trembling ground. How close? How much time? She had to make it as far as she could, yet still give herself time to connect with the volcano and perform the ritual. She would try to seal the evil within the mountain even as she calmed and directed the building volcanic eruption away from the travelers. She could only pray there were no other people on the other side of the mountain, because if she couldn't stop the blast, she'd try for a smaller eruption as far from them as possible.

The ground shook hard, the sound like a thunderclap, throwing her off balance. Gary's hand caught her arm to steady her and they ran together, Jubal right behind them. She wished they hadn't followed her, but a part of her was glad they had. She was fairly certain she wasn't going to make it off the mountain alive and their presence helped to give her determination and courage. She wasn't just fighting for herself.

The next tremor, much stronger than the one before, lasted a long minute, warning her she had run out of time. She stopped abruptly and flung her mother's pack on the ground. "It has to be here. We're not where we need to be, but if we're lucky, I can do this."

"We can help," Gary said. "We've participated in a couple of rituals. Tell us what you need us to do."

Riley wasn't going to ask how they knew what to do when she barely knew herself. There just wasn't time, but if by some chance she managed to pull off a miracle, both men were going to answer a lot of questions. She yanked open her mother's pack and removed a small handheld broom made of bunched willow tied tightly together. Hastily she began to sweep out a circle large enough to hold herself and the three men. She moved counterclockwise, brushing the debris free while she whispered her prayer to the four elements, calling them to her as she worked.

Riley had seen her mother perform the ritual of holding the volcano many times, but now that it was her turn, there was so much she didn't know. She had to undo the strands of the evil power permeating the entire volcano and weave powerful strands of her own strong enough to keep the evil contained, holding it within its own constraints, and not allowing it to go free.

"Use the salt," she instructed Gary. "Follow the circle. Jubal, there's sage . . ."

"Got it," Jubal said. He lit the sage and walked the circle three times, cleansing the area as he chanted softly under his breath.

"What the hell are you people doing?" Ben demanded. The ground shook continually, the tremors growing longer in duration and much stronger. "We have to get out of here."

"Try to catch up with Miguel and the others," Gary said without looking up. He continued to form the circle with the salt.

"No, whatever you're doing, I'll help," Ben said. "But this is insane."

"Can't you feel the evil?" Riley hissed. She could feel him now, real and powerful, coming at her in waves—his malicious triumph in the murder of her mother. He thought himself safe with her mother dead, and so far, he had no inkling she was on his trail.

"Keep working, Riley," Jubal said. "We'll explain as much as we can to Ben."

Riley was grateful. She had to shut out everything, even the terrible urgency of the moment. She had to find a complete calm and focus if she had any chance at all against so great an evil. She gestured to the men as she stood, inviting them inside the circle of protection just constructed. Even if she was defeated, hopefully she could make this small space safe enough to shield the others.

She walked the circle, envisioning the brightest light she could imagine, holding the black-handled, double-edged athame high. As the circle gained depth, Riley drew the quarters, setting the towers. She called to the elements. Air to the East. Fire to the South. Water to the West. Lastly, she whispered to the North, calling on Earth. Mother Earth. She forced her mind to concentrate on protections and block out the men moving around her.

Kneeling in the middle of the circle, she plunged her hands deep into the earth, focusing wholly on binding the evil. She struck fast and hard, using every ounce of strength she possessed.

"I bind thee darkness from doing harm.

To myself and those whom you would charm

I bind thee darkness to be free

As I lock thee away for none to see."

Reaction was instantaneous. Shock. Fear. Rage. Insects poured through the ground and raced at the circle, surrounding them, clicking and chirping aggressively. Bats flew at them from every side, but none penetrated that sacred circle. A heavy, oppressive malevolence pressed in on them. Lightning forked across the sky, a long howling bolt, sizzling and crackling through the night to slam to earth just feet from the circle. Next came a series of fireballs pounding down like a meteor strike as evil fought back.

Ben started to run, but Gary and Jubal both caught at him, holding him motionless.

"Don't leave the circle. This is the only safe place right now," Gary warned.

"And don't draw attention to yourself," Jubal added in a whisper. "It's fighting for its life. Either she can hold it inside the volcano or it will be loose on the world, and you saw just a little of what it can do from a distance. You don't want that creature interested in you."

Riley ignored them, barely aware of their presence. Without warning something moved against her throat, *inside* her body. Fangs ripped at her. Burning acid choked her. Claws wrapped in pure hatred raked at her. This was the creature who had murdered her mother, and it was fully aware of her now, and centering its attention on her.

She refused to allow loathing into her mind. This was her duty, her job. There could be no malice—she couldn't give him a way to enter her mind. Illusion was his game, but she was stronger.

Riley refused to give in to the need to touch her throat, to feel if the blood pouring out was real or not. She whispered another soft chant to chain the evil entity inside.

"I draw upon thee light, surround me with your might
Set this evil in the ground, keep me safe from that which seeks to harm
Find the sender, track him back, let the darkness return his attack
Let the fuse be short burning bright, let his evil fall short this night."

The evil entity pushed back hard, striking again and again at her throat. Raw. Burning. Torn open. Her breath barely pushed through her shredded vocal cords, the gaping jugular pouring out blood, soaking her clothing, splashing into the ground.

"Find him. Bind him. Hold evil chained.
Forged in fire. Hewn in rock."

The earth whispered to her. Assured and comforted her. Riley kept her hands buried deep in the soil, fingers curled into tight fists, holding that evil thing captured, refusing to let loose, no matter how he struggled, twisted and turned, no matter how he stabbed at her, trying to tear out her insides. Pain burst through her like a star, and she knew if she looked down she would see that her stomach had ripped open, her lifeblood pouring out onto the ground.

"I call upon spirit and earth. Create a cocoon from which there is no birth.

Fit this space with black crystalline, to encompass this evil, to hold and bind."

Arabejila. Emni hän ku köd alte. Tõdak a ho ćaδasz engemko, kutenken ćaδasz engemko a jälleen. Andak a irgalomet teräd it.

The voice filled her mind. Turned her blood to ice. Riley forced her fear down. She was in the circle of protection. She refused to be intimidated.

With effort, she managed to push aside her fear and concentrate on the words he'd spoken. He'd spoken her ancestor's name. She didn't understand the rest of the words, but instantly recognized the language as the same the porter had mumbled to himself over and over. This evil entity *knew* her—or, more likely, her ancestor—and believed she was still alive. That realization gave her an important bit of knowledge she hadn't possessed before. Whoever—whatever—this evil entity was, he wasn't all powerful and he made mistakes. Moreover . . . alongside the threat in his voice, she heard fear. He feared Arabejila. Considering that she was the one who'd locked him in the volcano and kept him there for centuries, that made perfect sense. In fact, she might even be the only thing he *did* fear.

If the evil entity feared Arabejila, that meant he had reason to fear her and that meant he was vulnerable in some way. She took another deep breath and locked on to him, curling her fists tighter to hold him prisoner.

Another tremor jolted the mountain hard, throwing the men off their feet. With her hands plunged so deep in the soil, Riley felt the rising of the volcano. The blast would blow the top of the mountain away and flatten everything for miles. No one would be safe, not even the archaeologist and porters who had taken off earlier. They'd be caught as well as every animal and tribesman within miles. She had no choice but to try to calm the powerful force, and failing that, turn it away from them, redirect the blast if at all possible.

"Fire flame, show your light
Burning bright within my sight
Brightness burn deep within
So I may see where to begin
Bring me light as fire burns
So I may bind it with twists and turns."

She chanted the words softly, eloquently, her hands deep in the soil, stroking and calming the ground, easing her way into the churning mass of gases and molten rock.

"We have to get out of here," Ben shouted. "Right now. This thing is going to blow."

Jubal and Gary kept a firm grip on him, holding him within the circle.

"You can't outrun a volcano," Gary pointed out. "She's our only hope now. I have no idea how she can do it, but clearly the mountain responds to her."

"What the hell can she do?" Ben demanded.

Riley ignored them, channeling power and energy into the earth. The ground shivered and shook continually, and she could actually feel a force rising.

"Fire leads me to the light
Guide my hand as I fight this night
Show me how to find my fire
So I may guide this volcanic power."

She wasn't going to be able to stop the blast, but she could already feel the response to her presence. She had to use every bit of energy and power she possessed to harness the volcano, to guide it away from the others—and that meant letting go of the evil entity she held so tight. Closing her eyes, she made the decision. If they were all dead, he would escape anyway. She couldn't do both. She abruptly pulled away, sending up a silent prayer that the binding would hold even through a volcano blast.

She felt the instant echo of malicious glee, of taunting laughter. That failure couldn't matter. Now, it was all about redirecting the blast and calming the volcano and preventing a catastrophic event.

"Red like flame, amber light, diverts this fire and holds it tight
Sword and dagger, double-headed axe, dragon's blood hold this volcano's blast
Salamander who lives in fire, create a tunnel for this river of flame."

Ash spewed high into the air. Several vents shot steam high. Fiery rocks streaked into the air, small blowholes, as if the great mountain just had to express itself. Lightning zigzagged, great forks spreading across the sky.

Riley held firm, refusing to flinch. "Triangle lightning, use your light to hold all powers, adding strength to their might."

She took another breath, closed her eyes and sent her prayer to the sky and deep into the ground. "Mother Earth, your humble daughter seeks your aid once more. You are living, breathing, ever changing in your natural state. The fire roars in you, yet your daughter pleads with you to tamp down that fire and send it far from us. The release is necessary to the growth of this world, true, but we ask for this boon."

It was the best she could do. Either she'd calmed the volcano enough to minimize the damage, or everyone was lost.

Arabejila had totally deceived him. Mitro wanted to rip and tear into something warm-blooded. His rage grew as he struggled against the tight binds woven around him. She was far stronger than she'd ever been. Her touch hadn't been hesitant at all. Throughout the years she'd seemed to decline in strength, but now she was all powerful—a force he hadn't counted on.

She felt different to him, but it had been centuries since he'd tasted her hot blood—and that had been his one mistake. He should have killed her outright immediately. Once he'd taken her blood, he had locked them together for all time. Even then, he thought her weak, but she wasn't now. She hadn't flinched or pleaded with him. She had struck hard and fast without the least bit of hesitation—something she would never have done before.

Snarling, he gnashed his fangs together, anger and hatred feeding his strength. She hadn't even deigned to speak to him. He was her lifemate whether she liked it or not, his possession. He could choose to keep her alive or let her die. It was his choice. He was superior and always would be.

He struggled harder against the tight bonds. Arabejila had always had a connection to the earth, but it seemed stronger than ever. The moment she was forced to turn her attention elsewhere, he should have been able to break free, but the bindings held tight. He couldn't move, couldn't rise toward that barrier he'd worked so hard to thin.

He cursed Arabejila, cursed the fact that she alone had the ability to shake him up. He should have made certain she was dead. She was the reason the hunter had found him again and again over the centuries . . . She'd trapped him here. She'd kept him here. And now she was the only thing standing between him and his triumph. She was truly the bane of his life, and if he didn't uncoil the chains she'd placed on him fast, he would be trapped for all time.

He renewed his efforts, concentrating on finding each strand binding him in his fiery prison. Arabejila had woven the spell tight, the earth itself adding to her weave. He had always found it utterly disgusting that all living plant life responded to her instead of him. He'd tried, in the earlier years, watching her walk through a field with flowers and plants springing up around her, to do the same, but the earth refused to speak to him. The rejection had been so total and so instantaneous, it had filled him with a loathing for all vegetation. He despised anything that would choose a weak woman over him.

Mitro had always considered Arabejila one-dimensional—good in every way. She didn't know how to be anything else. He studied the binding weaves chaining him inside the volcano. Those weaves told him much about his adversary. Arabejila had evolved over the centuries, just as he had evolved, and he found her much changed and more powerful because of it. More, her weaves only told him she was a force to be reckoned with, not anything personal about her. She had left no emotion behind to aid him in defeating her.

That rankled. She was supposed to be pining away for him. Her weaves should have contained sorrow and that ridiculous, futile dash of hope she couldn't suppress whenever they had come into contact in the past. No matter what he did, how depraved he'd become, she'd always clung to that tiny hope that she could "save" him. She'd never realized that he neither needed nor wanted to be saved. *Stupid woman.* He found it insulting that she thought she had the power to turn him into a cowering rabbit like the rest of his species.

Remembering those days, pure hatred welled up. He would destroy Arabejila in his time, but first he would have to escape. She would not defeat him, a stupid cow of a woman who thought she was special because she could make flowers grow.

The mountain jolted hard, and he felt a subtle difference almost immediately. Arabejila had turned her full attention away from him and the weaves binding him. He fought down the urge to struggle, to panic when the explosion could happen at any moment. He narrowed his concentration to one strand of his bonds. One at a time. He would have to break through that chain in order to escape.

Mitro tried to recall every detail he could about his recent encounter with Arabejila. He'd been shocked. Horrified even. He was so certain she was dead. She had not responded or spoken to him and he hadn't searched her mind when he had the chance. He stayed very still, reaching out carefully. If he knew what words had bound him, he could undo the weaves quite easily. He just had to get inside her head. She was his lifemate. Her blood would answer his call, but his touch would have to be delicate.

He tamped down all anger, not an easy feat when Arabejila was to blame for everything that had gone wrong in his life and he was already plotting to kill her and everyone she might care about. His touch on the thick weaves was very careful, seeking a tie to her. His blood stirred, but remained cold. Silence. Emptiness. There was no contact at all. If he didn't know better, he would say she was dead.

Puzzled, he changed tactics. The sense of urgency grew as the mountain rumbled and the gases spewed high. Below him, the gathering fiery storm threatened to break free. Abruptly he felt a difference, as if the weaves had loosened just that little bit as if she hadn't quite set them before she turned her attention elsewhere. She'd been gripping him hard, and now, that death grip was gone.

Triumphant, he struck hard, slashing through the weaves. They held, stronger than he expected against his all-out assault. He exerted pressure on his bonds, fighting panic, afraid his struggles might attract the attention of the hunter. Danutdaxton had become something much more as well, there in the volcano, and eluding him was essential.

The bindings tightened once, but then unexpectedly dropped free. Exalted, Mitro rose quickly toward the barrier and the one spot he'd spent centuries thinning. It would take seconds to break through, and when the volcano erupted, he would go out the vent with the gases. Elation swept through him. Glee. Triumph. *Nothing*, no one, could stop him.

Dax streaked through the furious volcano, moving as only a dragon could through the lower chambers, upward, toward the barrier. He felt the subtle difference in the earth, a pouring of comfort, a soothing hand stroking the volcano, easing the rising catastrophic explosion that would have blown the top off the mountain and flattened everything for miles.

Arabejila? He sent his inquiry, but he was positive she had been long gone from the earth. He'd felt her passing. He'd felt the mourning of the mountain when she was gone. His blood should have called to hers had she been alive. Still, the feel of her, the welcoming, the power—it was all there. More so.

Silence greeted his call. Had Arabejila been close—and he knew *someone* was trying to soothe the volcano—their blood exchanges would have allowed him to reach out to her. They'd been friends long before Mitro's betrayal, but their centuries of traveling together had deepened that friendship even further. Being around Arabejila had allowed him some emotion. She had been unique that way, providing solace to the warriors of their people—and Dax had practically been born a warrior. He had a gift for ferreting out evil. He could smell it, see it *inside*, and from the moment he'd met Mitro he'd seen inside to his rotten core.

The volcano whispered to him as he moved through the scalding chambers, told him of a woman, powerful, healing, a true daughter of the earth. Dax knew the moment she plunged her hands into the soil—the volcano responded with a flutter of activity. He felt the instant reaction, not only of the volcano, the soil, the very heart of the earth, but in his own blood. Familiar, yet unfamiliar. Arabejila, yet now—more. This woman was a force to be reckoned with. Where Arabejila was soft through and through, this woman had a core of heat and fire.

He continued to streak through the labyrinth of lava-formed tubes and hollowed caves, moving up toward the barrier. No doubt Mitro thought he could escape with the explosion of the volcano, right through that small space the vampire had worked centuries to thin. Dax had never let on he was aware of Mitro's work.

He never caught the undead working to thin the barrier, and all traces were removed, but Mitro hadn't counted on one thing—the intense blood bond between lifemates. Mitro had deliberately filled the mountain with his evil, so it would be impossible for Dax to detect him, not with his scent permeating every razor-sharp rock and molten pool. He had done so too late for this one escape hatch. He hadn't considered that Arabejila and Dax had exchanged blood so often throughout their hunt for Mitro over the centuries, and when he'd first started the thinning process, Dax could use that blood bond to hunt him. Dax had marked the spot in his memory.

Arabejila's blood continually called to Mitro's, and as the earth claimed Dax more and more as her child, his blood had begun to do the same. He had only to listen. Now, with the soul of the dragon dwelling in him as well, he had an added advantage he hadn't before—his senses of sight and smell were far above what they had been. The heat of the volcano fed him rather than drained him. The Old One and Dax had become better at sharing the same body and all senses. Right now, he knew *exactly* where Mitro was. He could feel the vampire struggling against the bonds the woman placed on him.

Mitro had positioned himself right at that narrowed barrier, right where Dax was certain he would. Dax sent a small thanks to the woman and to Arabejila. At long last he would destroy the vampire and his duty to his people would be done. He would be free to go to the next life. He moved quickly, rising steadily, winding his way through the maze of miles of chambers. Magma pools bubbled ominously. Steam and heat swirled together to create a dense fog. He used the dragon's eyes to see his way through the storm, racing the volcano to reach Mitro while he was still trapped.

The volcano took a deep breath, the whirlwind stilling, a terrible calm heralding a violent storm. Dax felt the exact moment when the woman turned her attention from holding Mitro to suppressing the catastrophic explosion. He couldn't blame her, she had people to save—just as he did. He pushed his speed, rushing through the last two chambers leading to that point of weakness where he knew Mitro would be.

He heard Mitro's gleeful snicker as the bonds broke loose and he streaked for the thin spot in the barrier. Dax hit him from the side, slamming into the body of the undead, driving him down and away from his goal.

Mitro shrieked in frustration and anger, trying to twist away, to get distance between them. Dax was too strong, too fast and he stayed close, chest to chest, driving his fist deep, penetrating through muscle, bone and tissue to drive for the heart.

Dax stared into Mitro's all-black eyes, the eyes of insanity, a monster without a soul. He'd been born defective and he'd purposefully destroyed every good thing in his life. Dax felt the edge of that withered, blackened heart. Diamond-hard nails ripped deep, tearing through the vampire's chest in an effort to surround the one organ that would ensure Mitro's demise.

Mitro screamed and thrashed, his talons raking at Dax's face, gouging long furrows from eye to jaw. He slammed his own fist deep into Dax's chest, trying to reach the hunter's heart before the Carpathian could extract his.

Hot melting rock erupted through the chamber, rocketing high, smashing into the barrier erected by Arabejila. The heat was so intense the barrier clearly was melting and along with it, their skin. Mitro's face drooped as if it had grown too thin, sliding from his skull and bones. Dax knew his own skin, acclimatized to the volcano, could not long withstand the enormous heat from the very core of the earth. It didn't matter.

Nothing mattered but destroying Mitro. The vampire could tear out Dax's heart and throw it into the bubbling orange and red pool of hot rock steadily climbing toward them, and it would be well worth it as long as Mitro was gone from the world. Dax's fingers dug deeper, reaching for the vampire's heart, as Mitro tore a wider hole in Dax's chest. For a moment it felt as if the vampire was ripping through his body with a dull knife, but Dax cut off all pain and focused on the job at hand.

Dax closed his fingers around the blackened heart and began to extract it. The vampire shrieked, maddened, enraged, ripping at Dax's face and eyes with one hand while he continued to tunnel his hand into Dax's chest in an effort to kill him before it was too late.

Dax pulled the heart free of the body and, looking straight into Mitro's eyes, let the useless organ drop into the fiery pit below. He felt no animosity toward the vampire, he felt no triumph or sadness. The decayed organ incinerated the moment it hit the bubbling cauldron of melted rock.

But instead of collapsing, lifeless, in Dax's arms as the vampire should have once his heart was destroyed, Mitro's lips drew back in a parody of a smile, his blackened receding gums and jagged, stained teeth snapping together with an ominous clicking sound. Triumphant, vile, and still very much alive, the vampire abruptly leaned forward and sank his teeth into Dax's throat.

7

Little by little the sky darkened, a great shadow drawn slowly overhead. A loud rumble heralded the continuous shaking of the earth. A dense ash cloud erupted, shooting straight into the sky like a voluminous black tower, expanding and churning as it rose. Within a matter of minutes the blackness was nearly impenetrable. Rain began to fall, a fast flurry of powdery drops.

Exhausted, mentally and physically, Riley could barely lift her head. Her body felt leaden, drained of all strength. She knelt in the dirt, trying to think what to do next, but her brain refused to work. She peered at the three men through the veil of darkness. They appeared misshapen from head to toe. All three crouched low on the ground trying to ride out the never-ending tremors. She realized the drops weren't water at all, but a heavy, powdery ash covering their bodies, blanketing the mountain, the trees, every bit of foliage surrounding them, and making it impossible to look up.

Lightning cracked across the sky. Thunder crashed. Electricity crackled around them all, sparks dancing around their bodies while halos surrounded their heads. The sound of cannonballs exploding hurt her ears and reverberated through her head. The smell of sulfur saturated the air.

Ben pushed himself to his feet, trying for balance when the ground rolled relentlessly. "We've got to make a run for it. We can't stay here. We're too close." He coughed, covering his mouth and nose. Anxiety edged his voice, but he clearly was trying to hold it together.

"Ben," Jubal said, his voice calm and steady. "You can't outrun a volcano. It isn't going to help to go charging off. We're either safe or we're not."

"If we're lucky, the main blast will be on the other side of the mountain and we'll survive if I can build us a shelter fast enough. Hopefully Miguel and the others are out of the danger zone," Riley tried to assure him, when she wasn't even certain herself.

Ben gaped at them, and then exploded with fear and outrage. "A shelter? Are you kidding me? That's a volcano! If we stay here, we're going to die!"

"She's not talking about a tent," Gary snapped.

"And if we run, we're definitely dead," Jubal added calmly. He turned to Riley. "Riley? Can you do it? We really need that shelter, and we really need it now."

Riley sat back on her knees and wiped at the ash falling on her face with a weary hand, trying to find the strength to call on Mother Earth once more. She closed her eyes. She wasn't certain she could do anything at all to save them. She'd come here to stop evil from entering the world, but so far, all she'd done was fail. She'd failed to save her mother, failed to keep the evil caged, failed to stop the volcano. Odds were she'd fail to save them, too.

Even though she'd suggested it, the idea that she could build shelter that would withstand a volcano did indeed seem as ludicrous as Ben declared. What had she been thinking? She took a deep breath and coughed, her chest tight, lungs burning.

"Riley?" Jubal prodded.

Fiery streaks of molten rock spewed into the air and hurtled down toward them. Purplish-red scoria and fiery stones rained down on them. They covered their heads, the three men trying to shield Riley with their bodies. She heard Gary gasp as a stone hit his back. Another glanced off a rock near Ben's head.

Jubal was right. They would die if they tried to run, and they would die if they stayed here without one heck of a volcano-proof shelter. If building one was even remotely possible, she *had* to figure it out immediately.

Riley covered her mouth and nose to try for a clean breath of air and then once more plunged her hands into the soil. There was desperation in her voice as she chanted.

"Square, cornucopia, spindle, scythe, salt and shield, I call upon Auriel's might." The words came out of their own accord, and they felt right. She felt as if she were tapping into a long-forgotten memory.

To her shock, the ground began to rise, following the circle of salt to form thick walls of rock and dirt, expanding fast, moving above their heads, curving and growing until they were inside a cave.

"Agate, jasper, tourmaline, line this place so none may burn."

Ash was everywhere, in her mouth and nose, clogging her throat. The shower of incandescent stones continued, making deep holes in the ground around them and sending hot shrapnel spraying over them. A small fissure opened up, running right up to the circle of protection, but stopped abruptly.

Riley closed her eyes, sending up a prayer that she would have the strength to do this. She felt the earth responding to her touch, a comfort that was fast becoming familiar. Around the circle of protection the walls continued to grow, lined with solid rock to add to the thickness, giving additional protection against a superheated blast. The walls climbed high, curving to form a ceiling overhead. Only a narrow opening remained.

"Ruby, garnet, diamond strong, seal us safe from fiery harm." As she chanted, all colors of red from fire lined the walls and began to build a door at the entrance.

The roar from outside dimmed, although the tremors continued relentlessly as the last remaining open space closed and sealed. Riley slumped to the ground, there in the darkness while the ground tossed and rolled. She was so exhausted she couldn't think. She'd done her best. Either they would survive or they wouldn't. She'd managed to protect them from gases and anything falling from overhead, but if the mountain blew and superheated lava found their cave, it wouldn't matter if they were inside or not, the heat would melt the rock and they'd probably suffocate before the fiery lava found them.

Darkness was absolute in the cavern Riley had created. Jubal flicked on a light, pushing it into the ground. The roof and walls sparkled with gemstones, giving off a beautiful, almost soothing glow.

Jubal looked around in amazement at the gem-lined cave. "Amazing, Riley. Whether we get out of this alive or not, let me just say thank you now."

Gary handed her a bottle of water he pulled from his pack. "Here, drink this. You have to be exhausted."

Riley found she could barely lift her hand to take the bottle. Her arms felt like lead and shook almost as hard as the ground. "If the mountain really goes up, it won't matter. You know that, don't you?"

"You managed to build us shelter from the ash and debris," Jubal pointed out. "I'm going to believe you minimized the explosion and pushed it away from us."

"This is nuts," Ben burst out. "How did you make this cave out of nothing? What are you? If someone told me about this, I'd never believe them."

"There are a lot of things in this world people have a difficult time believing," Gary said. "It's easier to dismiss the incidents as fantasy or pretend they didn't happen. Riley's obviously extremely gifted . . ."

"That's not gifted," Ben said. "No one can do what she did. Is this some kind of black magic, not that I know if I believe in that, either, but I've seen some freaky things when I've traveled, but this . . ." He trailed off again.

Riley snuck a look at his face. In the shadows from the dim light, his face appeared lined and stressed. She couldn't blame him. She'd grown up seeing the strange things her mother could do, but even as a child, she'd known others would never accept that plants grew beneath her mother's feet when she walked and reached out to her whenever she was close. There really wasn't an explanation she could give Ben that would make sense. The things her family could do were normal to her, but clearly weren't for others.

"Call her psychic," Jubal said. "She has an affinity for the earth and it responds to her. Hopefully, that connection was strong enough to direct the volcanic blast away from us."

"Affinity for the earth? Directed a volcano blast? That's bullshit," Ben said. "It's impossible. I just saw crazy shit with my own eyes, but damn it, it's impossible."

Gary's eyebrow went up. "Is it? How do you know what's possible and what isn't? In Indonesia the people believe their sultan has tamed and calmed the volcanos for centuries. They are certain he can protect them from the fury of eruption. And we've all seen inexplicable happenings on this trip."

Even as he spoke, outside the cave, more stones and debris pummeled the roof, landing with shocking force. Riley resisted the urge to cover her ears. Every jarring blow sent her heart jolting hard in her chest. Fear tasted like copper in her mouth.

An explosion rocked them a second time, the mountain shuddering, sending them reeling from side to side. Riley clung to the earth, digging her fingers deep, trying to get a feel for where the worst of the eruption had taken place and just how big it had been. At the same time, she tried using the soil to anchor herself. As it was, she sprawled hard against Gary, knocking her head against his. His glasses went flying. Ben fell over Annabel's pack, slamming his shoulder into the gem-studded wall of the cave. Jubal was the only one who maintained a semblance of balance, riding out the swelling ground waves as if he was surfing on his knees.

"Is everyone all right?" Jubal asked.

They all nodded, shock taking its toll on their voices.

"That sounded far away," he ventured after a few minutes.

Riley's heart settled into a steadier beat. She swallowed several times, testing her ability to speak. "It feels far away, the other side of the mountain. I can tell there are several vents open releasing pressure, and that blast wasn't catastrophic, but more of a burp. But *it's* out." She met Gary's gaze grimly. "I couldn't hold it and calm the volcano at the same time. So if we're right and the blast was on the other side of the mountain and we're not going to get burned up, we're going to have to deal with it—whatever it is."

She tasted the bitterness of failure. Fear skittered down her spine, yet deep within the earth, her fingers curled and held on tight to . . . hope. She caught the elusive presence of another. *Male. Power. Strength.* Yet his touch was subtle, a child of the earth as she was. At once she felt comfort. She wasn't entirely alone in the world. She had a brief glimpse of calm. Of determination. Of someone who would never surrender or back down.

Her breath caught in her throat. For one moment he seemed to touch her mind, a stroke, no more, *inside* her mind, a caress. She knew he was every bit as aware of her as she was of him. He didn't feel anything at all like the evil one had. This was so different. Gentle. She had the very vivid impression of a powerful being unafraid of his own strength and entirely confident. She wanted to cling to him for a moment, a strong anchor in an exploding world gone chaotic and mad all around her.

He was gone before she could catch his path. A soft, protesting cry slipped from her lips. She'd felt hope for the first time. In that brief moment, she couldn't explain it, but she wasn't so alone. He understood the whispering of the earth, the information she gathered when she sank her hands deep into the soil—that complete affinity with and the need, even compulsion, to care for the plants and environment around her. She was the guardian, the sentinel, and somewhere another walked the same planet and held that same job.

It occurred to her that she was a little mad after the murder of her mother—that she'd suffered some deep psychotic break—and she barely managed to swallow the bubble of hysterical laughter. She couldn't afford to lose it. Not now.

"Whatever the evil entity is—and it feels masculine to me—it speaks the same language as the porter chanted when he killed my mother. And I think it managed to escape with the blast." She swallowed hard, her eyes meeting Jubal's. "I'm sorry. I tried my best. If my mother hadn't been killed maybe she could have done more."

Ben carefully picked himself up, scooting across the dirt to put his back to the wall, careful to keep his movements short. "Someone needs to tell me what the hell is going on here." He pushed his hair back, his hand coming away filled with ash. "Because I feel a little bit as if I'm going insane. Did she really stop the volcano? I mean, we're still alive aren't we?"

"For the moment," Gary said. "I think she managed to minimize the blast and direct it to the other side of the mountain. The vents opening closer to us are just relieving pressure."

"How long have you had this particular skill?" Ben asked, his tone somewhere between awe and sarcasm.

"Since my mother died," Riley replied, feeling a little distracted. She wanted to brush up against that elusive feeling of comfort and strength and draw courage from it just one more time. Trapped in a cave, waiting to cook to death, exhausted beyond anything she'd ever known, she wanted to curl up in the fetal position and hide.

"How did you do this?" Ben demanded. "Are you some kind of devil worshipper? No one can make a cave grow over their head or stop a volcano from exploding."

"Clearly, I didn't stop the volcano," Riley pointed out. "And that's the second time you've accused me of worshipping the devil, and I really don't appreciate it. You were right here. You watched everything I did. I called on the Universe, not the devil." She couldn't keep weariness—or disgust—out of her voice, and it wasn't entirely fair to Ben. Given everything that had happened, his fear and need to lash out were understandable. If everyone weren't looking for her to save them, she might be tempted to lash out, too. Moreover, how could she explain what was happening to him when she didn't understand it herself?

Grief welled up without warning, and she blinked back a hot rush of tears. She wanted her mother—needed her. Everything was happening so fast, and Riley didn't have a clue what she was doing.

Gary stepped in smoothly. "Calm down, Ben. I know what's happening seems crazy, but just because you've never encountered something like this before doesn't make it less real—or less dangerous. Fighting among ourselves is only going to make things worse. Jubal and I have witnessed things that would send most people screaming their way straight to the loony bin. But the truth is, evil does exist, monsters come after us in the night, and people like Riley are sometimes the only thing standing between us and total annihilation. I wish you hadn't had to be a part of this, but unfortunately for you, you're a brave man and you chose to protect Riley instead of running away like the others. That choice, while admirable, has put you in harm's way and exposed you to powers beyond your comprehension. As long as you stick with us, you're going to be in the middle of this, and I can pretty much guarantee it's going to get worse before it gets better. So we need you to keep your cool, and lay off Riley. Sniping at her isn't going to help any of us."

Riley had to admire his calm, matter-of-fact explanation. There was something very reassuring about Gary. No drama. No ego. Just his presence. She took another drink of water. Her throat felt parched, her body thirsty. She needed . . . but what she didn't know. Only that she was suddenly craving something. Despite her exhaustion, her blood was on fire, rushing through her veins, her pulse leaping, finding a strange rhythm.

She felt more alive than she ever had and had no idea if it was because the volcano had come to dramatic life, breathing fire, or if it was because she'd connected with someone who had given her a brief moment of comfort in the midst of total madness. Maybe it was the intensity of her emotions, the fear, the grief, the adrenaline. Whatever it was, she felt every bit as vibrant as she did weary.

"It's just hard to wrap my head around all this," Ben said in a calmer voice. "The funny thing is, I've always been interested in folklore, everything from Bigfoot and the Yeti to werewolves and vampires and I've traveled all around the world in an effort to prove where there's smoke there's fire. I've been in a minisub searching for the Loch Ness Monster. You name it, if it was unexplained, I went to find it, but after all the disappointments, I didn't really believe anymore. Maybe I never really did. But this . . ." He shook his head and wiped his hand over his mouth. "I'm sticking with you, although I have to tell you, I'm just a little scared."

Jubal smiled at him, a flash of white teeth in his ash-blackened face. "Welcome to our world. You'd be crazy if you weren't a little afraid."

Riley pushed herself up and scooted to the far wall facing the three men. She drew her knees up and rested her chin on them. "I'm definitely scared, Ben. I've come to this mountain several times and nothing like this has ever happened before."

Ben sent her a strained smile. "Thanks for the cave, however you managed it. Melting in hot lava isn't the way I want to go out."

She tried to find a smile and hoped she pulled it off. "Pyroclastic clouds aren't exactly my idea of fun, either."

Jubal cleared his throat. "Are you certain whatever was locked in the volcano was able to get free?"

Riley nodded reluctantly. "He's free. I couldn't hold him." She tasted the bitter flavor of failure. "You know what he is, don't you?" When neither Jubal nor Gary answered, she sighed. "Look, we're in this together now. He's out. I felt him. I know he's real. You have to tell me what we're dealing with."

"I'd like to know, too," Ben agreed. "No matter what it is, it can't be much crazier than what I've already witnessed."

Jubal rubbed the bridge of his nose, his eyes meeting Gary's. He sighed. "No matter how we say this, you're going to think we're insane."

Ben shrugged. "I already think maybe I'm insane, so just come out with it. None of this seems real."

Still, both men hesitated. Riley didn't like the way they looked at one another. She felt her pulse jump. She couldn't get any more scared, could she? Fear of the unknown was worse than the knowing. At least then she could try to prepare.

"I need to know what this evil thing is, Jubal. I heard it speak. Its voice was in my head for a minute, and it felt foul." She shuddered. "I think it's going to come after me."

"What did it say?" Gary asked.

"He spoke in that same language the porter used just before he killed my mother." She closed her eyes, drawing on the same phonographic memory that let her reproduce bird and animal calls perfectly and made her so adept at linguistics. "He said, *'Arabejila. Emni hän ku köd alte. Tõdak a ho ćaδasz engemko, kutenken ćaδasz engemko a jälleen. Andak a irgalomet terád it.'* "

She didn't know what the individual words were or what they meant, but she reproduced the sounds, inflection and pitch precisely and the sickening foulness of the tone made everyone flinch.

"The only word I recognized was Arabejila. It's a family name and it's very unusual. My great-great-grandmother was named Arabejila and she was named after another great-grandmother."

Gary and Jubal exchanged another long look.

Riley sighed. "Just tell me what it means. At this point, like Ben, I don't think I'm going to be surprised by anything."

"He must have thought you were someone he knew," Gary ventured. "If you have an ancestor who was called Arabejila, when he sensed your presence, you must have felt familiar to him, which means her genes and gifts are strong in you. He probably believes you are this Arabejila."

"No relative of mine with that name has been alive for . . ." She trailed off, glancing at Ben. Whatever had lived in the volcano had to be a very ancient evil. How long had the women in her family been coming to such a remote part of the Andes and performing the ritual?

She pressed her lips together tightly and rubbed her cheek along her knees. If that ancient being had been sealed in the volcano by one of her ancestors, it stood to reason he might be a little angry and looking for revenge.

"Never mind. Can you translate what he said?"

"Repeat the phrase for me," he said. "I'll do my best."

She did so, speaking as slowly as she could without affecting the rhythm and inflection of the words.

Gary rubbed his jaw, stared for a moment at his blackened hand, rubbed the ash onto his jeans and then shrugged when his hands remained dirty. "*Emni hän ku köd alte.* I know that means 'cursed woman.'"

"I thought that phrase was familiar," Riley said. "The porter chanted it over and over. He was calling my mother a cursed woman."

"And now you," Jubal said.

Riley instinctively buried her fingers in the soil, needing comfort. She already knew that evil entity was going to be coming after her. She didn't need Gary to tell her that; she'd heard the hatred and rage in the thing's voice. But she'd also heard fear. She wasn't Arabejila, but if evil feared her, Riley was more than happy to claim kinship with the woman.

"*Tõdak a ho ćaδasz engemko, kutenken ćaδasz engemko a jälleen*, I believe is, I don't know how you . . ." He frowned at Jubal. "'Escaped'? 'How you escaped me'?"

Jubal nodded. "That's what I got. And something about 'not again.'"

Gary nodded. "'I do not know how you escaped me, but you will not again.' That's as close as I can get. Clearly he thinks he knows you."

"And the last part?" Riley insisted. "*Andak a irgalomet terád it.*"

"That means, 'I will have no mercy for you this time.'" Gary said the words in a rush, as if he wanted to get it over.

"So who is he? *What* is he?" Riley demanded.

Gary wiped at the ash on his jeans, not looking at her. "I'm afraid you're dealing with a vampire. A very powerful vampire. The real deal. He'll tear out your throat and drain you dry. He feeds off the suffering and terror of people. There's no doubt in my mind that's what was locked in that mountain."

Riley stared at him, openmouthed. She hadn't expected him to say *vampire*. Vampires were mythical demons in horror movies or novels. She didn't have a clue what she thought he'd say, but certainly not *vampire*. He was serious, too. She snuck a look at Jubal. He was just as serious.

"All those weapons you have, you were expecting this. Clearly, from the beginning, you knew."

Gary shook his head. "No, that's not true. We actually came here to research a particular plant we thought long extinct. A small group of adventurers had come here last year and one had a picture of the plant on his blog on the Internet. A friend of ours just happened to stumble across the photograph and sent it to me knowing my interest in rare plants. Jubal and I were both excited about it. I got in touch with the miner who described the plant and I became certain it was what we were looking for. We contacted a guide and came."

"But our guide was ill," Jubal said. "Just like yours and Dr. Patton's guide."

"And ours," Ben added.

Gary nodded. "So we threw in with everyone and figured since we were all going to the same general area, we could travel together and then go our own way when we got to the mountain. At that point we didn't have a clue anything was wrong."

"We began to suspect we were dealing with the undead when all the strange things began happening and they were clearly directed at your mother," Jubal added. "There's a certain feel to evil, and we've both felt it before."

Ben shook his head. "No. No way. I've studied vampire lore around the world, and I'll admit, there's a part of me that wanted to believe something like that existed, like in the movies. I ran into a group of people in my travels that totally believe in vampires and claim they hunt and kill them. They were all nut jobs. Completely whacko. There are no such things as vampires. The people they killed were ill, or lived differently or had trouble being out in the sun. I investigated each victim and none of them were vampires. The few people who act like vampires, killing for blood, are in mental institutions for the criminally insane."

"True enough," Gary agreed. "I know exactly the people you're talking about. I was mixed up with them once, a long time ago, and yes, they kill indiscriminately. They target someone and then twist facts to fit what they want to believe, but that doesn't negate the fact that vampires exist."

"If that's true," Ben argued, "why doesn't anyone know about it?"

Riley had to admit it was a good question. She kept her head on her knees, but watched Gary's face carefully. He truly believed what he was saying. Jubal did as well. Neither struck her as insane. She'd felt evil when she'd plunged her hands into the soil. Even more, she'd heard it—heard its voice. There was no denying it, as much as she'd like to.

"How was he able to get the bats and monkeys, even the piranha and that snake to target my mother if he was trapped in the volcano?" she asked, not waiting for Gary or Jubal to answer Ben's very logical question. She believed Gary, and that was just plain terrifying.

"Vampires can be very powerful. If this one has survived locked in that volcano, we're dealing with an extremely powerful one. He has been around for more centuries than we can imagine, growing in power."

Riley closed her eyes briefly. She'd let something truly evil out into the world. "There are stories, folklore we believed, about the devastation of both the Cloud People and the Incas living here, that something had killed their best warriors and destroyed their villages. They thought it was an evil god who demanded sacrifices of children and women, yet never was appeased. Could it be that old?"

"Yes," Gary replied simply.

Riley wanted to curl up into a ball and lay in the comfort of the soil. She hadn't had time to grieve for her mother and she felt overwhelmed with sadness so abruptly she could barely think. She didn't want to think. She didn't want to talk or hear any more. She wanted to be a child and cover her ears. She sighed instead and forced her weary body to sit straighter. "So do you carry stakes on you along with those weapons?" It was a halfhearted attempt at humor, the best she could muster under the circumstances.

Ben snickered. "Wooden stakes? Are you kidding me?"

"Stakes don't work," Jubal said. "You have to incinerate the heart. You can shoot them, stab them, stake them and even cut off their head, but if you don't burn that heart, they can repair themselves."

A groan escaped her. Of course you would have to incinerate the heart. Anything else would be just too easy.

Ben rolled his eyes. "Now I know you're crazy."

"I wish I could tell you I'm making this up," Gary said. "But I'm not. Everyone is at risk now. All of us. Every tribesman. Every member of our party that tried to get away from the volcano. He'll be looking for blood and he'll kill anyone he comes across. Not only will he take blood, but he'll take their memories and learn at a rapid rate so that he'll fit in anywhere he goes. His lack of knowledge of the past centuries won't mean anything within a matter of days."

Riley ran the pad of her finger back and forth over her eyebrow, trying to ease the beginnings of a headache. "Then we have to find the others and make certain they're safe."

Ben frowned at her. "You're actually buying into this? An honest-to-God vampire who won't die even if you drive a stake through its heart. Even if we stab or shoot it."

She nodded slowly. "I don't want to buy into it, Ben, but I do. Those animals behaved completely against their nature, and something drove Capa to murder my mother. So call it whatever you want to call it, but I want to know how to kill whatever it is. I want to know exactly what to expect when I come across it, because I don't want any more surprises."

Ben scowled at her but nodded his head. "I suppose you have a point."

"Vampires can be very cunning," Jubal explained. "They're masters of illusion. They appear to be charming and handsome, but in fact, they mask what and who they are. They can get inside your head and make you do whatever they wish. You'll go to them when they command it and allow them to rip out your throat. You will give them your children or any loved one if they demand it."

"Great," Riley said. "The worst monster imaginable, right? That's what you're saying. Just say that. So, along with a gun I need a flamethrower. I noticed you had one, Gary. Can I borrow it? I'm fairly certain it's me Vamp doesn't like. He made that pretty clear."

"I say we get the hell out of here the minute we can," Ben said. "Whatever it is can live off the piranha."

"But he wouldn't," Gary said. "A vampire feeds off of humans."

"I agree that you and Riley need to get out of here as fast as possible," Jubal said. "We should find the others and get them moving out of the rain forest and back to civilization as fast as possible."

"Has anyone considered how we're going to get out of here?" Ben ventured.

Riley felt their eyes on her. If the vampire couldn't get in, she might just consider staying for a very long time. She shrugged. "I don't know, but I'm not even sure that it's safe to go out yet. The ground is still shaking, and when I put my hands into the soil, I feel heat."

As she spoke, she thrust her hands deep into the soil. As before, her body reacted to the energy coiling around her palms and fingers. That soothing warmth seeped into her pores. She stayed very still and listened. The ground creaked and moaned—whispered softly. She caught the sound of her mother's voice, just a faint echo as if she was laughing and the merry notes traveled through rock and soil to find her. Tears clogged her throat.

She closed her eyes, inhaling. At first she could hear the men breathing. An occasional jarring crash resounded on the roof above her head. She forced herself to block out the distractions and pushed her awareness deep, searching for a connection, a way to tap into that vein of information that seemed to be just out of reach. She could hear rumblings and knew if she just tuned in, she would understand what was happening in the world around her.

She had a message center willing to impart information to her, she just hadn't learned how to use it yet, but each time she pushed her hands into the rich soil, she found she unlocked more of the mysteries surrounding her mother. Whatever gift exchanged from mother to daughter was locked here in the ground waiting for her to discover the legacy that had been left to her. She just needed to find the right words to draw the secrets to her. With others depending on her, she needed to figure it out.

She took another breath and let it out, pushing away the need for action or hurry. The men disappeared, taking with them the sounds of their presence. The walls of the cavern melted away. Fear and grief left her until there was only the sound of her lungs moving in and out rhythmically. For a few minutes she breathed, allowing the mechanics of that simple process to clear and open her mind completely.

She became aware of a pulse beating—an eternal thrum, coming from the very center of the earth's core. Through the pads of her fingers she felt an expanding cloud of extremely hot gas, and felt an intimate connection with that older star exploding violently, yet giving birth to new stars, to the sun and moon and planet Earth. She actually could see the creation in her mind, the nebula collapsing and cooling into a flattened, slowly spinning disk. Earth's surface covered by the pulsating ocean of molten rock.

Riley felt the bubbling magma beneath the surface, the shifting of plates and pushing up of mountains and the roots spreading out, like great chains and vines, deep beneath the sea, under every continent, connecting every part of the planet together—connecting it all with her. The first soft whispers came to her, murmurs filling her mind, voices of women long past, welcoming her to their sisterhood.

Her heart sang when she recognized the familiar, comforting feel of her mother and grandmother.

8

Dax stared into the hate-filled, triumphant eyes of the vampire. Just as the volcano had changed Dax, Mitro, too, had evolved into something else. He had spent hundreds of years inside that superheated environment, and to withstand the pressure, gases and heat, Mitro had shifted into a form that was better suited. Over the centuries, his body had taken on the shell of a mutated lizard.

Heavy ridges dissected Mitro's skull, drawing his skin tight over heavy bones. Singed hair stood straight up in spiked razor-sharp rows. Eyelids had grown heavier and the eyes themselves, windows to the soul, reflected back a pure black, no white showing at all, no soul within. Scars from the magma formed deep pits over most of his exposed skin. Slime-covered skin had yellowed and gave off a faint scent of rotten eggs. The chamber began to spin. Poisonous gas infused in the vampire's thick, mottled skin induced lethargy and clouded the mind.

Dax forced his brain to work. The withered heart of the vampire had been incinerated, yet he still lived. How? And how could any hunter possibly kill the undead if he didn't die when he should have? In all the endless years of destroying the undead, he'd never encountered such a thing, nor heard of it.

The mountain shook. A boom reverberated through the chamber. Maniacal laughter grated, slicing through his head. Staring straight into his eyes, Mitro drove his clawing fist deeper into Dax's chest. Agony, bright and hot, robbed Dax of breath. The talons ripped and tore, shredding sinew and muscle, digging a hole, tunneling deep in an effort to reach the Carpathian's beating heart.

That dark parody of a grin widened, jagged, stained teeth in receding gums rushing toward his neck even as the greedy talons grasped at his heart. In that moment everything changed. Dax didn't have the luxury of dying, leaving Mitro loose on the world. Dax had to live no matter what.

He drew back, ignoring the agony ripping through him, took a breath and unleashed a torrent of fire straight into Mitro's malevolent face. The vampire howled, jerking back, twisting his arm viciously as he withdrew his empty fist. Mitro threw himself to one side to avoid the steady stream of flames pouring from the hunter's throat, his scream filling the chamber.

Bright red blood sprayed into the air from Dax's torn chest. Great globs of burning blackened blood, a poisonous acid, from Mitro's open chest splattered through the chamber and burned into ashes, raining down over him. Gases exploded into fiery balls, hurtling through the enclosed space, pitting deep craters into the walls. Vents burst below them, more noxious gas rising along with bright orange-red sprays of molten rock.

Mitro hammered at the thin barrier, slamming into it over and over like a battering ram, dodging the fiery bombs blasting upward from the lower pools of roiling magma. Dax leapt after the vampire, reaching with the tips of his fingers to hook an ankle and yank the undead backward. A thousand tiny needles punctured his palm, burning on contact. His first instinct was to let go, but he forced himself to hold on, dragging the vampire back down toward the bubbling pool of heated rock.

Mitro drove his foot into the hole in Dax's chest. Pain exploded through the hunter. For a moment everything went black. His body shut down, his hand slipping off the ankle. He tumbled through the air before he caught himself. Mitro was at the barrier, ramming his ridged skull over and over into the same spot. Dax streaked upward to try to intercept him again.

The mountain rumbled ominously—held its breath for one still second—and then heaved. The concussion sent both combatants reeling. Dax slammed hard into the wall before he could catch himself. Heat seared his body. Blood dripped from his ears. His vision blurred. The chamber filled with gaseous vapor, and the sudden increase in pressure nearly tore him apart.

In that instant, he felt the Old One rise to protect him. His body had grown accustomed to the conditions of the volcano over the centuries, but neither he nor Mitro would fare well when the volcano erupted and the dragon knew it.

The Old One took possession fast, his soul rising, spreading out to encompass Dax. Crimson and orange scales first engulfed Dax's body, sliding smoothly and efficiently from his head to his toes. The hard shell covered the gaping hole in his chest, but his blood continued to seep out between the scales, staining his chest scarlet.

Dax was used to shapeshifting, but this felt different. When Carpathians shifted, there was no sense of the body completely remaking itself, but this time, there was. He could feel his mass increase, his bones lengthen and reshape. He could feel the wings sprouting from his back, the supple, scaled hide stretching out like vast sails catching an ocean wind. He could feel his nails lengthen, become razor-tipped diamond talons. Strength, agility and raw, primal emotion coursed through his veins. He wasn't a hunter who'd assumed the shape of a dragon: he *was* a dragon. Mighty. Powerful. Master of fire. King of the sky. And though his consciousness was still there, the Old One was there, too, ancient and powerful and just as deadly.

His wings spread, and his dragon body spun in midair. The long, ridged tail splashed into the magma pool, slinging red-hot rock against the sides of the cavern. But instead of pain, the heat invigorated him, strengthened him. He screamed in triumph and challenge and spewed another jet of hot flame toward the vampire.

But just before the boiling clouds of flame enveloped him, Mitro shifted into a large, scaly black dragon and rammed hard against the barrier, breaching it at last. He bellowed his triumph as the mountain belched, geysers of vapor and fiery material venting through thin spots. There was another short breath and the mountain erupted. Huge, violent plumes of gas, ash and molten rock spewed forth, ripping through the mountaintop and into the sky above. Both dragons went hurtling sideways, driven through the side of the mountain by the force of the blast.

The fiery red dragon tumbled end over end through the sky, disoriented, nearly blind, inside the cloud of fiery ash and gas spreading over the forest. Lightning cracked across the sky. Bright streaks of red and orange fountained into the air. Ash and white-hot mud rained down. Fiery cannonballs of molten rock shot through the air. A river of lava poured out of the gaping wound in the side of the mountain, looking like long ribbons of thick, glowing taffy, twisted and bright, dropping to the forest below. Trees exploded, fiery bombs bursting into flames.

Glowing eyes pierced the veil of the dark cloud and ash to spot the struggling black dragon. Red wings swept down in powerful strokes, propelling him high into the air. The experience was unlike any Dax had ever shared before. He was Dax with the Old One, watching, feeling and thinking with him, yet at the same time he was separate. It felt almost as if his consciousness was a visitor in the dragon's body. The body wasn't his own, and yet it was. The duality left him feeling dazed and a little disconnected.

Yet despite the alienness of his current situation, Dax remained keenly aware of the blood dripping through the scales covering the dragon's chest. Mitro had wounded Dax badly, and that wound had carried over through the transformation. Dax knew he needed to stop the blood loss, and soon. The dragon, however, cared little for the fluid leaking from his chest. Rage and dominance consumed the Old One's mind as he raced toward the floundering vampire that wore the appearance rather than the true form of a black dragon. Banking left and using the ash cloud for cover, the Old One rode the volcano's superheated updrafts to rise above Mitro. When he was positioned above the black dragon, the Old One tucked his wings tight and dove, rocketing downward, plummeting through smoke and ash at deadly speed.

Mitro glanced up just as the red dragon extended its wings and brought its fore and hind legs around, talons extended for a strike. At first Dax thought Mitro would run, but when the black dragon only screamed a challenge and launched toward him, Dax realized Mitro had no idea he was confronting a true dragon rather than the weaker shapeshifted form of a dragon that Carpathians could assume at will.

Mitro thought he had the upper hand.

The Old One was confident that he had the greater size, greater skill, stronger position and momentum on his side. The kill seemed virtually assured.

Inside the dragon, Dax struggled to come to grips with a storm of fierce emotions. Dax had always fought, always killed, with emotionless efficiency. The dragon did not. To the dragon, the fight *was* life, full of wildness, rawness and pulse-pounding emotions so vivid he could almost taste, touch, see and smell each one. Elation, pure and white, whirled with flames of fiery red aggression, and streaming banners of golden-bright pride. Dax's mind and senses whirled with the overload.

The red dragon slammed into the smaller black one, and they locked together, both falling out of the sky. Wings fluttered wildly, each dragon seeking balance and superior attack position. Long necks writhed. Fangs snapped and tore at scaly hides, seeking a killing bite. The talons of their back legs clutched each other with grim determination, while their forelegs tangled and ripped at vulnerable bellies.

The Old One was stronger and bigger, driving his claws deep into Mitro's belly ripping and tearing through the armored hide to the soft, vulnerable organs beneath. His claws penetrated with each stroke, removing scales and chunks of bleeding flesh.

Within his black dragon form, Mitro screamed in shock and pain and insane rage. He'd been certain of his victory—certain of his physical superiority over Danutdaxton—but each of Dax's blows struck deep, while each of Mitro's own were turned away by diamond-hard scales and a seemingly impenetrable red hide. Mitro didn't understand. *How was this possible?*

He writhed wildly but could not break free of the red dragon's fierce grip. Locked in a death battle he suddenly realized he might not win, Mitro began a desperate, brutal assault on Dax's one possible weak spot: the scales over his heart where, even in dragon form, blood was seeping from the terrible wound Mitro had dealt him. With vicious determination and demonic speed, Mitro landed a series of punishing blows on the bloody spot. The chest plate bent, but before it could break, Dax's fangs sank deep in Mitro's shoulder, ripping out a massive chunk of flesh and tendon.

Writhing, screaming, ripping, biting, the two giant beasts plummeted toward the burning ground. Seconds before impact, the two dragons ripped apart, wings spread wide to catch the wind and send them soaring in opposite directions.

Mitro pushed hard, pumping his wings with desperate speed to climb back up into the air. The red dragon pursued him with single-minded determination. The calm, relentless, determined hunter who never surrendered the chase.

He couldn't outrun Dax and, though it still made no sense, clearly couldn't best him with strength alone. Mitro needed an edge, an advantage. His eyes narrowed to obsidian slits, focused on the ash cloud billowing from the erupting volcano. Putting on a burst of speed, he flew straight into the boiling black heart of the plume.

Through the Old One's eyes, Dax watched Mitro dive into the superheated ash cloud. As he disappeared from view, the wind shifted, beginning to spiral around the cloud.

What was he doing? The circling winds gathered the particles of hot ash in an ever-tightening vortex around the wounded vampire. *Did he think he could hide in the cloud?*

The Old One let out another roar of challenge and dove straight toward the vampire, eager to end the threat.

The concentrated debris in the air dropped visibility to zero, but the dragon's vision saw more than even Carpathian eyes. He could see the changes in the density of air, the solid form at the heart of the whirling black ash cloud. The black vampire was motionless, wings outstretched, letting the unnatural cyclonic winds keep him aloft. Dax could almost feel the vampire healing his wounds from the inside. Closing tears in vital organs and stopping blood loss where the dragon had sliced and torn.

The red dragon was practically on top of Mitro when all the rock and debris in the air solidified into a packed wall that completely blocked the vampire from view. Fearless, certain of his dominance, the red dragon brought his hind legs and forelegs into position for another strike, and plowed through the relatively thin barrier, shattering it on impact.

But instead of finding a vulnerable, wounded opponent on the other side of the ash wall, they slammed full force into the hard point of the black dragon's tail—a point Mitro had transformed from simple flesh, scale and bone into a razor-sharp trident of silver spikes, each two feet long and glinting with evil, serrated at the tips.

Screaming in surprise and pain, the red dragon impaled itself on Mitro's spiked tail. Dax gasped in agony, feeling the spikes as if they were tearing through his own flesh.

Luckily, instead of taking the speared tail through the heart, the spike embedded deep in his stomach. The serrated edges were making quick work of the Old One's insides, but because they'd missed the heart, it bought Dax and the dragon a few precious minutes.

Once more, the two dragons were locked in a death battle as they plummeted from the sky. Mitro stuck fast to the other dragon, claws and tail spike digging deep. The Old One continued to claw and shred at Mitro's belly and limbs, teeth snapping at Mitro's neck and head. The black dragon rammed his tail spike up under the red dragon's ribs, seeking the elusive heart, but just as before, Mitro's shapeshifted dragon form was no match for the might of the Old One. Mitro reeled back in pain.

That flinch gave the Old One the opening he'd been waiting for. His teeth bore down lightning fast just above the shoulder, wrapping around the smaller neck, powerful jaws snapping shut with extreme force. The black dragon returned a bite on the other's face, his fangs sinking deep beside the Old One's left eye.

The dragons crashed into the mountainside, rolling down the steep sides, crushing trees in their path. A hard jolt broke them apart. Mitro came to a stop first, while the larger, heavier Old One continued to roll almost to the base of the volcano. Wounded, one wing torn and bloody, the red dragon struggled to its feet and screamed its defiance, eyes still locked on its combatant, refusing to lose sight of his goal.

Inside the body of the dragon, the Old One's rage and pain buffeted Dax with a maelstrom of emotion. The Old One was determined to win despite its injuries. Dax wasn't sure how much more their shared body could take, but the Old One fought off his attempts to control the red dragon. All around them, ash and burning chunks of pumice continued to rain down from the erupting volcano.

The red dragon tucked its weakened wing tight against its back and began to climb up the mountain toward Mitro. Still reeling from the brutal fight and equally brutal landing, the black dragon righted himself with shaky, labored motions. Black wings extended and flapped as Mitro tried to gather his strength and take to the air.

Unwilling to let his prey escape, the Old One put on a burst of speed, latched on to the black dragon's rear leg and threw him into a stand of nearby trees.

Riley blinked rapidly as the cave around them disintegrated. Ash continued to fall, soft drifting petals that choked the air and covered the trees and foliage like down. The forest around them was intact—the blast hadn't flattened the trees on their side of the mountain—but a few scattered fires and mud had done major damage. Several hundred feet up, she could see the devastation of the ruins of the Cloud People's village. Fires glowed all up and down the mountain, orange and red valiantly struggling through the darkened ash swirling in the air.

"We can't stay up here," Jubal said, covering his mouth and nose. "The wind is shifting our way and there's every possibility of a gas cloud coming at us from the other side."

"I can't see a trail," Ben said. "How are we going to find our way back without Miguel?"

"We've got GPS," Gary said. "And once the ash settles enough, we've got friends we can call in to pull us out with a helicopter, but we should try to find Miguel and the others just in case."

Riley's head jerked up. There was that ominous note in his voice—in the way he worded it. She let her breath out, coughed and covered her mouth. "I think I can track them," she admitted with a small glance at Ben.

"Of course you can," Ben said. "You can build caves and stop volcanos. I'm just looking for the thigh-high boots and cape." He flashed her a little grin and wiggled his eyebrows.

In spite of the circumstances she laughed. "I wish I had my cape. I'd fly us out of here."

Gary took the lead. Riley and Ben fell into step behind him. Jubal brought up the rear as they began to make their way down the mountain. Ash was thick powder on the ground, in the foliage, falling from the trees above them until they were nearly drowning in it. They wrapped shirts around their mouths and noses and continued doggedly on.

It was impossible to tell how close to dawn it was with the ash so dense in the sky, obscuring any evidence of light, but her watch told her they had a few more hours before the sun began to climb. It shouldn't have mattered, but if there was an honest-to-God vampire roaming around, then she wanted the sun to come up fast.

She cleared her throat. "Gary, if this ash hangs over the rain forest and keeps it dark, will the . . . a . . ." Saying the word *vampire* out loud just sounded ludicrous. She definitely could understand Ben's disbelief even in the face of evidence that some form of evil haunted their journey and pushed the porter to murder her mother.

Gary glanced over his shoulder, his expression sober. "I know it's difficult to believe that such things exist. But it's out there and it's a killing machine. It cannot come out in the sun, that much is true about them. They go to ground and place safeguards around their resting places. If this one was locked in a volcano for hundreds of years without blood to sustain it, it has to be one powerful creature."

"And hungry," she murmured. "Tell me about them. Everything you can think of."

Gary looked up quickly. Fear and panic raced over his face as he fought to find words. Before Riley could look up he spoke.

"I will. Later. Right now, we need to move." His voice somehow seemed calm compared to how she felt when she saw giant red dragon wings outstretched, speeding toward the opposite side of the mountain.

They ran. They raced through trees and brush, leaping over fallen trees and debris, unmindful of the many small cuts and bruises they earned as fronds and branches whipped at their skin. The first time they heard the powerful roar that ripped through the air above them, the sound nearly froze them in their tracks. Then survival instincts kicked in, and a jolt of adrenaline sent them racing even faster.

Adrenaline and lack of breath dueled with one another as they attempted to race over a small rise. A crash came from their left, its strength so great it dropped them to their knees. They couldn't tear their eyes away as trees, dirt and ash were tossed into the air. For a split second Riley thought she made out the shape and color of a red wing, but then it was buried in chaos.

The madness came to an end, but what rose over the treetops below was a sight to dazzle the mind, dust and ash still in the air; the red dragon rose from the rubble, his head and back and folded wings coming fully clear of the smaller trees. Jaw, lined with wicked teeth, opened wide, eyes almost alight with fire, in their depths a crimson red.

A second, much smaller dragon, a gleaming black, burst from the ashes, wings out from its torn, bloody body, the wedge-shaped head reaching with snapping teeth toward the red dragon.

"Holy shit," Ben whispered.

Under the circumstances, Riley found the profanity utterly appropriate. The two enraged dragons turned their heads in tandem and pinned their focus on Riley and her companions.

Fear had been her constant companion this entire trip, but now, as the gazes of the giant red and the smaller black dragon rested on them, fear turned to terror. A rotting, twisted evil shredded her insides, and heat so hot it felt like she was trying to hold the sun in her chest burst through her body.

Riley fell to her knees. Sickness washed through her, seeming to spread from the ground up as if living mold and fungus raced over her skin. A terrible, poisonous voice began clawing at her mind, speaking the same language the porters had used.

Then it was over. The terrible voice fell silent as the black dragon let out a furious roar. The red dragon answered, his shout like a force of nature, the shock waves of the sound strong enough to flatten trees.

Riley's hands came up, covering over her ears. She felt a pressure in her chest as she saw the black dragon turn and climb up the mountain. The red dragon followed close behind.

A hand grabbed her arm and yanked her to her feet. *Jubal.* The man always seemed to hold on to his nerves no matter what happened.

"We need to get away from here *now*."

The ground began to rumble and quake. On the volcano less than a mile above them, new vents split open, releasing geysers of steam and hot gas.

"Holy shit." The whispered words sounded crystal clear to Dax's dragon-enhanced senses.

Four humans were huddled together on the ash-covered mountainside. Dax caught a glimpse of shocked faces. Three men huddled protectively around the smaller, curvier frame of a woman. Inside the red dragon, Dax felt a strange awareness—like a crystalline note singing through the dragon's veins. Rich, vibrant, alive. All at once Dax smelt the rich, fertile aroma of the forest, of earth. Through the dragon's eyes, he could see it, a verdant glow of green that seemed to radiate from the spot where the woman's feet touched the ground. Dax couldn't see her face, but Dax knew instantly who she was. The power of the earth was so strong with her, she could only be the latest descendent of Arabejila.

Protect them! he cried into the Old One's mind.

The red dragon snarled and snapped at the air in a clear warning, and the four humans took off running down the mountainside. The black dragon hissed and charged toward them, but the Old One leapt into his path. The two beasts began a bizarre dance between predators as Mitro looked for a way around the giant red dragon, stepping to the side, bobbing his head, only to be matched step for step, move for move.

With no choice but to trust the Old One to keep Mitro from the humans, Dax directed his full attention to healing the dragon's wounds from the inside out, while simultaneously trying to find a way to separate himself from the bombardment of visceral emotion and bring the red dragon under his control. The Old One was a ferocious fighter, but he had no sense of self-preservation and no intention of letting any other being dominate his actions, even for his own good.

Their shared body was badly injured, dangerous amounts of blood gushing from deep wounds, internal organs damaged almost beyond repair, but his spirit fought Dax's attempt to divert him from his prey. The Old One was completely consumed by the need to rend and kill his enemy, regardless of the cost to himself. Within the dragon's body, aware of how close they were to death and even more aware of the vulnerable humans who had resumed their frantic run down the mountain, Dax was equally determined to stop the Old One long enough to heal. He could not afford for them to die before Mitro was defeated—especially not with the woman so close. Yet each time he attempted to exert control, his efforts seemed only to feed the Old One's rage.

Suddenly, the black dragon turned and extended his wings. Long, curving hooks sprouted from the apex of each wing. He used the hooks as a third pair of claws, scrabbling up the volcano in leaps and bounds. With a final, ferocious roar, the red dragon set off after his adversary once again.

The hot rush of emotion rolled over Dax like an ocean of fire, burning him with its wild need. But this time, instead of fighting that fury, he relaxed into it, let it wash over and through him. He didn't try to stand fast. Instead, he tried to make himself as insubstantial as mist.

The Old One's anger and destruction surrounded him. The dragon's innate determination to dominate any threat plowed into him, and this time, Dax let that fury pass through him without resistance. Lightly, with serene patience and endless calm, his senses branched out through the dragon's body. He was not an interloper in the dragon's body. He *was* the dragon. Not a separate consciousness, not a separate will, but one and the same. He did not want to imprison or control the dragon, but rather merge their consciousnesses, let their thoughts and actions become one. The dragon offered raw power, primal and indefatigable. Dax offered calm, judicial restraint, the ability to plan, think and act without passion, without rage, without emotion. If he could successfully join the dragon's might with his own legendary control, together they would be unstoppable. Together they could—and would—end the threat Mitro posed to the world.

But they would only succeed if they could act as one, rather than fighting each other for control.

Above them, higher up the volcano's slope, Mitro had turned his attention to the bubbling fury of the earth's hot core. The ground began to tremble as Mitro directed the volcano's heated gases and acids to the surface. Steam began to rise from the cracks and fissures in the rocks. The main blast of the volcano had exploded on the other side of the mountain, but now Mitro was opening another vent on this side . . . one that would mean certain death for the four humans racing down the mountainside.

Mitro knew Dax too well. Knew how to distract him. Mitro called it weakness—to care for those helpless before a hunter's great power—but that need to serve, to protect, was the only thing that had ever stood between Dax and the same darkness to which Mitro and so many other Carpathian hunters had succumbed. The innocent must be protected at all cost. It was the reason Dax had been born. The reason he lived still.

The dragon's bloodlust was in full force as the Old One fought to pursue Mitro and end him. Fire spewed from his throat, roaring up the mountain, licking at the black dragon's tail.

Mitro leapt into the sky just as the volcano split open. The side of the mountain burst open, throwing boulders and trees through the air like a child's toys. Burning clouds of ash and superheated gas roared down the mountainside at phenomenal speed.

As diversions went, it was a superb one. To go after Mitro now would mean certain death for the humans. With only a split second to decide, Dax made his choice.

We must save them, Old One. The woman, especially.

He didn't try to force the dragon to his will, instead he merged his will with the dragon's, weaving their most instinctive drives together. With a scream, the Old One wheeled around and launched into the air, diving at a steep incline toward the fleeing humans below. As they neared the small group, dragon's wings spread wide, forming a protective shield over their bodies. Ash and burning rock pelted the dragon's hide. He locked his claws deep in the earth and swept his wings tight around the small party, ignoring their shouts of fear and surprise as he caged the humans in a protective dome formed by his curled body and overlapping wings. The dragon tucked his head beneath his wings as the pyroclastic cloud slammed into him.

His good eye was pressed against his tail. His left eye was temporarily blinded by the wound Mitro had dealt him, so he couldn't make out the faces of the people trapped beneath his wings. There was so much dust and ash from his landing that he doubted any of the people could see anything. They'd probably have a hard time breathing soon, too. But they would survive, and that was the important thing.

Dax tried to calm the Old One, to silence the instinctive growls rumbling in the dragon's chest. He didn't want to frighten the humans more.

Then, to his utter shock, a hand slipped out and touched the wound next to his eye. The touch was such a small, tiny thing, but so unexpected—so fearless and unafraid—that both Dax and the dragon froze in stunned paralysis.

Long, long ago, before even Dax had been born, the world told tales of dragons and maidens. Some said, a maiden's call was impossible for a dragon to resist. But now, as the woman laid that small, soft, gentle hand upon him, Dax knew it wasn't her call—it was her touch. A caress that gentled the savage heart of the beast. It was such a paradox—frailty that conquered strength.

Finally, the volcanic blast subsided, and for another, long moment, no one moved. Dax wasn't sure what to do. Everything in him—every thought, every one of his senses, every nerve in the dragon's body—was focused on that small, slender hand laid alongside the dragon's wounded eye.

Abruptly, foul, crowing laughter rang out in his mind, snapping him out of his strange daze.

Once again you have failed, Danutdaxton. Just as you will always fail. Mitro's sneering voice choked Dax's enhanced senses with rotting filth. *Because I am the superior being, and you will always be weak!*

The Old One unfurled his wings and flung himself back on his haunches. Despite his wounds, the dragon roared a defiant challenge with enough force to be heard for miles, then spouted a jet of intense flame high into the sky, a beacon in the dark of night. It cut through the ash and clouds, lighting the area in a fiery glow. But Mitro was already gone.

Sapped of strength, the Old One turned slowly back to the humans, who had covered their ears against his shattering roar and curled up in tight balls to protect themselves from the intense heat of his flame. They were huddled in the only small spot of greenery left on this part of the mountain. As the echoes of his scream died away, they lifted their heads and slowly got to their feet.

Dax's heart skipped a beat as he caught his first good look at the woman—at the extraordinarily beautiful face that was as familiar to him as his own. The lush, womanly curves, the soft, fathomless dark eyes, the long, iridescent black hair and skin as pale as milk beneath the layer of volcanic ash that covered her from head to toe.

Arabejila? Hiszak hän olen te? He whispered the question in astonishment on the private path they had forged between themselves centuries ago. Was it truly her? She had been an ally in his pursuit to bring Mitro to justice, but he'd felt her die centuries ago. Hadn't he? It seemed impossible that she could have survived all these years . . . and yet, there she stood.

She turned as if she might be seeking the protection of the three men with her, but the Old One surprised him by curling his tail more tightly, trapping her and forcing her a step closer. Her scent dizzied him as they breathed her in.

Her heart thundered in his ears. Clearly, the red dragon frightened her. Perhaps she could sense, as Mitro had not, that the Old One was a true dragon, not simply a shape assumed by the Carpathian hunter she had once known.

Dax radiated his will through every cell of the dragon's body and their mutual, merged consciousness. The Old One was too weary from battle to fight for control, and the great, fiery red scales and immense mass of the dragon folded in upon itself. Shrinking down and metamorphosing back into the tall, muscled density of Dax's natural form.

"Arabejila. *Hiszakund olenaszund elävänej.*" He truly had thought she was dead.

She stumbled back, raising her hands as if to ward him off, clearly shocked that the massive bulk of the dragon would disappear to leave a human form standing before her. Two of the men in her company sprang into action, pulling weapons of some kind and rushing toward him, lethal intent plain in the cold glitter of their eyes.

Had he misread the situation? Were these men holding her prisoner?

Dax reacted instinctively, moving with preternatural speed. "Arabejila, run!" he shouted in Carpathian. "Run, my sister! If they are Mitro's slaves, he will soon return."

He disarmed Jubal, breaking his arm with a clear, audible snap. The man fell to his knees, clutching his arm to his chest.

"Sisar?" the man repeated in Carpathian almost under his breath. Then

in an odd dialect Dax was unfamiliar with, "Gary, wait, he thinks she's his sister. He's trying to protect her."

Dax caught Jubal by the strange clothing covering his chest. The hunter pulled his hand back, fingers curved into diamond-tipped claws, ready to rip out the human's throat, when Arabejila cried out in the same, odd dialect as the first man.

"No! Stop! Don't hurt him! Please!"

Dax froze. Not because he understood her command—though the plea in her voice was unmistakable—but because at the first sound of her voice, an enormous wave of emotion crashed over him. Not the fiery, rage-fueled emotion of the dragon, but something deeper, fuller, more visceral. It shook him to his core. And the black-and-white world of his Carpathian vision deepened as well, becoming richer, more varied.

Before his brain could process the change, before he could understand or even put a name to it, a loud blast sounded behind him. Something hard and hot tore through his back, ripping a path through his chest. Dax staggered, releasing the man in his grip and falling to one knee. In a daze, he put a hand to his chest. It came away wet, covered in dark liquid.

"Gary, stop! Stand down. Put the damned gun away!" The man with the broken arm pushed forward, shoving the others out of the way. *"Olenasz? Nimed olen?"* A demand to know his name.

Jubal glanced up at the others. "Someone, give me a light. I need a light over here."

A small, shockingly bright light flared into existence. It blinded Dax for an instant, and then focused on the bloodied mess of Dax's chest.

His blood gleamed bright, shocking scarlet in the light. His skin, once the pale white that had never seen the sun, was a burnished mahogany brown.

Dax stared up into Arabejila's eyes. Not black but a rich, dark brown, the color of fertile earth so necessary to every Carpathian's survival. But she wasn't Arabejila. She wasn't the friend who had traveled and hunted beside him for centuries. She was someone else entirely. Someone he had long ago ceased to think could possibly exist.

He reached for her, his bloody hand brushing a streak of red across the ash coating her cheek. *Päläfertiilam.*

9

Riley stared in stunned amazement at the fiercely beautiful man kneeling before her. He'd said "*Päläfertiilam*" and touched her cheek with exquisite gentleness; she found herself literally frozen in place. Little red and gold specks of glowing ash were falling in a dazzling display around them, adding to the dreamlike feel of the moment. The terror of mere seconds ago had evaporated entirely, leaving behind a dazed sense of wonder. Then, with a blinding speed every bit as shocking as his unexpected gentleness, the man whirled on Gary, divested him of the pistol and caught his throat in a viselike grip. The entire series of moves happened in less than a heartbeat.

"No, please!" Riley leapt forward instinctively, grabbing the vampire's arm. Beside her, Ben brought up his weapon.

"Ben, wait," Jubal barked. "He's not the vampire! He's not the vampire!" Jubal pointed to his left wrist where the bracelet that had been radiating colors seemed to have changed back to what he had called its dormant state.

Whether driven by an innate protective streak, a rush of adrenaline or simply self-preservation, Ben did not respond to Jubal's shout. He brought his rifle up, taking aim at the back of the dragon-man's head. His finger squeezed the trigger.

Riley's whole body jumped at the loud report, then everything seemed to move in slow motion. The rifle spat bullet after bullet in rapid succession. Riley screamed and covered her ears as she waited for the dragon-man to fall. He seemed an impossible target to miss, standing as he was only a few feet in front of Ben. But the man didn't fall.

One moment the dragon-man was standing in front of her, the next he was not. She saw the small explosion of dirt as the bullet crashed into the wall of mud behind the spot where he'd been standing. Then another and another. It happened so fast, she was still trying to make sense of it when the rifle fell silent.

The dragon-man had released Gary to disarm Ben. He now had Ben by the shoulder and was staring intently into Ben's eyes. The man's other hand was pressed against the bullet hole that had ripped through his stomach. Ben sat with abrupt gracelessness. Ignoring Gary and Jubal, the vampire released Ben and turned his entire focus back on Riley.

She half expected him to rip her to pieces as her mother had been.

Instead, he gave a small bow and said in a surprisingly calm and polite voice, "You are not Arabejila, *sivamet*. My apologies for the confusion. It is only that you resemble her so strongly."

Some small, rational part of her mind was thinking she should be screaming or something, but Riley just stood there, mesmerized, staring at the preternaturally beautiful face. At the . . . the distinctive *fangs* that had lengthened in his mouth. Dear God. He was a *vampire*. An honest-to-God, bloodsucking *vampire*! The vampire looked like a man. A stunningly beautiful man. Short, closely cropped black hair, skin like burnished mahogany, dark eyes that flickered with ruby lights in their depths. And his voice . . . his voice was pure magic. It caressed her like a physical touch, soft, smoky, soothing. The stirring cadence of his voice calmed her.

It took her almost a minute to realize he was now speaking English, she was so fascinated with the shape of his mouth and that flash of white teeth. His voice was charismatic, a blend of honey and warmth.

"Please, *päläfertiilam*, allow me to introduce myself." He bowed slightly, with an otherworldly grace. "I am Danutdaxton."

Dumbfounded didn't begin to describe her state as the man straightened to his full height. She had never seen anyone so beautiful, so impressive or so wounded. He stood there with straight shoulders, his body bleeding from hundreds of small and large wounds, his gaze steady on hers, his eyes . . . mesmerizing. His eyes were incredible, with as many facets as a cut diamond, the color as luminous as a diamond, yet holding tiny red and orange flames. His mouth was cut perfectly and when he smiled . . . his teeth looked very white and very sharp.

"I—" She cast a frantic glance at Gary and Jubal. She knew they'd told her that vampires could appear good, but she was shocked at her reaction to him. Tiny electrical charges raced up her arms. Her breath caught in her lungs and even her mouth went dry.

To her surprise, the two men shared a silent, speaking gaze, then both lowered their weapons and bowed in the vampire's direction.

"It's okay, Riley." Gary began speaking to her in a very soft and calming voice. "He's not a vampire. The other one was—the black dragon. But he's a Carpathian . . . a *hunter*." He said *hunter* as if it held great meaning.

"B-but . . . he's got . . . f-f-" She tapped a finger on her teeth and spat the word out. "*Fangs.* And he can literally dodge bullets."

"I know. It's hard to explain, but he isn't a vampire. He hunts them. He's one of the good guys, but he's hurt very bad and he needs blood." This time Gary looked like he knew he was imparting things he didn't want to.

"Carpathians need blood to heal," Jubal added, "and he needs to heal right away."

"So . . . what?" Riley glanced between the two men, suddenly not feeling at all reassured. "Are you saying he has to take our blood to survive?"

She didn't look his way, afraid of being entranced by his gaze again. If he needed blood, she didn't want him taking hers—or did she? Was that what she was afraid of? That she wanted to go to him and take away his pain? Her need to help him confused her and made her wary. It took every bit of strength she had to hold herself in place and not rush to him and offer whatever he needed—including blood.

"Does he take blood the way a vampire does?" She winced at the question, afraid she was insulting him, but she needed to know. While trying to avoid the hunter's gaze, her glance fell to Ben, and she dropped quickly down to check on him. Ben's eyes were glazed over and he swayed as he sat on the ground. "Is he okay? What did you do to him?" she asked.

Dax answered, his diction without hesitation as if he'd always known her language. "He is perfectly healthy. He has minor cuts and bruises. Nothing worthy of your concern." When she looked unconvinced, he added, "I have put him into a meditative state to calm him. He was becoming quite agitated, and he could easily have hurt you or the others without intending to do so. But you are all perfectly safe now." As if that should put all her fears to rest, the hunter turned away and began speaking with Jubal in his ancient language.

She looked Ben over. He was breathing, and just as the hunter had stated, other than a few cuts and bruises, Ben appeared perfectly unharmed. But it was like the man was sleeping with his eyes open.

"I understand, thank you, Jubal." Clearly finished with whatever private conversation he'd been having with Jubal, Dax had changed back to English.

She didn't care if the hunter got angry, she couldn't allow Ben to be in such a state, not when he'd come to her rescue so often. "Let him go." She turned toward the hunter. "Let him go right now."

He released Ben so quickly, the unconscious man rocked forward, almost falling onto her. She put a hand on his shoulder to steady him, a little shocked that the hunter had complied so quickly.

Coming to, Ben looked like he had just awakened from a long nap. He actually yawned. "Wow, that was some dream." Ben smiled at her, totally relaxed as his gaze wandered to the half-naked, badly wounded man standing behind her. His smile faltered. His gaze traveled up Dax's impossibly torn body to his beaten and bloody face. Then Ben just froze, his mouth open, his eyes wide with renewed terror.

"Ben. Ben, it's okay." Riley grabbed his face with both hands, forcing his shocked gaze to hers. "It's over. Everyone's okay."

Ben gave a choked sound, like a scream pinched off before it could gain volume.

"He's not going to hurt us." She forced a smile. "Look. See?" She stood slowly and put a hand on the hunter's upper arm. Rock-hard muscle bunched beneath her fingertip and shook with a small tremor she would have missed if she hadn't been touching his skin directly. For a moment pain slammed into her, taking her breath. Just that fast it was gone, leaving her feeling slightly ill. "Everything's okay. You're okay. You're safe now."

"It would be much simpler and more effective just to keep him under my control," the hunter murmured close to her ear.

She shivered at the melting richness of his voice, then scowled, refusing to look at him. "Don't you dare. If you are one of the good guys, like Jubal claims, you'll leave him alone."

"If that is your wish, I shall, but your safety, *päläfertiilam*, is now my first concern. The moment this human's fear puts that at risk, he will go back under my control. Does this please you?"

Riley drew in a deep breath. Even looking at him was difficult. What was it that pulled her toward him like a magnet? She needed to push him away from her, to get some perspective.

"My mother's dead, some ancient evil we were sent here to contain has escaped into the world and I'm standing in front of a man who can change from a dragon to a man, dodge bullets and control people's minds at will. Nothing about this situation *pleases* me!"

His eyes filled with genuine sorrow. "I am sorry I was not able to save your mother." He lifted one hand to the side of her face and tucked a strand of hair back behind her ears. "More sorry than I can express. I know what it is to lose someone you love."

Her whole body ached to lean toward him, to let him wrap those impressively muscled arms around her and envelop her in his strength. Riley fought the instinct, but it took considerable effort.

She allowed herself the luxury of looking at him, uncaring that she was so attracted to a being that clearly wasn't human. She saw pure strength, and power. She couldn't help but notice that. The way he moved was so careful and precise, so fluid and effortlessly graceful, like a giant, predatory jungle cat. When he stood still, his dark, burnished skin seemed to shimmer with flashes of iridescent scarlet, as if the dragon he had been was still there, waiting for its chance to be free. Her gaze fell to his chest. He wasn't wearing a shirt, and the rippling muscles that bunched beneath his skin held her attention captive.

As she looked down, she caught her first unobstructed view of his chest.

"Oh, my God." There was a hole over his heart, as if someone had taken a pickax to his sternum. The wound should have been gushing blood. With a wound like that, he should be dead. Instead, it was as if something had closed off the blood vessels, leaving only trickles of red seeping from the gaping cavity. She turned a horrified gaze toward the others. "He should be dead with a wound like that! How is he not dead?"

"Carpathians can be killed. It just takes a lot more than it takes for a human. They can control their heartbeat, their blood flow, the functions of their internal organs, just about everything," Gary explained.

"But Dax isn't going to last long in this state without healing," Jubal added. "This part is going to be hard for you to comprehend, Riley. Dax needs to pack those wounds with earth and he needs blood to replace all that he's lost."

"You mean he's got to suck someone's blood?" She took a half step away from the Carpathian. "He's got to drain one of us to survive?"

"Carpathians take only what is needed," Dax explained hastily, clearly making an effort to still the rising distrust in her.

"Carpathians have lived for centuries in harmony with humans," Jubal added quickly. "Please, there will be time to explain everything later. For now, we need to help heal Dax. If that vampire released from the volcano comes back—"

"He will," said Dax.

"—we're going to need the hunter at full fighting strength."

"Do not fear, *sivamet*," Dax said, and the soft, husky timbre of his voice ensnared her once again. "If it comes to it, I will die before allowing Mitro Daratrazanoff to hurt you, but it would be best for all if I faced him in full health."

Her gaze dragged back up his torso, pausing as it reached the terrible wounds gaping in his flesh.

"Can you really heal him, Jubal?" Her voice didn't seem like her own, and neither did her reaction. For reasons she didn't understand, the sight of the man's terrible wounds was almost more than she could bear. The thought of his pain horrified her on a deeply personal level—affecting her as viscerally as the sight of her mother murdered before her eyes. She couldn't bear the thought of this man suffering, and she didn't know why. She was certain that brief glimpse of agonizing pain had been his.

Vampires and hunters, volcanos and dragons: this whole situation was crazy, but she couldn't tolerate the idea of this hunter—*Dax*—suffering one more second of pain. She looked at Gary. "Fix him now." Her voice carried with the power of her ancestors, and something in him seemed to rock with her words.

There was a brief moment when no one moved. Even the world around them seemed to hold its breath. Everything went still. Gary moved first, looking almost formal, standing in front of Dax with a slight bow.

"Saasz hän ku andam szabadon," Gary murmured in the hunter's ancient language. Without flinching, he offered his unbroken wrist to the hunter.

Whatever the words meant, the hunter clearly took them as an invitation, because without delay he bared his fangs and bit down, his mouth closing around Gary's wrist. Gary's expression flashed briefly with pain before going totally relaxed.

Riley's heart nearly stopped beating. Her hand went defensively to her throat. She felt her pulse pounding there. For a moment, the flash of fangs had been shockingly sexy. She wanted Dax's mouth on her neck, his teeth sinking into her—not Jubal. Blinking, shaking her head at her strange compulsion, she nudged Jubal.

"What did Gary say to him?"

"It is a custom of Carpathians. Gary said, take what I offer freely. That means, Gary would exchange his life for that of the hunter if it was necessary. He is asking no favor in return for his blood," Jubal explained.

Riley couldn't help but watch. The movement of Dax's mouth on Gary's wrist fascinated her. The hunter's fangs joined the two men together, as if they were close brothers, one saving the other without thought for his own safety. Dax appeared stoic, but the flames in his strange, multifaceted eyes leapt and danced. She felt her heart tune to the rhythm of the hunter's as if they were connected instead of hunter and friend. Her blood sang in her veins, surging hotly.

Dax's gaze jumped to her face.

Dax released Gary and straightened. There was no trace of blood on his lips and no sign of a wound on Gary's wrist. She didn't know what to think. Beside her, Ben stood in shivering paralysis.

The gaping wound in Dax's chest did begin to bleed then, but some invisible force kept the blood from spilling out of the wound. Dax scooped fresh dirt from the ground, spat into it, and packed his wound with the mixture. His eyes closed, as if packing his wound with mud brought some sort of relief.

"I have not had blood in many centuries. It is both wonderful and awful."

His gaze drifted over Riley's face. "I am starved, and yet I dare not take too much. Just enough to heal my wounds until I am used to feeding again. Then I will need to sustain myself in order to hunt the undead."

Riley pressed her lips together, nodding as if she understood when she didn't really. Jubal seemed to though. He stood in front of the hunter and offered his unbroken wrist.

Dax reached for the other arm with surprisingly gentle fingers. "This pains you. The bone is broken." Even as he spoke he ran his hand over the injury.

Riley watched closely. Heat seeped out from between Dax's palm and Jubal's skin. She could see a faint glow, and she was close enough to feel the warmth as well. The little white lines of pain eased on Jubal's face.

"Is that better?"

Jubal nodded. "Much, thanks."

Riley noted that Dax didn't apologize for having broken Jubal's arm in the first place, nor did Jubal seem to expect him to do so.

Jubal murmured the same exact phrase in Carpathian as Gary, and just as before, Dax bowed, took the offered wrist and drank.

This time when he finished, Dax thanked the two men and then looked at her. Her whole body tingled. Heat washed up her spine and her gaze fixed on his mouth. *What is wrong with me?* She should be screaming in horror. This was an honest-to-God vampire right in front of her eyes, drinking blood from her friends. And she was just standing there, marveling at him.

She touched her tongue to suddenly dry lips. His gaze jumped instantly to her mouth and those flames in his eyes leapt higher. Her thighs tingled. Her breasts ached. She swallowed hard and instantly his gaze was on her throat. He seemed aware of every move she made, every breath she took.

Beside her, Ben began shaking horribly. "Oh, my God. Oh, my God. He's going to kill us. He's going to kill us all."

Ashamed that she'd forgotten he was even there, she reached over to lay a soothing hand on his shoulder. "Calm down, Ben. If Jubal and Gary say he's a friend, I think we should believe them."

Poor Ben didn't believe them. He must have thought the vampire was going to drink him dry, because his mind completely snapped. With a shriek, he spun around and started racing through the jungle, bouncing off trees in his mad rush to escape.

"Ben!" Riley spun around. "Someone stop him! He's out of his mind."

"I can bring him safely back and keep him calm," Dax said, "but that requires me to control his mind, which you have already told me I must not do." One dark brow arched. He stood there, waiting for her to make the decision.

She bit her lip. On the one hand, she hated the idea of him controlling Ben's mind—of him controlling *anyone's* mind. On the other hand, in his current state, Ben was going to injure himself or worse. And if that evil vampire was still roaming around . . .

She glanced again into the forest where Ben continued to shriek and stumble, running into a bush first and then a tree. She winced when he went down and then scrambled back up only to run again.

"Do it."

The hunter reached for her hand and gave it a reassuring squeeze. His expression softened with unexpected gentleness, making him look almost . . . kind. In a rough-edged, dangerous, bloodsucking, gorgeous vampire sort of way, that is.

"It is for the best, *päläfertiilam*. I will do him no harm, I promise you." Then he switched his attention to Ben's fleeing figure, and his expression turned to stone. Fixed, focused, unyielding. He spoke in that ancient language of his, and though Riley couldn't understand the words, there was no mistaking the tone of absolute command.

In the distance, Ben came to an abrupt halt, then turned and calmly made his way back to the group. His expression was serene, as if he were out for a stroll through the park on a balmy summer day. He walked back to Riley's side and stood there, silent and still.

Even though Riley had given Dax the okay—even though she knew this was for Ben's own good—watching him obey like a mindless puppet made her stomach churn. It was so wrong. Like slavery, only worse. At least slaves still possessed their own minds.

"As will he, when I release him," Dax said.

Her eyes flared in alarm. She spun around. "Did you just *read my mind*? Did you? *Did he?*" She whirled on Jubal and Gary, looking for answers.

"Riley . . ." Gary held out his hands in a conciliatory gesture.

"I did. Forgive me if I offend, *päläfertiilam*. Your thoughts are very strong. I—" His voice hitched, and his expression flickered for an instant before he continued, "I must remind myself you are not familiar with Carpathian ways. I did not mean to intrude."

She frowned. That flicker in his expression had been a wince. He was in pain. Glancing at the still-dreadful gaping wound in his chest, concern overrode fear. "Sit down. Sit down and do whatever it is you need to do to heal yourself."

She laid a hand on his arm, intending to help him down, but the moment her flesh touched his, agony rocketed up her arm. She gasped and yanked her hand back. The pain vanished instantly.

"Dear God, was that you?" She touched him again, and almost screamed. "It is. My God, it is. How can you bear it? You're in agony." She hadn't thought about what terrible pain he must be in when he first stood up, tall and strong. He was a freaking vampire or hunter or whatever he was. Mythical creatures weren't supposed to suffer, they weren't supposed to hurt—but he did, and it was excruciating. She knew it. When she touched him, she could feel it as clearly as if it were happening in her own body.

Unable to help herself, she touched him again. Something inside her demanded that she help him, that she heal him. It was almost a compulsion.

Clearly, Dax wasn't the one compelling her, because he gently pulled her hand away. "Do not, *päläfertiilam*. We cannot keep all the pain in check, and I would not have you hurt yourself on my account."

"We? Who's we?" she asked in a distracted voice. Her attention was already, inexorably pulled back to Dax's injuries. Looking at the wound, she could almost feel it herself. As if she were traveling inside his body, touching each raw nerve ending, broken bone and shredded muscle, feeling with gifts that had been passed down from generation to generation. Dax's pain called to her, tore something deep inside, some barrier she hadn't realized existed.

Riley lifted her hand again and slowly placed it over the mud-packed hole over Dax's heart. She pressed her palm against the wound, packing the earth deeper into the wound, completely unaware of what she was doing. Only aware that she needed to continue. There was something wrong inside him, something that seemed intent on consuming him. Sheer force of will held it in check. His will, stronger than the mountains, stronger than the earth itself.

Her hand lifted, leaving a perfect handprint in the mud. She raised the same hand to his face and touched his cheek, wiping the blood and dirt from his cheek and trailing it slowly down his throat back over his heart. Words and patterns blossomed inside her mind. Power rose as Riley looked into Dax's eyes, iridescent, beautiful eyes and focused on the gleam of scarlet fire that flickered in their depths.

She slid an arm around Dax's side, placing one hand over his heart and the other in the same spot on his back. Then she unleashed the power that was now a throbbing beat inside her. The raw, earthy force flooded through her hands, and Dax's body devoured it. The power consumed the earth packed in his wounds and transformed the dense, rich, organic matter into skin, bone and muscle. She had no control over what happened next, no comprehension of how it happened. She only knew that the power in her called to the power in him, using the earth that bound them both together. Bones knit, nerves re-formed, tissues and blood vessels regrew with astonishing speed.

When it was done, Riley's consciousness came rushing back to her body. She sagged against him. Now, it was his arms coming up to steady her. She stared up at him, dazed, still feeling everything he was, as if she were connected to him, as if she were part of him. She knew she had somehow, miraculously, healed him. Healed him completely. Yet, it still felt like she'd missed something. He was still in so much pain, and he shouldn't be.

Riley's brow crinkled as she tried to work through the confusion. Her eyelids became very heavy and it was suddenly all she could do to try to keep them open. The effort was too much for her. Exhausted, blackness swallowed her up, and she collapsed in the arms of the hunter.

Dax found himself smiling down at his lifemate. *What a gift she possesses.* She had healed him—and not with methods known and used by Carpathians, but by manipulating the earth itself. She had touched him, and the earth in his wounds had transformed at her command. Dax checked his wounds, flexing his muscles experimentally. The hole Mitro had torn in his chest was gone. The countless, bone-deep slashes torn by razor-sharp talons had knitted together, leaving not even the smallest seam to prove they'd ever existed. He'd not even needed to go to ground!

Even Arabejila, more gifted in earth than any Carpathian he'd ever known, had never possessed such an amazing talent.

And his lifemate was human, to boot. That made her existence even more of a miracle. He'd never heard that a Carpathian and a human could be lifemates.

Not that it mattered. She was here, in his arms, and he was more content than he'd ever dreamed possible just holding her and breathing in her scent. Even the Old One seemed entranced by her. She smelled of wildflowers over spring rain, a miracle of fresh beauty in the midst of Mitro and the volcano's destruction.

While she was healing him, his soul recognized and cried out for hers. He felt her soul answer. She didn't recognize the calling, only the flash of pain at the knowledge that she was so close and yet they weren't joined. Deep inside him, the second soul had reached for her as well, already so much a part of Dax, that the dragon knew Riley was their salvation.

His thoughts turned immediately to her welfare. She must be the one he'd felt trying to keep the volcano contained, and no doubt the effort of those exertions as well as the miraculous way she'd healed him had clearly exhausted her, leading to her collapse. He checked her carefully, just in case, but her only injuries were minor cuts and bruises from her race through the jungle, and those he mended with a thought. She needed sleep, then water and food, but the latter could wait until she awakened.

He couldn't take his eyes off her. Even smudged with dirt and ash, she was the most beautiful sight he'd ever beheld, and she seemed so fragile in his arms. The mere thought of the slightest harm befalling her made his muscles clench and the Old One strain against Dax's control. He and the dragon, both, were united in their determination to protect her. With a thought, Dax cleansed the ash and dirt from her body, leaving her and her clothing clean.

Dax finally tore his gaze from his lifemate, and turned his attention to the two men who had offered him their wrists. Jubal and Gary were friends to the Carpathian people. He'd learned their names and searched their memories when he took their blood, and used that connection to absorb their language, a more modern dialect of the language he'd correctly identified as English. They were now under his protection as well. As for Ben, Dax owed the man a debt for the way he had stayed to protect Riley despite the danger to himself.

"Eat, drink and rest for a few minutes, my new friends, but then we must get moving. Mitro, the vampire I was hunting, is free of his bondage, and it isn't safe to remain here." He looked down at Ben, who had slumped over onto his bag. "He will be fine once he wakes. If you would be so kind as to prepare him food and water as well."

"You're going to hunt the vampire." Gary made it a statement.

"He won't expect me to have healed so quickly. He'll need blood and a place to go to ground. If I'm lucky, I will be able to destroy him this night."

Gary glanced at the sky. "There's not much in the way of night left."

Dax nodded. "I task you with watching over my lifemate." There was a small edge to his voice, the first of the night. "I will return tomorrow eve. See to it that she is well." He looked around. "You will need to find a place easier to protect. Mitro is capable of sending anything at you. He will know I will work to keep you safe, and above all else, he wants Riley dead. He believes her to be Arabejila. I'm certain of it."

"Just up ahead, there's a small hollowed-out clearing," Jubal said. "I noticed it when we first hit the base of the mountain. It's protected on three sides by boulders with a small stream on the other side. We can set up a tent there with netting for Riley."

Dax checked the location with a judicious eye and then added safeguards to keep out any threat. "I will return."

He took to the air with great reluctance, streaking away from them. He had little time. Mitro would hunt for blood before he went to ground, and he was in a rage. He would do as much damage as possible. Dax went back to the spot where the two dragons had fought. Blackened pools of acid stained the ground, and burned through any plant or tree that had been left standing on the side of the mountain close by.

The mountain was ravaged by the mud and fires. Still, everything seemed so different, new to his eyes. Even with the powdery ash settling on the trees and brush at the base of the mountain, and choking the air, he could still discern color, a gift from his lifemate. Blacks were vivid and bright. Whites and glimpses of green and brown sent a small frisson of joy through him in spite of his grim task. In a way he was grateful for the ash. The colors were so unique to him, so vivid and brilliant, they almost hurt his eyes.

He picked up the scent immediately. Mitro was gravely wounded and had no energy to waste on hiding from Dax. He would expect the hunter to go to ground near the humans, not chase after him.

Once more Dax took to the sky, using the form of an owl. The owl's vision provided him with the ability to see so much more and its small body would barely be noticed. As it was, with the ash in the air, Dax was forced to send a wind in front of him to clear the skies enough to see anything unusual. Mitro wouldn't have gotten far without blood. He crisscrossed the area patiently, widening his circle until the owl caught sight of something lying near the stream.

Immediately, Dax descended, the owl settling in a tree above and to the right of the scattered objects below. A heaviness in his chest, along with the knots in his stomach forewarned him. There were two bodies, both had tried to run, and had died hard, screaming in fright. Their eyes remained wide open, mouths still forming their last cries, both throats shredded. Bright ribbons of blood streaked their bodies. Mitro had always been a messy eater.

Inside the body of the owl, Dax sighed. He had known Mitro would find blood; he was too cunning not to. The rain forest was a big place, and there were few humans anywhere near the mountain, yet unerringly, Mitro had been drawn to them.

Dax shifted into mist and drifted down to study the two bodies. Both appeared to be native to the forest, although dressed in the same way as Gary and Jubal. A machete lay inches from one of the bodies, its blade stained dark. He moved over the second body, and found what he expected. Blood had seeped from under the body where he'd been cut multiple times by the machete. That was just like Mitro, forcing someone to hack up a friend or loved one for the vampire's amusement.

Mitro was definitely up to his old tricks. He hadn't been an hour or so out of his prison and he was already killing and torturing. Sorrow pressed down on him, an unexpected emotion. So many lost years attempting to destroy a depraved, vile creature, and failing time and again. Having to look upon the aftermath of the undead's path of destruction over and over was far more wearing than he'd realized. Now, with his ability to feel, Dax was weighed down by every single one of those lives lost over the centuries.

At once he felt a stirring, a brushing of souls. His. The Old One's. *Hers.* His heart leapt. The burden of destroying Mitro was his, but he wasn't alone.

Ours, the Old One corrected.

A soft whisper stroked a caress in his mind. *Ours,* Riley's voice echoed.

Dax was not alone. He would find Mitro and destroy him, that was his bound duty, but this time, he would have something of his own to fight for. The owl spread its wings and took off as dawn was about to break. He was grateful for the ash, obscuring the gathering light. He'd been deep inside a mountain for so long that even deep within the owl's body, that shrouded, first light hurt his skin and pierced his eyes.

He hurried back to his woman. *Päläfertiilam.* Lifemate.

IO

"Dreams are the angels' way of showing us what is on the other side," Riley's grandmother had told her when Riley was just a child. If that was true, then heaven was a warm and sultry place, considering the dream Riley had just had.

The dream had been so wonderful, in fact, she was loath to leave it. She clung to sleep, to the wispy remnants of that dream, filled with soft caresses and strong hands, until the clamor of voices around her grew too loud to ignore.

Her eyes fluttered open, and she sat up, frowning and disoriented, to find herself in what looked like her own tent. Light shining in through green fabric revealed a neat and ordered space that for the first time since its purchase was now also perfectly clean—with no hint of the dirt or the smell of wet canvas that had clung to it throughout the trip through the jungle. She was still fully dressed, although her boots were sitting beside her pack and her jacket had been neatly folded and put on top as well.

She could hear people moving about and talking outside the tent, and judging by the number of voices, her small party must have met up with other survivors. She sat up abruptly, hope blossoming. Or maybe everything that had happened since heading up the river had all been one horrible, bizarre nightmare.

Before she got her hopes up too far, however, the tent zipper came undone, and the panel fell back to reveal an outside world covered in a thick blanket of gray volcanic ash with more still falling from the sky. Not a dream then.

Riley found a sad comfort when Gary stepped through the tent's opening with a hot bowl of soup and a spoon in his hands. "Oh good, you're awake. I have your breakfast—or dinner, since the sun is about to set."

"Hello, Gary." Nodding her thanks, she took the bowl and set it aside. Her body was still waking up, and she wasn't hungry. "What's happening? Where are we? Is everyone okay? How long have I been asleep?"

There was plenty of room in the three-person tent, and Gary sat down on a camping stool someone had brought in. "Jubal and Ben are fine. In fact, they're outside now." He indicated the door flap. "We're in a camp some of the locals set up as a gathering place for survivors. As for how long you slept, you have been resting for two days now."

"*Two days?*" she repeated, incredulously. She'd never slept so long in her entire life. Her brow furrowed with sudden suspicion. "Did the vampire hunter put me to sleep?"

"No, he didn't. Apparently, you drained every reserve of strength you had saving our butts and healing him. Which is why you need to eat now, whether you feel hungry or not." He cast a pointed look at the soup bowl.

"Two days," she muttered. "Good God." She lifted the spoon to her lips and numbly took a bite. The flavors exploded across her tongue, and she glanced down at the soup in surprise. It was really good, and as she swallowed her first bite she realized she really was hungry.

"I'm not sure you are aware of what you did, or if you even remember," Gary continued when he was satisfied she was eating. He lowered his voice so others outside couldn't hear him. "Dax, the Carpathian hunter, was badly injured and you used your gifts to directly heal him. He told me that you didn't just draw power from the earth like you did to hold the vampire, or when you redirected the volcano's eruption. You used that power, but you drew most of the energy from yourself and poured it into him. Riley, you healed him completely. And by that, I mean you regrew bone and tissue from nothing. I've been around Carpathians, and not even the strongest healers among them could have done what you did by themselves and in so short a time. It's nothing less than miraculous. After you passed out, Dax checked you out himself, but he couldn't find anything wrong, so he told us just to let you rest. So we have." He glanced down. "More soup?"

It took a moment for Riley to realize she was staring blindly at the now-empty bowl. "Yes, thank you."

Raising his voice, Gary called out to Jubal, and seconds later exchanged her empty bowl for a full one. Jubal himself only poked his head into the tent long enough to give her a huge smile and a wave, which she returned automatically. Then he ducked back outside, and the tent flap closed behind him.

"Riley, you've suspected for a while now that Jubal and I know a lot more than we've been willing to share. We keep secrets for many reasons, mostly because keeping those secrets helps protect people we care for. But because Dax sees us as your "protectors," he's given us permission to share some of our knowledge with you now." He looked like some of her fellow professors did right before they started their first two-hour lecture on a topic that would take years to fully explain.

"Wait." She held up a hand. "Before you get started, tell me about the others. You said Ben and Jubal are okay. What about the rest of the people from the boats? Did they survive?"

"Dax found Miguel, Hector, Don, and Mack Shelton when we were coming down the mountain. And following the trail of the professor and his students is what led us here." Something in the tone of his raised voice caused a sinking feeling in her stomach.

"What happened?"

"The professor fell. Oh, don't worry, it's nothing too bad, except he's in the jungle, and needs to be able to walk, but he'll be okay. He broke his leg."

"And?" she prompted when he fell silent again. "You don't get that worried look in your eyes because the professor broke something. What else?"

"Dax found two of the porters dead that first night. They were returning to see if we all made it away from the volcano. Fernando and Jorge."

She shook her head. "That's so terrible." She knew the bad news wasn't over and waited in silence for him to tell her the rest.

"One of the guides and one of the professor's students are missing. Pedro went to find clean water for breakfast. Marty went with him. They never came back." Gary's expression went grimmer. "Dax believes the vampire he's hunting might have found them." The look on his face said he believed it, too. "But just in case he's wrong, we have most of the men out looking for them now," he added.

Giving her a moment to process the news, Gary handed her empty soup bowl out to Jubal again and exchanged it for two blue metal camping cups.

Vampire. Riley shook her head in disbelief. Vampires were one of the monsters from stories. They were the thing you dressed up as on Halloween, the evil creature in a scary movie. They weren't supposed to be real. But then again there weren't supposed to be dragons, and her mother wasn't supposed to be dead, and . . . her heart seemed to skip as she thought about that man. He wasn't supposed to be here, either, whatever he was.

She took the camping cup Gary held out and took a grateful sip of the tepid water. It was warm and tasted of ash and chemicals, but it quenched her thirst and soothed her parched throat.

"What else aren't you telling me?" The image of two dragons facing off in front of them rose to mind. "What about the hunter, Dax? Did you know he was here the whole time?"

"No, of course not. We had no idea Dax or the vampire was here. I don't think anyone did. From what Dax told me, he and Mitro—the vampire—were locked in the earth under the mountain for a very long time. A Carpathian woman named Arabejila, who came here with Dax to hunt Mitro, sealed them both in. Dax suspects Arabejila was your ancestor, and that she's the one who passed down the ritual you and your mother performed to keep the volcano from erupting and freeing them. According to Dax, Mitro is worse than most vampires, and he has a gift for escaping bad situations. Maybe that gift helped him wear down the barrier, but in any case, he's free now." Gary noticeably swallowed after he spoke.

"So what exactly *is* a Carpathian? You keep using that word like it should mean something to me." Riley needed an explanation as to how vampires and dragons had become a reality.

"The Carpathians are an ancient race—a different species, really—that has existed alongside mankind for a very long time. In fact, the Carpathians say they are of the earth itself. They have very long life spans, and possess amazing gifts and abilities, which is no doubt what spawned all the legends and myths about vampires and shapeshifters. It would take a very long time to give all the details, so I'll just hit the high points. I am sure Dax will be happy to answer any other questions you may have." He gave a small grin.

"Jubal and I have been friends of the Carpathians for some time now. We work with them and for them and count ourselves lucky for the privilege. They are really remarkable beings."

Riley couldn't stop herself from glancing down at Gary's wrist where Dax had taken his blood. If he'd lived with the Carpathians for a long time, was he a friend or more like a pet cow they milked whenever they needed to feed?

Noticing the direction of her gaze, Gary smiled. "I'm fine. Sometimes you can get a little dizzy from blood loss, but Dax was careful not to take too much. They need blood to survive, and the way I see it, giving to them isn't much different than donating to the Red Cross or the local blood drive."

"Except the Red Cross doesn't drink what they take."

"No, but they do use it to save lives. Humans need blood to survive, and so do Carpathians. The only real difference is how they get it. Besides, most people never know they have had their blood taken. It's really quite unobtrusive and painless. Carpathians use their abilities to put a person into a dream state."

"So they enthrall people. Like vampires do in novels and movies."

"Yes, there's nothing malicious about it. Most usually flood the person with happy thoughts, take what they need and leave pleasant memories behind when they leave."

Gary rubbed his wrist as if he could still feel the teeth breaking through the skin. Maybe he could. He hadn't looked like he was in a trance state when Dax was drinking from him.

"Why aren't there any marks?" Riley asked. "I watched him take your blood, but I don't see any sign of a cut or even a scratch on your wrist."

"That's because a Carpathian's saliva has rapid healing agents in it that seem to work on just about anything organic. Wounds close almost instantly. It's really something. They have other gifts, too. Abilities that would seem to fall more in the realm of magic than science. But all those gifts come at a price."

"What price?"

"A pretty steep one. The way it was explained to me, each Carpathian male is born with a seed of darkness in him. At first it's nothing—less than nothing. Like a grain of sand in the ocean. But as the males age, the darkness in them grows."

"By 'darkness,' what do you mean, exactly?"

"I guess you'd call it evil—or, rather, the capacity for evil. Sort of like all the aggressive emotions—hate, violence, selfishness. Once a Carpathian male reaches adulthood, that darkness starts pushing, trying to dominate him. Like I said, Carpathians live a very long time. The longer the male lives, the stronger the darkness inside him becomes."

Gary paused to take a sip of his water, but whether he did so from thirst or nerves, Riley couldn't say. He looked a little uncomfortable.

"The Carpathian males lose the ability to see in color, then the ability to feel emotion. I don't have a clear understanding of how that works exactly. I think it's a little different from person to person. For some, I gather it's a clean cut, like the lights just went out and every emotion they ever had is simply taken away. Love, sadness, joy, regret, all of it's gone, and what is left is just emptiness. For others, it's apparently not such a drastic change, and their emotions just fade. There are some who use their memories to recall what emotion used to feel like, but I'm told it's like hearing under water. It's not the same, but they cling to it, because it's all they have. But even that doesn't last. The darkness eventually corrupts everything, and the Carpathians know it. That leaves them only two choices: either meet the sun and die—and yes, that part works just like it does in all vampires—or embrace the evil and become a vampire, as Mitro did."

Riley looked down at her hands, inexplicably sad. "How terrible for them. So they *are* vampires, after all."

"No, they aren't. But they can *become* vampires if they embrace the darkness inside them. That's what we tried to tell you before. The vampires aren't just evil; they've *chosen* to be evil. They choose to give up their souls because they feel a rush when they kill while feeding. They relish the hate, the destruction, the corruption. There's no worse monster on this earth than the vampire. And the Carpathians like Dax hunt them. And Riley, something you need to understand is that some of the vampires they hunt were once their friends. Maybe even family members. It takes a very strong person to bear a burden like that."

Riley struggled to wrap her head around the information Gary was sharing. Rationally, she had a hard time believing in vampires and shapeshifters, but she'd seen them herself. She couldn't deny they existed. But then, she knew magic existed—the sort of magic that defied rational thought. She possessed it herself, as had her mother before her. The hardest part to come to grips with was the idea that Dax wasn't yet a vampire but might become one. Seeing the image of Dax, standing before her as red and gold flecks fell down all around him, his eyes so focused and yet so lost.

Riley pushed her hand under the corner of her sleeping pad she was sitting on. Her fingertips touched the tent floor. The vinyl felt cool against her hand. Her fingertips began to tingle as her connection to the earth grew stronger. She pushed into the plastic, gaining comfort the closer she got to the packed dirt underneath the tent. To her surprise, the thin plastic material seemed to dissolve beneath her hand, giving her access to the earth, which parted easily, as if welcoming her exploration.

"So Dax hunts these vampires, the ones like this Mitro who escaped from the volcano," Riley summarized. "But Dax is Carpathian, which means he has this same evil growing inside of him as Mitro. And if he doesn't suicide in the sun, he'll eventually become a vampire as well."

The image of Dax's broken body, his wounds open to the night sky, flooded through her. But even though he'd surely been in agony, he'd regarded her with such warmth and such wonder, his eyes filled with emotion. Hadn't he? Her heart seemed to stutter at the idea of him turning vampire. He was noble. Filled with courage. He'd touched her with such gentleness. She couldn't believe that there was evil in him. He was capable of violence, but evil? The idea was so devastating she could barely breathe.

Seeking solace, she used her fingertips to move through the earth. It was odd they moved through the packed soil with almost no resistance, as if she were running her hand through still water. The earth seemed to be singing under her hands.

With her fingers in the soil, if she didn't think about the why, and the how, instead focused on the song that was all around her, she could sense all the others in the camp. She knew where they were, what they were doing. Then, abruptly, she froze, her body turning cold from fear at the thought that Dax was gone.

"Gary, where is Dax right now?"

"He's resting at the moment. Like I said, Carpathians and the sun don't get along too well, although it doesn't seem to affect Dax quite as strongly."

"Gary," she said very coolly. "Answer the question."

"Dax wanted to stay close just in case Mitro or some other threat came up and we needed him."

Riley's eyes widened and she jumped to her feet. Gary, taken by surprise, fell over backward in his attempt to get out of her way.

"He's right underneath us isn't he?" She looked down, scanning the tent floor. She *felt* him, and relief flooded every part of her. He was close. She would see him again.

Gary got to his feet and righted his stool. "I honestly don't know. The location of their resting place isn't something Carpathians share, for obvious reasons, but that would make the most sense. He wants to keep you safe."

Riley *knew* Dax was there. Maybe they weren't supposed to know his exact resting place, but the earth whispered to her. And she knew. There was a man, a Carpathian, buried underneath her. She looked down at her feet. She was standing on him. Well, not actually standing on him, she corrected herself silently. To be perfectly technical about it, the tent just happened to be pitched over ground that contained Dax's sleeping body.

"I hope he doesn't expect me to help dig him out," she said out loud, and Gary brought his fingers up in a shushing gesture.

Laughter rumbled through her, and she knew it was Dax. The man spoke right into her mind. *I thank you for the invitation but I am sure I can find my own way out.*

His voice was polite and smooth but each word carried a smile. She shivered. Okay, more than polite and smooth, his voice sounded like warm molasses pouring into her mind and filling every empty, lonely spot. Just the sound of his voice sent fingers of arousal dancing through her body and an electrical current snapping and crackling in her veins. Warmth spread through her as if that molasses found a way into her body.

He couldn't be in her mind. Not with the things about him she was thinking—like how very sexy everything about him was. Color swept up her neck into her face. "I'm not comfortable with you in my head."

She glared at Gary, as if he were to blame for Dax's behavior.

Unperturbed by her irritation, Dax continued speaking directly into her mind. *I left you a gift, Riley, to thank you for your assistance. Do you like it?*

Some external force directed her attention down to the sleeping bag. She flipped the edge over to reveal an intricately woven quilt that depicted a beautiful landscape of mountains and grasslands, all worked in reds and blacks with threads of shining silver and gold embroidered throughout. A silvery moon in the top corner of the quilt sent beams of silvery light shining down upon the landscape below. The detail was exquisite, full of depth and movement. She turned it over to see the back side, and the quilt moved like silk, soft and warm in her hand.

The backing showed a different scene filled with wildlife. Birds of prey flew alongside a giant red dragon. On the ground below, wolves, lions, tigers and snow leopards raced across the plains, some diving into rivers and streams. As with the front of the quilt, the detail work was so exquisite, the scene practically came to life. More than that, the quilt radiated warmth and comfort.

"You shouldn't have," Riley murmured.

The quilt is not to your liking? There wasn't any emotion in Dax's voice, but Riley somehow knew she had hurt him. She had never been good with social niceties.

Her heart thudded in her chest. She'd never seen anything more beautiful—except him. She moistened her lips and glanced at Gary. Color crept up her neck to stain her cheeks. She felt Dax in her mind, waiting for her answer. She reached back to him, wanting to share what she had to say with only him.

I like it very much. How could anyone not? Her fingers traced the lines of the red dragon. Simply touching the fabric, stroking the lines of the design, seemed to wash away her worries and fears. "Did you hear me?" Her heart thudded. She felt shy, when she'd never thought she had a shy bone in her body.

Yes. The word stroked over her skin like a caress.

This is truly a piece of art. But it's far too beautiful to use—especially in a tent. The idea was outrageous.

Ah. But it was made for your use. You healed me. I wanted to thank you, and as you were sleeping, it seemed like the appropriate gift. His tone seemed more at ease. *Did you sleep well, Riley?* He spoke her name slowly, as if with great care, his tongue savoring each syllable.

She gently folded the quilt and set it down on her bed, her fingers lingering on top of the red dragon, stroking. *I did sleep well, and thank you for the quilt, Dax.* She found herself trying to say his name with a similar inflection.

But I am not having a conversation with a man while he is buried in the ground beneath my feet. Not to be rude, but I find the whole thing more than a little creepy. Her hand went over her mouth. Did Carpathians know what teasing was?

She could have bitten her tongue. She had the worst sense of humor, and she really didn't want to hurt his feelings, but talking to a man lying in the earth beneath her feet was kind of . . . humorous. She sank down and began sliding on her boots. As she was hunched down tightening the laces on her left boot, she felt just the brush of his lips against the back of her neck.

I see. Well, if that is the case, you could join me here if you like, it would not be too difficult. I am sure you would find it very interesting.

Riley froze for a moment, her hands stilling on the laces of her boot. The idea of joining him . . .

Male laughter vibrated from the floor. Waves of warmth radiated upward, and she started laughing, too. Carpathians definitely knew all about teasing. That realization eased her fears that her Dax could possibly become vampire. Evil creatures taunted, but they didn't tease. Teasing was gentle, friendly. There was a difference. Somehow, she got the feeling that he wanted to touch her, even if he couldn't physically be there right then. And somehow he had. Tingles coiled inside her and her shoulders relaxed.

You called me your *Dax.*

She stiffened. She *had* called him her Dax. She thought of him that way and she had no idea why.

Yes, you know why.

That voice could melt a glacier. If she didn't quit she'd be tripping over her own tongue. "I am leaving. You"—she pointed to the ground—"stay there." See? She could be funny, too. Laughing at her own joke, she exited the tent.

Gary followed her out, and as they left the sound of Dax's laughter faded, leaving her with a small empty feeling that she quickly tried to push aside. Riley stopped Gary with a hand on his arm. "How do we keep him from becoming a vampire?"

Gary looked at her for a long time, obviously choosing his words carefully. "The Carpathians are born with a soul that must find its other half. The light to their darkness. Only that soul can restore colors and emotions and prevent a Carpathian male too long in the world without those things from turning. Without that one woman who is the other half of his soul, he will choose between giving up his soul and becoming the very thing he hunts, or he must seek the dawn and suicide. He must find his lifemate."

At the word her heart clenched. She pressed her hand over her heart, suddenly barely able to breathe, her mind racing. "Gary, what's the Carpathian word for lifemate?"

Gary looked her straight in the eye. *"Päläfertiilam."*

Riley slowly nodded her head, trying hard not to notice that her blood surged hotly at the word, or that her mind continually reached for Dax. She pressed her lips together to keep from smiling. "I understand."

"Do you?" Gary asked.

She shrugged. "Not really, but I'm certain I'll figure it out."

Outside the tent, ash blanketed everything. It was still falling through the canopy of trees, turning everything a snowy gray. Riley looked around, easily spotting Jubal and Ben along with some natives gathered around a central fire pit. The camp was surprisingly large. As she walked toward Jubal and Ben, another group of men came in from a trail off to her right.

She spied Alejandro, one of their guides, along with Miguel, Hector, Don, and Mack Shelton. They were obviously one of the returning search parties, but since there was no sign of Marty or Pedro among their numbers, it seemed clear their search hadn't been successful.

Jubal approached. "Hey, Riley. Good to see you up and about. You feeling okay?"

"I'm good, thanks." She turned to watch the returning search party. "Gary told me Marty and Pedro went missing."

"Yeah. Looks like they still are. Can't say if that's good news or bad."

"Vampires like to play with their victims," Gary explained in a quiet voice. "Turning people into walking puppets isn't uncommon. If Mitro is the reason those two are missing, whoever finds them will probably get a very unpleasant surprise."

Riley spun around in shock. "Did you tell them that?" She nodded her head in the search party's direction, lowering her voice so they wouldn't hear.

Gary and Jubal's silence was all the answer she needed.

"Why wouldn't you tell them? If you're sending out a search party and putting them in harm's way, shouldn't they know what they're dealing with?" She scrubbed her hand over her face. "Gary, Jubal, how fair is that?"

For the second time since waking, she felt the sensation of a warm hand touching her back, calming her and drawing the focus of her anger away from Jubal and Gary. She turned to glance behind her, but no one was there.

"We considered it highly unlikely they'd find Marty or Pedro," Gary said. "Before Dax went to sleep, he ran a preliminary search in a five-mile radius around the camp, and found nothing."

"Riley, you have to understand," Jubal added when she continued to shake her head. "Gary and I swore an oath, to keep the Carpathians' secrets at all cost and by doing so keep their race safe. We didn't make that vow lightly, and we don't keep it lightly. There are men, women and children . . ." He paused for a fraction. "And babies counting on us." He watched the returning members of the search party as they separated and sought out their own tents, and his expression turned resolute. "We will not fail them. We can't share even a hint of what we know with others. Too many lives depend on our silence—not to mention, do you really think the likes of Don Weston would believe us?"

"Gary, how long have you known about the Carpathians?" Riley asked.

"For some time now," he admitted. "Several years."

"And in that time you've never told anyone else about them? Ever?" Her question made the two men go still, as if she had touched something sacred.

After a long silence, Jubal finally said, "Riley, you're the first person either of us has ever told." The way he said it made her wonder how these two men lived with such a big secret. How the world looked to them, as they went into coffee shops and airports, listened to news reports about unexplained events, knowing what they knew.

The ground under her seemed to shift a little. Riley looked down and sent a thought spiraling into the ground. *Go to sleep. I'm not dealing with you right now.*

Riley tried to put herself in Gary's and Jubal's shoes, to imagine what she'd do in their place. If an entire race of beings depended on her for survival, would she betray their trust and reveal their secrets to others? Or would she keep their secrets even if that meant she might put other people in danger?

Truth be told, she'd already made that choice. She and her mother, both. They had come here to this mountain to work the ritual that had been passed down from generation to generation. Her mother had known about the evil imprisoned in the mountain, but she hadn't warned the others in their party. Neither had Riley, when the secret fell to her to keep. She'd done what needed to be done. Was she really any different than Gary and Jubal?

"Riley, I know it's hard for you to understand. It's hard for us to withhold information when we know it might cost lives. But have you ever been a part of something so important that your own needs become insignificant? That's what this is to us." Jubal paused to let his words sink in.

"Even though we can't talk about what we know, we still do what we can to protect the innocent," Gary added. "Like the way we accompanied you up the volcano. We suspected what was up there. We couldn't tell you our suspicions, but we came with you to protect you all the same."

Riley saw the same defenseless honesty in Gary's face that she had in Jubal's. That helped put her own feelings of guilt to rest.

She felt Dax before he spoke to her this time. *They are both great men, sivamet, both have tremendous capacity for caring for others. It is a very rare trait. It is no wonder my people have chosen to bring them in.*

Dax had a way of bringing a calming stability when he spoke to her. *They helped as much as they could on the trip here, and on the mountain. I owe them a debt.* It was odd speaking in her head to someone, but she had to admit she liked the intimacy of it. Strangely, when his voice filled her mind, she sometimes caught a hint of life, his memories, as if more than just his voice had entered her mind.

It seems we both do. Riley heard the conviction in his voice.

If you're going to keep talking to me, I don't see why you're pretending to sleep.

Riley could almost see him smiling. *I will rise soon. I find I can withstand the sun even longer now than I could before. However, since I doubt Mitro has gone far, I need to conserve my strength.*

All the more reason you should stop talking. I'm sure it takes energy to speak to me like this. She wasn't at all sure she was right, but she remembered how completely drained she'd felt after she healed him.

Riley, I find that I only gain from speaking with you. As for strength, I find myself stronger than I have ever been before, but thank you for your concern.

Riley took a deep breath. *You called me* päläfertiilam.

Yes. There was no hesitation. He exuded complete confidence.

She felt another surge of heat curling through her body like a wave. *I asked Gary for the translation. He said it meant* lifemate *and that there is only one.*

Gary is correct. You possess the other half of my soul. You are the keeper of my heart.

Again, she felt that wave of heat rush over her. *How do you know?*

I know. He spoke with that same confidence.

How will I know?

This time she felt his smile, his joy. *I will share my mind with you. Court you. Persuade you. I can be quite charming when necessary.*

Without warning, goose bumps prickled across Riley's arms. The smile faded from her face. She turned instinctively toward the trail the search party had returned from. The smell of rotting vegetation, one of the jungle's inescapable aromas, seemed stronger than usual. She realized the song from the plants and earth she had heard since waking had changed, becoming discordant.

Mitro is attacking, Dax told her. *Do not fear. You are safe.* He sounded certain, but she wasn't feeling it.

"Safe? I've seen what he can do. I've felt it. And what do you mean he's attacking? From where? How?" She gestured to Jubal and Gary, mouthing "Mitro is attacking."

It's nothing I cannot stop. He is simply trying to weaken me by forcing me to protect this village while the sun is still up. A group of men and women he has corrupted are moving toward us. You have the ability to track them through the earth if you so choose.

"They're coming," she told Gary and Jubal. "Men and women under Mitro's power."

Gary ran toward the big tent without a word. Jubal gave her a pat on the shoulder and turned to shout commands in the local dialect. The entire camp erupted with activity, men gathering weapons and preparing for a fight, women hustling children to safety.

"What should I do?" She felt the rush in her body, but was at a loss at what to do about it.

Stay close to the center of camp. And breathe, sivamet.

She felt like an idiot, but she took a moment and tried to calm down.

Good, remember, I will always be with you. I won't let any harm come to you. She felt invisible arms wrap around her, and the taint of evil washed away, replaced with warm strength. *I can sense Mitro's puppets coming from the neighboring village, but I want you to try and "feel" them. Then we will set a defensive perimeter.* Dax showed an image of her sliding her hands in the ground.

Riley knelt down. When she put her hands in the earth before, she'd felt compelled, like the earth itself was asking her to communicate. This time, she was the one doing the asking. She wasn't sure she really knew what to do—or that she could even do it. Taking a breath, she put her hands together as if she was going to dive into a pool and slowly pushed her fingers down into the earth.

The packed soil shifted, loosening so that her hands plunged in with ease. Surprise gave way to exhilaration as her world changed again. The song of the earth was strong and rich. It hummed up her arms, through her veins and along her nerve endings, a harmonious vibration that filled her with a sense of vast, ancient power and limitless strength. She closed her eyes, sitting back on her heels and savoring the sensation.

Use what the earth offers, Dax advised. *Stretch out your senses.*

There was nothing on earth not connected to it. She had the wild idea that she could even sense what was happening on the other side of the world, if she tried hard enough. As it was, however, she confined herself to a slightly less grandiose effort. Instead of the world, she reached out to the earth nearby. Her awareness radiated out to all corners of the camp and then beyond, moving through the sandy soil of the rain forest until she located the group moving with deadly purpose toward the camp.

"Dear God." She could feel the misery, the rage, the evil taint that clung to them like a foul muck.

Riley, remember you're in control. Your job is to gather information. We need to see how many people are coming, and what sort of surprises Mitro has in store for us. You're doing great.

Riley steeled herself and tried to look at the mob. In her mind's eye, she saw the top of a recently shaved head bobbing in front of her. Then another head, this one covered in bloody scratch marks that were already bubbling with infection. She was looking through the eyes of a tree frog, watching as the mob passed by below his perch in the branches.

Frustrated that she couldn't make out more, she pushed out with her power. Her hands sank deeper into the earth. The tips of her boots sank, too. A second view of the mob appeared, and it was like she had two sets of eyes, watching from two separate angles. Then a third pair of eyes expanded her vision, and a fourth. It was difficult to adjust to the multiple visual inputs.

Breathe, Riley, you are doing great. Let the fear go. You can do this. I'm right beside you. And he was. She could feel him under her, around her, inside her, sharing her mind. At the moment, it didn't feel creepy or disturbing. She wanted him there, wanted him with her. *Good, now focus on what you want. Trust your gifts to do the rest.*

There are so many eyes. Where do I focus? Her head hurt. Images were pouring in now, dozens of different wildlife feeding their vision into her mind, each with a different perspective of the advancing threat.

His voice was steady, reassuring, as if they had all the time in the world and this was simply an exercise, not a matter of life and death. *Pick a single image and then focus on one small detail.*

"Okay, I'll try." She chose the first "screen," the one that came in from the tree frog.

She was once more looking down on the tops of the people as they moved past. One head caught her attention. A woman. Her straight, thick black hair was covered with leaves and ash, like most of the others, but she had something stuck in her hair. An ornament made of bone, carved and painted. Riley could make out the swirls of red and white paint beneath the streaks of ash. She locked her focus on that hair ornament, and as the woman continued on the frog tracked her with its eyes until the hair ornament disappeared from its view.

The image of the woman immediately changed to a different perspective.

Now she was watching the woman from a spot ahead of her, but she still had a clear view of the ornament in her hair. Riley could see part of the woman's face but she didn't want to get lost, so she stayed focused on that single detail. As the woman walked, Riley's vision began switching from view to view. The viewpoint switches started coming faster and faster, until Riley thought she was going to lose herself.

Dax poured waves of reassurance into her, and as if blinds had opened to let sunlight stream in, her mind expanded, using the eyes of every insect, bird and beast nearby to form clear, three-dimensional images of the party.

The entire party of the hundred or so villagers advancing on Riley's encampment were bent on killing her and everyone with her.

II

Riley was shocked at the clarity of her new, stereoscopic vision, which was so far superior to her own, unenhanced eyesight. All of the details and color, the ability to magnify images and see multiple locations at the same time was incredible. It should have been overwhelming, but miraculously, she was fine. She could do this.

Mitro's minions were making a straight line for the encampment, destroying everything that attempted to slow them down. It was clear they had come from a local village. And even though everything about them felt evil and wrong, she found it hard to believe all of them had willingly succumbed to Mitro's foul control. Some of the women had baby cradles strapped to their backs!

Dax, wait. What are we going to do to these people? Kill them? There are mothers in that group!

They were *mothers, Riley. Were. The men and women coming toward us are already gone from this world. Only their physical husks remain. Vampires take pleasure in digging out the insides of what they despise and can no longer be, replacing it with the foul evil they have become.*

Can't you save any of them?

I wish I could, sivamet, *but it is not possible. Those people are truly gone. The only humane thing to do is put their bodies to rest. I am sorry.* Empathy radiated through their connection.

There were no children in the mob, and Riley's heart broke at the thought of what might already have happened to them. Their parents clearly had not given up without a fight. Almost all of the oncoming villagers bore signs of brutal struggle, including deep furrows scratched into their bodies and faces.

Riley could feel the plant life trying to bend away from the taint of evil the group carried with them. Suddenly her vision went blurry, as if the eyes through which she was watching had lost their focus. She pulled back, closing off all but a few of the viewpoints until she was staring at the approaching group from above. That was when she realized there were several people wearing similar hair ornaments in the row. She counted eight different people, each wearing the same small bone adornment. There was something about them that made her skin prickle. She stretched out her senses and nearly gagged at the overwhelming stench of evil that radiated from them. The earth cringed beneath their feet, insects scurrying away, plant roots withering beneath each step.

For whatever reason, these eight carried the most concentrated levels of corruption in the entire group. As she focused on them, using the reluctant eyes of creatures that would rather run than look at them, she made a disturbing discovery. The long, matted hair spilling down their backs was not their own, but rather multiple bleeding scalps grotesquely sewn together. Riley gagged again as the bowls of soup she'd eaten earlier threatened to come back up.

Those eight are the greatest threat, Dax said. *Riley, you don't need to see more. We have all the information we need.*

She held on a moment longer. *Are you sure? Maybe I can see something else to help us.* More details flooded into her brain. The flesh of the eight seemed to ripple and palpate, as if bugs were crawling in every direction under the surface of their skin. Their fingertips were devoid of flesh, the bones filed down to points.

Not out there. Come back to the camp. Come back now. Dax's tone changed. He wasn't making a suggestion.

Riley moved away from the group, releasing the eyes of the forest, but not her connection to the earth. Slowly, she pulled her awareness back to their own encampment, and found herself searching for Dax among the people preparing for battle, needing his calm, reassuring strength. Her awareness shifted downward, and she found him, wrapped in earth, solid and calm in contrast to all the chaos above. Strength radiated from him even while he rested. She could feel his hands running over her arms.

Are you up for a little more?

With the power of the earth running through her veins and his mind connected to hers, she'd never felt so strong before. *What did you have in mind?*

I was thinking about defense.

Defense? Were you thinking a moat or something?

This is what I was thinking. Her mind filled with an image of the trees behind the camp interlocking to form a dense wall. Two of the trees in the wall remained upright, growing taller than normal. Riley frowned. Weaving the trees into a fence to stop the oncoming attack made sense, but the picture Dax had formed showed the wall being erected at the back of the camp, not the front.

I don't understand. You want to trap us in? Why wouldn't you put the fence between Mitro's puppets and our camp?

I won't let any harm come to the people in this camp, if it can be avoided. Have faith.

Even as Dax spoke the group of thirty or so in the camp, some only armed with spears, began running toward the tree line he'd shown her. Four of the men broke off from the group and ducked into the big tent. Moments later, they came back out, carrying the professor on a makeshift gurney. His remaining student followed close behind, the professor's pack clutched in his hands. Together, the small group moved back into the tree line.

Riley reached for the trees and the plant life with a mental sweep of her hand. The foliage vibrated at her touch, then leaves unfurled and roots extended as she encouraged the plants to grow. Soil was rich with nutrition and water. Bushes thickened. Trees grew taller, branches reaching out. Limbs and vines entangled, weaving together rapidly, and a wall began to take shape.

Excellent, Riley. Leave an opening here. He showed her a small opening in the middle of the wall, just large enough for a single person to fit through.

When she formed the opening and grew the two trees on either side to his specifications, he said, *I have lived a very long life, even by the standards of my own people, but I must say I've never been as impressed with anyone as I am with you. You are amazing.*

Riley didn't respond, but warmth unfurled in her belly. It was nice to feel helpful. She still couldn't believe she was doing most of the things he'd shown her. Seeing through the eyes of forest creatures. Making plants grow with just her will alone. Even her mother hadn't accomplished such feats, and yet, with Dax's help, the abilities seemed to come almost instinctively.

She continued to grow the wall of vegetation, spreading it out in a semicircle around the back half of the village to form a natural funnel, with that opening in its center. The rest of the camp filed through the opening in short order.

All right, Riley. That's enough. It is time for you to leave.

Are you sure the wall will hold? She could feel the attackers drawing nearer. There were so many.

I am sure. Let go of the earth and come back into yourself.

Her hands still in the soil, Riley pulled her consciousness back into herself. It was just as disorienting leaving so many minds as it had been extending out into them. When she was fully back in her own body, she slipped her hands free and staggered to her feet. Her arms and legs felt like she had just run up a mountain, and her head was pounding.

She stood for a moment to catch her balance and stretch her back. The camp was deserted. Only her tent and the big tent at the center were still standing. Everything else had been packed up and carried away.

She turned to face the living wall behind her. It was a sight to behold, dense and impenetrable, already covered in moss, leaves, and little flowers of every color. The wall had grown so quickly, the ash hadn't had time to cover it yet. Gary and Jubal had climbed the two large trees on either side of the center opening, and they had each taken a perch high up in the branches.

Ben emerged from her tent, carrying her backpack. He moved with calm efficiency.

"Time to go, Riley." He gestured for her to precede him toward the opening in the wall. Evil was on the wind and getting closer, and they were the last ones left in the camp.

As they approached the opening, Riley could see the tips of rifles and blowguns poking through the wall of foliage. Everyone who had preceded her through the wall had taken up defensive positions on the other side. Now, she understood the plan. This evacuated camp ground was to be a killing ground, plain and simple. She turned sideways to get through the small opening. Ben followed close enough behind that he bumped against her with every step.

Slipping one shoulder down she ducked through the last few inches of the tunnel and emerged on the other side of the wall. She stepped clear of the opening to let Ben pass, then laid her hand on the wall and willed the branches to grow and intertwine to close the opening. Through the barrier, she could hear the sound of marching feet, growing louder as their attackers neared the encampment's perimeter, and it gave her pause. Dax clearly wanted her on this side of the wall, safe and tucked away. Lord knows, she didn't belong out there in the fight. But she had skills that could help. She wasn't sure where she belonged.

"You belong exactly where you are."

His voice sounded in her ears this time, rather than her mind. She spun around and found him standing less than ten feet away. The sun hadn't yet set, and he stood there in the muted light of the ash-filled sky. Tall, strong, otherworldly. Sparkles of red-gold light flashed around him like fireflies as the dust from his scales rained down from his rising. Riley couldn't take her eyes from him.

With a few long strides, he closed the distance between them. "Right now you are here with me. I wouldn't want you anywhere else." The man's presence was enough to make her forget where she was. He bent his head toward hers, his lips hovering close. Energy crawled from the tips of her toes and traveled up her body, warming and swirling. For a moment, she thought he was going to kiss her right there, and she couldn't think, couldn't move. She could only stand there, staring at him in anticipation.

His head tilted to one side, and he pressed his lips to her cheek. The contact was intimate, soft. With him standing so close it was impossible not to feel the strength of his big frame. The combination of strength and tenderness shifted something down deep, and Riley almost wrapped her arms around his neck.

She needed him. Her heart was thudding like a drum. She wanted to cry for the villagers who had lost everything because she hadn't been strong enough or fast enough to keep Mitro imprisoned.

"Had you kept the volcano sealed, we would never have met," he reminded gently, his thumb tipping her chin up while his other hand cupped the side of her face. "I believe in fate, *päläfertiilam*. Mitro was meant to escape. I have no idea why. Maybe the Universe decided I deserved one such as you. If so, I am forever grateful to it. I am deeply sorry that you have to see the ugliness a vampire leaves in his wake."

Riley nodded her head, half mesmerized by him. One would think that with a war party headed their way, led by zombies . . .

"Ghouls," he corrected, in that same, soft, *hypnotizing* voice.

They were talking war, and her mind was hearing something else. That slow drawl, like molasses, warm and comforting. He exuded such confidence that she couldn't help but feel safe even when she was scared to death. He looked at her and touched her as if she was the most precious, beautiful woman in the world.

Dax had only known violence for most of his existence. He'd seen things most people couldn't comprehend and yet, with her, he was unfailingly gentle, tender even.

She nodded her head. "I can do this."

"I know you can," he agreed.

The cry of a bird and a shout from one of the villagers snapped them both back to attention. They turned to peer through the leafy wall and found that the first of the oncoming attackers had spilled like insects into the encampment clearing. Some of the attackers carried bloody spears and machetes; others held nothing but branches and rocks. Quickly they broke into two groups, each heading for one of the tents.

Riley watched as they tore the first tent to pieces. One of the eight, who had accompanied the first group, became enraged upon finding the tent empty. In a fit of fury, he shoved his spear through the closest person. Pools of black blood spilled out upon the ground as the wounded man screamed and fell to his knees.

Dax pulled her close. "Riley, go. You don't have to see this. I asked you to build the wall because most of the villagers from our camp came from the village Mitro destroyed. They don't need to see what I'm going to do, and you don't, either."

Her heart felt heavy, almost too heavy for her to bear what was going to happen. She studied his face. No expression. His eyes looking into hers, going almost blank. It was *his* heart she felt when he refused to feel it. Riley raised a hand to his face, cupping his jaw. "Do what you have to. I'm not going anywhere."

Dax's hand lingered for a moment, and then a chorus of bone-grinding noises rose from the gathered attackers. Dax pressed a quick, hard kiss on her lips, then turned and disappeared into a cloud of mist that blew through the foliage. Riley stepped close to the wall, and with a touch of her hand, the entangled branches parted so she could see through the wall to the encampment beyond. Her heart dropped as she realized every enraged face was turned her way, looking straight at her as if the dense thicket of leaves and branches was invisible. The group charged.

Riley stumbled back in fear, but then the men leading the charge tripped over something and went down hard. The ones who followed either were stumbled over or tried to jump their downed companions. Shocked, Riley moved back to the small hole she'd made in the wall. As she watched, a man jumped over one of the fallen, and was caught midleap by Dax, who was moving so fast, he was little more than a blur. His foot landed on the fallen man's neck, breaking it with a crack at the same time he snatched the other man out of the air. Bones crunched again as the leaping man's head twisted nearly 180 degrees. The limp body dropped to the ground; all she could see was a blur darting from one end of the encampment to another. And everywhere the blur went, bones cracked and bodies dropped like heavy sacks and did not move again. The trail of corpses made it easier to see where Dax had been rather than what he was doing.

He moved faster and faster, dispatching one possessed villager after another until there was no one left but the eight, scalp-bedecked leaders she had identified earlier. The killing field fell silent. Tears spilled from her eyes. The once-peaceful camp was now littered with bodies, men and women who would never return to the ones who loved them. Horror and sorrow at the loss of life welled up inside her. Then Dax returned to the center of the camp, and waited, alone and unafraid, as the eight leaders of the mob circled him.

Seeing them now with her own eyes, they appeared even more horrific than they had when she'd watched them through the forest's eyes. The bloody scalps of their previous victims bumped against their backs. Their faces had been painted in blood, their teeth filed to sharp points to match the skinless, sharpened bones of their fingertips.

Riley's fear overrode sorrow as Dax stood there, unmoving, calm and ready. Darkening clouds blocked the fading light of the sun, turning the sky a deep, awful red. The scene took on an even more nightmarish quality, with evil and death permeating the air beneath that blood-drenched sky. Wave after wave of foul corruption sped across the ground. She found herself rocking back and forth as each wave washed over her. Her swaying motion began to match the movement of the eight leaders.

One of the eight stepped closer to Dax. A trail of insects and black ichor spread out in his wake, shining darkly in the fading light. Even behind the relative safety of the tree wall, Riley's whole body shook with tremors. She wasn't afraid of insects, but she was terrified of those dropping from the ghouls. Her blood curdled at the thought of them crawling over her skin.

Riley wasn't sure what Dax was waiting for. The rate and magnitude of the spreading evil increased with each passing moment. Already, the flowers blossoming all over her plant wall had wilted and died. The eight were closing in, and Dax, with his back to her, seemed to be just standing there. Had his attack on all the others exhausted him? The sun was still up, even if it was hidden by the clouds. Surely, that drained him, too.

Suddenly, the eight leapt forward in unison, moving with speed she had not thought them capable of. Two leapt through the air above Dax. The others attacked from different angles.

A voiceless scream ripped through Riley. There was no way the creatures could miss. All eight were moving as fast as Dax had, bloody claws extended in preparation for their strike. Still, Dax continued to simply stand there. One of the creatures ran between Riley and Dax, obscuring her view. Her heart rose up in her throat.

"Dax!" Blinding light streaked down from the sky, slamming into the ground where Dax was standing. "No! Dax!" *Dax!* Blinded by the lightning, she gripped the intertwined branches and screamed his name.

She blinked furiously, trying to clear her vision, then stabbed her hands into the ground and took control of every creature she could find and used their eyes to replace her own. A broken sob escaped her lips when she realized he was still there, safe, standing near a pile of charred bodies and holding a ball of blue and white fire. Quickly he lifted the ball into the air and released it. The shining orb drifted upward like a balloon and moved toward the center of the clearing. The insects that had followed in the wake of the eight were moving rapidly forward, blanketing the ground with their scuttling forms.

A movement from above drew her attention. Still perched high in the branches overhead, Jubal was tying himself to the trunk of his tree. In the other large tree flanking what had been the tunnel through the living wall, Gary was doing the same. She looked back to the clearing. The pile of bodies near Dax began pulsating. A horde of insects erupted from the center of the pile, spilling down in every direction. One of the eight half shoved, half crawled his way out of the pile as well.

Dax raised a hand toward the ball in the sky and called, "Gary, whenever you're ready."

Riley had just enough time to look up and see Gary squeeze a detonator trigger before the encampment exploded. Dirt, rocks and bodies slammed into the tree wall as an enormous ball of flame roared out from the center of the camp. Riley screamed and ducked, instinctively covering her head with her arms. Then Dax was there beside her, shielding her body with his own, both of them facing away from the blast. For a moment, all she could do was cling to him and catch her breath.

The intense heat was still radiating from the blast point, but as the worst of the noise and debris died down, his tight hold on her loosened. Together, they turned to look back. To Riley's amazement, a wall of red and blue fire was raging in the center of the camp, but contained, as if trapped behind a wall of glass just at the edge of the tree line. She could see little blue-white streaks running up and down the outside of the invisible wall.

Dax pointed his right hand toward the firestorm and the wall pushed in on itself. Quickly, it retreated back, shrinking from the blaze and funneling the heat skyward. The fire shrank tighter and tighter until it closed in upon itself and disappeared altogether, leaving behind a barren stretch of charred ground devoid of all signs of battle. Riley stood up, staring at the blackened ground in surprise, realizing that the area had been completely cleansed. Every last hint of the evil that had permeated the ground was gone. Dax had destroyed it utterly.

Dax's arms tightened around her, pulling her closer as they watched the remaining ash rain softly down on the scorched clearing. She leaned her head back against his chest and breathed in his clean, masculine scent. His arms were warm, so hard and solid. He made her feel safe and protected. She turned in his arms to look up at him in wonder. He also made her feel tiny, even delicate, which considering her height was no easy task.

Her eyes searched his face. The burnished skin, his strange multifaceted, burning eyes. The strong, masculine beauty that made her heart flutter every time she saw him. She laid a hand along the side of his face, brushing one thumb across his high cheekbone, marveling at how his skin felt. And how clean. There wasn't a smudge of dirt on him, while she could see just from her hands that she was a sooty, soil-covered mess.

"You're clean. You just took out an entire army, stood in the center of a blazing inferno, and there's not a speck of dirt on you. How is that possible? I can't walk two steps without getting filthy." Riley raised her hands, which were streaked with dirt and soot.

He smiled. Really, he had the most gorgeous smile. "There are certain gifts Carpathians have that can be quite handy." Without warning, the dirt, sweat and salty tracks of her dried tears evaporated from her skin. One second, she was a hot mess. The next, she looked like she'd stepped off the cover of a magazine, every hair in place, her skin smooth and fragrant, her clothes crisply pressed and sweet-smelling.

"Where have you been all my life?" she quipped with a grin. "And do you do windows?" She knew she was relying on humor to slow the adrenaline. The sheer terror of seeing him surrounded by the insanity of Mitro's macabre human robots was almost more than she could bear. He must have known it, too, by the tenderness in the way his thumb traced her cheekbone and moved down to her lips.

He laughed, and the rich, deep sound rolled over her senses like dark chocolate melting in her mouth. Pleasure rippled up and down her spine, and all she could think about was dragging his perfect mouth down to hers and kissing him like there was no tomorrow.

Only the sound of a twig snapping in the vicinity of the wall brought her back to her senses. She pulled away, coughing nervously, looking anywhere but at him.

"So . . . uh . . . what just happened out there? You rigged some sort of bomb?" She looked up at him under the sweep of her heavy lashes.

"We used something called 'explosives' that Gary and Jubal brought with them. I didn't know what Mitro might send against us, and I wanted to be ready for anything." Dax indicated the two men. "They are good fighters, very prepared."

"And the wall of fire, with the blue and white lightning running through it?"

"The four of us were too close to the explosives, so I used a ward to hold in the majority of the blast. That also let me concentrate the heat of the explosion on Mitro's ghouls, to cleanse their taint and remove the possibility of any future threat from them."

Riley shook her head. "Why is it I have a feeling that the more time I spend around you, the more questions I'm going to have?" The sorrow of the fleeing villagers who had set up a temporary camp and taken them in beat at her. The earth cried out at the abomination of evil and the destruction of plant life. She needed him to mute the sounds and sensations for just a few moments to give her time to recover.

His answering smile was warm and inviting with just enough sexy to make her hungry for more. She wanted to kiss him again. She wanted to wrap her body around his and lose herself in his strength.

Dax's fingers curled around the nape of her neck. "You can, you know. You can take from me whatever you want, *sivamet*. I give myself to you willingly." His eyes drank her in, and his hot gaze dropped to her lips.

On some level, Riley knew the fear drove her more than passion. She needed comfort. She needed to feel him alive, hear his heart beat strong and steady after watching him so calmly facing the enemy. The thought of him dying had all but shattered her. She told herself it was because she'd just lost her mother, but . . . it would be a lie. It was him. Dax. She stepped closer to him, captured by the small flames burning in his eyes.

"I thought you were dead. For just one terrible, unimaginable moment, I thought you were dead," she murmured, sliding her hands up his chest, over his heart.

Dax seemed to know exactly what she needed. His arms moved around her body. Hard. Strong. Comforting. He pulled her tight against his chest. She rested her head there, just for a moment, just to listen to his rock-steady heartbeat. His hand beneath her chin urged her head up. His eyes met hers. The small red-gold flame leapt and burned, robbing her of breath. She watched his mouth move toward hers, inch by slow inch.

Everything feminine in her reached for him, her stomach doing a slow somersault. A thousand butterflies took wing. His lips were warm and firm, but soft. She felt as if she just melted into him. His tongue teased the seam of her mouth, demanding she open to him. She did so, and he swept inside. There was no breathing—he did it for her. There was refuge, sanctuary, a world of sensation with the ground moving beneath her feet, sweeping her away from death and madness. She all but crawled up his body and wrapped her legs around his waist.

The sound of Gary and Jubal climbing down from the nearby trees was barely enough to break the moment.

"What now, Dax?" Gary asked when he reached the ground. "Is there anything here still left to be done?"

Dax shook his head, sweeping her behind him with one arm protectively, giving her time to collect herself. "I believe Mitro has already left this area, or he wouldn't have sent his ghouls out on such a useless attack. He is far too cunning to have sent them alone if he were still here. This was nothing more than a delaying tactic, something to hold my attention while he escaped to somewhere else."

Without thinking, Riley laid a hand on his arm, still needing their bond. He gave her a warm glance and covered her hand with his own. She could feel a portion of her own, earth-born strength pouring into his body, renewing his depleted energies.

Through that connection, Riley realized that even as Dax was standing here, talking to them, his mind was scouring the surrounding countryside for some sign of his ancient foe. She could almost feel the death and destruction that Dax had to search in order to find Mitro. It pained him to witness Mitro's evil, she realized. He might have lost his emotions centuries ago, if what Gary told her about Carpathians was true, but that didn't stop him from feeling responsible for the lost lives and the destruction Mitro had wreaked. He considered Mitro's escape *his* failure, not hers.

"So what's the plan?" she asked, trying to bring his attention back to her, away from Mitro's trail of carnage. The attempt to distract him worked.

"You think I have a plan?" Male amusement lightened his eyes.

"Men like you always think you have a plan." She laid a hand on the tree wall. The branches and vines parted, re-creating a wider tunnel that led back to the clearing. She ducked through, Dax close on her heels. Jubal and Gary brought up the rear.

"Men like me?" Dax murmured as they exited the tunnel. "Just how many men like *me* have you met?" He was showing off his teeth in a way that made her want to cover her neck.

"Not the point. So, what's the plan?" She looked back toward Jubal and Gary to include them in their conversation.

"We should find out what happened to Marty and Pedro first," Jubal said. "Unless they were in the group . . ." His words died off, and everyone looked to Dax.

"They were not. Though I doubt you will find them alive. Mitro's stench is very thick in this part of the jungle."

"So how do we go about finding them?" Riley asked. "Even if you think they're dead, we can't be sure. And we can't just leave them out here alone. Who knows what sort of traps Mitro has set."

"I have to go to the village where these people came from." He indicated the blackened battleground.

"The remaining villagers have fled," Jubal said. "They melted into the rain forest, and Miguel said they wouldn't go back to their village."

Gary nodded. "We told him to take the others away from here, deeper into the forest as well, and to wait for us there. They think another more aggressive tribe attacked us."

Riley tightened her fingers around Dax's. "Why go there? Haven't you sacrificed enough? You don't have to see what else he's done."

Dax brought her hand to the warmth of his mouth. "Mitro had to have spent at least one night in that village to have corrupted so many. He would have left dangers behind, as well as his personal signature of evil. I have to clean that up. From there, I should be able to find in which directions he traveled. It's possible you might be able to help me in that regard, Riley, although I'm not certain I want you to see any more death, but with Arabejila's connection to him and your gifts, you might be able to pick up his trail. In that lies our best chance of discovering what happened to the two missing men. And finding them might help me anticipate Mitro's next move."

The thought of seeing more innocent dead people twisted her insides, but Riley took a breath and agreed. If he had to endure the aftermath of the vampire's destructive path, she wanted to share it with him. She was just as responsible. "I'll do whatever I can to help. But how can finding Marty and Pedro help lead you to Mitro?"

"It's just a guess. The only thing that ever changed his course besides a hunter getting too close was information he could turn to his advantage. If he took your friends and didn't kill them immediately, then he was likely using them for information."

"What information could he possibly get from an archaeology student and a local guide?" Riley answered her own question. "The local area. Pedro would know all the roads, all the villages and cities. He'd be like a walking map of this part of Peru."

Jubal continued the line of thought. "The kid would have buckets of information the vampire could use. Internet, English, how electricity works, biology, explosives. Hell, cameras, police, world trade. Marty's college education would definitely be of interest."

"We should get moving. The more time that goes by the fainter Mitro's trail will be, and it is a very big world out there for him to hide in," Dax said.

"Let me take a minute and see if I can . . ." Riley trailed off looking toward the blackened ruins of the battleground. "It will only take a moment." She felt guilty for holding everyone up, especially since she knew they were on a limited time schedule, but the compulsion was growing strong in her. She couldn't bear to leave that scarred piece of ground when she knew she could aid the healing process.

She didn't wait for permission, her feet already taking her toward the blackened soil. She was vaguely aware of Dax pacing protectively alongside of her, but her mind was already tuning itself to the earth. Everything else faded into insignificance. She knelt beside the terrible blackened soil and sank her hands deep. Closing her eyes she sent out energy, the seeds of plants, trees and flowers moving through her mind. She could see them sprout, wind their way up through the dirt to burst toward the sky. The soil was rich with minerals, fuel for the plants to aid them in recovery.

She had no real idea of time passing until she found herself swaying a little and blinking at the sight of the circle of dense foliage growing in front of her. Dax put a hand on her shoulder to steady her. Behind him, Gary and Jubal were looking at the amazing growth of plants. There was no feeling of evil thanks to Dax, and the ground was more fertile and thick with an abundance of young trees, ferns and plants.

"I should probably get my pack—we will need supplies," she said, with a small, shaky smile. She felt as if she was coming back from a long distance. She allowed Dax to help her to her feet. "What about them?" She pointed back toward the wall. "Are we leaving any weapons with them or anything? The professor didn't look like he should be moved much."

"I was thinking just the two of us. Gary and Jubal can stay and protect the others and your things. We won't leave them for long." He gestured toward the wide circle of plants. "That's amazing. You're amazing." *And mine.*

Her gaze jumped to his. She heard him so clearly, that firm, soft and warm and so sexy voice pouring into her mind so intimately. Her hand fluttered to her throat. "You're not going to turn into a giant red dragon right now are you?"

"Do you want me to shift into a dragon?" His voice sounded different, causing her to think more closely on the conversation: something in what they were saying mattered to Dax but Riley wasn't sure what.

"I was thinking we could hike if it's not too far."

"I was thinking something a little different." Dax sent a picture of him lifting her off the ground and taking to the sky with her in his arms.

"No. No way. Don't even think about—" She squealed as the man swept her off her feet and began to run.

"I can't believe you're carrying me again."

He glanced down at her in genuine surprise. "I can turn into a dragon, stop an explosion with 'magic,' and do all manner of incredible feats, but you can't believe I'm carrying you?"

"That was a figure of speech. Now put me down. I will not be carried through the jungle by Tarzan."

"I do not know this Tarzan, but if he makes a habit of carrying off his woman, I think I would like him." His laughter rumbled through her. "Wrap your arms around my neck and hold on tight."

He launched into the sky, spearing up through a hole in the canopy. The moment they broke through the canopy, Dax caught her around the waist and turned her so she could see the ground below them and the direction they were flying. "Oh my . . ." From this height she could see the volcano clearly as it was billowing ash from one side. The rivers of magma spilling down its sides looked like ribbons of orange light in the dusk sky. The sight was humbling and beautiful on such an elemental level Riley found all she could do was watch in awed silence.

"I had hoped you would like this."

"Dax, I don't know how anyone could not like this. It's beyond words."

"The height doesn't bother you?" There was a teasing note in his voice.

"If you let go, the height will bother me very much." She realized her nails were digging into his arms wrapped around her waist. Slowly she loosened her muscles, trusting he wouldn't let her go.

"I won't let go." Warmth spread down her spine and nestled deep inside.

The sky turned red and gold all around them, and little red and gold flakes swarmed about them. At first, she thought the glittering flakes were embers from the volcano, but they remained close despite the fact that Dax and Riley were racing across the sky.

"What are these red and gold sparks in the air around us?"

"The side effects of a choice I made. Mitro was getting out, and I wasn't strong enough to stop him. I needed something more than I had to give . . ."

"You locked yourself in a mountain for untold years, but you blame yourself for his escape? Dax, it's my fault he's free. My mother and I didn't get there in time. I wasn't strong enough to keep him caged."

"No, Riley. Stopping Mitro is my responsibility. It always has been."

Silence speared between them. Riley wasn't sure what to do. She wanted to comfort him but wasn't sure how.

"What was the choice you made?" she asked instead. "When you were trapped in the volcano with Mitro, you said you made a choice . . . one that caused these red sparks that flicker around you at times, especially when you're moving fast. What was it?"

"Mitro and I weren't the only ones trapped in the mountain. A fire dragon had chosen that volcano as his final resting place long before we arrived. When Mitro was trying to escape, the dragon offered to merge his soul with mine in order to give me his strength and abilities."

"You mean dragons are real?"

He laughed. "I tell you I chose to merge my soul with a dragon's and you're more interested in the fact that dragons are real?"

"No . . . well, yes. Really? They're really real?"

"They were. I don't know if any still live. The one I found had been there for millennia. His body had crystallized, becoming part of the mountain."

"So you're telling me that right now your soul is mixed with a dragon's, and as a side effect from time to time these sparkling red and gold flecks appear." She shook her head and laughed in disbelief. She couldn't help it. What else did he have in his life? "So if I ask why you're so sexy, are you going to tell me your mother was a goddess from Mount Olympus? That she ensnared your father, after a shooting star fell to the ground on a starless night?"

Dax laughed again. "My mother was a sweet woman whom my father loved very much. Although, it's true my mother did claim to ensnare my father, and he did claim he saw stars the first time he set eyes on her." Then his tone changed, losing its flirtatious note. "We're here."

They glided back to earth and landed softly in a small clearing about a half mile from the smoking remains of a village. Dax set her down on her feet, but kept her hand in his.

"Riley before we continue, there is something I'd like to give you." Reaching into his pocket Dax brought out a folded black and red silk cloth in the shape of a dragon. "You open it by pulling the wings out to the sides."

"I don't want to ruin it."

"I can make another one."

Carefully, Riley pulled the wings back, and the cloth dragon unraveled in a way only Dax's magic could make it do. In the center of the cloth lay a gold and silver bracelet.

"This is for me, but why?"

"Let's just say for now it's tradition. I wanted to say I am very sorry for the loss of your mother, and again I hoped you might honor me by finding a home for her last gift in here." He gestured to the empty setting in the intricate design and then slipped the bracelet on to her wrist.

Riley wasn't shocked when it fit perfectly. It was a work of art, and she tracked the different trails of silver, each holding several smaller diamonds meeting at the central space.

Reverently, Riley pulled out the silver dragon with agate eyes holding an obsidian stone. Her mother's death was an enigma. The magic and power she now had wrapped through all her memories and experiences. Something had touched her when she was there, something that had soothed the grief and allowed her to move forward. But holding the piece of jewelry handed down in her family from mother to daughter was a reminder of her mother, and no matter what that something was it couldn't fill the gap that was left behind.

She thought about everything her mother had stood for, the way she was raised, her sense of humor, how she always was there to pick her up when she had fallen down. Annabel was classy and strong; if this dragon was her last gift it deserved a better place than inside her dirty pocket.

Riley's mind was puzzling out what it meant to wear her mother's stone out where others could see it. "How did you know about the dragon, and my mother?"

"You touch it from time to time when you walk, although you don't seem to notice. As for knowing about your mother, how could I not know?"

Opening her hand she presented the dragon to him. "Would you mind?"

Dax covered the bracelet and her wrist with both hands, having palmed the dragon. She felt the heat but couldn't tell if it was his touch or what he was doing as tingles ran up her arm and into her fingertips. His hands came away, and it was perfect. The shadows of grief were still inside, but as she looked from his face down to her mother's gift on her wrist, Riley felt a little more at rest. Without thinking Riley wrapped her arms around Dax, this time feeling completely at ease; she pulled hard, bringing his head closer to hers, initiating the contact this time.

His kiss took her away, sensations pouring into her body. He was so warm, his skin almost hot, his body hard against hers while his mouth moved over hers in long, heady kisses.

Riley pulled back a little, and Dax let her, but she could feel the struggle in him. It caused a wicked sense of danger and control she found a little intoxicating. The fact that he was having a difficult time with control was reassuring. Riley released his neck, slowly bringing her hand over his chest. She could feel his heart beating. Looking up she saw that his eyes were dancing as he held still, and Riley felt even more powerful. Playing with fire, she curled her nails into him.

The growl that rumbled out ran over Riley, causing her to jump back. Dax's whole demeanor was one of victory and entirely too male, she thought. "You beast." Shocked laughter infused her voice at the man that had growled at her.

"If you wish me to be, *sivamet*. It would be my pleasure."

Riley felt he wanted to pounce on her right then, and by God there was a part of her asking him to. Dax spoke in her mind. *We will have lots of time for pouncing, I promise you.*

"I'm going to leave that one alone for right now. Thank you for the bracelet." She was trying to find a way to break some of the sexual tension, but she didn't think there was a knife big enough. "What does *sivamet* mean?"

Dax smiled down at her, tucking a flyaway strand of hair behind her ear. "You're welcome. I enjoy giving you things you like. As for *sivamet*, it means 'of my heart,' or 'my love' might be a better interpretation in your language."

Her heart performed a slow dizzy somersault. She had no words, but held his answer close to her. She just nodded.

"We need to get moving," he said gently.

"It's probably best. Where is the village we were going to?"

"Not very far, but we should explore the perimeter first and see what we find. And, Riley, be aware, Mitro's evil will be drawn to you like no other. Keep your mind open to me at all times."

"Dax, I made my choice." She rubbed the bracelet on her arm. "Mitro killed my mother, those villagers and how many others, and now he's out there right now and by all accounts doing it all over again. I don't think I can fight him, but I can do this."

"Take my hand. I have been blocking the area around us from your senses, but I am dropping the barrier now."

The difference was instantaneous. Riley was filled with information. Her power was not one she could turn off and on, only turn up or dim down. It was easy to tell where the village was. The slimy feeling sinking into her skin gave that away.

"He was here," Dax said. "But he's long gone. I feel his evil permeating the ground. He's left a few traps, and I'll get rid of those. He's good at masking his tracks, but there will be evidence. As powerful as he is, even he has to leave something of himself behind."

She closed her eyes and filtered through the information.

They walked the perimeter, in a very wide circle, looking for signs Mitro left behind. They'd circled halfway around the village when Dax suddenly stopped in his tracks. Evil lay so thick in the ground, she felt like she was swimming through it. She looked down at the ground and saw the soil moving. "What is that?" She was horrified.

The moment she spoke, ants erupted from the ground, the surrounding bushes, even dropped from the branches overhead. Dax snatched her up and jumped across a clearing of grass and dirt. The area was ant-free, and as Riley looked back, she saw that the spot they'd leapt from had already returned to normal.

"One of Mitro's traps. Let's continue." He was matter-of-fact.

Dax found two other traps, sprang them and cleared them unemotionally. But then, just before they completed their circle around the village, Riley halted abruptly without even knowing why. "Dax." She looked up at him, confused. "I'm not certain what I'm doing." She frowned. "There's something here. Do you feel it?"

"Yes," he said.

She looked up at him. "You would have found this without me. What is this? Some kind of test?"

"I didn't want to leave you there. It was too dangerous. If one person from this village escaped or lagged behind the battle, you would be the target. Here I could protect you as well as find out what you can and can't do." There was no remorse in his voice. She realized he wasn't going to apologize for choosing the best way to keep her safe.

She straightened her shoulders. "Let me try, then."

As he had done when they first reached the village, Dax blocked all the other information, letting her concentrate her senses on that one strangely empty spot. As she focused, Mitro's trail became clear. Riley began to shiver. The tiny spot wasn't empty. The evil was so concentrated, it froze her senses, the way ice numbed nerves.

Riley sidestepped away from the direction they had been going, and started following the icy trail, certain that this was the path Mitro had taken. Her instincts were directing her thoughts. Her abilities stretched out. Though they weren't as strong without using a ritual to focus and amplify them, with Dax blocking the "noise" from the rest of the forest, it was easy to follow the trail Mitro had left. Her mind raced along the icy remnants of his wake, twisting and turning as the vampire had until Riley was very far from where she started.

"That's far enough, Riley. We have enough to go on." His voice broke her concentration.

That wasn't what she wanted to hear. She was getting closer to him. The trail had a different feel, like it was growing stronger. She wanted to know her abilities every bit as much as Dax did.

"*Sivamet*, you've given us a start, but it's getting too dangerous." There was a firm command this time.

With a sigh, Riley let go of the trail and came back. Her body ached and her muscles felt as if they were hard knots, her legs like rubber. Dax was the only thing holding her up. "Why did you call me back? I was getting so close."

"You were getting tired. And Mitro might have been waiting for you. He has a gift for such things. He might have been able to strike at you in that form."

"I really don't like him." Her breathing was back to normal and her arms didn't feel like lead weights.

"I knew him before he turned vampire, and I didn't like him then, either." Dax stood and helped her to her feet.

She shuddered as the noxious sensations radiated out from the village, but she stood her ground. As she processed the information, she realized there was more, that the rhythm and pulse of the surrounding area vibrated in opposite tune. She could feel the earth fighting to expel the blemish on the land.

Holding hands, Riley and Dax walked together toward the village. They walked into three more traps, each of which Dax quickly dispatched, and then they broke through the forest into the cleared area of the village, and Riley found herself standing in the middle of the most horrifying sight she'd ever seen. Words failed her. The sheer number of bodies strewn across the ground defied belief.

"Mitro must have visited the outlying areas during his first night and brought more villagers here," Dax said. "I have never seen him work this fast before."

In the center of the village was a horrific altar of sorts. A wooden dais bore a crude throne fashioned from what looked like wood and human bones. Great black wings soared out on two sides, each covered in layers of black feathers. The wings were covered in blood that refused to dry in the humidity of the jungle. Like a macabre waterfall, blood continued to drip from the blood-soaked dais to the black ichor-covered ground below. Riley and Dax carefully circled the dais. Pinned like a crucified Jesus to the back of the bloody wings was Marty's tortured body, naked except for the insects that were feeding or hatching in his open wounds. Bile rose in Riley's throat. Most of Marty's organs were hanging free outside his body; his back had somehow been fused with the dais, and it was his blood dripping down the front. As they approached, the bloody, disfigured face lolled to one side and a bubbling groan wept from his lips.

"Oh, my God. Dax! Dax, do something! He's alive. He's still alive!"

With a wave of his hand, Dax sent all the insects fleeing their feast. He stepped up to the dais and placed a hand just over the boy's collarbone. Bloody eyelids fluttered. Haunted eyes rolled up to focus on Dax. How Marty was alive, let alone still conscious, Riley had no idea. Her heart was breaking as she looked at him, and tears streamed down her face.

Dax held the contact for several minutes, clearly searching Marty's mind for information he could use. When he was done, he turned his head just slightly toward her, not making eye contact. "Riley, look away." It was the closest Dax had ever come to a plea, and she almost did as he asked. Instead, she squeezed the hand she still held. She knew what he was going to do, and she wouldn't let him do it alone.

In that instant all pain was gone, memories of horror were gone from his mind, so Marty only remembered happy moments in his life. Dax waved his hand, and Marty gave one last sigh before succumbing to his horrible wounds. Riley didn't need to be told that there was nothing they could do. The boy was too far gone. Her tears continued to fall as Dax walked them away from behind the dais.

Clouds formed unnaturally fast, dark and mean. Lightning raced from one side of the sky to the other. The electricity was palpable in the air, but it was Dax being so closed off that truly unnerved her. For the first time she felt him mentally slipping away, and she let him go. She understood the need to distance oneself when faced with such horrors.

"Marty was here to study ruins with his professor and Todd, his friend," Dax said, staring at the gathering storm. "He had a love for history and especially the study of how myths and gods were created. Mitro spent a lot of time in this part of his brain. I believe the vampire may be considering making his own cult, using the volcano and the dragons and local legend." His voice was neutral, but even without the connection she thought she detected shame.

"This is not your fault, Dax."

He went on as if he didn't hear her. "Mitro used Marty to learn about the modern world, or at least as much of it as he could. He took his time while he made the village people sacrifice each other in his name. Pedro was one of the first to die."

"Dax . . ."

Dax cut her off. "Yes, Riley, this *is* my fault. Every child, every man, every woman . . . their deaths are my fault." Dax raised his hand and lightning sprang to his fingertips, gathering into another ball of light and fire.

"Do we know where he is?"

"Before coming here Marty and Todd spent time in a city, filled with people. Mitro spent time reviewing those memories. I think the city appealed to his latest aspirations."

Dax threw the ball of flame straight down at their feet. Waves of lightning and fire in every color spread in an instant, burning everything but them. Dax took her arm and guided her back toward their camp. The fire retreated from their every step. "I believe he wants to go to a place where there are young people that will worship him as he believes he deserves."

When the village was out of sight, Riley looked up at Dax. Otherworldly and beautiful, his expression looked carved from stone.

Riley had had enough of his stoicism. She could feel how much he was suffering. She reached up, grabbed the back of his hair and kissed him hard. At first, he held firm and then their world turned to a fire as hot and wild as the one they'd just left as he let her take him to someplace far, far different.

12

Riley knew she wasn't alone the moment she woke. She was surrounded by Dax's scent. Warm. Masculine. Wild. Dangerous—which was strange because she instantly felt safe.

"Open your eyes."

Her body responded to that soft, hypnotic voice, melting, turning liquid. She lifted her lashes and looked into his face. Desire, raw and electric, sizzled through her body until heat pooled low. He looked sinfully beautiful, the most beautiful man she'd ever seen. There was nobility in that carefully carved face. Each feature was distinct and etched with an artistic hand. His short, spiked hair, obsidian black, nearly sparkled, giving her palms a tingly feeling and forcing her to curl her fingers tightly into fists to prevent her from running them through that thick pelt. God, he was gorgeous.

Her breath caught in her throat. He was lying beside her on his side, his body curved protectively around hers, on one elbow, his head propped up by his hand, his eyes drifting possessively over her. The look in his eyes stole her sanity. There was desire, stark and raw that set her blood surging hotly, bringing every single nerve ending in her body alive.

Riley was reluctant to sit up, savoring the feel of his hard muscles, the impressive length and thickness of his heavy erection lying tight against her bottom and the heat from his body warming her. He smiled at her, a flash of white teeth, his strange eyes claiming her. The multifaceted eyes glowed at her with small orange-red flames illuminating the colors of diamonds. His free hand was in her hair, as if he couldn't resist the feel of it. His long fingers massaged her scalp, sending the most delicious sensation through her.

She blinked up at him. "Hello."

He inclined his head. "Good evening. I brought you something."

His hand reluctantly slipped from her hair, and she actually followed the descent of that warm touch with her head, wanting to rub against him more. Was there shyness in his voice? Not quite, but certainly a hesitant charm she found intriguing. She turned over and as he sat up, so did she, stifling a yawn. He traced the pad of his finger down her cheek to her lower lip.

"You have this very tempting lip that makes me want to lean over and just bite," he said very softly.

She found herself blushing. She wasn't a woman who blushed, but then men didn't say blatantly sexual things to her as a rule. Her mother always told her she was intimidating, unapproachable and too striking. The combination, according to Annabel, was lethal when meeting men. Only the bravest would dare to get shot down. Of course mothers had to say things like that—maybe they even believed it. Riley had never bought into her mother's explanations.

His finger caressed her lip, soft brushstrokes threatening to steal her sanity. She had an incredible, and completely out of character urge, to draw that finger into her mouth. He was temptation personified—the serpent in the garden—and she was falling faster than Eve ever thought of eating that apple.

She made a sound, she knew she managed something, but his eyes, with those small red-orange flames flickering with such heat, surrounded by the longest lashes she'd ever seen, were so distracting and intense.

"Do you want your gift?" he asked softly.

Her gaze dropped to his perfectly molded mouth. If she leaned forward just a few inches . . .

"*Sivamet*, are you awake?"

There was laughter in his voice. Riley had it bad, because that laughter resonated through her body, setting every nerve on fire. She managed a nod, completely mesmerized by him. She had wanted out of the classroom, wanted some adventure, but she had never considered she might find . . . *him.*

"This is an ancient tradition," he explained as he gave her a single flower.

The blossom was large, much like a lily but shaped like a star. The petals were open to reveal the inside, the ovary a deep ruby red with two striped filaments. The shape and size of the stigma brought the color flooding to her face—that particular part looked like a very large erection. She knew flowers, her mother grew every kind, but this one, stunningly beautiful, definitely could be used to explain sex.

"Taste it."

She blinked at him. Swallowed. She didn't know why that sounded sexy. Everything he said and did seemed to be sexy.

"Use your tongue to stroke along the . . ."

"Um. I get it." She couldn't possibly.

Her eyes, captured by his, refused to look away. She was caught there, in those mesmerizing eyes, trapped, unable to defend herself. Her tongue darted out and she touched that bulbous head tentatively. At once taste burst through her mouth, vibrant and spicy. Addicting. She licked along the underside and all around the head, seeking more of the elusive flavor.

Dax leaned closer until she could feel his warm breath against her neck. "Do you like it?"

"It's amazing," she admitted. "I've never tasted anything like this."

"The flower takes on the taste of the giver."

His gaze bored into hers, compelling her to get every last drop, the intensity of desire sending a shiver through her body. Why in the world would she find his declaration hot? And why couldn't she stop devouring the fragile flower, craving that spicy taste. The petals, soft velvet, held his scent. She felt surrounded by him with each stroke of her tongue, drawing that nectar into her body.

"Hand it to me." He didn't take his eyes from hers.

Reluctantly she took one last lingering lick along the stigma and handed him back the flower. Holding her gaze, he dipped his head, his mouth in the bloom. His tongue found the filaments and ovary, devouring the nectar collected there. She'd never seen anything so sexy in her life. Her entire body went hot.

"Your taste is addictive." His gaze burned into hers. Blatantly sexual.

A flood of liquid heat added to her discomfort. Tension coiled in her belly, slithered through her deepest core until she crawled with need. She pressed her lips tightly together as he took his time obviously savoring the inside of the flower. His gaze burned over her, those tiny flames growing hotter and wilder as he ate out the night flower.

By the time he lifted his head, his eyes were glowing. "Kneel up for a moment."

She didn't think to question him, too caught up in his sexual web. Whatever the pull of lifemates, the physical attraction between them sizzled and she didn't want to miss one intoxicating moment.

She knelt.

He nodded approvingly. "Sit back on your heels and open your thighs." As he gave her the command, he held the flower cupped in both palms, solemnly, as if it was of great importance.

Heart pounding, she complied. He placed the flower exactly at the junction of her legs, petals whispering against her open, jean-clad thighs.

"Tied vagyok." His gaze for the first time left hers, to drift possessively over her. *"Sívamet andam."* The flames in his eyes leapt high, while the multifaceted diamonds glittered and burned. *"Te avio päläfertiilam."*

His softly spoken words sounded beautiful, but more, she recognized a ritual quality to the presentation and knew he was telling her something important to him. Her entire body had reacted to those nearly whispered words. His voice was a weapon, she decided, especially when he spoke in his own language. The tone was as hypnotic as the words and she found herself straining to understand. "In my language please," she asked.

"*Tied vagyok* means . . ." He frowned, searching for the words in a language he'd just acquired. "'Yours I am,'" he said simply.

Her heart jumped. This amazing warrior, so beautiful, so protective and sexy was *hers*?

"*Sívamet andam* would be, 'my heart I give you.'" He touched her face gently, tracing her cheekbones, her jawline and chin and then back up to the curve of her mouth, as if memorizing every detail.

Blood surged hotly through her veins. She *felt* him inside of her, a part of her. Riley pressed her lips tightly together. Something important was happening, but she didn't know what. She didn't want to say or do the wrong thing. A part of her wanted to run. She had no doubt Dax believed exactly what he was saying—he was giving her his heart. He was larger than life. One of the heroes from a movie who could save the world. She thought of herself as . . . ordinary. Here in the rain forest where there was no one else, she probably looked like a great find, but there was an entire world waiting for him.

"There is only one lifemate for our species, Riley," he said.

Her entire body clenched. Wept. Electricity sang in her veins. She wanted to believe that she could have him, but truly it was absurd. They barely knew one another. He was from ancient times. She was caught in some kind of intense dream she didn't want to wake from.

"What does *te avio päläfertiilam* mean?" Was that her voice? So husky and sensual?

He frowned, concentrating, trying to come up with a suitable translation. "You, wedded wife, my." He shook his head. "'You' is equated to lifemate. *Wife* is your closest word. Your marriage ceremony is the closest to the binding ritual I can find in Gary's memories. I am saying you are my lifemate."

She blinked at him. "Is this a marriage ritual?"

He shook his head, a flash of white teeth sending another surge of desire skittering through her body. His teeth looked strong, straight and just pointed enough that she found herself a little frightened, which only added to the exhilarating experience.

"When the ritual binding words are said, that is equivalent to your marriage vows—but more. That cannot be undone. This is more like . . ." He broke off, clearly searching Gary's memories for an analogy. "This ceremony is important for us both."

He rubbed the bridge of his nose, a gesture she found endearing. "I've courted you in the way of my people and this ritual ensures fertility and acceptance."

Her heart jumped again. Her body burned. "Fertility?" Her voice sounded squeaky even to her own ears.

"Our women don't have many children in spite of the longevity. This flower is important to our preserving our future."

"It is?" She glanced around her, keeping her voice low. Their conversation seemed so intimate—so sexy. As always, she and Dax were secluded away from the others. When he arrived, he always seemed to find a way to isolate her before waking her.

"You need to repeat the words back to me," he said, his voice dropping an octave lower.

He shifted to his knees, opening his thighs wide. Her breath hitched in her lungs.

"Take the flower in both open palms and place it . . ."

"I get it," she said hastily, color creeping up her neck and face.

She tried to pull her fascinated gaze away from the impressive bulge in the front of his jeans. The material was stretched taut, looking as if at any moment it would give way. She'd never been so enamored, sexually frustrated or interested in a man. She'd even dreamt of him. The erotic dreams only added to her shyness with him.

Very carefully, so as not to bruise the petals, she scooped up the flower and, cupping it carefully in both hands, she transferred it to the vee between his open legs. The sides of her hands brushed along his thighs. She could feel his powerful muscles and the tremendous heat emanating from his body. Her hands shook, so she deposited the flower quickly and placed her moist palms on her own thighs.

"You say the words back to me," he encouraged.

She had listened intently to the accent and the words, but saying them aloud to him instead of Gary was intimidating. Not only that, but did she mean them? Was she his? She enjoyed being with him, was intrigued by him and felt safe with him. He had a sense of humor, was intelligent and was a walking god of sensuality. She didn't feel alone anymore. Everything about him appealed to her—but could she trust it? Did she have the ability to hold a man like Dax? When this adventure was over, what would they do?

Dax leaned toward her, his breath warm on her face, a whisper against her lips. "*Ainaak sívamet jutta*, which means 'forever to my heart connected,' is exactly what you are. All these doubts of yours must be laid to rest. There is no other for me. You can turn me away, but you will be condemning me to a half-life. You possess the other half of my soul. You have only to touch my mind, Riley, and you will know me far better than others will know their partners in their lifetimes."

"Don't you think this is happening too fast?"

"I am not familiar with your society or culture," he admitted, "but in mine, we have certainty. You are my other half. There can be no mistake. You restored my emotions and the color to my life. Your soul completed mine. My heart calls to yours. I crave the taste of you and I burn for your body. There is no doubt in my mind."

How could she not respond to that? He made her feel beautiful. Intelligent. The only woman in the world. She wasn't ready to give that up. In any case, what did she have to go back to? Her parents were gone. There was nobody. But . . .

She leaned closer to him, over the flower, her mouth scant inches from his. "I want to do this. I really do, but I'm not certain what you want of me in the future. I have no idea what your world is like, other than vampires, dragons and things with big teeth occupying it."

His gaze moved over her face, branding her, claiming her, burning his possession into her. "We'll take it a day at a time until you're comfortable. I'll explain everything to you as we go along. Anything you're not ready for, I don't mind waiting. It's important to me that you want me in the same way that I want you."

She studied his expression. He felt right to her. For once in her life she was going to let her heart overrule her mind. She bit her lower lip and nodded. Instantly his gaze dropped to her mouth. Her stomach muscles bunched and fingers of arousal teased her thighs. If he could do that to her with just a look, what could he do when he was really touching her?

"Do you remember the words I said to you?"

She nodded slowly, took a deep breath and jumped off the proverbial cliff, praying he'd catch her. *"Tied vagyok."* Her lashes veiled her eyes. "Yours am I."

The flames in his eyes leapt, revealing desire bordering on lust. His chest rippled, all those delicious muscles beneath that thin cotton shirt of his. She felt as if she was free-falling through a storm of glittering diamonds.

"*Sívamet andam.* My heart I give you."

His eyes blazed fire. She felt his gaze burning right through her skin to her very bones, branding her. Her heart matched the rhythm of his. Her breathing followed his. She swore her pulse found his. She felt him breathing in and out. Felt the blood rushing through his veins. She heard his heartbeat in her head.

"*Te avio päläfertiilam.* You are my lifemate."

The moment she uttered the words, Dax poured into her mind. *Warm. Filled with strength.* He was both gentle and tough. Courageous. Images flashed through her mind, his memories, his youth, his centuries of hunting, his stark, utter loneliness, even when he traveled with Arabejila, believing he would never have a woman of his own, believing he had failed his best friend and that friend's daughter. Her heart ached for him. She wanted to be the woman to comfort and love him.

"Now, pick up the flower again and come sit between my legs while I braid the vines and small flowers in your hair. While I braid your hair, you feed me one petal as you eat one. Once this is done, our courtship ritual will be complete and you will have indicated your willingness for me to continue with our relationship."

Riley frowned at him, but without a word scooted closer, turning to face away from him. Her heart pounded with the enormity of what she was doing. She was no young girl to jump into a relationship because she was overwhelmed with physical attraction, and yet she seemed too helpless to stop herself. She wanted him. Craved him. And every minute in his company just seemed to amplify her needs.

He reached out and pulled her into the junction between his open legs, back against him, until she was so close, every muscle seemed imprinted into her skin. He radiated heat, his warmth surrounding her like a blanket. She pressed her lips together as he gathered her long hair in his hands, dividing it into three sections.

A shiver of arousal went through her. She was burning up. Needing him. Was it the flower? The ceremony? His taste? Or the man? Everything was blending together into one potent aphrodisiac. His hands were in her hair and every gentle tug sent electricity arcing and snapping through her. Her need of him bordered on obsession. She broke off a petal and reached behind her with it.

Their eyes met. A flood of liquid heat dampened her panties. She had the sudden urge to reach back and pull his head to hers. The flames in his eyes leapt and burned. His lips parted—those perfectly sculpted, *tempting* lips—and she placed the petal in his mouth. His white teeth bit down, and her stomach clenched in response. Deliberately, eyes still locked with his, she put a petal in her mouth. His taste burst on her tongue, hot and masculine, shattering her every idea of the hunger between a man and a woman. She felt almost desperate for him.

Still locked with his gaze, she saw that same heady combination of lust and hunger flaming in his eyes and then something else crept in—something dangerous and feral. He looked all at once predatory. Beneath his skin she caught the faint lift of scales, almost as if a beast lay in wait. He turned his head slowly but she knew he was aware of everything and everyone around them. Only then was she aware of the approach of Gary and Jubal. Disappointment and frustration rushed through her.

"Another petal for both of us."

His voice was husky. He was just as affected as she was and that made her feel better. He didn't want their time together alone to end any more than she did. She put another petal in his mouth and crushed a second in her own. The second petal only seemed to increase her desire. Knowing Jubal and Gary were approaching fast should have taken the heat out of her skin and the hot surge from her veins, but nothing seemed to dampen her desire for Dax, not even company.

Riley was grateful for the night, although the full moon seemed to turn night into a soft glowing day. She managed to place the last petals into Dax's mouth and her own just as Gary and Jubal reached them.

"Good evening," Dax said pleasantly.

Had Riley not seen his reaction she would never have known he was smoldering with desire for her and not at all happy with the interruption.

"Where did you get that flower?" Gary asked, excitement edging his voice

Dax frowned, the flames in his eyes growing. Clearly he didn't like the demand in Gary's voice.

"Gary and Jubal came here looking for a particular flower," Riley explained hastily.

"It's important," Gary added. "That flower is extinct in the Carpathian Mountains. We've speculated for a while now that it's important for the women's ability to conceive."

Dax shook his head. "I've lost so much time. I thought, from your memories, that Xavier was the culprit behind the loss of our women and children, that it was his poisonous microbes in the soil."

"He definitely attacked your people," Gary admitted, "nearly destroying an entire species over time, but he had some help along the way."

"The flower?"

Gary sighed. "I think the toxins in the soil, the microbes Xavier introduced, killed off the flower. Gabrielle . . ." He stopped, glanced at Jubal and then shrugged. "Jubal's sister is conducting research with me. Some of the ancients have returned to their homeland and when she interviewed them, a fertility ritual with this flower came up again and again. We began to believe there was something to it, so we focused on finding out what happened to it."

"We use satellites and computers," Jubal added. "The good thing about being around a long time is the accumulation of wealth and knowledge so Carpathians can afford all the latest gadgets. We have a couple of kids in the community that are amazing on computers. They've programmed theirs to look for certain trigger words. The man who filmed the ruins on the mountain and sent the pictures to the professor also filmed the flower and posted it on his website, asking if anyone knew what it was. He thought he'd found a new species. Josef, that's our resident genius, picked it up and we came looking for it."

"They can't be native here," Gary speculated aloud.

"Arabejila planted them. She loved them and knew she'd end her life here. She wanted a little bit of home. They only bloom at night, and she planted them up near the village where she planned to live out her days," Dax said.

"Are there a lot of them?" Gary asked. "Enough that we can harvest the roots and transplant them back where they belong? Did they survive the blast?"

Dax nodded slowly. "I can gather them tonight with the roots intact. The larger flower carries the seeds. The dragon covers ground fast. I could be at the top of the mountain and catch up to you fairly quickly."

"You'll need to pack the roots in soil," Riley contributed. "I could go with you to help," she offered, feeling suddenly shy. There was a part of her that was afraid of rejection, but the idea of flying across the night sky on the back of a dragon and spending more time with Dax was irresistible.

Dax rose, reaching down to take her hand and draw her up next to him. "I would enjoy your company very much, Riley."

He pulled her back against his body, the movement so natural she felt as if she belonged. His body felt strong, firm, an anchor in the midst of a storm. Excitement fluttered in her stomach. He reached around her, circling her body with his arms, trapping her against his chest, his hands clasped at her waist.

"You will have to be careful," Dax continued, as though he hadn't just made his claim very public. He was extraordinarily gentle, and so easygoing and natural about it, Riley could tell the movement was a gesture of ownership, but more his need to be close to her.

"Mitro is well ahead of us," he continued instructing the others. "And he's making his way out of the jungle, but he needs information, just as I did. He's been long away from this world and he'll have to catch up. He'll need languages and every bit of data he can accumulate to fit in easily."

"He'll know you're hunting him," Jubal said. "Won't he just run? It seems the prudent thing to do."

Dax shook his head. His thumb slid back and forth in a little caress across the bare skin of her stomach just beneath her shirt. Riley wasn't altogether certain he was aware of that little strumming motion.

"He'll need blood first, and the knowledge of this century is all important to his survival. He will avoid me, and especially Riley. I think he believes she's Arabejila, and he knows she can track him. He'll head for a populated area, but he'll want to slow us down. He'll set traps to kill us and false leads to delay us."

"We'll be careful, Dax. We'll keep moving toward the river." He glanced over his shoulder in the direction of the others. "Weston and Shelton are asking questions why we're not making a straight line for the river. Miguel hasn't said anything to them, but they have GPS."

Dax frowned, clearly not understanding. He touched Jubal's mind and "read" the information and then rolled his shoulders in a casual shrug. "Instruments can be misleading, especially with all this ash in the air."

"Which is why our emergency contact hasn't sent in their helicopter to bring us out," Gary said.

"Avoid any tribesmen," Dax advised. "You can't trust anyone you meet. Riley's given us Mitro's general direction, but she can't know if he's killed anyone else, turned them into puppets, ghouls or programmed them to kill you. We'll be back well before sunrise."

Dax stepped back, taking Riley's hand. "Be safe, all of you. If you call to me, I'll hear you, but I may be too far away to give much aid," he warned.

Jubal gave him a small salute. "Just get us those flowers. We'll handle this."

"Don't be cocky, Jubal," Dax said. "Mitro is unlike any vampire you've come across. I'm a skilled hunter. Even while tracking Mitro, I executed many vampires, none of whom held anything close to Mitro's power."

"Believe me, Dax," Jubal assured. "When it comes to vampires, I'm always ready to pass on them. Any of them, let alone this one. I've seen what he does. I have no desire to meet him, especially without you to back me up."

Dax nodded his head and turned abruptly, as was his way. He was still a little uncomfortable in the presence of so many people, but he liked both Jubal and Gary. They both were men of integrity and they'd fight with him if needed. He read their determination to protect Riley. They also understood the lifemate bond. Riley didn't fully comprehend yet, but she was willing to try with him and he couldn't ask for more.

He tugged on Riley's hand, bringing her under his shoulder. "So are you ready to be a dragonrider?"

Riley's impossibly long lashes lifted and her eyes met his. His breath caught in his lungs. Her eyes glowed at him with excitement. Her cheeks were flushed beneath her flawless skin. She looked more beautiful than ever.

"I can't wait, although I'll admit I'm a little afraid. You'll talk to me the entire time?"

That was his lifemate, ready to meet each adventure head-on. He brought her knuckles to his mouth and nibbled gently. "I'll be with you. The Old One regards you as his family. He won't allow anything to happen to you, either. You'll be safe."

"I know." Riley made it a statement.

Dax walked with her beneath the protection of his shoulder, her hand pressed against his heart while he took her away from the camp and the prying eyes of the others—especially Weston, who had no idea he was placing himself in danger every time he turned his leering, all too hungry gaze on Riley.

Her body moved like liquid grace against his. Flowing. Sensual. The taste of her was still in his mouth. His pulse leapt at the close proximity. He had always known the lifemate pull was strong, he'd witnessed that powerful force between couples, but he hadn't expected the need to be so intense. Still, he was determined that Riley make her own choice. He wanted her to save him because, to her, he was worth saving.

Once they were out of sight of the others, he lifted her in his arms and took to the sky. He needed a large clearing where the dragon could take off and land. He could feel Riley's excitement, the faint trembling of her body, the shimmer of anticipation running through her, and found himself smiling. He couldn't remember experiencing shapeshifting for the first time, or flying, or just being happy. Now that he was with her, he was learning all over again to laugh, to feel. He really was just as genuinely excited for her as she was.

She turned her face up to the wind and laughed out loud. The sound resonated through his body. He could feel the Old One stirring as well. Her laughter was so contagious, that not only was he affected, but so was the dragon. Setting her gently in the tree line at the edge of a meadow, he strode into the center of the large field.

At once he felt the Old One stretch deep inside of him. Strangely, this time, instead of feeling apart from the dragon, he felt a part of him, feeling the intense emotions much more vividly than before. Dax wasn't certain if it was because Riley had restored his own emotions to him, or if he was merging with the dragon to the point they were becoming one and the same. He knew once he made his claim on Riley and said the ritual bonding words, their two souls would be forged together. Could that be happening with the Old One?

None of that mattered. Riley was waiting, and he couldn't wait to share the experience of flying a dragon with her. She could barely contain her excitement, jumping from one foot to the other like a small child. Her eyes shone and her face was flushed. Her lips were slightly parted, an invitation he forced himself to resist. Once they were alone on the mountain, among the field of night star flowers, he would take advantage, but not now, not while she was waiting and anticipating. He wanted to give her this gift.

It is a gift, she said softly, her voice filling his mind with—*her.*

She had a way of pouring into him like warm honey. She gave him a feeling of joy, and he'd never known what that was before. She admired him, respected him, and thought him beautiful and extraordinary. Now that he'd found his lifemate she would know his heart's desire and would always be aware of his every mood.

I feel the same way. Her voice was shy. *It's nice to know I'll always have someone who'll defend me.*

You have both of us, Dax assured. *The Old One and me. He's a part of us, and you're his family now. Like me, he'll defend you with his life.* It was important to him that no matter what happened, how bad things got, she would never have to face any danger alone.

He summoned the Old One, sinking his spirit deep to allow the other freedom. The dragon would have been reluctant to emerge had it not been for the fun of allowing Riley her first dragon ride. His time was long past, and he'd spent centuries content with hibernation in the warmth of the volcano.

Riley held her breath as Dax shimmered into transparency so that she could actually see through him, and then he disappeared altogether. Red and gold flakes sparkled in the moonlight, floating toward the ground all around where he'd been standing. She thought of Dax like that, moonlight and flame, fire and ice, glittering gold and fiery red. He was beautiful. His heart was beautiful. His soul.

Someone else stirred in her mind and for a moment she tensed, looking around her, but the feeling was far too familiar. Too much like Dax.

Our soul. The voice was matter-of-fact. Ancient. Modern. Timeless. A hint of humor crept into her mind.

I see you can still speak, Old One, Dax said. *And you prefer to do so with Riley.*

Now she felt the dragon's laughter vibrating through her mind. He was very amused at Dax's expense.

She loved that Dax found the entire thing as amusing as she did. Nothing ever seemed to ruffle him, and in truth, they were all three very connected.

He is the strong silent type until he gets in a fight and then all thought process goes out the window, Dax informed her.

Riley laughed, the sound taking wing in the night sky. She loved to hear Dax sound so carefree. All he'd known was duty, and, although he was determined to find and destroy Mitro, he took time with her to enjoy the moments they shared together.

The dragon shimmered into solidity. Huge, his great bulk settled, giant wings outspread and fanning, creating wind. Riley clasped her hands together and pressed them hard against her fluttering stomach. The Old One craned his long neck toward her, and even though she was still partially in the trees lining the meadow, his wedge-shaped head nearly touched her. He stared down at her with his opalescent eyes—eyes as multifaceted as Dax's, although where Dax had a volcano's flame flickering behind the gemstones, the dragon's eyes appeared golden in color.

His snout was long, with the upper jaw curving down over the lower jaw, revealing gleaming teeth. He had one horn in the center of his nose, a short, wicked-looking weapon, and two more, just as lethal, beneath his chin. Horns protruded all the way down the back of his head and down his neck, great sharp gold and red spikes protecting his head. She could see just how dangerous the dragon would be in a fight.

His scales were absolutely, incredibly beautiful. Every shade of red from a deep crimson to a pale red covered his body, the plates overlapping to protect him in a fight. Riley touched the lighter-colored ones closer to his belly, a little in awe.

Very politely, the dragon extended his leg to her. Riley's pulse raced, her heart kicking into overdrive as adrenaline rushed through her veins, but she didn't hesitate. She stepped onto the Old One's leg and swung one leg up and over to settle into the small leather saddle positioned just at the neck junction. She didn't have to be told that Dax had provided the saddle for her. There were no reins—it wasn't at all like riding a horse. She found stirrups, more to brace herself with than for any other reason.

Riley grasped one of the long spikes and held on tightly. The Old One didn't need to be told she was ready; their connection was growing stronger, just as her bond with Dax grew stronger with every passing moment. She felt the tremendous strength as the dragon gathered himself to make the leap into the air. Great wings pumped strong and they were aloft.

Riley lifted her face to the star-studded sky, laughing with sheer joy. She had dreamt of adventures, yearned for so much more, *hungered* for that one partner, that perfect man who would fit with her, would give her the courage to embrace life. In this perfect moment she had it all. She felt Dax entwined deep inside of her, holding her close—safe.

The dragon was such an unexpected gift. Dax had given her so many in such a short time. He was everything she'd ever dreamt of. It was impossible not to fall more and more for him. He had spun ties around her heart without her even realizing he was doing it. There was something so incredible about the combination of the gentleness he inevitably showed her and the fierce, explosive warrior he could suddenly become the moment circumstances demanded.

The Old One flew high above the forest, and looking down she could see the damage the blast had done to the mountain. Mudslides had swept away trees in sections, cutting paths through deep forest. Steam vents had opened, and ash covered everything, but this side of the mountain had been spared the worst of it. For all the mess of the ash, looking down on the canopy was incredible. As if reading her mind, and he probably was, the dragon dropped down closer so she could even make out the animals and birds taking shelter in the branches.

The wind tore tears from her eyes and blew her hair back from her face. The sound of her laughter echoed through the skies. She could see why Dax had entrusted the dragon to make the journey. The powerful wings beat down and up, creating a wind of their own, so that dragon and rider streaked through the sky, high above the miles of rain forest. The river looked like a ribbon and the various streams feeding it appeared to be thin threads cutting through the dark forests of trees.

She should have been afraid, but Dax was too close, in her mind, whispering to her, pointing out waterfalls and cool, hidden pools as well as the silvery, moonlit leaves exposed after the wind from the Old One's powerful wings blew the ash away.

All too soon they were back to the mountain, and the dragon circled, descending over a ruin of a village. To one side of the ruins she spotted a sea of stars, petals open, bathing in the moonlight.

Dax. She breathed his name in a kind of awe. *It's so beautiful.*

Yes, it is. Thank you for showing it to me through your eyes.

The dragon banked hard and she clutched at the base of the spike at the junction of his neck, gliding as he approached the field of flowers. She held her breath, afraid he'd land in the middle of them and crush all those swaying night star flowers. Again she had the impression of amusement from the dragon. He settled just to the right of the field without as much as a bump. Very politely he extended his leg.

"Thank you, Old One," she said softly. "That was . . . extraordinary." Riley scratched around the base of the horn on his nose.

The red dragon inclined his head, his eyes glowing affectionately. She stretched, pacing away from him to get a good look at the flowers. The field was tucked around ancient circular stone structures, and raised platforms dotted the slopes, very indicative of the Cloud People. Mist moved around her, enveloping her, nearly obscuring her vision of the ruins. Up so high, where she was born, in the familiar stunted growth of the lush forest, she took a moment to look around, hoping the blast from the other side of the mountain had spared the forest itself.

Thankfully, there appeared to be very little damage. The ruins were intact, a historical treasure for generations to come. The forest itself, the flora and fauna supplied by the heavy mist forming the veil of clouds shrouding the upper mountain. And that field of rare flowers . . . It smelled like . . . *him*. Every breath she drew brought him deep into her lungs. She tasted him on her tongue, setting up that terrible craving.

Riley turned and saw him. Her heart nearly stopped beating. She actually pressed her hand over her heart in a kind of protest. Dax stood tall and straight in the middle of the field of white stars, those glittering flakes of variants of red falling all around him like a shower of gold dust. The moon caressed him with fingers of light, stroking through his blue-black hair and highlighting the color of his skin. His shirt stretched taut across his heavily muscled chest. Arms and thighs were roped with muscle, rippling beneath his casual clothes. Only Dax could manage to look elegant in jeans and a white T-shirt.

The expression on his face as he looked at her robbed her of any sane thought. He looked at her with such a mixture of tenderness and desire her body just went up in flames. In that moment, she wanted him to belong to her as she'd never wanted anything in her life. There was only Dax and the amazing night, the joy bubbling brightly in her after her incredible, impossible ride on the back of a magnificent dragon. After that sensual, sexy ceremony she'd so willingly participated in.

His world was both terrifying and breathtaking. She'd never felt more alive, more sensual, more in tune with herself and the world around her than she did when she was with him. She felt beautiful and intelligent and even brave. It didn't matter that she didn't fully understand what a Carpathian was or what it would entail being with one. She only knew she wanted him to be hers. For once in her life she wasn't going to think every angle to death and be too cautious to make a move.

Dax's glittering eyes locked with hers and she knew she was completely, utterly lost, and she didn't even care.

13

Dax held out his hand to her. Riley couldn't look away from his eyes. The flames burned and leapt, a fiery glow that threatened to consume her. Her very core caught fire, burning in answer, burning for him. The combination of his potent masculine scent surrounding her and his glowing eyes mesmerized her. She took a compulsive step forward, needing him just as much as she needed the air to breathe.

She didn't remember moving after that first step, but she stood in front of him, close, so close she could feel the incredible heat of his body. He burned with desire—for her. It was there in his eyes, in those leaping flames, the way he looked at her as if she belonged to him—with him.

He seemed to know her, know everything about her, know exactly what she wanted and needed. He seemed to have found a way inside her soul, her heart. Everything about him appealed to her. His smile made her world light up. He gave her courage and made her a better person. She'd fallen for him like the proverbial ton of bricks.

His hand cupped her chin, turning her face up to his. His gaze burned through her, branded her, stamping his possession into her very bones. The air refused to leave her lungs. She found herself staring up at his chiseled, perfect face, a little lost.

She couldn't hide anything from him. He knew her every innermost thought. She felt vulnerable and exposed, caught in a bright spotlight, but she didn't want to escape. He knew everything about her, what she wanted, who she was, what she stood for. Her deepest fears—and none of it mattered to him. Why should she try to hide that she wanted him with every single fiber of her being? He would know anyway. She wasn't ashamed of it. He was a good man, the only one she'd ever considered giving her body to, let alone her heart.

Dax cupped her face in his hands and bent his head to hers. "You are certain this is what you want, Riley? *I'm* what you want?"

Even his voice, that dark warm molasses, a slow pouring of molten lava into her veins, sent desire spiraling through her body.

Kiss me. She thought it. Whispered it. Merged her mind with his and sent the image. She needed him to kiss her. She'd been waiting all of her life for Dax to kiss her.

Dax's mouth, that oh-so-perfect mouth, curved into a smile. His white teeth flashed. So straight, but definitely sharp enough to take a bite out of her. Her heart leapt toward his. Her pulse thundered in her ears. As his head came down toward hers, the ground shifted under her feet. Her lungs burned for air. He was so beautiful, this man who was so strong, so fierce, yet protective and gentle with her.

His lips brushed across hers, featherlight, warm, so familiar now, a maelstrom of erotic sensation. She could kiss him forever and it would never be long enough.

Dax stroked a caress down her face, his fingers lingering on her smooth skin. She seemed so young to him. He realized in her world, she was old enough to know what she was doing, but he felt very protective toward her.

"Riley . . ." His heart protested, but he couldn't live with himself if he didn't protect her. "You don't have to do this."

"It's what I want," she assured.

She looked at him with stars in her eyes. His belly clenched hotly. She was such a mixture of innocence and temptress.

His thumb stroked back and forth across her stubborn chin. "Once I bind us together there is no going back. It isn't the same as in your world, Riley. You can't choose to be with me to save me from damnation. You have to want to be with me. You have to know what you're getting into. I'm Carpathian, not human. My rules are not always going to be the same as yours. My world is dangerous."

When she would have protested, he laid his thumb over her lips, stilling her. "Riley, I won't be able to take it back once we cross this bridge. You won't be comfortable being apart from me. You can't live in two worlds. Eventually, I'll have to bring you fully into mine with all it entails."

She frowned at him. "Gary told me if you don't claim your lifemate, you're in danger of becoming vampire."

He shook his head. "I will not turn. That is not a consideration in your decision. I do not want you to give yourself to me because of physical attraction, or a sense of duty."

Riley reached up to touch his face, tracing the lines there with a featherlight touch he felt all the way to his bones.

"Silly man. How can I not want to be with you? We fit. Can't you feel it?"

Dax took her hand and pressed a kiss into the center of her palm. "There is no other for me. I know you're the one. But we're talking about a different world. You see one side of me, *sivamet*. You don't look very carefully at anything else. You don't want to see."

"That doesn't mean I don't know it's there. I'm choosing to enter your world slowly, but I know it's right for me. What do I have to hold me? A career I'm no longer enamored with? I have no family. I feel alive when I'm with you. I want this, Dax, for myself. I hear what everyone says when they sit around the campfire. They're afraid of you, not Gary and Jubal, although even they're leery, but I'm inside your head. I'm safe with you."

He tried one more time, but already his heart sang, his blood surged and he allowed himself to believe. "It won't always be easy. *I* won't always be easy."

"I'll take one step at a time and as long as you're patient with me, we'll get there," Riley assured.

Dax curled his fingers around the nape of her neck and drew her closer. "You don't lack for courage, do you?"

"Actually I do," she corrected. "You seem to make me much braver."

"It will take great courage to come fully into my world, Riley," he cautioned.

He bent his head to hers because it was impossible to resist her any longer. Every cell in his body cried out for her. His mouth found hers. He took his time, resisting the urgent need sweeping through him like a tidal wave. He kissed her gently, pouring himself into her, his need of her, his love of her, his knowledge that she was his world and he would always, *always* stand for her.

Her mouth was sinfully delicious. Hot and velvet soft. He could kiss her for an eternity, over and over and never come up for air. The wind played a song over his body, fanning that relentless fire smoldering in the pit of his belly. Crimson-golden flames rose, leaping to race beneath his skin, spreading like a firestorm through him.

Dax sucked her lower lip into the hot cavern of his mouth, groaning softly with need. His teeth tugged her lush lip, biting gently, showing restraint when he wanted to devour her. She was trembling, her breath coming in shallow, ragged gasps. Her eyes, when he pulled back to look at her face, were enormous, watching his every move. He could hear her heart pounding, her blood pumping so fast through her veins it was a wonder her heart hadn't burst.

Riley stared up at Dax. Flames leapt and burned in his eyes. His skin glowed crimson and gold, radiating light, as if deep inside beneath the hard frame, a fire raged. He looked absolutely confident and so beautiful she couldn't believe she hadn't conjured him up in a dream. He was the hottest, sexiest man she'd ever come across. Just looking at him made her weak, desire lashing inside her belly with curling hot licks.

Gently he ran his fingers down her cheek to the corner of her mouth. "I want you so much, Riley, even my deep slumber was disturbed by the thought of the things I want to do to you."

Deep inside, her muscles clenched tightly, arousal teasing her thighs and breasts. His eyes glowed, mesmerizing her. The fire leapt wildly behind the many facets so instead of one, there were multiple flames burning with a mixture of lust and such intense hunger a shiver of fear slipped down her spine.

"There is no one safer in this world from me, than you, Riley," he assured, a hint of tenderness creeping into his voice. "I would never harm you."

He cupped her chin, his thumb sliding back and forth across the small dent there hypnotically. She couldn't look away from him, away from that perfect mouth with his lengthening teeth. He made no attempt to hide his teeth or his desire from her. Her heart slammed hard in her chest.

Dax laid his hand over her breast, exquisitely gentle. "Let your heart hear mine, *sivamet*. Mine calls to yours, allow yours to answer."

Her heart felt as though it was being squeezed in a vise. His voice was smoky, velvet soft, playing along her nerve endings. And his palm, barely there, curving around her left breast left her lungs burning for air.

"Take a breath," he advised, his voice wrapping her up in sheer seduction.

Riley tried to do what he said, inhaling when he did, exhaling to keep from fainting at his feet. Never in her life had she been so affected by a man. He was so in control and she was both terrified and desperate for him.

I am not altogether certain I'm fully in control, he confessed. The words brushed against the inside of her mind, a slow molasses that poured into every shy and lonely crack, filling her with anticipation. *And desperation does not begin to describe how much I want you.*

Her gaze locked with his. Those flames burned intensely—for her. Her heart settled into the rhythm of his. Her breathing followed his. He was her anchor as he led her into an unfamiliar world.

"I want this, Dax," she said as firmly as her trembling body would allow. She meant it. The shivering was a mixture of fear and anticipation.

He waved his hand, and in the middle of the field of night flowers, there, in the veils of mist on the mountain where she was born, was a large four-poster bed, draped in white. She recognized the canopy as one from a picture she'd shown her mother from a magazine when she'd been a teen. The bed was just as beautiful as the one in the photograph, the wood a deep golden hue and carved with waves and whorls.

Dax took her hand and led her through the flowers, the scent of him, so potent, surrounding her, making her a little light-headed. Deep inside her most feminine core, the ache was sweet and terrible, as she wound through that narrow trail to come to stand by the side of her fantasy bed.

He bent his head, his mouth finding hers with urgent demand even as his hands slipped to the hem of her shirt. His kiss left her dizzy with need. When he lifted his head, he slowly pulled her shirt off, leaving her standing in her lacy lavender bra. She shivered as the mist touched her skin. Dax stepped back, looking down at her with his blazing eyes, and at once she was warm, the temperature in her body soaring in spite of the cool vapor surrounding them.

He brushed his skin over the swell of her breasts. "You're so beautiful. Your skin is unbelievable, soft and flawless." He breathed the words. "I lay awake, unable to move, my body locked in stone, and I went over and over what I hungered to do to you. I knew every inch of you. I want to taste every inch of you, kiss every inch, claim every inch."

Riley drew her breath in swiftly. Every move he made, everything he said, the *way* he said it in that hot, sexy voice, even the way he looked at her, made her weak, left her body damp and throbbing. She was more than willing to give herself to him in any way that he wanted.

"Te avio päläfertiilam," he whispered softly in his own language. His hand found the scrunchy in her hair and pulled it free from the end of her long braid. "You are my lifemate." His fingers tugged at the weave until her hair cascaded to her waist in a long flowing waterfall of blue-black silk.

The timbre of his voice changed as he spoke in the ancient language. The words sounded like a command, the deep masculine voice coming from somewhere inside of him. As he spoke everything in her responded, a flight-or-fight instinct, yet at the same time, her inner muscles clenched tightly, a spasm of sensuous pleasure she couldn't prevent.

He bunched her hair in one fist, pulling her head back as his mouth came down on hers, demanding entrance. He swallowed her soft gasp as she stroked her tongue along his a little tentatively. He pulled her closer, his other hand shaping her body, smoothing down her back to the curve of her buttocks, his palm sliding over her rounded cheek to press her even closer as he pushed his heavy erection against her. A small keening moan escaped her throat.

A part of her was still terrified of what she was doing, especially when she could feel his lengthened teeth with her tongue, or scraping along her skin ever so gently. She knew he was using restraint, going slow for her, but her body was raging at her, desperate for his possession.

Dax feathered kisses from the corner of her mouth, across her jaw to her chin. His teeth nipped at the small dent there. *"Éntölam kuulua, avio päläfertiilam."* He said the words against her chin, his voice deep and commanding.

"I claim you as my lifemate," he translated as his hands slipped around to unlatch her bra. He drew the lace from her body and tossed it aside. His heated gaze dropped to her exposed breasts, his breath catching in his lungs.

Standing in front of him, half naked, with the way he was looking at her, made Riley feel both wanton and sexy. She reached up and traced the lines in his face, the shape of his jaw and his contoured lips.

"You truly are the most beautiful man I've ever seen," she admitted.

He cupped her breasts in his hands, his thumbs brushing her nipples before he dipped his head and ran a trail of fire from her chin down her throat to the tips of her breasts. His mouth was hotly erotic, tugging and pulling, his tongue stroking, teeth scraping gently. Just when she thought her legs would give out, he feathered kisses down her ribs to her flat stomach.

"Ted kuuluak, kacad, kojed." His tongue swirled around her belly button and then dipped inside her. Those crimson-flamed eyes looked up at her as he translated. "I belong to you."

Her heart stuttered at his declaration. The idea of Dax belonging to her was an incredible rush. She brushed her fingers through his closely cropped hair. She loved how his thick hair stood in spikes, yet felt as soft as down.

Dax went to his knees, hands at the waistband of her cargo pants, undoing the button while his smoldering gaze held hers captive. She couldn't breathe again, the sight of him kneeling in front of her, looking at her as if he was going to devour her any minute sent her body into a melting pool of feminine arousal. With almost languid movements, he unzipped the pants and slipped his hands inside, hooking his thumbs in the waistband to slowly slide them from her body. He took her lacy lavender panties right along with the cargo pants, leaving her body fully exposed and vulnerable to him.

Where had her boots gone? The thought was fleeting. She knew she had them on, but suddenly her feet were bare and she was naked. His teeth sent little stinging caresses from her navel to her hip where his tongue found an intriguing indentation and remained there for a few moments, indulging his whims and driving out any questions she might have had. Who could possibly think while he was kissing and licking her belly and hip bones, his hands kneading and massaging her buttocks?

"*Élidamet andam.* I offer my life for you."

His hands went to her legs, pushing them apart, and he ran his tongue up the inside of her left thigh, while that soft, spiked hair brushed up her right.

She was not going to survive. Riley gripped his shoulders, keening softly into the night. She threw her head back as her body pulsed and throbbed. His mouth left little flames up and down both thighs, his teeth nipping, his tongue easing the sting while she held on to her sanity by a thread.

He raised his head, his hands on her bare hips, his warm breath teasing the vee of curls at the junction of her legs. *"Pesämet andam."* Still retaining possession of her hips, he stood, fully clothed, making her feel all the more vulnerable and sexy. "I give you my protection." His hands slid to her waist and he walked her backward until the backs of her knees hit the bed and her legs buckled.

Dax guided her down to the bed, helping her to lie on her back. Riley felt caught in an erotic dream. His hands were gentle as he positioned her on the soft silken sheets, but so firm and strong, she felt as if she couldn't move, her body molten lead, heated beyond the ability to do anything but wait in desperation.

Above her, the mist hovered like a white blanket, swirling into shapes of glittering stars, great constellations untouched by the thick ash that still hovered in the air just beyond the clouds of vapor. She knew Dax had created that beautiful outdoor ceiling for her. The wind touched her heated skin, the cool brush against her burning skin only adding to the urgency of need.

He grasped her ankles and pulled her legs apart, exposing her most vulnerable entrance to him. Again, his hands were gentle, but his grip unbreakable should she have tried to twist away. Her gaze jumped to his face.

"Uskolfertiilamet andam." He swept his shirt over his head and tossed it away. "I give you my allegiance."

Riley felt her heart jump toward him in response to his declaration. Something inside of her shifted. She could feel the difference, but there was a roar in her ears, blood pounding in tempo with his.

One hand shackled her ankle, holding her still as he shed the rest of his clothes with a single thought as most of his kind usually did. Her gaze drifted from his face to his broad chest and flat stomach, lower still to his thick, long erection.

Her eyes widened; her skin went from raging hot to ice-cold and then back to hot again. Both fists curled into the sheets to hold herself still as he lowered his head to kiss her calf. His lips felt cool against her skin, but sent those fingers of arousal skittering up her thigh. She nearly pulled her leg away, but his grip held her firm. His mouth moved higher, his kisses interspersed with little nips of his sharp teeth and languid licks from his velvet tongue.

He paused for a moment, his lips against her inner thigh, his hair sliding over her damp opening so that streaks of lightning arced through her. *"Sívamet andam."* His eyes met hers. "I give you my heart."

Air rushed out of her lungs. Besides being the sexiest man alive to her, the sincerity in his voice—in his eyes—mesmerized her. There was something much deeper, a tenderness, that made her weak. He was handing over his heart into her keeping. The idea of it was humbling to her. Dax was an ancient warrior, a different species altogether, more feral and powerful than the animals and yet he was giving himself into her keeping.

He turned his head, a lazy languid motion, as if he had all the time in the world when she was clawing at the sheet and tossing her head, her body no longer her own.

"Your scent is intoxicating," he whispered against her mound, his warm breath adding to the tension coiling tighter and tighter.

He was killing her slowly. Slowly. Every word he said. Every move he made. His touch. His mouth. His kisses. The feel of his body, so hard and unyielding against the softness of hers. He inhaled deeply once more and she realized that as the flowers in the field had taken on his scent for her, the strange petals held her scent for him.

He lifted his head to look down at her, those red-orange flames tinged with gold now. She could see stark, raw hunger stamped in the lines of his face. So sensual. Her entire body seemed to clench, waiting, anticipating. She held her breath. Her heart seemed to stop.

"Sielamet andam." The flames in his eyes leapt and burned with a fiery glow. "I give you my soul."

She was burning now, her head tossing back and forth on the sheet. She had his heart and soul. His allegiance. She wanted his body as well. Right. Now.

"Please, Dax," she whispered, a plea, a prayer.

"You have to be ready for me, *sivamet*. I want only pleasure for you for your first time."

"I am ready," she nearly sobbed. Her hands went to his hair, tugging on those silky spikes, trying to bring him over the top of her. Everything in her ached for him, pulsed and throbbed and demanded him. The tension coiled tighter and tighter, the pressure building until she thought her body might just implode.

She felt his tongue swiping over her and she bucked mindlessly. He clamped one arm firmly around her hips to hold her still.

"So impatient. Don't move."

"You're asking the impossible," she gasped.

He lifted his head just enough to give her one look of reprimand. His eyes burned over her, nearly all red now, glowing with a fire threatening to burn out of control.

Riley curled her fingers tighter in his closely cropped hair, holding on for all she was worth. She truly didn't think she would survive the gathering pressure, the intensity of the heat. Beneath the layer of his skin she caught the impression of scales and, like his eyes, his skin was fiery red. The temperature of his body, like hers, had gone soaring, as if both of them had caught fire. The red-gold dust from those scales rained down around them.

His mouth touched her again, his tongue stroked wickedly, and then stabbed deep. She nearly convulsed, bucking, her hips jerking in spite of the restraint of his arm. Her muscles clenched hard. A small keening wail escaped. He began a slow, leisurely assault, tongue and teeth, driving her out of her mind. Sounds escaped his throat, hot and desperate, as if he couldn't get enough of the taste of her. His arms tightened, holding her still as he licked and sucked and took small nips with teeth while she writhed under him, her head tossing and her body spilling more and more hot cream into his mouth. Pleasure gripped her stomach, rising sharply as he pushed a finger into her.

I'm not going to survive. Fear skittered through her mind as her body coiled tighter and tighter. He was so sexy, hot beyond her imagining, and there was no possible way she could keep up.

Hold on to me. His voice was rough with stark lust.

Dax lifted his head, possession in his glittering eyes. Her stomach spasmed as he wedged himself between her thighs, lifting her hips, positioning himself at her entrance. She could feel him tight against her, so hot and thick, velvet over steel. A small sobbing plea escaped. She couldn't wait another moment.

His fingers gripped her hips as he slowly, inch by slow inch, began to enter her. He threw his head back, his face a mask of raw pleasure.

"*Ainamet andam.* I give you my body."

Dax fought for control. She was scorching, wrapping him in fire, so tight he wasn't certain he would fit. Very reluctantly, her tight muscles gave ground, allowing his invasion, a slow, exquisite submission.

"*Sívamet kuuluak kaik että a ted.*" He bit out the words while sensations poured over him and into him. He held himself still when his body demanded he pound into her, but she needed a moment to adjust. "I take into my keeping the same that is yours."

He meant every word. Binding ritual or not, the words meant more to him than ties between them. She would be his treasure, cherished, protected and loved above all else. Her heart was his. Her soul. And her body, this beautiful instrument of a pleasure he had never conceived existed. He set his teeth as he pushed deeper, feeling her muscles reluctantly unfolding like the petals of the flowers surrounding him until he was lodged against her thin barrier.

He wanted to give her such pleasure she would never regret her choice. He shifted, blanketing her, the movement causing her to gasp and writhe under him, her muscles gripping him with a fiery passion. He stroked a caress over the swell of her breast. Again her sheath tightened, nearly strangling him with pleasure.

She was saving his soul with her decision, no matter what he'd told her. He might never turn vampire, but her gift was even more important to him because she *chose* him. She followed him into an unknown world, one of danger when she was apprehensive and fearful. She had put her faith in him, trusting him when he'd been in danger of losing faith in himself and the world he'd fought so hard to maintain. She had no idea what she meant to him, but he would never let her down, and her pleasure was just as important to him as her safety.

Riley's hands found Dax's biceps, feeling the coiled strength there. His hard flesh filled her, stretched her. The slightest movement he made sent streaks of fire racing over her skin and lightning arcing through her body. His lips traced a path over her breast, drawing the creamy, aching mound into the heat of his mouth, suckling strongly, his tongue lashing, and his teeth grazing her nipple. The sensation drove her crazy, pushing her need past desperation.

"Dax, more. I need more." He had to stop the coiling pressure building, always building with no relief.

He raised his head for one moment, those multifaceted eyes glowing fiercely with a thousand flames. He opened his mouth to reveal the long, sharp teeth. Her breath caught in her lungs. The teeth sank deep, right along the swell of her breast, while his hips surged forward, breaching her thin barrier. Pain lashed through her body to give way instantly to near ecstasy.

Riley's body bowed, the soles of her feet finding the mattress for leverage as she rose to meet the thrust of his hips. Her fists doubled in his hair, holding him to her, while her blood flowed into him, locking them together in the way of his species. He was everywhere, in her body, her mind, wrapping himself in her heart, while the scent of him invaded every one of her senses.

As merged as closely as they were, she could taste herself, feel the explosion of pleasure in him as her blood filled his cells and organs. His already large erection grew even thicker, stretching her more. Fire streaked through him, her feminine sheath wrapping him in a strangling, velvet soft, fiery grip, milking and squeezing, as he thrust deep and hard with each stroke, bringing both of them closer to that free fall.

Sensations tore through her, the combination of his pleasure with hers pushing her higher still. Heat seared her, scorched her. The tension just stretched out more and more, with no end in sight. She clutched his shoulders, nails digging into his flesh as she tossed wildly beneath him.

Dax reluctantly lifted his head, watching her blood seep from the two pinpricks over her breast and trickle down the creamy slope to her taut nipple. Her chest rose and fell as he followed that enticing trail, his body slamming harshly into hers again and again as he indulged himself. Finally, he closed the small wounds with his tongue.

"Ainaak olenszal sívambin." He uttered the words in a roughened, husky tone, stilling, refusing to give either of them relief. He was close to growling, the pleasure in his body one he'd never conceived of. "Your life will be cherished by me for all my time."

She was nearly mindless, tightening her muscles to grip him. Through the connection of their minds, she knew he was on the very edge of his control.

He slipped his arm beneath her head, his eyes all fire now, burning over her like a brand. "Be still."

She panted, her hips unable to obey, her muscles clamping around him, desperate for release, her head tossing wildly. She couldn't be still, no matter what he said. She strained upward, but he kept her immobile as he lifted one hand to his chest. With one diamond-hard nail, he opened a thin line along the heavy muscle over his heart.

"Take what I offer, *sivamet.* Come closer into my world."

Her eyes widened. She stared at him in shock. Still, and it shouldn't have been, he looked so erotic, hot and sexy, there in that open field of flowers, with his hard body and ruby red drops of blood summoning her. She nearly shook her head, but she was mesmerized by the sight.

"Please," she whispered. Her body was on fire. She needed release, but she wasn't certain the plea was for him to take her over the edge. The temptation of tasting him was a dark whisper she was finding hard to ignore. The idea of drinking his blood should have been repugnant, not erotic, but her mouth could already taste him. His scent was everywhere, and her body was hot and needy.

"You have to make the choice on your own, Riley," he said implacably. "This is the way to bring you closer to my world, and you have to know it's truly what you want." Cradling her head in the crook of one arm, he gathered her hips with the other and thrust deep.

Riley could feel his thick, hot shaft like a steel brand spreading fire through her. She knew flames burned in him. She could see the glow beneath his skin, in his eyes, the scorching heat of his body. Every inch of his hard flesh as it buried deep in her sheath spread those flames into her. She caught fire and burned. There was no end in sight. She moved, and he stopped.

A sob escaped. She needed him. Wanted him.

You hunger for me.

A bead of blood trickled over the muscle of his chest to the edge of his flat, hard nipple. Her gaze followed it, her tongue sliding over her lip. He wouldn't let her hide from the truth. Deep in her veins she could feel a throb, every bit as strong as the terrible ache in her body. She remembered the taste of him in the flower and that intoxicating scent of his, amplified a thousand times by the field of flowers surrounding her. She couldn't deny what he whispered was true, but human inhibitions held her back.

I feel your hunger beating at me.

His voice was seduction, let alone that harsh, jackhammer stroke he drove into her and once again stilled. Desperate, before she could think what she was doing, she licked at that thin trail of crimson with her tongue. His taste burst through her like champagne. She followed the trail back to the source, her mouth latching on, tongue dipping and stroking.

His groan was a rough, sexy sound. He threw his head back, whispering to her, helping her now that she'd made the decision. The essence of his life poured into her, filling her, restructuring, nurturing.

"*Te élidet ainaak pide minan.* Your life will be placed above my own for all time," Dax bit out between clenched teeth. His body shuddered with the effort to hold back. His skin gleamed red and gold, scales showing beneath.

Riley stared up at his face. Lines of sheer lust etched deep, sending spirals of arousal spinning deep. The taste of him hit her hard, an aphrodisiac that added to the firestorm in her body. She would never get enough of him, not his taste and not his body.

Enough, sivamet. *You cannot take too much at once. Just enough for an exchange.*

She heard his words as if from a great distance. Her blood roared in her ears. She wasn't certain what he meant, but she couldn't stop. Dax was forced to gently insert his hand between her mouth and his chest.

"*Te avio päläfertiilam.*" He caught her hips in both hands, sliding her closer, pushing her legs over his shoulders. "You are my lifemate."

With a small sob she fell back, her gaze locked with his. Her body was threatening to explode, so tight she was afraid she'd shatter into pieces. That movement of his body had his shaft stroking and caressing deep inside her. Brushstrokes of white-hot fire. She was so close to that edge, yet she couldn't tumble over.

"Dax." She cried out his name, reaching for him, her mind hazy, needing him to take her over the cliff with him. "Please. I can't . . ." She didn't know what she needed from him, only that she was burning from the inside out.

Dax surged forward, a steel spike of living flesh, burying himself over and over. Deep. So deep. She swore she felt him piercing through her stomach. Over and over. So hard. He pistoned into her, driving deeper still until she was certain he found his way into her soul. There was no pause, no moment to catch her breath, just that relentless pounding at her body.

Riley dug her nails into his arms, her head tossed mindlessly, her lungs burned for air. Deep in her mind, she heard herself scream. Her mouth was open, but no sound actually emerged. Her body clamped down hard on his. The orgasm ripped through her, shattered her, melting bones and muscles, burning cells and tissue in an explosion of shocking pleasure. She felt Dax erupting much like a fiery volcano, pulse after hot pulse while her body seemed to shatter into a million pieces.

Dax slumped over her, breathing raggedly, his heart pounding so hard she could hear it. She couldn't move, her body still alive with pleasure, but leaden, her arms so heavy she couldn't find the strength to move her hands into that thick pelt of hair she loved touching.

Dax turned his head into her neck. *Ainaak sívamet jutta oleny.* The whisper filled her mind. "You are bound to me for all eternity."

Another shock wave of pleasure washed through her. She shuddered, her body climaxing again and again. She could feel something different inside. She was . . . more. Evolving. Tied to him. She never wanted to let him go. It seemed as if there were millions of tiny threads weaving them together.

Dax brushed kisses over her eyes. "*Ainaak teräd vigyázak.* You are always in my care."

Her body shuddering, Riley forced herself to find the energy to lift her hand to his face. His impossibly long lashes were wet. She touched the tips gently.

He turned his head to catch her fingers in his mouth, sucking gently before releasing her. "The binding ritual is our version of marriage, only more permanent. It binds your soul to mine. Perhaps I should have waited until you really have more of a concept of what you're getting into. It's no excuse, but I don't want to be alone again, Riley."

"Neither do I," she assured, blinking back tears. "I want this. No matter what happens, Dax, I choose to be with you. You warned me there would be no going back. I'm prepared for that."

He rolled over, taking her with him, so that she sprawled across his chest. Riley buried her face in the junction between his neck and shoulder, exhausted. She was certain when she was alone, she would be aghast at the enormity of her decision, but she clung to him, one hand in his hair while the other smoothed over his chest.

Dax wrapped his arms around her, holding her tightly. "Are you going to sleep?"

"Yes. You can gather the flowers for Gary and Jubal," she said. "I'm not moving for the rest of the night."

Dax laughed softly and brushed a kiss on top of her head. "As you wish, my lady."

14

Riley woke just before sunset. How she knew it was only minutes away, she wasn't certain, but there was no doubt in her mind *exactly* when the sun would sink from the sky. She thought the continual drone of the insects might have woken her, the sound seemed so amplified in her head she clapped her hands over her ears. Birds flitted overhead in the trees, the squawking and chattering much louder than normal as they prepared for a long night of predators hunting them. *Everything* was so much louder, including several of the men's snoring.

Her hand hurt, and when she lifted it to inspect it, it was quite swollen. A spider, or some insect had clearly bitten her and she had an allergic reaction. She couldn't remember having allergies to bites, but in the rain forest, she knew the insects could carry all sorts of venom. She would have to do something about it. Her first aid kit was in her backpack.

Annoyed, she sat up in her hammock and surveyed the campground. Her body was deliciously sore in places she hadn't known she had. Her heart was pounding a little bit too hard at the enormity of what she'd done—giving herself to Dax. She wasn't irritated with anyone but herself.

She had to be honest, she'd practically thrown herself at him. He'd even tried to talk her out of it. In truth, counting actual days, she'd barely met him, but she felt as if she knew him better than she'd known anyone in her life. Sharing his mind, she learned so much about him.

Riley bit down hard on her thumb, scraping her teeth back and forth along the nail, trying to reconcile her staid little life with her behavior in the rain forest. Was she going to go all stupid and regret such an amazing, incredible, *hot* first time? It wasn't as if she was in high school. She was a college professor for heaven's sake. If she wanted to have sex with the hottest vampire hunter in the rain forest, she certainly didn't have to be ashamed of it.

Was she ashamed? *Hell* no. She would never regret giving herself to him, but it hadn't been just her body. With a little sigh she shoved long tendrils of hair that had worked their way out of her braid away from her face. She blushed at the memory of Dax pulling out the thick weave, at the memory of his hands in her hair. He had been the one to braid it again, right after he'd collected the flowers for Gary. She'd remained sprawled out naked on the bed, too exhausted to move. Again she felt the color rising into her face.

If it had been just sex she'd had with Dax, she wouldn't be so nervous. She'd given him her heart and soul. Basically she'd jumped off a cliff and had no idea if there was a safety net. He'd shatter her if he didn't feel the same way about her that she felt about him. And there it was. The entire problem. He professed to feel the same way, and last night, she'd been in his mind and had been so certain, but today, she could hardly bear being away from him.

The separation clawed at her. She found she couldn't turn her mind away from him. She felt as if she were holding her breath, waiting for his arrival. She detested that the women in her family were so close to their mates that they wanted to be with them every moment. She had made herself into an independent woman, well educated, able to take care of herself. She spent time with friends and truly enjoyed their company. She wasn't dependent on a man for fun, or for her livelihood. Her ancestors had all died within weeks of their husbands—even her own mother.

Riley had been so determined she would never be the same way and yet . . . she was *obsessed* with Dax. She *needed* to see him. She rubbed her hands over her face again, trying to think clearly, to assess the situation. There was no going back and if she could, she knew she wouldn't. She was in love with him, more than in love. The moment his mind had shared hers, she was lost. There was no being alone ever again. She had only to reach for him and he was there. His devotion to her was easy to read. Dax didn't attempt to hide his need or his admiration of her. For him, there truly was only Riley.

She pulled the first aid kit from her pack and picked through it until she found the allergy cream. So why was she upset? She had no real idea of what she was getting into and she always, *always*, had a plan. Her mind just worked that way. She needed stability. A goal. She didn't fling herself headfirst off a cliff and have no idea how she was going to land. She didn't give herself to a man. No, not a man—a Carpathian who considered humans a food source. Ever since she'd set foot in the rain forest, things had been out of control.

She smeared the cream over her swollen hand, sighing as the wind shifted, slightly teasing her face, telling her she wasn't alone. "Weston," she greeted without turning her head. Carefully she put everything back in the first aid kit and stowed the kit in her backpack. "I thought we had an agreement. You were going to stay away from my sleeping area. I like privacy."

"I wanted to talk to you, before the others got up."

Riley sighed and turned her boots upside down to make certain nothing had crawled into them in the middle of the night. She had to admit Don Weston sounded conciliatory, but still, she braced herself, grateful she had the gun Jubal had given her. She even went as far as to feel for it where it was hidden in her sleeping bag on the hammock. "Sure, what is it?"

"Look, I know you don't like me. And I have to admit, you have a good reason. I drink too much when I have to go out to these places. I hate the wilderness. I hate everything about it, especially the bugs. I know I was a jerk, but it was supposed to be harmless fun and it gives me a certain image." Weston scowled and toed the buttress root of the tree closest to him. He glanced over his shoulder toward the other men and lowered his voice even more. "This is going to come as a big shock to you, but I've got a couple of sisters . . ."

Riley's head went up and she stared at him, very surprised. She couldn't equate this man with a mother let alone sisters. "I never suspected."

Weston looked back toward Mack Shelton and pushed at the rotting vegetation with the toe of his boot. "Yeah, I have sisters, and I keep them away from my friends."

"So that's why you came with us up the mountain instead of turning back with the professor. It seemed so out of character for you," Riley said.

He scowled at her, shrugged and gave a little sigh. "Let me just get this out. This man, Dax, I know you all said you knew him from before, but I don't think you really know what he's like. I talk a good game, and maybe I don't come off as someone you'd trust all that much, but men like that . . ." He trailed off, shaking his head.

Riley slipped the gun from her sleeping bag to her backpack. She began to take her hammock down, needing something to occupy her hands while she listened to Weston's revelations. Besides, as soon as Dax arrived, they'd be on the move again.

"He's all charm and looks great, but he's dangerous. I've seen a few men like him, and they explode into vicious fighters when they're crossed. He's not the kind of man I'd want my sisters dating, that's all."

Riley shoved her hammock into her backpack, took a breath and turned around to face Weston. He was trying to warn her, which was sweet in a way, but he was far too late; she was already lost. She knew Dax was dangerous to her, but not in the way Weston obviously meant.

Electricity arced over her skin and sizzled in her veins. *He* was close. *Dax.* Very close. Her entire body instantly tuned to his. His scent drifted to her on the evening breeze, all the spice and masculinity, the outdoor, wild scent she recognized as Dax. She took a breath and breathed him into her lungs.

At once she felt wholly alive and unbelievably sensual. She was aware of her breasts tingling, her nipples growing taut, the smoldering fire in the pit of her stomach she'd only been dimly conscious of flaring to life. How did he do that? She hadn't even laid eyes on him yet.

She forced her attention back to Weston, managing a smile. "I appreciate the warning, Don. I'll be careful."

How careful? Do you think to resist me now?

The words shimmered into her mind. There was an edge to Dax's voice that both frightened and thrilled her. His fingers slipped over her injured hand. At once the sting was gone. His hard body brushed against hers from behind.

He pushed his hips close so that his heavy erection was imprinted against her body. Strong fingers stroked caresses over her right breast. Her stomach tightened. Her thighs ached. How could he do that when he wasn't even visible?

How is it that you are always surrounded by men, sivamet*? I find I do not like this habit of yours, always to be with other men.*

Now his breath was warm against her neck. His tongue licked along her leaping pulse. Strong teeth bit down on her neck, right over that now pounding pulse. The bite stung, but his tongue eased the ache.

Um, I am traveling with them, she felt compelled to point out. Deliberately she pushed her buttocks back into him. *Or hadn't you noticed?*

Happiness burst through her. He had come. Her stomach settled down, her heart quit pounding. She found herself following the rhythm of his lungs.

How many others have warned you about me?

Sharp teeth grazed the side of her neck a second time and her womb spasmed. Her knees went weak. He definitely wasn't happy to find Weston alone with her in her private little sanctuary cautioning her about Dax. She poured into his open mind. Her hunger for him. Her secret amusement that Weston, of all people, would try to counsel her.

You find him sweet. The last word was uttered with sarcastic contempt.

His teeth bit down a third time, hard enough to take her breath away. But there was that clever tongue, bathing the small wound in healing, numbing saliva. His teeth scraped back and forth over her pulse. Her body went weak in anticipation, weeping in welcome for him. She waited, closing her eyes, needing his erotic bite.

"Riley, are you all right?" Weston asked, a hint of concern creeping into his voice. "I really didn't want to upset you. I felt it was important that someone say something to you."

She startled, forgetting for a moment that Don Weston was still close by.

Answer him so he goes away. He's very uncomfortable in the role of protector. And he lusts after you. He can barely keep his hands off you. It is best for his health if he puts distance between you immediately.

You can't possibly be jealous of Don Weston. That trait seemed so out of character, almost petty, and beneath Dax.

There is no reason to be jealous of a man you do not have regard for. Dax sounded a little arrogant.

It was difficult to think straight with his body so close to hers. His intoxicating scent enveloped her, heightening her awareness of him. *He only came to warn me. He's never once tried anything he shouldn't.*

His teeth, scraping rhythmically back and forth over the pulse in her neck, were very distracting, making it nearly impossible to think clearly. His hands slid up her body, inside her shirt, to cup her breasts. He stood behind her, unseen, his heat surrounding her, his heavy erection pressed tightly against her and all she could think about was having him again and again. Was it possible to fall in love with a man's body?

He is not a good man. He envisions himself as one, but he makes himself believe women want him because he feels he's entitled to them. Sooner or later, he will do harm to a woman and that woman will not be you. There was no mistaking the menace in his voice. *I am a hunter of evil. Human or Carpathian. It does not matter to me. It is my duty to destroy evil where I find it.*

A shiver of fear slithered down her spine. She had known all along that Dax was dangerous, she didn't need Weston to tell her that. He could go from old-world courtly to explosive violence in seconds.

He has sisters.

Dax bit down right in the sweet spot between her neck and shoulder. His body felt as hard as a rock, unyielding, his arms strong, surrounding her. Heat rose around her, seeping from his body to hers. Pressure coiled tighter and tighter in her most feminine core, hunger rising sharp and terrible, an ache only he could assuage.

If I tell you what goes on in his mind when he's around his sisters, you would not be championing him.

"I'm fine, Don," she managed to get out, her voice far too husky. "Thanks for the warning, I'll be very careful. But I do have to pack fast; we need to make the river today."

The smell of food made her slightly nauseous. The others were finishing up breakfast and breaking camp. She really wanted to yell at Weston to leave so she could be alone with Dax before the others were ready to go. She needed to be alone with him. She bit down hard on her lip. She was a grown woman who had no business acting so wantonly.

You're making that up, aren't you? Surely Dax couldn't know such a thing about Weston.

Night fell in soft shades of dove gray, dropping around her like a blanket, but she was still out in the open with only a few trees and that thin veil of protection to shield her. No one could see what Dax was doing, and so far she had managed to retain some semblance of decency, when all she really wanted to do was strip off her clothes and impale herself on Dax.

Dax's heavy erection burned like a brand along the curve of her buttocks. His hands began a slow, deliberate massage of her breasts, fingers tugging and rolling her nipples while his mouth blazed fire up and down her neck. She had to stifle a moan of sheer pleasure. Sensation swept through her like a tidal wave.

Believe me, sivamet, *I wish that I was. He is a very depraved man. He just hasn't made the last leap to his full potential.*

The moment Weston shuffled off, she allowed her head to loll back on Dax's shoulder, weak with need. Dax's mouth went back to her neck, teeth scraping along her pulse. Her blood surged hotly, every nerve ending screaming for him to bite down. Her breath came in ragged gasps of pure need.

She had no control when it came to Dax. The moment he spoke, or even was near her, her body went up in flames and she threw all decorum out the window.

No one can see. I'm shielding you from their view. Even if they walk over here, they will not be able to see you.

His hands slid down her flat belly to drop to the waistband of her cargo pants. She thought to protest, her eyes flying open, looking around her, but his palm cupped her mound, his thumb finding that hot little button craving attention.

You have to stop. I won't be able to be quiet, she gasped, the tension in her belly winding tighter and tighter. He had barely touched her and she was already so close . . .

The little sounds you make are music to my ears. I need to hear them, he whispered wickedly, his teeth tugging at her earlobe. *No one will hear but me.*

He slipped one finger into her slick heat, his thumb stroking and thrumming, playing relentlessly, driving her higher and higher so fast she couldn't catch her breath.

A keening cry escaped. She felt his burst of satisfaction and a second finger joined the first, stretching her. Teeth sank deep into her neck. The flash of pain tightened her muscles so they clamped down hard on his fingers. Pain gave way to a flood of sensual pleasure so overwhelming she would have fallen had he not been holding her up.

Give me what's mine.

The command filled her mind, nothing less than a demand. His mouth on her, drawing the essence of her life into him, his fingers claiming her, his hand at her breast, tugging on her nipples were all too much. Her body erupted with strong waves, racing up to her breasts and down her thighs. She nearly sobbed his name as the ripples of pleasure flashed through her. His tongue slid across the pinpricks on her neck, to seal the two small holes he'd left.

The moment she could stand on her own, he stripped off her shirt, solidifying right in front of her, his hands already lifting her breasts to his mouth. His mouth was hot, on fire, suckling strongly, his tongue dancing over her nipple. His chest was bare, his skin nearly glowing, all hard mahogany. She cried out, a soft, strangled cry caught in her throat as his mouth tugged and pulled at her breast, teeth skimming her nipple, delivering a tiny sting of pain and easing it instantly with a velvet tongue.

Riley's heart pounded as Dax lifted his head to lock his gaze with hers. She could see the smoldering heat there, the stark hunger. He lifted one hand to his own chest. Her stomach clenched. Her mouth watered. Holding her gaze, he drew a line over his chest with one diamond nail. His hand went to the nape of her neck while the flames in his eyes leapt and burned. He put steady pressure on her until she bent her head to tentatively flick her tongue over the ruby beads seeping from that thin line over his heart.

The moment she tasted him, she knew she was lost. There would never be enough time to spend with him. He made her feel alive. Her body sang when she was with him. Her sense of smell, her vision, everything was so different—so more. She craved him. Was addicted to the taste of him. The world around her faded away, leaving only Dax and his hard body and exquisite taste.

She slid her palm down his chest to his flat, washboard stomach. She absorbed each defined muscle with her fingertips. Women dreamed of a man built like him—and he was hers. He'd given himself into her keeping. Her hand moved lower to find that impressive bulge. Boldly she rubbed gently, reveling in the ability to touch him.

His mind poured into hers, sharing the pleasure her hands and mouth gave him, sharing erotic images in his head. She gasped at what she saw there, at how it made her burn even more for him.

Enough, sivamet. *You do not want to be sick. You have to come into my world slowly. I do not want there to be complications.* To ensure her obedience he slipped his hand between her mouth and his chest.

How could she slow down when she was already on the wild ride? She didn't want to slow down at all, she wanted to burn for him. Go with him wherever he went. Horrified at her obsessive thoughts, Riley stepped back—or tried to. Dax simply glided, his movement fluid.

He caught her chin, forcing her head up. *I woke to your doubts beating at me. You are no more obsessed with me than I am with you. I cannot ever betray you, Riley. You are mine in this life and in all the lives given to us. It will still not be long enough for me.*

His confidence was a turn-on to her. She'd never met a man who could be so completely in charge without being overbearing.

I know this is right, Riley assured. *I know you're what I want.* She had to look away from those burning eyes to admit her failings. She looked down at her boots. *It's hard to believe that I'm the one you really want out of all the women in the world. You haven't really seen any other woman besides me. Wait until you go into a city. Your world was different than it is now. There are so many beautiful women in the world for you to choose.*

Dax smiled down at her, once more forcing her chin up so that her eyes met his. Her heart nearly jumped from her chest there was such tenderness there.

There is only one Riley and she is mine. He bent his head slowly to hers.

Riley watched him come to her, his eyes blazing into hers, his perfect, chiseled lips slightly parted, his warm breath and then his mouth on hers. She gave herself up to his kiss, letting the world tumble away. He kissed her again and again and she found herself melting into him, her body going soft and pliant. His hands skimmed down her spine to the curve of her buttocks to lift and press her tight against his erection. Her breath caught in her lungs, still slightly shocked that he would want her so much he would take her right there out in the open.

Did you doubt I could go long without having you again? Again there was an edge to his tone, as if her uncertainty on awakening reflected on his integrity in some way.

I hoped you couldn't. Although . . . She looked back toward camp. The others were finishing their evening meal and packing to travel.

Dax leaned forward and took her right breast into the heat of his mouth. His fingers tugged and rolled the nipple of her left breast. Her body arched, pushing deeper into the scalding heat. Temptation beat at her. Moisture gathered between her thighs. Clearly, her body was his. There was no resisting that hot mouth and wicked hands.

He lifted his head, and the dark desire burning in his eyes was exhilarating. *Step out of your jeans.* His fingers continued to roll and tug at her nipples.

I have my boots on. She dropped her hands to the waistband of her pants, prepared to at least get them off of her enough to assuage the burning ache between her legs. In any case, she wasn't certain she wanted to be stark naked out in the open even when he assured her she couldn't be seen. It seemed so indecent.

And sexy. You're so sexy.

She had to admit, it was sexy. He made her feel that way, as if he couldn't wait to have her, as if he had to have her or he wouldn't make it through the next moment. Still, being out in the open with people so close, shielded only by a few trees and a swirling fog . . . so wrong. The cool air hit her body, raising goose bumps. She looked down and her boots and jeans were gone. A slow smile curved her mouth.

You're the sexy one. In my world, the women would say you are hot. He was. She'd never been around any other man who could drive out all sane thought until she was only pure feeling.

She was naked standing in just a little grove of trees. She should have been covering up, but instead, her nipples grew harder than ever as she thrust them into his palms, evidence of her desire pulsed between her thighs and arousal teased her thighs and breasts. If Dax could remove clothes so easily, she had no more doubts that he could hide them from the others. She wanted him any way she could have him.

Dax made a sound, a rough and intoxicating growl that sent a spiral of lust teasing her stomach. He bent his head once more to her breasts, cupping the weight of them in his hands, and lifting them to his mouth.

She cradled his head to her, eyes wide open just because she had to see him—she loved watching him. Everything about Dax was sensual, his heavily lidded eyes, the heat glowing beneath his skin, the hot pull of his mouth on her breast. She stood naked, the wind on her body, her skin singing, her blood surging hotly, and a burning ache between her legs. She should have felt exposed and vulnerable in front of him. She didn't have a stitch on, her body open to his, but he made her feel beautiful and his. She loved feeling as if she belonged to him.

Of course you belong to me. Your soul is the other half of mine. You were born for me, as I was born for you.

His hands were everywhere, sliding over every inch of her skin, his mouth devouring her until she couldn't think straight. Long, drugging kisses had her body weeping with need. She wrapped her arms around his neck, tightening her hold on him, feeling possessive, feeling enraptured.

Dax lifted her, until her body slid sensually against his. "Wrap your legs around my waist," he whispered into her mouth.

I'm too heavy. She was tall and very curvy, not at all the average cover model, and she didn't want him to hurt his back.

His laughter vibrated through her like a hot mineral spring. The bubbles found their way inside her bloodstream, bursting and sizzling as she complied with his order.

Now you're just being silly. There was tender amusement in his voice.

His mouth was on hers again, demanding now, the kisses growing wild and possessive, sending flames rolling through her. He kissed her as if he was a starving man, as if she ensured his survival—and maybe she did. His tongue stroked along her lips, pushed into her mouth to tangle with hers. Electricity sizzled through her veins, little shocking waves that left her breathless and needy.

Deliberately he allowed her to feel the edge of his strength, as he held her easily against his chest. *Wrap your legs around me. Hook your ankles.* His fingers found her entrance slick with moist heat. *You're so ready for me.*

How could she not be ready for him? *I'll always be ready for you,* she whispered into his mind, allowing him to see him as she did, so perfect, so sexy she could never resist him.

I love how wet you get for me, but then I want to taste you. Devour you. Lick every inch of you until you're giving everything up to me.

His voice was low and dark, a blend of rough and dangerous that sent another wave of heat curling through her. She laced her fingers together at the nape of his neck and leaned into him, biting at his shoulder because everything he said just made her more impatient for his possession. When he groaned, she turned her face into his neck and bit at him gently. His body shuddered.

Hold on.

Now his voice was hoarse with need. She held on tightly as he lowered her body oh, so slowly. She felt the velvet head, hot and thick pressing tight against her entrance. She tried to press down hard, but his hands refused to allow it. He entered her slowly, inch by deliberate slow inch, holding her absolutely still, while he pushed deeper through her resistant muscles.

Dax groaned as pleasure burst through him. He'd known heat and fire for centuries, but the scorching burn of her fiery, tight sheath was nearly his undoing. He lowered her slowly, savoring the resistance, the way her body gave way to his invasion. Her soft little broken, gasping cries nearly drove him insane. *I want a long slow ride,* sivamet.

He could feel every tight muscle gripping, as he stretched her. The head of his cock was so sensitive, the feeling as close to ecstasy as he figured he was ever going to get. He pushed deeper, giving himself up to the building explosion.

Her eyes stared into his. Glittering. Wild. So much intensity. So much emotion—all for him. He was in awe of her. There was no way to conceal who he was from her, his mistakes. His guilt. His failure. He was a hunter of one of the most lethal monsters on earth and yet she had such faith in him she had bound herself to him. It was humbling and at the same time exhilarating.

She could make him lose control with just those small movements of her body. Those little panting cries. Her mouth curved, a sensual siren, tossing her head, lifting her hips at the guidance of his hands, her sheath suckling at him, wrapping his shaft in white-hot flames.

Riley rose slowly, her hands on his shoulders for leverage, the friction causing him to shudder, fight for his own control. She threw her head back and lowered her body with equal slowness, impaling herself on him, gripping and teasing as if her muscles were fingers fisting his shaft tightly. She threw her head back as she rose again, dragging over him, deliberately making small circles as she lifted herself, driving him wild.

"Is this what you wanted?" she asked, teasing innocence in her voice. She found the rhythm, that perfect, excruciatingly slow rhythm that made her body tighten in anticipation.

His growl sounded more animal than human.

She took her time, finding that if she squeezed her muscles and did slow circles as she rose and fell, his pleasure, along with hers heightened more. Electric sensations sizzled up her belly to her breasts and down to her thighs. Tension vibrated through her body, coiling tighter and tighter, her womb shuddering with her imminent orgasm. Just when she thought she couldn't take any more, that the friction was going to drive her insane, Dax made a rough sound in the back of his throat and flexed his fingers on her hips before gripping her hard.

Dax took control, slamming her body down on him hard and fast, lifting her and dropping her again and again, his velvet spike a piston, tearing through her with a fiery, driven purpose. Her body trembled, and she thrust back, impaling herself as the mind-numbing sensations ripped through her. Her body grasped his, gripped tightly, dragging over him, sending the fiery fingers squeezing in a brutal, erotic grip.

His entire body shuddered, his shaft erupting in a fiery release flooding her sheath so that a series of intense explosions rocked her. Riley held Dax tight for an anchor as her body continued to pulse and throb while she tried desperately to calm her heart and still her gasping breath. She had no idea sex could be so all encompassing.

I'm crazy about you. She made the admission in her mind, feeling shy and exposed.

I'm so in love with you there isn't any way to express it adequately, he returned with his absolute confidence.

Personally, I think you did quite well.

Riley buried her face in Dax's neck, her hands stroking his back possessively. Her body was damp with sweat and she knew she smelled like sin and sex, but it didn't matter. She clung to him, reluctant to let him go, her heart beating with the same rhythm as his. She knew she should put her legs down, but she wanted to hold him as long as she could, be connected physically as long as possible.

"I can't believe you were able to do that and have the strength to hold me up," she whispered. She didn't have the strength to speak in a normal tone.

"There are advantages to being Carpathian," he said smugly. Dax turned his head to brush kisses in her hair. "Your friend is coming this way."

"Can you keep us from his view forever? Maybe we should just stay this way, locked together for eternity," she murmured.

Dax laughed softly, the sound in her mind rather than heard. "Insatiable woman."

"I am." She pressed kisses over his pounding pulse, unrepentant, playfully nipping with her teeth. "I'm trying to distract you."

"You don't find hunting vampires exhilarating?"

She lifted her head to stare into his laughing eyes. He looked so much younger and carefree when he laughed, yet it was so rare for him to do so. Very slowly she dropped her legs until she was standing. The movement shifted him inside of her, sending another ripple of pleasure through both of them.

"Fine, we'll go hunting. But this was much more fun. I don't think the two things are comparable." She gave him a little pout as he slipped out of her.

His mind stroked hers with caresses as with a wave of his hand she was fully clothed, clean and fresh. He was reaching for her pack as if they'd just finished gathering her things when Gary walked up. Dax shifted slightly, positioning his body just a little in front of her to give her time to recover.

"Good evening," Dax greeted. "I trust there were no incidents while I slept."

Gary shook his head. "Everything was quiet. Were you able to find the flowers? To bring enough back so that we can plant them in the Carpathian Mountains?"

Riley laughed at the eagerness in his voice. "We brought you back an entire sack of seeds and roots as well as the flowers intact. I packed them in the soil so they should make the trip, although how you'll get them through customs I don't know."

"I have friends that will do that," Gary said. "I just need to get the flowers to them. They know how important it is. They never have trouble getting anything they want."

Dax looked up, his gaze pinning Gary's. "Carpathians? Your friends are Carpathians?"

Gary nodded. "Yes, they provided us with weapons and gear for this trek. They're our emergency contact. They were waiting to hear from us," Gary said. "We need to make it to a clearing . . ."

"You called them already? When did you do this?" Dax asked. His voice was very low. Smoldering. The last word ended in a long, slow hiss.

Riley stiffened, her heart skipping a beat. He sounded . . . scary. Gary seemed to be used to the sudden change in Carpathian males. He didn't blink.

"We knew they would already be looking for us. As soon as we could get a call out to let them know we were alive, we did. We called at sunset." Gary shrugged casually. "They'll be sending a helicopter to pick us up. They're aware of the injury to the professor, and they'll deal with the others as well."

"What did you tell them about me? About Mitro?" If anything, that low voice, warm as molasses, dropped another octave lower.

"That you were with us, of course, and that a dangerous vampire was on the loose." Gary removed his glasses and looked Dax straight in the eye. "I exchanged blood with you voluntarily. Would you be more comfortable reading my mind? You can get the information a lot more efficiently."

Dax shook his head. "I appreciate that you would allow me to invade your privacy, but until I need to 'see' who we're talking about it isn't necessary. This is more than one Carpathian hunter?"

"The De La Cruz brothers," Gary explained. "They were sent to South America centuries ago. Did you know them?"

"We had lineages, not surnames. I do not recognize such a name. Show them to me."

Gary pictured the images of the De La Cruz brothers in his head in the best detail he could muster. It had been centuries since Dax had been in the Carpathian Mountains, so it was reasonable that he might have missed the hunters sent out by Vlad.

Dax slipped past the barrier in Gary's head to study the images. A black scowl added to the uneasy feeling in the pit of Riley's stomach. She didn't understand how Gary wasn't affected by the tension in the Carpathian hunter.

Unexpectedly, Dax's multifaceted eyes flicked to her face. She felt the impact instantly. At once warmth poured into her mind. She had the sensation of arms surrounding her.

You're connected to me, Riley. He is not. He reads what I want him to read.

She studied Dax's face. There was no black scowl, no expression whatsoever. Gary had no cause to be concerned that anything was wrong because Dax appeared to be matter-of-fact.

What's wrong?

I am a hunter. I have to hunt my own people. I see shadows of darkness where others do not. Mitro had a lifemate and that did not stop him from choosing evil. I do not want to take you into an even more potentially dangerous situation.

Dax directed his attention to Gary, but shifted his body subtly, so that Riley felt his warmth enveloping her. The energy that had felt so intense, much like the volcano's pressure building in the ground, was gone.

"I recognize only one of them. The one you think of as Zacarias."

Gary frowned. Dax's tone was still low, and as mild as ever. The darker energy was gone, yet Gary caught something of Dax's misgivings. Riley found it strange, but Dax had been in his mind and maybe left an echo behind of his earlier irritation.

"I know he's considered very dangerous, but if you're worried he may turn," Gary said, astute enough to know Dax's main worry, "Zacarias has a lifemate. He is safe as long as she lives."

Riley glanced up at Dax. He didn't change expressions, but she knew Gary's assurance hadn't swayed him in the least.

Jubal came up to them, Gary's pack in hand. "We'd better get moving," he said with a nod of greeting to Riley and Dax.

"We'd better leave then," Dax said, effectively terminating the conversation about the other hunters, "if we're going to make the clearing in time to start transporting people to safety. How big is the helicopter they're sending?"

"I don't know, but I doubt it will take all of us on the first trip," Gary said.

Riley crouched low and sank both hands into the soil, feeling for the vampire. He had been making his way steadily toward the river and leaving, in his wake, death and destruction. Nature shrank from the abomination that was the undead. Around her, the world faded, leaving her in another environment where she could hear the whispers of the rain forest. The trees spoke, grateful for her presence, willing to share information.

The uneasiness that had plagued her earlier was gone—a dark dread that seemed to be a part of her ever since her mother had died. Now, with her hands buried in the comfort of the soil where she was once again close to Annabel's spirit, she realized that terrible dread was the vampire's blood calling to hers.

Horrified at that sudden revelation, she jerked her hands from the soil and sank back onto her heels, shuddering with distaste. An ice-cold frisson of revulsion slid down her spine. She had known she was connected in some way to Mitro, but she thought the connection was in the earth, the soil, not in her own body.

What is it, sivamet*?*

The warmth in Dax's voice, as it poured into her mind, helped to steady her.

I need a minute. She couldn't look at Jubal and Gary. They'd helped her so much, stood by her, and all the time, her blood called to the vampire.

"You two take the others and start out," Dax ordered. "We'll catch up."

Jubal glanced down at her, but Dax shifted, gliding in front of her without seeming to have moved. Jubal looked up at the Carpathian, and something flickered in the depths of his eyes that instantly had Dax coiled like a snake ready to strike.

"You okay with that, Riley? Catching up with us?" Jubal asked, in spite of the gathering tension.

"Yes, thank you Jubal for asking," she answered. *Gary and Jubal have looked after me all this time, Dax. There's no need to get upset because he shows concern for me.*

I have never been questioned before, Dax said. *I find it difficult to be in the company of anyone other than my lifemate for prolonged lengths of time. I have never spent this much time with others, and it is wearing.*

Riley hadn't considered that. Of course it was difficult for him, he'd spent centuries alone. Even before the volcano, he'd been a hunter of vampires, spending months, even years on his own with no one around. The world was a changed place for him. He had fought for hundreds of years for the protection of his people and then, while he was locked in a volcano, his species had nearly gone extinct.

Jubal lifted his hand and walked away in the direction of the river, shepherding the others to follow Miguel. The professor was carried out, the remaining porters taking turns with the others as they made their way steadily into the rain forest. Within moments, the trees and foliage had swallowed them.

Dax waited until they were gone before crouching down beside her. "Arabejila's blood runs strong in you. Mitro believes she lives, which is to our advantage."

She nodded her head. "I understand that, but I didn't realize it wasn't only the earth telling me where Mitro has been. I can feel my blood reaching for him." She took a deep breath, forcing herself to look him in the eye. "It's disturbing. I want my blood to call to you, not him. It makes me feel dirty."

Dax gathered her into his arms. *"Hän sívamak,"* he whispered tenderly. "My beloved. My blood and your blood are forever connected. Our hearts, our minds and our souls are inseparable. As for Arabejila's blood, as we traveled together, we often were forced to exchange blood. Her blood is why Mother Earth accepted me and granted favors to me. My connection to Mitro is not as strong, but it is there."

Riley slipped her arms around his neck. "You always know the right thing to say to me to make me feel better. Let's go find him, Dax. The sooner we find him, the faster we can get on with our life together."

15

The wind picked up, swirling through the canopy, blowing storm clouds into a churning, riotous mass of spinning dark threads. Lightning forked across the sky, a wicked fork of electricity, lighting the canopy for a brief moment. Thunder rolled, a great boom, shaking the ground. On the heels of the thunder the low moan of the wind rose to wail and then once again died down.

Riley wiped sweat from her face. It was hard to breathe with the ash still clinging to the leaves and flowers. Her boots felt horribly heavy and she made a note to herself to purchase lighter ones next time. Her mind was a little hazy, the hike almost surreal.

Fate had made a terrible mistake. For Riley, tramping through the rain forest at night was an exercise in courage. She tried not to connect with Dax, afraid he'd see how afraid she was of every shadow. Her heart beat so loud she feared Jubal and Gary would both hear it. She wasn't certain how she got to be the lifemate of a Carpathian warrior, who seemed to have all the courage in the world, when she was afraid of the shadows.

Riley cast a quick look around her at the others as they tramped through the dense vegetation. No one else seemed to be feeling as if at any moment they were going to be devoured by a pack of crazed jaguars leaping out of the shadows. It wasn't as if she was completely crazy—the coughs and grunts coming from a short distance away told her at least one, mostly two jaguars paced along beside them.

She tried to control her breathing as best she could, but with every step she took, apprehension grew stronger and her chest grew tighter. The jungle seemed much denser, Miguel and Alejandro struggling to hack a path and keep them all on the much-faded trail. The more miles they covered, the more the dread inside her grew and the harder it was to keep the pace the guide had set.

Her night vision was amazing, her restless gaze following the thousands of insects forming a moving carpet under their feet. Everything seemed overly loud to her, especially the persistent drone of insects, and even the bugs took on a sinister quality to her overactive imagination.

Birds screeched in warning to one another, a constant, alarmed communication, unusual for nighttime. Above their heads was continual motion, the flutter of wings, the swish of branches as monkeys leapt from branch to branch as if they, like the jaguars, were following the travelers.

Tree trunks covered in black spikes seemed to leap out of the shadows at them. Oversize leaves, split into razor-sharp fronds, reached for them, driven by the wind. The dread seeping into her made her stomach churn. The sound of the machetes slashing through the screaming branches and foliage only added to her frayed nerves.

Riley and Dax had caught up with the others quickly. He'd simply shifted into a giant bird and taken to the air, carrying Riley until they were close enough to join her fellow travelers. To make better time, Dax took over carrying the professor. He could go for miles without breaking a sweat. She resisted looking over her shoulder at him. He was close, but with the weight of a grown man in his arms, he couldn't be leaping into action if someone went crazy with a machete or the monkeys ambushed them.

Gary walked directly in front of her. She caught him twice looking over her head, back toward Jubal. They exchanged a knowing look that made her shiver. Okay, she wasn't entirely losing her mind; they both felt the danger, too, they just reacted better. She put her hand in the pocket of her light jacket, assuring herself the Glock was there should she need it.

Your fear is beating at me, yet you do not allow me to share your mind. What is it?

His voice was always so calm and reassuring.

We don't make any sense. She would have glared at him if she wasn't so busy looking in the trees for an imminent attack. Sometimes being so utterly calm was annoying.

Match your heartbeat to mine. Your heart is beating too fast, Dax ordered. *In what way don't we make sense?*

Smug male amusement was *much* worse than calm. She risked a quick glance over her shoulder to glare at him. He wasn't even breathing hard, while her lungs were burning. He was all muscle and hotness, and her body felt like lead. He didn't seem to mind that at any moment he might have to pitch the professor into a spiny tree to save the day like some comic book hero.

Comic book hero? Is that how you see me? I must have a cape.

His laughter filled her mind, raw and masculine and unexpected. She found herself smiling just because he was. He'd managed to find his way into her mind when she had been so certain she was closed off to him. He could make her laugh in the worst of circumstances. Ignoring the gathering anxiety pressing down on her, she deliberately began to conjure up an image of Dax in pink tights, a long tunic and a pink cape.

This is what you wish me to wear? He sounded perfectly serious. *It is much like the Inca garb. The color might clash with my skin tone.*

Riley burst out laughing. *Clash with your skin tone*? she echoed. Small beads of sweat ran down the valley between her breasts. She had to rub more out of her eyes. *What in the world does Gary have going on in his head? You got all your information from him.*

Jubal as well. He has sisters. Once again he sounded smug.

She took a deep breath, hoping he'd deny it, but knowing he wouldn't. *You know we're going to be attacked.*

Yes, of course.

Riley stumbled, but caught herself before she fell. She felt light-headed, dizzy enough to sink to the ground in a faint. She bit down hard on her lip, the stinging pain grounding her. *You've been talking to Jubal and Gary.* She made it a statement.

Coordinating what they need to do.

Riley cringed a little at her ridiculous reaction to his matter-of-fact tone.

Speaking mind to mind seemed so intimate to her, a secret shared with a lover. Could she be jealous? How utterly beneath her. And in the middle of an incredibly dangerous situation. She was acting like an idiot. She wasn't even the jealous kind.

She frowned as she walked, counting her steps to clear her mind. There was no buzzing in her mind to indicate the vampire was influencing her as it had the porter who killed her mother. She continued counting each step, finding a rhythm, wishing she could stop and put her hands in the earth. She felt exhausted, and the soil would rejuvenate her.

Riley? Why do you keep cutting yourself off from me? Your heart is still beating too fast.

She shook her head, not wanting Dax in it. She needed to work this out on her own. Her frown deepened. Dax, Jubal and Gary had all agreed that vampires preyed on weaknesses. She was definitely insecure, feeling as if she somehow wasn't worthy of Dax. To her, he was noble and courageous. He'd sacrificed his life for his people. He'd endured all kinds of suffering and wounds in battle, been completely alone while she'd had a wonderful, happy childhood with every advantage.

At once her mind was flooded with warmth. *You have great courage, Riley. There is no other for me, nor will there be.*

She got that. She really did. She'd committed to him. She hadn't gone to sleep insecure, but she'd awakened that way. Her mind turned that over and over. What had been different from the time Dax had carried her back to the others and helped her set up her hammock for the night and when she'd awakened? Something had happened to make her doubt herself, or worse—doubt Dax. What was it? She must have fallen into a trap Mitro had set.

She looked around her at her traveling companions. None of them seemed affected.

Gary turned around abruptly to face her, stopping so fast she ran into him. He caught her shoulders in a steadying grip. "You're burning up."

A lump had formed in her throat and when she tried to swallow, she had difficulty. *You're talking to Gary again.*

You're shutting me out.

No remorse. She would have to store that away for future reference. *Apparently not, because you're back in my head again.*

Everyone had stopped at some command from Jubal. Dax set the professor down gently on the makeshift travois the guides had made. Riley watched him stride toward her. Her heart leapt toward him. He was impressive any way one looked at it. Sometimes, when she saw him, like now, so confident and purposeful, he intimidated her just a little, yet at the same time, he made her feel safe.

He seemed to get taller as he approached her. His grip on her upper arms was as gentle as ever, yet she knew if she tried to free herself it would be impossible.

"Look at me, *sivamet.* Into my eyes."

She was aware that the scales running beneath his skin were very close, which meant he was more upset than his demeanor indicated.

Lightning forked across the sky. The wind howled, sweeping through the trees with deadly intent. The branches swayed, rubbing one another to make a clacking sound that seemed to reverberate through the jungle. Long vines dropped down from the overhead canopy, looking like hangman's nooses in the dark.

Dax transferred one hand to her chin, tipping her head this way and that, studying her eyes. "You're ill," he said.

"The spider bite. That's the only thing I can think of. Mitro must have had insects waiting to attack me. Can he program them to do that?" Even to her own ears, her voice sounded far away. "I should have known something was wrong when I was acting so out of character."

"Out of character?" he repeated, catching her when she would have collapsed.

"You know, doubting that I was good enough to be your lifemate. I'm sure I have a high opinion of myself." She reached up to stroke his jaw. "You really are beautiful, Dax."

He hissed something between his strong white teeth she couldn't catch. She seemed to be floating through the air, while several of her travel companions looked on with trepidation on their faces.

She waved at them. "No worries. He has a pink cape," she assured.

Overhead, the flutter of wings distracted Dax for one moment as he found the spot he was looking for. Crouching low, he looked up as a great horned owl, known as the night tiger, settled on the branches above them.

Somewhere in the distance, an eerie scream sent a shiver of goose bumps chasing down the travelers' spines. They all moved closer together.

"This is my fault, Riley," Dax said. "This evening I was so eager to be with you that I dismissed the bite as a typical hazard of the rain forest. I took the swelling and itch away, without delving deeper."

Riley looked up at him, her hand stroking his face. "I'm right, aren't I? Mitro attacked me, didn't he? I should have known right away. I hate it when I'm slow on the uptake."

He passed his hand over her face, taking the sheen of sweat from her skin. "I think, in this instance, you were quick figuring it out. You aren't used to dealing with the undead." He laid one hand over her heart and the other over the small wound on her hand. "Mitro is clever, and his traps can be subtle."

Jubal. Gary. Keep an eye on that owl. Be ready to kill it if necessary. Dax sent the order to the two men he felt had a chance of keeping Mitro's next weapon at bay. He still found it a little disconcerting to rely on humans, but neither man flinched when it came to combat with the vampire's puppets.

Dax took a deep breath and sent himself outside his body, becoming spirit, a white light of energy, slipping into Riley's body to track the sliver of poison the spider had injected. Mitro had kept it very subtle so the threat would have time to take hold and spread before anyone noticed. It was very Mitro-like. Most vampires were anything but subtle. Mitro was in a category all his own.

Dax hadn't known he was lonely until Riley had come into his life. He loved the conversations she had with herself, her smile and the way she would suddenly blurt out that he was beautiful. He also loved that she was intelligent and quick to comprehend the unknown. She didn't waste time denying what was happening, she took it all in stride, and he admired her for that. Now, moving through her body, she remained quite still, observing what he was doing, but not protesting.

She was already fighting the effects in her mind. He could see the damage there, but Riley was strong, much stronger than Mitro gave her credit for. That was one of the vampire's weaknesses. He viewed women as inferior to men. He always had. He had underestimated Arabejila, and he would always underestimate Riley, which gave her a small advantage.

Dax moved through her body, white light illuminating the dark blue clusters of cells spreading slowly, multiplying and invading healthy cells. Dax attacked the clusters with bursts of energy. The darker cells tried to hide from him, but he ruthlessly followed them, moving through every organ to ensure he got every last one. He would never be complacent about her health or safety again. Had she not begun to question why she was acting out of character, the virus might have had a much better chance of taking hold.

He knew the moment he returned to his body, the owl would attack, because Mitro would know Dax would be at his weakest and would orchestrate the strike that way. The bird was a predator and would hurl itself at Riley, going for her eyes with its lethal talons.

Jubal. Watch for the one you can't see. He couldn't help himself, he had to warn Jubal. As much as he'd learned of the two human men traveling with him, he still preferred to rely on himself, especially when it came to protecting his own lifemate.

Clever Mitro. I know you so well by now.

Dax burst into his body, accepting the disoriented effect that came with shedding one's physical shell and then returning to it. Simultaneously, he allowed the armor lurking beneath his skin to the forefront. Diamond-hard scales erupted from his feet to his neck, sliding over his skin to encase him in a shield. He spun around in a quick circle feeling for the real attack. The cat hit him hard in the chest, a monster of a jaguar, the hot breath on his face as wicked teeth rushed for his throat. Claws raked at his belly.

As if from a distance, he heard the rush of wings as owls dropped from the trees, talons extended, trying to get at Riley. He clamped his hands around the neck of the jaguar, holding the teeth away from his neck. A gun went off right near his ear and two more fired from a short distance away. With a quick wrench of his hands, he broke the neck of the cat and flung the body from him, turning to face the threat of the owls.

Three birds lay dead on the ground surrounding Riley. She held a gun in her hand. Jubal and Gary stood with guns out as well. Handy thing, guns. Dax liked the idea of them. A gun might not kill a vampire, but it could definitely kill a vampire's puppets. Mitro was clever, but he hadn't counted on Gary and Jubal or guns. This trap hadn't slowed them down or caused real harm.

Dax nodded his thanks to the two men and reached down to help Riley to her feet. She stood a little shakily, and Gary leaned in to remove the gun from her hand.

"Maybe we should be a little careful with this thing," he said.

Riley held out her hand. "I hit the thing instead of you, didn't I?"

Gary grinned at her. "I believe you did, Miss Parker."

Dax found the exchanges between the men and Riley interesting. He "felt" their affection for one another. Teasing seemed to be an art form.

Riley checked her gun before slipping it back into her pocket. She made a little face. "Here comes Weston. How are we going to explain this?"

Dax waved his hand toward Weston and the man stopped abruptly, looked around him and scratched his head as though he'd forgotten what he was doing. Riley's laughter spilled into Dax's mind.

I wish I had that particular talent.

You will, he assured. Aloud, to Jubal he added, "Let's get them moving again. We want to make the river before the sun is up. If we're being flown out of here, we'll have to give the helicopter somewhere safe to land."

I suppose I'll learn everything I want to know without having to go to school as well, Riley said. *You'll be making my profession obsolete.*

He brought her hand to his mouth, placing a kiss in the center of her palm. "Only for you," he murmured.

She laughed, just as he knew she would. He found he was becoming just as addicted to the sound of her laughter as he was to the way she looked, that soft glow and the curve of her mouth.

Before we join the others, you might want to get rid of your scales. I think you look adorable, but Weston probably will be incredibly rude. You know how you get when people are rude; better just to change out of that outfit.

Her laughter teased at his body this time, the vibration rushing through him like an aphrodisiac while fingers of sound stroked. He found himself laughing with her. Mitro had just made another try at her and Riley had shaken it off and was teasing him.

You're quite something, lifemate. He held out his hand to her.

She sent him a quick smile and placed her hand in his. They made their way back to the others, Dax ensuring none of the other travelers, other than Jubal and Gary, would remember anything that happened. Once again, Dax lifted the professor and they started off for the clearing where the helicopter was to meet them.

The flutter of wings overhead told Riley they weren't completely out of danger. She was shaken at the thought that even when Mitro was long gone from the forest, he could still leave such successful traps behind. He was much more powerful than she had ever imagined. She should have known when Dax was so amazing and yet in battle after battle with the vampire, neither had won. Mitro had to at least be his equal.

"Stay alert," Dax advised Jubal and Gary. "Keep everyone in a tight formation and pick up the pace."

The travelers fell into line, Weston and Shelton grumbling as usual.

"It's best to stay quiet," Dax said. "You never know what's going to trigger a jaguar attack."

Weston swore under his breath, but both men immediately fell silent.

Riley hid a smile. *You have such a way with people.*

I am learning to be in your world.

Smug. Arrogant. Male. Hot as hell. Why in the world did she find him so attractive? He made her feel as if she could do anything when she was with him.

I think I've fallen in love with you. Right here in this rain forest in this terrible, awful, ugly situation. She made the confession as she walked along the trail, keeping her head down as if she was watching the narrow trail. All the while, she held herself still. *You're so beautiful, Dax. Your heart. Your soul. I don't think I could ever find a better man.*

Dax poured himself into her mind, needing the closeness every bit as much as she did. Carpathians knew. There was no doubt for them. But humans wondered. Worried. And Riley was moving from her world into his—an enormously generous decision. A gift beyond price. How could he not treasure her?

Dax felt his soul brush hers. *You are* hän ku kuulua sívamet, *which means, "keeper of my heart." And you are* ainaak enyém, *"forever mine." I am fully aware of the courage it took for you to bind yourself to me without fully knowing what you were getting into, and I will forever be the keeper of your heart, Riley. I will be forever yours.*

Riley hugged his words to her as she kept moving through the dense foliage. She listened to the sound of water racing down the slopes and over rocks to run in narrow ribbons or wider streams. Water was everywhere. Drops fell from the leaves above them to add to the rushing rivulets. More water burst from the side of the hill in a long fall over boulders, a frothy stream of glittering silver. Below the waterfall, the large, moss-covered rocks formed a pool.

Bright green moss covered everything near them, the rocks, the fallen tree trunks, even the trees standing. Riley spotted flowers springing from the green slopes and rocks, some in bushes almost as tall as some of the smaller trees. The splashes of color along with the bright silver of the water in the dark were beautiful. She wished she was alone with Dax and could just sit quietly with him, holding hands and listening to the sounds of the waterfall splashing into the cool pool below.

Dax answered her with a caress down her cheek. *I can always have the Old One make an appearance. He isn't fond of people. He'll clear them away fast.*

Riley laughed, unable to contain her happiness that she had him. He made her feel safe in a world turned upside down. She could forget the ugliness of the situation for just a few minutes and see the beauty around her because of him.

"It's damned hot," Weston called. "Come on, Riley, want to strip down naked and go swimming tonight with all of us? Bet you'd like that. You'd be the center of attention."

Riley glanced back at Dax. Their eyes met. Amusement bubbled up. *Serpent in paradise. There's always one.*

The Old One particularly finds him foul.

Riley reached deeper. The dragon opened a sleepy eyelid, winked and went back to sleep. He wanted little to do with man. *The Old One, or you?* she teased.

Perhaps both, Dax conceded. His hands were gentle on the professor, his steps sure as they continued hiking toward the river. *If Weston truly wishes to be naked, I can help him with that.*

The trail led down a ravine and back up the other side. The going was easier. Miguel's machete was silent. Ferns grew everywhere, in between the boulders and along the banks of the pool and stream, creating a glimpse of paradise.

Don't you dare! Laughter bubbled over.

Perhaps not, Dax agreed, but he quickened his pace until he was up beside Weston.

The engineer snickered. "You got something to say to me? I'm just saying what every man here is thinking, including you." He grinned at Riley. "Isn't that so, baby? Your fantasy. Naked with all these men licking that gorgeous skin. You'd love it."

Riley's heart stilled. She shook her head, her breath burning in her lungs. Weston had no idea what he was dealing with. Dax could go from easygoing to extreme violence and back in seconds. *Don't. Don't hurt him.*

He will not feel a thing. His voice had gone from soft and sensual to grim and forbidding.

A shiver went down Riley's spine. This was a man—a being—one couldn't control. He would go his own way, make his decisions based on the rules of his world—not hers.

Weston opened his mouth to taunt Dax again and a deep, bullfrog croak came out. Startled, Weston's hand went to his throat, his eyes going wide.

Shelton burst out laughing. "Dude! What's wrong with you?"

Riley pressed her lips together, trying not to laugh. *Your sense of humor is out of hand.*

I don't find anything about Weston humorous. You wish him to live, so better he croaks this way than another.

There was no amusement in his voice, or in her mind, but his answer made her laughter escape in spite of her determination not to encourage him.

Weston cleared his throat and tried again. A series of loud sounds much like croak, croak, croak burst from his throat.

Even Jubal's mouth twitched as though he had to suppress his laughter. Gary and Miguel smirked, but neither commented. Miguel continued leading the line of travelers down through the narrow canyon that was a shortcut to the river. The small gorge would save them miles.

You can't leave him like that.

I think it's best, Dax replied.

Once again warmth flooded her mind, all that slow, heated molasses filling her brain with erotic fantasies.

He can't say your name and naked *in the same sentence, not without me remembering just how soft your skin is. The only man to lick water off your skin is going to be me.*

A frisson of pure arousal slid down her spine. Heat curled in her belly. Even when he was being bad—*especially* when he was being bad—he was downright sexy.

Now you're just being outrageous. She paused and then let her imagination take flight, wickedly feeding him a few fantasies of her own.

She felt his breath catch in his throat. Fire smoldered deep.

You could get yourself in trouble. I can always shield us from prying eyes, and believe me, sivamet, *I am more than willing.*

Her womb clenched. Hot moisture gathered. Her breasts felt instantly achy. She would love to be in his arms, legs wrapped tight around his waist, him buried deep inside her. She would love to be in the cool water with him, under the waterfall, or better yet, in a soft bed . . .

Hard bed, he corrected. *The things I could do to you in a hard bed. Or on a hard floor.*

She swallowed, nearly stumbling at his sexy implication. The things he could do with his voice alone left her breathless; she couldn't imagine what he had in mind on a hard bed. Her mouth went dry and the blood in her veins throbbed. The ground shifted beneath her feet.

Riley glanced down to see water bubbling up around the soles of her boots. The ground appeared so saturated that the water had nowhere to go. It actually took a moment for her mind to assimilate what was happening. She looked around her. Water leaked from the moss-covered boulders and trickled between smaller rocks. She blinked and several small mudslides gave way to ribbons that swelled in volume.

We have to get out of here. This is a natural basin and it will flood fast. The other side of the canyon looked a good distance away. More leaks were springing, the mountain too saturated to hold all the water. *I should have been warned. I should have known.*

She felt as if the earth had betrayed her. Granted, she was diverted by her exchange with Dax, but still, she should have felt her connection with the earth was so strong, she should have been warned the water was rising all around them.

Another trap, Dax soothed softly. *Mitro knows I can counter this, so why would he bother? It makes no sense. Can you feel anything beneath the water? Or perhaps in the sides of the canyon?*

Riley fought down panic. Miguel picked up the pace, clearly reading the danger. Both Jubal and Gary looked at Dax briefly and then at each other. They must have known Dax could stop the rising of the water, or at least delay it enough for them to get out, but neither said anything.

She forced her mind to stretch, to see beyond the obvious danger of the moment. It was difficult to get past the urge to flee. Her brain told her flight was best, but she grabbed on to Dax's calm and took a deep breath and let it out. She actually felt her mind unfurl, reaching for her connection to the earth. For a moment, she felt a little dizzy, disoriented, as if she was in two places at one time—aboveground and below.

Sounds faded, the pounding footsteps, the splash as boots hit the water inching up on the trail, the roar of the falls, everything receded until she was left with the whispers of the earth. She went still inside, even though she continued forward, on automatic pilot, her eyes on the man in front of her.

A river rushed beneath the canyon, fed now by the continual rain. Steam rose around them, curling through the boulders and reaching out like fingers toward them. Something moved, shifting continually, hiding in the vapor. She was aware of the movement just outside her vision. The sensation was dreamlike, as if she watched from a distance, seeing the steam drifting as the water table rose.

There was something more . . . Something she just missed. It was there, lurking beneath the water, waiting for its moment. The thing waited, watched, radiating malevolent hunger. She had the impression of red eyes staring beneath the water, fangs dripping. No, not thing—*things.*

Riley gasped and shook her head adamantly. *No, Dax. Don't.*

You control the water. Don't try to stop it, that will trigger the attack. Just slow it down.

Riley knew she had no choice. Dax was going to face the monsters below them. He trusted her to stop the rush of water pouring into the canyon from both sides as well as the water rising up beneath them. He was utterly calm and matter-of-fact. She took a breath and nodded her head, the terrible rolling in her stomach stilling. She would do this. If he could face those fangs and the single-minded purpose to kill them all, she could slow the rising of the water, but she'd have to get to it—the water was up to their ankles, slowing them down.

Dax handed the professor off to Alejandro and Jubal, taking care to ensure Patton wouldn't feel the jarring of the two men as they waded through the rising water. He waved his hands, weaving an intricate pattern, so that for a moment the air around them shimmered, cutting off the humans' ability to see him, and he slipped beneath the soil to drop into the water below.

Jubal's brain had contained a wealth of information, and Gary was a walking data bank. His mind carried billions of facts, some so strange and outrageous, at first it was difficult to believe, but when he looked into Riley's memories of airplanes and trips to the moon, those facts had been confirmed. There was so much he had missed while imprisoned in the volcano. He had knowledge of those things, but he hadn't experienced them.

Evidently the college student Mitro had found was a walking data bank as well. Jubal recognized a form of the creatures waiting for him there in that river. Goliath tigerfish, although as always, Mitro had manipulated the species and enhanced their natural aggression and savagery. The tigerfish weren't native to these waters, so the student had to have traveled elsewhere for them to have been in his mind. Surprisingly, it was Jubal's memories that gave him the most data on the dangerous species. Clearly he was just as well traveled.

Riley's memories had not contained any information on the fish. *Riley.* His Riley. She was such a miracle to him. He could feel her fear beating at him, but then she would shore up her defenses, set her shoulders and get the job done. There was so much about her to love. The moment she recognized what he intended to do, she no longer feared for herself—it was all for him. He couldn't remember anyone ever worrying about him, and it was a strange, two-edged sword. His heart swelled with joy at that thought of a woman caring so much, but on the other hand, he really didn't like to cause her anxiety.

Dax dropped deeper in the water until he felt the first stirrings of evil. The sensation seeped slowly into him rather than poured in. He expanded his vision as well as his senses, shifting into a tiny, nondescript leaf as he neared the gigantic fish. They were formed loosely in a pack, pacing slowly with the humans above them. As the water rose, so did they, gaining ground. So if the water table dropped, how could these fish possibly escape and do harm to those aboveground? What did Mitro have in mind?

Mitro was cunning. Dax would expect fish. Something nasty and brutally savage, but if he stopped the water rising, how would that trigger an attack from monster fish? He was missing something important. The water would rise, and if Dax or Riley didn't stop it, the fish would attack. But if they did succeed in stopping it, then the fish would be useless to Mitro.

Waves of evil assailed him as he hovered over the pack of fish. The feeling emanated not from the hungry pack of tigerfish, although certainly he felt the taint of the vampire on them, but it was something more, lurking below them, held back like a leashed tiger.

Without warning, a tigerfish lunged at him, mouth open wide, swallowing Dax. He reacted immediately, poisonous spines covering the leaf as it shifted into a very large lionfish, the terrible spines lodging into the tigerfish's throat and mouth, paralyzing it. He burst through the jaw of the monster fish only to be surrounded by the pack. He shifted again, diving down, leaving behind a trail of the tigerfish's blood. The pack tore into the goliath fish.

Beneath him, the real threat exploded toward the surface, a monstrous streak of scales, wedge-shaped head and streamlined wings. Front legs were tucked under, just as the wings stayed tight against the sides of the beast as it rose like a locomotive toward the surface. Dax caught the blue-green sheen to the scales as it rushed by. The force of the backwash sent him tumbling backward.

The Old One roared a challenge, the sound bursting through Dax's skull. Although the dragon had lost his mate long ago, the deep pain and sorrow would forever be etched into his soul. He would not lose Riley. Riley was part of him now, just as Dax was. No water dragon would take her from them.

No, not in your form. Dax took charge, knowing the water dragon would have the advantage over a fire dragon in their circumstances. *My form, but we both work together.*

Dax streaked after the dragon, pouring on speed, cutting through the blood-soaked water, his hands outstretched for that spiked tail. The long tail swept back and forth in the water like a rudder as the water dragon cut easily through the water. Dax allowed the red and gold scales to pour over his body as he caught that wedged spike on the tail and instantly reversed direction. The Old One rose just enough to lend his strength as well.

The water dragon hissed as it halted its forward progress abruptly and was jerked backward. The water churned, great turbulent bubbles, so agitated he could have been in the middle of a geyser. The tail whipped back and forth angrily and the water dragon spun around, and, moving like lightning, rushed the hunter.

Dax watched the huge, wedge-shaped head lunge straight at him. Underwater, the eyes were open and fiercely malevolent. The horned snout opened to reveal a jaw filled with serrated teeth. Just as the dragon snapped at his head, Dax threw himself to the side, still retaining possession of the lashing tail. Beneath the water, he heard the steady drum of a heartbeat. The water amplified the sound. The rhythm of the heart of the water dragon sounded strange to him, the beat booming first loud and then softening only to swell in volume again.

Dax was Carpathian, and he honed in on that sound unerringly. His blood sang in his veins. He reached out to the dragon, matching heartbeats, slowing the giant boom gradually, all the while dodging the lightning-fast strikes with those wicked teeth and the lashing head. He stayed just out of reach, staying in tune with the giant heart slowly taking control of that wild beat. It seemed to beat not where it should have been, but instead was lower and to the right, as if the heart had slipped and lodged in a different place than normal.

The water dragon slowed his great body, shuddering. Still, the dragon was so enraged that something as insignificant as Dax would dare to enter his territory and stop him from gaining the meal promised him by his creator . . . Dax nearly dropped the tail. Mitro had *created* the dragon. He would know that if Dax faced the water dragon, he would go for the heart and he'd deliberately placed it in the wrong position.

He is real yet not, the Old One confirmed.

Dax struck hard at the weakened heart, driving through the thin mantle of scales to the soft underbelly. His diamond-hard nails bit through the belly to drive toward the now very sluggish heart. It was much larger than he expected, but he managed to grasp the organ in his fist. The dragon's head whipped around and ripped at his shoulder.

Dax hung on grimly to the tail with one hand while he curled his fingers around the object he sought. The moment he wrapped the heart in his hand, he knew he'd made a terrible mistake. Spines embedded themselves in his hands. Poison entered his system rapidly. He ripped the heart from the thrashing dragon before the creature could take his head off. It was close though; he felt the blasting breath of cold water pouring over him, the snap of those jaws as the teeth nearly managed to tear his face open.

Dax put on a burst of speed, heading for the surface, feeling the poison taking hold, paralysis setting in. Below him, the gigantic tigerfish scented prey, shooting toward him in a pack hunting formation. His fist punched through the thin ground surface as his legs went numb. He stretched as far as he could, opening his hand, fingertips searching for something solid so he could pull himself out of the water. With the poison slowly spreading through his system, there was no way to shift.

A hand smacked his wrist, caught hold and jerked on his arm. Jubal's face swam into view. Gary, crouched beside him, reached down, caught him under the shoulder and heaved him up and out of the water. Under him, rising up out of the water, following the same path, a goliath tigerfish opened gaping jaws. The mouthful of thirty-two wicked teeth burst at him like a locomotive.

The gunshot was loud, almost in his ear. Jubal and Gary dragged him up and away as Riley calmly emptied her Glock into the fish. It dropped back into the hole Dax had made, and the water instantly bubbled up red.

We've got you. Riley's voice poured into his mind.

Give me a minute to drive the poison out of my system. I don't want you near this. It's slow-acting but paralyzing. It took longer than he anticipated to rid his body of the poisonous brew Mitro had prepared for him and to heal the wounds the dragon had inflicted.

Miguel had continued with the others, racing out of the canyon. Dax waited until he had his strength back before destroying Mitro's mutations. He didn't want them to breed and grow in the river and eventually kill someone. By the time the four of them had caught up with the others, the helicopter was waiting in the small clearing.

16

Dax was glad to see the helicopter lift off, taking with it the engineers and the professor and his party, minus their memories of anything but being caught in the violent explosion of a volcano. The only one who would remember Jubal, Gary and Riley was Ben, but only the experience of running for their lives from the volcano. He'd hesitated over that man, but something prevented Dax from removing everything. He'd relied on his instincts for centuries, and he wasn't about to stop now.

He was thankful only Jubal and Gary stayed behind with him and Riley. There wasn't enough room in the helicopter for everyone, and the pilot, a woman, Lea Eldridge, informed him that she'd seen the smoldering ruins of a home several miles to the east and a friend of Juliette De La Cruz resided there. She'd asked if they would check on the woman. As there was a good clearing for her to land, she would meet them there the next night. He had agreed that when he rose the following night, they would do so.

Miguel and his brother left to make their way home along with the last remaining porters. As far as they remembered, their missing men had died in the volcano, just as the professor and Todd Dillon believed Marty Shepherd had died in the ensuing mudslides. Capa and Annabel had been lost to the volcano as well.

Weston left with an additional gift from Dax. He couldn't watch the man his entire life, but he could plant the suggestion that every time he went to say something inappropriate to a woman or about a woman, he would croak instead. Dax found the solution rather fitting.

"Thanks for staying behind," he said to Jubal.

"There wasn't really room for us," Jubal said with a small shrug.

"There was room if you really wanted to go," Dax said. "I appreciate you watching over Riley when I'm unable to do so." He wanted to convert her, so he wouldn't have to worry that she slept aboveground and he was below. He needed her with him for his own peace of mind.

The sound of Riley's laughter drew his attention. Dax turned his head to see her standing beside Gary, laughing at something he said. His heart clenched hard. He had never thought to have her. In all the centuries that had passed, he never really believed she would exist for him. His life was one of duty and honor, not pleasure and joy.

She turned her head slowly, the first rays of the morning sun catching the gleaming lights in her hair. Her eyes met his and he had the sensation of falling into those deep, mysterious pools of cool, dark earth. Strangely, he actually felt his stomach tighten. Her smile was for him alone, her mouth curving, white teeth flashing. He knew every sweep of her cheek, the line of her jaw, the little indentation in her chin. He felt like he was soaring high, just as he felt when he'd been in the body of the fire dragon, strong and true, flying free over his world.

She had a way about her, something he couldn't define, but when he was with her, he felt totally alive, on fire with passion, as if he could do anything. Dax held out his hand to her. She didn't hesitate, but came to him, never once looking away from his gaze. She put her hand in his, and he drew her into the shelter of his body. "Are you two all right with setting up camp?" he asked Jubal. "I'll bring her back soon." He glanced at the sky even as he tucked her hand over his heart, holding her palm tight there with his.

The rain had washed some of the ash from the canopy, and the first streaks of dawn looked as if rays of light from stars bursting overhead shone through the heavy foliage surrounding the clearing. He loved the night, but the few early morning dawns he managed to catch held their own beauty.

Riley didn't ask questions, but she went with him, walking beneath his shoulder, fitting perfectly as if she was born for him—and he believed she was. She was ethereal, royalty, her body moving fluidly with hardly a sound. Already her skin had taken on the look of that of Carpathian women. She was more than halfway in his world, and he needed to let her know what was to come. He'd noticed she wasn't eating, particularly meat, which no self-respecting Carpathian would ever touch.

He caught her up in his arms and took to the sky. She loved flying as much as he did, and he took her up, feeling her delight in soaring so high.

This is how you make me feel whenever I look at you, he confessed.

She snuggled tight against him, her face turned toward the wind and the soft drops of rain still falling. *I'm glad then, because I absolutely love flying. I can't wait until I can do it by myself, although*—she rubbed her head against his chest—*there are certain perks to flying with you.*

He laughed, unable to contain the joy he felt when he was alone with her.

I can already feel the effects of your blood, she added. *My hearing and vision are much more acute. It's becoming harder to be away from you. Is that normal?*

He tightened his arms around her, feeling slightly guilty. He'd read things in Gary's mind he wished he hadn't. Like the present prince of his people who had been the one to inadvertently discover psychic human women could be converted without the danger of insanity; he wished he could be without the knowledge of what the woman went through before he'd started the process. The facts and images in Gary's mind were very disturbing.

I asked to come into your world, Riley assured him. *It's been my choice from the first time I laid eyes on you. I felt your soul and the Old One's soul. I felt as if I'd come home. You're my home, Dax. I want to be with you in your world. You never said it would be easy.*

He dropped his chin on top of her head, her silky hair weaving strands into his shadowy jaw as if tying them together. He was in her mind enough to know she took responsibility for her decisions. She had made a choice, and it was important to her that he saw it as her decision.

You're a courageous woman, Riley. I'm proud that you're mine. I'll live my life making certain you never regret giving yourself to me, or making the resolution to join me in my world.

Riley sent him the impression of a warm smile. Her hands tightened on his forearms and she turned her head a little to try to catch raindrops on her tongue. Laughing when she managed it, she bent her head to brush a kiss along his arm.

I know I can be of some use to you now. I was worried I might be a burden. I get afraid, but I know I can help you. Not fighting. Well, I can shoot a gun, but I don't want to get close to anything like those people we saw from the village. But I can be an asset to you in other ways.

Dax spotted the small entrance he'd been looking for. He'd seen the cave earlier and thought it had potential.

I have to take you back to Jubal and Gary in about an hour, but we've got this time. I want to tell you what to expect with the conversion and allow you to decide the when and where.

She took a deep breath. *Now? Why don't we just get it over with?*

He nuzzled the top of her head again and dropped down to the entrance of the cave, scanning automatically for traps and any living creature that might be occupying it.

"Not here, not now. Somewhere much safer." He sighed. "So it isn't entirely up to you, the when and where, but I'll get it as close as possible, I promise."

Very carefully, he set her down in the thick vegetation in front of the cave, waving his hand to the interior, preparing it for their entrance.

"I have no worries that I won't be safe with you," Riley said.

The ring of honesty in her voice humbled him. "You will need to rest and heal for several days, *päläfertiilam*. We have a vampire to catch."

Riley smiled up at him. "I like when you refer to me as your lifemate in your language. And beloved as well. I feel beloved, when I never thought love would come my way."

He took her hand, ducked to gain entrance through the narrow opening and led the way. The ground curved down and around, dropping several feet as they walked until the hallway began to widen.

"My language is still very natural to me. I have to try to think of a proper translation in your language, but I'm getting better at it," he said.

"You speak with a perfect accent."

"I still don't always choose the correct sentence structure," he pointed out. "Correct me if I get something wrong."

"I think it's cute."

He turned back to look at her, knowing she wore that teasing smile he loved so much. He stopped abruptly so that she ran into him, his arms sweeping around her, holding her tight against him. The feel of her soft body melting into his astonished him.

"I'm crazy in love with you," he said.

She turned her face up to his. "That makes two of us. I can do this, Dax. I can make it into your world and be happy. I've given it a lot of thought. I've seen all the dangers, but I know I want this." She cupped the side of his face as she traced the strong line with her thumb.

He kissed her hard. Demanding. A little rough. She responded like she always did, not in the least intimidated. She kissed him back. Hard. Demanding. A little rough. Her slender arms circled his neck and brought his head down more fully to hers. She poured herself into the kiss, accepting his storm of turbulent emotion.

The volcano was inside him, buried deep but smoldering. He wanted her with every cell in his body, and he hadn't even seen it coming on. The force of his need shocked him. Hunger clawed at his belly, a new kind of hunger, but just as urgent, just as feral. His fist bunched in her hair and he pulled her head back to take better advantage of her soft, hot mouth. He lost himself there for long minutes before he finally, still kissing her, lifted her into his arms, high against his chest so he could keep moving through the hallway toward the open gallery.

Riley opened her eyes as the cool air hit her body. She was absolutely naked. Not a stitch covered her skin. The flames from hundreds of lit candles leapt and danced, surrounding her on three walls. Above her head, on the ceiling, blue stars glittered with a soft radiance, creating a midnight sky. The walls of the cave seemed to be studded with gleaming gems.

Dax had created a bedroom. The chamber was warm and inviting. The sound of water dropping into a deep blue steaming pool only added to the ambience.

"This is where I live," he whispered. He wanted her to love the night the way he did. She had gotten inside of him, wrapped herself around his heart. Her smile lit his world. Turned his body hard and filled him with such love, such emotion, that he felt shaken, vulnerable even, when he never had.

One woman. It amazed him that he could feel such intense emotion after feeling barely anything for centuries. She just had a way about her that took every sane thought from his head and replaced them with . . . her. He found he was uncomfortable when others were close, because the wealth of emotion for her was nearly impossible to hide. It made him feel . . . exposed.

He looked down into her earth-colored eyes. Her lashes were long and feathery, half concealing the heat of desire looking back at him. "You're so tempting," he said. Her lips were full and curved and made for kissing.

She moved in his arms, her silky skin rubbing over his, sending little electrical charges arcing between them. "I'm hoping you're tempted," she admitted.

He set her feet on the smooth floor he'd created for her, walking her backward until the backs of her legs hit the platform placed in the center of the chamber. She sank down, sitting on the edge of the hard surface. The action placed her exactly at the height he'd intended. Her head was just a little below him, just enough.

Dax widened his stance, stepping close to her, his hands going to the back of her head, guiding her forward. There was never hesitation in Riley. She cupped the weight of his balls in her palms, rolling and kneading before sucking gently. The breath left his body in a rush as her tongue traced a path up from his sac, along his thick, swollen shaft to the underside of the flared head.

He reached down and tugged at the binding around her long hair, releasing it so that black silk cascaded like a waterfall down around her. The contrast between her soft glowing skin and her blue-black hair was beautiful to him. Her lashes rose, and for one moment their eyes met. Watching him, she opened her mouth and took him in. Fire burned down his shaft. She tightened her mouth and sucked hard for a moment or two and then danced her tongue over him.

Riley had fantasized about loving Dax with her mouth. Tasting him this way. Her skin felt hot and sensitized. Her breasts ached and swelled, nipples twin taut peaks—for him. Every breath she took, every swipe of her tongue, made her crazier for him. The flower ceremony had shown her how addicting he could be and tasting him only made her crave him more.

She could taste his hunger, barely held at bay—for her. His shaft pulsed and throbbed, filling her mouth, stretching it in the same way he stretched her feminine sheath. He was hotter than a volcano. Her tongue curled around him again and again, lashed and danced and then her mouth sucked wildly, drawing the spicy nectar out of him.

The sounds he made, low and feral, only added to the wild need rising in her like a dark storm. She was desperate for him, desperate to feel him inside her mouth, her mind, her body. She wanted his mouth on her, feeding from her veins, taking the very essence of her life. She wanted to be his substance, his air, his everything.

His hips jerked. His hands did the same, tugging at her scalp. A low, dark moan escaped his throat. A growl rumbled deep in his chest. His breath sounded ragged and harsh. Riley lifted her lashes again, to watch his face as she pulled slowly off of him, licked around the flared head and then gradually, tightly swallowed him again. The flames in his eyes had gone red-hot, nearly consuming his entire eye surface in a haze of lust.

"O köd belső," he uttered between clenched teeth. His voice was harsh. Demanding. *Darkness take it.*

She laughed softly around the mouthful of a very hot spike. More like humming than a laugh, the vibration moving through him as she slid her mouth tightly up and down, his hands rough in her hair. *Is that a Carpathian curse? Are you cursing at me?*

There was such power in bringing him to the edge of control. Joy burst through her. She loved having him at her mercy. He was driving her just as crazy, her body so aroused she could feel the wet evidence of her desire on her thighs. *Fill me.* She whispered the urgent need into his mind. *I need you inside of me. Hard. Fast. Rough. I want to be yours.*

You are mine. He made it a declaration as he thrust deep one last time, feeling the heat of her silken mouth wrap him in glory. Using the fist bunched in her hair, he jerked her head back, forcing her to break the exquisite, tight suction.

He didn't wait. Couldn't wait, as desperate for her as she was for him. He pushed her back on the platform, so that she sprawled out, panting, her breasts rising and falling with her agitated breathing. She brought up her knees, planting her feet a good distance apart, lifting her hips in invitation.

"Hurry, Dax. Hurry."

He dropped over top of her, slamming his cock deep so that she screamed, arching her back and pressing harder into him. He thrust hard and fast, burying himself deep while her hot sheath suckled and gripped, the friction building their release fast. Too fast. He wanted this to last forever, but already he could feel her tightening, clamping down on him, the hot wash of her body, and the strong waves rippling through her, taking him with her. He surged forward again and again, slamming deep as her body locked down on his, squeezing and milking, demanding his hot release. His hoarse shout joined hers, and he collapsed over her, fighting for breath.

He wrapped his arms around her and rolled, taking her weight, loving how she sprawled over him like melted lava. "I think I left a little gold dust in your hair."

Her laughter was muffled. She didn't lift her head. "Everyone will think I have body glitter on. Those scales of yours are beautiful, but they do leave evidence behind." She yawned lazily. "It might come in handy if you ever decide to stray."

"Carpathians don't stray," he said, and bit her earlobe. He rubbed her enticing butt. "Sit up, we need to talk. We're racing the sun."

She yawned again. "I see how you are. Get what you can from a woman and then insist on *talking*." She rolled off of him reluctantly and watched him rise in his fluid, easy way.

"I want to talk to you about what will happen when I convert you," he said. "It's important for you to know. I looked into Gary's mind to find answers to why you, a human, would be my lifemate. In my time, there was no such thing. No one ever conceived of such a thing. The few times anyone tried to save the life of a human by converting them, it was disastrous."

Riley sat up slowly, pushing her hands through her cascading hair. The action lifted her breasts and made him hungry for her all over again. "That might be pertinent. What kind of disaster happened?"

He leaned forward and brushed a kiss over the sweet slope of her creamy breast. "I think you're going to have to put clothes on if we're going to discuss this. I have to go to ground and that means I have to put you safely in Gary and Jubal's care, so we don't have much time left." Before she could protest, and he was a weak man when it came to her desires, he covered up temptation with a wave of his hand.

"If you converted me, we would have plenty of time." She moved like a siren, in spite of her clothing, her hot gaze drifting over him.

"You are a very wicked woman," he decreed, catching her wandering hand. He needed clothes as well, a good distance from her if he was going to have a chance to resist her. "You need this information."

She made a little moue with her lips, those lips he always found irresistible. She definitely had an unfair advantage over him. If she pouted, or cried, he'd be lost.

"All right. I'll behave," she conceded with the smallest of teasing smiles. "Bring on your worst. But I won't change my mind."

He hoped not. He'd told her once started, there was no going back, and she was well on her way to being in his world. He couldn't reverse the process.

The smile faded from her face. "I'm listening Dax. I can see this is upsetting to you." She sat up straight and folded her hands in her lap. "Get on with it. I'm listening. What kind of disaster?"

Dax felt tension gathering in the pit of his stomach. "The men and women they tried to save over the last few centuries apparently became deranged and had to be terminated. It wasn't until the prince discovered his woman could be turned because she had psychic gifts that our species became aware a few human women might save us."

There. He'd said it. He'd told her the horrible truth he'd found in Gary's memories. There was more, but he needed to see her face. Feel her reaction. Check that he wasn't showing how, for the first time he could remember, fear held him in its deadly grip.

She nodded her head. "I see. As in deranged, you mean like those people in the village? Mindless? Intent on murder?"

He nodded. "Drinking blood much like a vampire. Sometimes turning cannibal."

She reached for her hair, bringing it over her shoulder, beginning to weave it into a long, thick braid. It was something to do with her hands, he knew. She hadn't blinked, but her hands were trembling.

"Okay then. Is that it? Because you haven't settled down."

"It's painful." He nearly blurted out the information when he didn't blurt. Ever. She was turning him inside out with the stoic look on her face. "*Very* painful." Just to clarify. And adhere strictly to the truth. "It's like dying, convulsions, I can show you the memories if you wish." He made the offer reluctantly.

She studied his face in silence. He worked at being completely expressionless, not wanting to persuade her one way or the other with his aversion to revealing the actual images.

Riley threw her braid back over her shoulder and stood up. "I don't want to see. I'm not stupid. I knew in order to cross into your world, I'd have to leave mine. Your body is very different from mine. I knew from the beginning that a change wouldn't be easy. Nothing worthwhile ever is." Her eyes met his. "Believe me, Dax, you're worthwhile."

She stood up and crossed to him, putting her hands on his shoulders. "Women have babies knowing it could hurt, but that a small few moments are nothing compared to the joy they'll receive when they have their child in their arms. Whatever I have to do, I'll do." There was absolute resolve in her voice and in her eyes.

Her face blurred for a moment, forcing him to blink rapidly.

"When you deem it safe, I'm ready. I want you to just finish, and while you're doing it, remember the kind of woman you tied yourself to. I take responsibility for my own choices. I don't do what other people tell me to. I like information shared with me, and I want respect and a partnership." She lifted her chin. "I would never be silly enough to argue with you over safety, or even health, which I've observed are your two big issues, but I like to make my own decisions."

He gripped her upper arms. "Is that a warning?" His heart felt as if it had swelled so large it was too big for his chest.

"Take it any way you like. I know you're afraid I haven't really looked at the real you. I have. You tend to be a very dominant man, and that's okay with me, it really is. But I'm just as afraid that you haven't taken a good look at who *I* really am. I make my own decisions and I've never done well with someone telling me what to do."

He read the small hint of fear quite easily and it turned his heart over. Heat skittered through his belly and settled low. He pulled her tight against him. "I'll cherish you forever, Riley."

She had made up her mind, but she still feared her decision. It was a huge one, and her life would be changed forever. If he abandoned her . . .

"It is impossible for me to abandon you," he assured softly. "I'm taking you back to Jubal and Gary, but I'll be sleeping just beneath you. Reach for me if you have need and I'll wake." He kissed her thoroughly, wanting to remove every doubt from her mind. He knew it was impossible, but he would keep trying until she was just as certain of him as a Carpathian lifemate would be.

She wrapped her arms around his neck when he lifted her into his arms. "I hate to leave this place. You made our time together beautiful for me. Thank you."

"I want you to remember that I love you, Riley. You. The person you are. This is going to get uglier, and you'll need to hold on to any good moments we can find," he warned.

He took her through the hallway back out into the early morning light. The sun, obscured by the haze overhead created by the ash, still hurt his eyes. The light on his skin burned, but the scales moving beneath the surface protected his body, allowing him the freedom to take to the sky. He took in the early morning, breathing in the rain and scent of the forest.

Movement was constant in the canopy below. The sounds were far different as the birds called to one another. Monkeys scolded and added to the chaotic movement. The forest was waking up just as he was going to sleep. He could see it would be difficult for Jubal and Gary to sleep during the day and his respect for them grew. They were going out of their way to protect what was his.

The two men had already set up a net and tent with a sleeping hammock for Riley. They had chosen an area easily defensible and one where he could find a resting spot without the water table being too high. He found both of them extremely efficient. They were definitely well versed in the ways of the Carpathian people.

He greeted them formally, giving them the respect they deserved, clasping their forearms as one warrior to another, before relinquishing Riley into their care. He found it much more difficult than he'd anticipated to leave her, even for a few hours. She looked alone, although she stood straight, her chin up and even managed a small smile he kept with him as he opened the ground and allowed the cool soil to greet him.

They cautiously approached the clearing Lea Eldridge had told them about. Long before they were close, the stench of death filled their nostrils.

Riley glanced uneasily at the three men. "Not again. I could feel Mitro as we've gotten closer to the river. He came this way for certain. I hate that my ties to him seem to be getting stronger."

"That's the Carpathian blood," Dax explained. "Not any tie to him. Your abilities are growing, and that has nothing at all to do with Mitro. He's a killing machine. There is no goodness in him, no mercy, not for anyone. There's no redemption for him. If his lifemate couldn't save him, no one could. Arabejila is long gone, and evil has completely taken him over, although, in all honesty, I think he was already completely evil."

"Some people are born with something not right," Riley said. "We want to say it's always the environment they're raised in, but sometimes, it just happens. Maybe it happens in every species."

Gary nodded his head. "Even animals are born with problems, both physical and mental." He shrugged. "It happens."

Mitro had been twisted from the first time, as a boy, Dax had met him. There had always been a cunning savagery about him. His need to hurt animals and the other boys drove others away from him.

Dax shoved the memories away. In the clearing ahead, the smoldering remains of a home came into view. He halted abruptly and caught Riley's forearms, effectively stopping her. "You'll need to stay here, *sivamet*. The stench of evil is strong here."

Her body rocked against his. She frowned up at him. "He's gone. You know he's gone."

"He leaves both carnage and traps behind. Neither is for you."

She raised an eyebrow. "I think you're mistaken about that. I think he left both behind for me to find. He knows I'm following him."

"That he does, *sivamet*. And we'll get him."

"He should never have gotten out." Riley glanced over his shoulder toward the smoldering ruins of the little house there on the side of the river. "I should have been able to stop him."

"Riley." Dax said her name softly, shaking his head. He stroked a caress down her long sweep of hair. "You have to know you aren't responsible for any of this."

"Of course I am. He got out. He's killing people, destroying lives. How many more will he kill before we catch him?" She blinked back tears and gestured toward the cabin. "Whoever lived there had a life and it's gone because I wasn't powerful enough, or fast enough to keep him a prisoner in that volcano."

"If you believe that, you have to believe that ultimately, the failure is mine. I have had centuries and yet, I failed." Dax kept his voice very low, very matter-of-fact. His guilt was not in his inability to defeat the vampire, that was part of the job. Sometimes the hunter won and sometimes the undead prevailed. All hunters knew and accepted that premise.

At once Riley's expression changed and she shook her head. "No, no, Dax, please don't think I ever thought that. Of course it isn't your fault . . ."

"It isn't yours, either. Mitro is evil. I have no idea if he was born that way, or what shaped him, but he wanted to be evil. He embraced that darkness in himself. He had every chance to move to the light, but he clearly made the choice to be what he is."

He dropped his arm around her shoulders and began walking away from the scent of smoke and death. "He seems to need carnage and suffering. It feeds some deep need he has. He's been around centuries, and maybe it is not our destiny to stop him. But we will continue to try, Riley. There is nothing to gain by blame or guilt. Neither serves any purpose, not in a life-and-death hunt. I need you to be at your strongest and most determined. He can't ever see weakness in you. The moment he does, he'll use it to attack. Remember, vampires can get into your head."

Riley nodded. "I hate that you, Gary and Jubal have to see what he's done and I'm protected from the worst of it."

He leaned down and brushed a kiss across her mouth. "I never want you to have to see any more of his work than necessary. I can help to distance the horror from Gary and Jubal should they ask, and they know enough of our abilities to ask if they have need. I have dealt with this most of my life and can look upon death and torture without repercussions. I have the ability to push all emotion aside."

Riley turned, stepping in front of him, halting his forward progress. She linked her fingers behind his neck as her eyes searched his carefully. "I don't know how you've done this so long, Dax, but I admire you for it. I wish I had the courage to tell you I'm going with you no matter what, but I already feel sick just with the thought of it."

She pressed her face against his chest, right over the steady beat of his heart. He was such a rock. So calm. So completely confident. There was no doubt in her mind what he would find when he approached that little cabin. Lives were lost, others changed forever. She sighed, wishing she could somehow prevent him from having to witness the depravity and cruelty of Mitro.

Dax caught her chin, tipping her head up, his strange, beautiful eyes staring down into hers, captivating her with those spinning colors and the bright flame that shone with such intensity every time he looked at her. "I appreciate that you would spare me this, Riley. It is enough that I know you don't have to see."

"I wish neither of us had to do this. And poor Gary and Jubal. Traveling with me, they had no idea what was in store for them."

He bent his head and brushed a gentle kiss across each eyelid and then blazed a trail of fire to the corner of her mouth. "Don't worry about them, my gentle heart. I watch over them. They're good men and good friends to our people. I won't let them see more than they can handle. They're tough, both of them, and they've done this many, many times already."

"You're a good man, too, Dax. You're so worried about everyone else that you don't take yourself into consideration," she protested. "I love that you want to shield all of us, but I'm just saying, I wish I could do the same for you."

"But you do," he assured, bending his head down to brush his lips back and forth across hers like a soft whisper. "That's what you don't understand. You wipe out every bad place I've ever been. I see only you when you're with me. Loving you is the easy part, Riley, and when I'm with you, everything else disappears. Just wait for me here. Don't put your hands in the ground; you know he's gone. Just sit quietly and wait for me."

"I'll stay here and wait," she promised. "I'll stay in sight of you at all times. I don't feel that horrible dread that signals he has a terrible trap for us. I think you'll be getting the worst of this one."

"At the first hint of trouble, if you, even for a moment, feel something isn't right," he said, "reach for me. I'll be close."

Riley flashed a small smile meant to be reassuring. "I'm really not all that brave, Dax. I'll be yelling at the top of my lungs for you as well as screaming in my head."

"Do you have the weapon Jubal gave you?"

She nodded. "I keep it ready at all times. It might not kill Mitro, but it might slow him down and for certain it would slow down the creatures he creates."

"He won't make a try for you himself unless he's cornered, or if he finds himself with a certain opportunity, otherwise, he's too cunning for that. He'll let someone else do the killing, and that's what worries me the most. He was trapped in the volcano and he managed to delay your mother and then get others to kill her for him. He can do the same to you. You can't trust anything, not animal, insect, bird or even man."

"Dax." She raised her hand to his face and traced his jaw. "If you're trying to scare me, you don't have to. I'm terrified. I'm not the heroine type."

He couldn't stop the small smile and shake of his head. "You really don't see yourself at all, do you? Fear has nothing to do with courage, and you have more than your share of courage."

She shook her head and tipped her head up to kiss him briefly on the mouth. There was nothing sexual in her kiss at all, just a warmth of companionship, a trust that squeezed his heart hard. "Be safe," she murmured.

Dax turned away from her abruptly. It was getting much harder to give her the room she needed. He'd been so long without anyone and the threads binding them were getting tighter so that needs and wants became the same. Hunger for her was growing with each passing hour he spent in her company. He had set out to coax her to fall in love with him, spending time in her mind, an intimacy difficult to resist, but he found he was the one falling off that cliff.

Long strides took him back to where Jubal and Gary were waiting. "This one is going to be bad," he advised. "I'll go in first and try to find any traps Mitro left behind. You two stay just at the edge of the tree line. Don't step into the clearing. There's no way of knowing what will trip any ambush he's set."

"We'll have to find them before we leave this place," Jubal said. "Otherwise someone innocent could come along and be injured or killed."

Dax nodded grimly and shifted into mist and streamed into the clearing beside the river. The cabin was very small, no more than a single room with a small covered porch that had been up on stilts. Now it was tipped on one side, blackened and burned. Nothing was left of the house but three half walls, a mere husk surrounding a smoldering ruin. The roof had been constructed of tree branches and leaves as many of the huts were when natives were on the move. This one had been built hastily and there was little there to say anyone had lived there long. He moved around the cabin carefully, testing the air for any sign of Mitro's inevitable traps.

Dax found the body a hundred feet from the burnt-out ruins. She'd been young. He knelt beside her for a few moments, waving away the insects and touching her hair briefly in a salute to her. She'd had courage. She'd been pregnant, and she'd tried to protect her unborn child. He shook his head and signaled the two waiting men.

Jubal arrived a stride or two ahead of Gary. Dax saw Gary's face. He knew exactly what he was going to see. There'd been too many of these times, humans ripped apart by a vampire.

"Mitro's a bastard," Jubal stated.

"She was jaguar," Dax said. "And pregnant with a jaguar baby. The baby is over there." He indicated the infant with his chin. "A boy."

"He killed the baby in front of her, didn't he?" Jubal asked grimly.

Gary took off his shirt and wrapped the baby's body carefully in it. "He took the baby while she was still alive, drained the baby dry and then attacked her. He likes to play with his victims. Jaguars need to be burned. They never leave bodies where others can examine them."

"Let's get it done before the helicopter comes for us," Dax said grimly. He glanced over to Riley. "There's no need for her to see this. It will be bad enough telling her about it."

17

The Old One was agitated, and it didn't do to have an extremely large dragon upset in a large city—or anywhere, for that matter. Dax paced up and down the terrace overlooking the lights of the city. The De La Cruz family owned an enormous estate on the outskirts of Rio de Janeiro. Apparently, they owned homes in nearly every major city throughout South America. They seemed to have adapted well to living among the human species.

Just as Dax had evolved there in the volcano, the De La Cruz family had evolved as well—yet he wasn't comfortable with their modern transformation. He didn't believe it. They were hunters, every one of them, wolves in sheep's clothing. For all their modern look, and the charm the De La Cruz brothers exuded, he knew what they were deep down under all that sophistication—predators, every one of them.

"What's wrong?"

Riley's soft voice brought him up short. He turned to look at her. She sat in one of the deep chairs, chin on her drawn-up knees, watching him with her dark, cool eyes. There was genuine concern in her voice—in those liquid eyes. He'd never had anyone concerned over him before other than

Arabejila, and certainly not like this, not that he could remember, not that he could feel. It was a strange—and wonderful—feeling.

"I'm concerned about being here in this dwelling."

"House," she corrected as promised. "Why?"

He paced the long length of the terrace restlessly. Riley was his lifemate and she'd asked a question requiring an answer. He sighed and came to a halt in front of her. "I should have executed Mitro centuries ago, long before he went on his crime spree. I knew the darkness grew in him. I was born with a curse, although Arabejila's father told me it was a gift of tremendous value. I knew better. Even as a young boy I saw the mark on many of my friends. As we grew, I became uneasy around them and they were much more uneasy around me. No one wants to be marked as damned."

"Did you do that?"

He shrugged. "I tried not to, but I saw that shadow in them very early and I couldn't help but watch them. I made everyone uneasy. At first the elders didn't believe me, but when my predictions came true, they started paying attention. The moment that happened . . ." He trailed off, turning his back on her to grip the railing with both hands, staring out into the night.

Riley bit her lip. That little boy had to be somewhat of an outcast. The other boys and men in his village would have shunned him, kept their distance just in case he discovered that shadow in them and called them a potential vampire. She could feel the stark loneliness in him. As a man—a hunter—he didn't seem to be aware of it. He didn't recognize his own emotions let alone acknowledge them; he'd been too long without.

"The thing is, just because I saw the shadow didn't mean they chose to give up their soul. Some found lifemates eventually and lived honorable lives."

Riley held herself very still, refusing to give in to the urge to comfort him. Dax had no idea he needed comfort and he would shut down. She reached tentatively for their mind connection, not wanting him to pull away from her. Empathically she felt his childhood pain, but she wanted to "see" his memories through his eyes. The moment she reached for him, she felt not only Dax, but the Old One. The dragon was just as concerned for the Carpathian hunter as she was.

She focused on the rail Dax gripped as he looked out over the city. She couldn't imagine what it must be like for him seeing the modern world, but he handled everything calmly, stoically, which gave her insight to his personality. The pressure from his fingers denting the wood told her much more about him.

"I saw the darkness in Mitro from the very beginning. He was from a powerful family and took great advantage, always a bully," Dax continued.

His voice was very soft, but she almost felt each word, brushing at the inside of her mind with a paintbrush of pure shame and sorrow. He didn't hear it—or know—but she felt that raw emotion tearing through his soul. The Old One felt it just as deeply as she did, because unlike Dax, they were both in tune with their emotions.

He had spoken to her about Mitro several times, just small snippets, but she'd seen the vampire's depravity and his need for cruelty even as a young boy. Sometimes monsters were born, not made, and she feared Mitro was the former.

"I tried to tell the elders. I even went to the prince, but I was young and they discounted what I said. As I was proved right more and more and the others avoided me, I learned hard lessons about accusing someone before knowing for certain if they actually would make the choice to turn. Instead of telling others when I saw that darkness in some of our males, I studied each of those with the shadow in them, their ways and habits. I followed them and often, when they made that forbidden choice, destroyed them."

Riley closed her eyes briefly. The sight of his hands gripping the rail until his knuckles were white saddened her.

"I had to let them kill someone while turning. It was the only way to assure I wasn't committing murder." He turned to look at her, sorrow weighing him down. "Do you know how many people I could have saved if I'd just destroyed them before they could make a kill?"

She fought the urge to rise and go to him, to put her arms around him to comfort him. He needed to tell someone. The weight on his shoulders—and he'd carried it for centuries—needed to be shared.

"You're right, though, Dax, it would have been murder," she advised gently.

He was silent for so long she nearly prodded him, but the dragon held her silent, stirring just enough to make her aware he was waiting, too—and he had the patience she needed. Dax wasn't used to sharing, certainly not whatever fear he held so deep that even he couldn't really recognize it.

Dax let out his breath slowly and nodded, but he didn't seem too sure.

She clamped her mouth closed, pressing her lips together tightly. She wrapped her arms tighter around her knees as a surrogate for him. She needed to hold him, to comfort him in the way he offered her comfort and support.

"Mitro seemed . . . much more foul . . . than any other. There's a nobility to most Carpathians and I respected them, but not Mitro. I watched him closely, and he enjoyed the pain of others, animals, humans and Carpathians. He was cunning and vain and unfortunately, quite intelligent. He found a lifemate in Arabejila. She was the other half of his soul—light to his darkness. The courtship began and I . . ."

Dax shook his head and turned his back completely to the rail, leaning against it to look directly into her eyes. "I looked away. I thought him safe. No Carpathian male with a lifemate would turn vampire, so as uneasy as I was, I quit watching him."

Riley allowed her lashes to sweep down, veiling her eyes for a moment so he wouldn't see her sympathy. Dax was not a man to recognize shame or guilt, yet he felt it just as much as she did.

"Arabejila's father was my best friend. We hunted together. When others shunned me because of my strange talent, he didn't. He told me my gift was useful, that I could keep our people safer than any other. We shared blood when we were injured. He knew his lifemate far before he ever would have lost emotion and color so he had nothing to fear from me, I know that, but still, he felt genuine affection for me as did his lifemate and Arabejila. They became my real ties to my people."

She could see flashes of images—his memories of a laughing woman who looked very much like her. A man and a woman, holding hands, turned toward one another, a look of utter love on their faces. Their expressions took her breath away, so much love. Sometimes, when Dax looked at her, there was that intensity in his eyes, that amazing look of love focused on her, and she felt the luckiest woman in the world.

She forced herself to look at the next images, the ones in such stark contrast. The man, Dax's best friend, dead on the ground, his hand inches from his lifemate's, blood pooling around him, his throat and heart torn out. His lifemate dead, and Arabejila, her throat torn and bleeding, desperately trying to free her baby sister from her mother's body.

It was a scene straight out of a horror film, and Dax had stumbled onto it—worse, felt responsible for it.

Riley could hardly bear the thought of those deaths and how Dax felt, even suppressed as his emotions had been. She couldn't imagine knowing that happy family, being a part of it and coming upon them, discovering them dead and dying . . .

"When I could have prevented it."

Her gaze jumped to his. He had known all along she was in his mind. "How?" she asked quietly. "How could you have prevented it?"

"I could have executed him."

She shook her head. "That would have been murder. He hadn't done anything yet, had he? You were genuinely shocked. I could feel your horror. You could barely believe what you were seeing. Until someone commits a crime, there isn't much anyone can do—not even you."

Riley gripped the arms of her chair to prevent leaping up to hold him. "Dax, you know you couldn't touch him without proof. You didn't know for sure. You aren't God. You aren't a judge."

"That's exactly what I am. The Judge. And I failed my friend and his family." He shoved his hand through the short spikes of pitch-black hair. "Arabejila was Mitro's lifemate. He killed her mother and father in front of her and bragged that he would be the most powerful vampire ever to live by killing his lifemate as he made the choice to give up his soul. When he couldn't finish her off—that lifemate bond was too strong for even him—in his rage, as vampire, he claimed her, binding her soul to his lost one so that she would suffer every moment she lived."

Riley found herself blinking back tears. She was Dax's lifemate, and to her, the binding ritual had been beautiful and sacred. "What Mitro did is a sacrilege, no less."

"I still see them like that," he confessed in a low voice. "Torn apart. Katalina's stomach ripped open. Arabejila trying to free her sister." He closed his eyes for a moment. "I took the knife from her and finished the job. I hacked up my friend's beautiful, wonderful lifemate."

"To save a child, Dax. You saved a child. She would have wanted you to save her baby. She would have begged you had she lived."

He pressed his fingers to his eyes hard. "To see that infant torn from its mother the other night, there in the rain forest, I actually felt . . ." He shook his head.

Sick. The word shimmered in her mind.

Riley surrounded him with warmth, the only thing she could think to do. There were no real words to comfort him. There couldn't be.

He shook his head. "Carpathians don't feel sick. Not when they're on the hunt. Mitro knows the one thing that . . ." He broke off again and straightened his shoulders. "What he did to Arabejila was the absolute, ultimate betrayal of his lifemate. In our world, there can be no greater sin than trying to murder one's lifemate and condemning her to a half-life of sheer suffering and deliberately killing our children."

Dax paced restlessly again, as if the smoldering rage buried so deep was climbing too close to the surface for him to contain.

"The lifemate bond doesn't allow one to survive long without the other," Dax continued. "Mitro chose to give up his soul, so he wasn't affected—although he couldn't bring himself to kill Arabejila. She traveled with me, devoting herself to tracking him and helping me send him to the next life, but she suffered greatly through the long years."

"And you felt her sorrow."

"Males lose their ability to see color or feel emotion after a couple of hundred years, or sooner if they make kills continually. I used to go to Arabejila's home often when I returned from hunting because just being close to Katalina, her mother—and eventually Arabejila—allowed me to remember feelings easier. I didn't see colors, but I knew what affection was. They made my life much more bearable until Arabejila lost her lifemate. I wanted to be numb, not to feel her great sorrow, or how she had to fight to stay alive. In a way I felt I should be punished by her emotions, although she tried to hide them from me."

Riley brushed his mind with hers, the lightest of caresses, needing to surround him with her love. She knew he could barely stay there on the balcony, with the night sky trying to soothe him. It was a night for recriminations. Ever since he'd seen the infant and the torn body of the child's mother, Dax had been restless and more than uneasy. She just didn't know how to help him.

"We're safe here, aren't we? Inside this house? Mitro can't know we're here, can he?" she asked. "I can sense that you're unhappy here. We need a place to stay, and Riordan De La Cruz has given us this beautiful house. You have a resting place . . ."

"Which I would never use, and he is well aware of that," Dax said, his face darkening.

"Why? He's Carpathian. He has a lifemate. Gary and Jubal both know him. His sister-in-law, Jasmine, is here."

"The Old One is uneasy," Dax said. "I can't seem to settle him down. He's leery of Riordan. And Carpathian hunters do not ever allow others to know their resting places."

The dragon soul moved against hers. The dragon was sleepy, yawning, waiting for Dax to discover it was the hunter worried, not the dragon. The dragon would flame an enemy immediately and take care of any problem. There wouldn't be the incessant talking.

As if the dragon had given him a little push, Dax continued, "When I go to ground, I will not have the luxury of being close to you, not unless I use what has been made available to me. I can't keep you safe."

Riley frowned, trying to understand. "Riordan appears to be very hospitable. He's clearly devoted to his lifemate and his sister-in-law. What worries you—um—I mean the Old One?"

"I knew the oldest brother long before they came to this place. Then, they did not call themselves by these names. The eldest was not only shadowed, but held great darkness in him, even as a boy. If Mitro could still make the choice to give up his soul, it stands to reason that any Carpathian male could commit such an atrocity."

There it was. No one was safe. Riley frowned, trying to put pieces of information she found in his mind with data she'd learned from a few conversations.

"Dax, can you please explain the lifemate bond to me one more time so I can better grasp the real concept? Gary tried to, but I don't really fully understand." She was missing something here, or Dax was. And given his state of mind, his explosive response to danger, she needed to be very knowledgeable about his world now. She'd been going on instinct, but the information was extremely important.

Dax crossed to her and sank into a chair beside her. Instantly his fresh scent enveloped her. He smelled of the outdoors. Of danger. Of heat and fire. Her entire body reacted to his close proximity, an electrical current surging through her bloodstream. Her lungs burned, and deep inside she ached. He reached out and took her hand, the movement so gentle, his touch barely there, but every sense heightened until she could feel every breath he took.

His skin was warm, almost hot, as his fingers tangled with hers. His thumb stroked caresses over the back of her hand. He was silent a moment, idly playing with her fingers, sliding his in between hers in slow, almost brushstrokes. She could barely breathe, barely think.

She found it strange that even here, back in a city teeming with life, with people, she was all too aware of her hunger and need for Dax. His love for her was so strong in that moment it was almost tangible, wrapping her up in strong warm arms when he was barely touching her. Her love for him brought her to tears when she was alone. Every beat of his heart was heard by hers. Every breath he drew, she drew, too. More than anything, right now she wanted—no, needed—to find a way to comfort him.

"A male Carpathian loses all emotion and the ability to see in color after the first two hundred years. Sometimes sooner. The more one hunts and kills, the faster the process. In my case, it was very fast. We are taught that there is one soul between a man and his lifemate. He holds the darkness, and she is his light. There is only one and she must be found."

Dax brought her hand to his mouth, kissing her knuckles. "I found you."

"Because you bound me to you, our becoming lifemates would prevent you from turning," she reiterated.

"So I thought it would. Now"—he shook his head—"I don't know. Mitro knew Arabejila was his lifemate and still, he turned."

That was one fact she couldn't dispute. "But," she felt compelled to point out, "Mitro bound Arabejila to his lost soul *after* he became vampire. They were lifemates, but he never truly claimed her until he'd deliberately chosen to give up his soul. He was already the undead. He couldn't bring himself to kill her, that bond at least transcended his need to kill, but he wanted her to suffer. Perhaps she could have saved him if he'd claimed her before he turned."

Dax leaned forward for a moment, and still holding her hand, he covered his face briefly. "I don't think there was any hope of that. He was so black, Riley. So dark."

"Did you see darkness in Riordan?" she asked. Very gently she put her hand in his hair, all those soft, thick spiked strands she loved to stroke caresses in. "He seems so devoted to his *päläfertiilam*." His word for lifemate rolled off her tongue. She was beginning to like the sound and fuller meaning of the Carpathian description even better than the translation of "wife." Somehow it seemed so much more.

Dax shook his head. "Still, we're in his home. He shares these places with all of his brothers. I'm hunting Mitro, an extremely powerful vampire. He's evolved into something I don't understand, and that makes him even more dangerous. If I have to divide my attention between Mitro and one of these hunters we could be in trouble."

The way he was touching her was making it difficult to think straight. His voice was hypnotic, a blend of smoke and velvet. She leaned her head against his shoulder. "You have a way of making me forget about danger, Dax. Do you really think Riordan is an enemy to us?"

"That's good. I don't want you to worry."

You worry enough for all of us, the Old One contributed. *If you'd like I can burn down the house and kill them all.*

"Don't you dare," Riley said.

"He wouldn't," Dax assured her. "He's teasing you. Riordan appears to be a good man, and very devoted to his lifemate, but that sliver of a shadow is in him. Nowhere like his eldest brother, but it's there. He's capable of great . . ."

"Violence?" Riley smiled at him. "Like you? Do you have a shadow in you?"

"Once, before all this started, Mitro said I did. He told the elders the reason I could 'see' into other hunters was because I carried the curse of darkness myself."

The Old One snorted, the sound reverberating through both of their skulls.

"I don't think he's taking anything Mitro said very seriously," Riley confided in a whisper, as if that would keep the dragon from hearing.

"We have company," Dax said, his face totally expressionless, as if it had been carved in stone. Emotions could be shared with her, but no one else.

Movement caught her eye. Dax shifted subtly, putting his body slightly in front of hers, his arm sweeping across her to pin her in the deeper shadows. Jubal held the door of the terrace open for a small, very pregnant woman to precede him.

Jasmine Sangria sent them a tentative smile. "Are we intruding?"

"No, of course not," Riley said hastily. "This is your home, and you're very kind to share it with us."

Jasmine, Riley had learned upon their arrival, was Riordan De La Cruz's sister-in-law. Her sister, Juliette, was fully Carpathian, brought into the Carpathian world by her lifemate. Jasmine was not. She was jaguar, as Juliette had been before her conversion, and she'd been kidnapped and raped before her cousin and Juliette with Riordan had been able to rescue her. Juliette admitted to being overprotective of her.

Jubal pulled a chair from the patio dining set and gestured for her to sit. Jasmine made a face at him, but slipped into the chair. Jubal covered her with a quilt. It was quite beautiful, woven of special material. Jasmine bunched the material in her hands, obviously finding the quilt soothing.

She took a deep breath and sent them another shy smile. "I've never spent much time in a city and sometimes it feels as if I can't breathe here."

Juliette had informed them that Jasmine had spent her life in the rain forest.

Jubal pulled up a chair beside hers and sank into it, leaning a little toward her, looking almost protective. "That's understandable."

Dax threaded his fingers through Riley's hand and held it tight against his chest. "You're going to have that baby very soon."

Jasmine nodded. "I certainly hope so. I feel like I've been pregnant forever." She gave a little laugh, and for the first time, she sounded young instead of tense. "She kicks all the time."

Juliette, Jasmine's sister, came out onto the terrace carrying two glasses. She handed one to Jubal and one to her sister. "You need to stay hydrated, Jasmine."

Jasmine made a face at her when she continued to stand over her, frowning. "I'm all right, Juliette. At this point, if I go into labor, it's all good, right? I couldn't stand staying indoors another minute. Jubal came with me and Dax is out here so I am perfectly safe."

Something in Juliette's manner alerted Dax that Juliette didn't think Jasmine was safe in the least, but she merely shrugged, pulled out another chair and sat down. The terrace was filling up fast. Something was going on here, and that added to his uneasiness. Riordan had greeted them and left in haste. He obviously knew Gary and Jubal, but what Carpathian male would leave his lifemate and sister-in-law unprotected with an unknown hunter so close to his family? Times had certainly changed. And what emergency had drawn him from the residence?

Juliette smiled at Dax and Riley, but her smile didn't light her eyes. "Riordan will be home any minute. I'm so sorry he had to leave abruptly."

"Jubal, how long have you known Jasmine and Juliette?" Riley asked. He seemed so comfortable with the family, and they'd greeted both Gary and Jubal as old friends.

"We've made a few trips here," Jubal said, "and they've always put us up in one of their homes."

"We enjoy their company," Jasmine said. "Speaking of, where is Gary?"

"On the phone," Jubal answered with a little grin. "He and my sister Gabrielle talk endlessly and they're very excited about a flower Dax found for us up on the mountain."

"A flower?" Juliette leaned forward. "Gary and Gabrielle have been working hard to discover why we can't carry our children. I thought it was the microbes . . ."

"In part," Jubal agreed, "but Gary says that doesn't explain everything. Both he and Gabby think there's a combination of things that have led up to the reason infants can't go to ground, mothers can't carry or breast-feed and only male children were being born."

Riley's heart jumped. She had known the Carpathian species was on the verge of extinction, Gary had given her a brief overview, but she hadn't considered what that would mean to her and Dax when they chose to have a baby. She wanted children. Lots of them. She had been an only child, just as her mother had been. She'd been lonely at times and envied her friends who had siblings.

We will have many children if that is your desire, Dax assured. He brought her hand to his mouth and nibbled on her fingers, sending little darts of fire racing through her bloodstream. *You are very fertile. I am capable of having children. If there is a problem, as I understand, with the soil, I've been in a volcano, and the earth would let you know not to rest where there is anything that would harm you.*

He had a way of speaking so matter-of-fact, with absolute calm, that she couldn't help but believe him, the tension instantly fading away.

"The worst is carrying to term and having the child for a few months only to lose it," Juliette said. "So many of our women had to suffer miscarriages, stillborns or losing their children in that first year." She shook her head. "I don't know if I could bear that."

Jasmine placed her hands protectively over her baby. "That would be so awful."

"It isn't going to happen to you," Jubal assured, putting his hand on her arm, a gentle, reassuring gesture.

Jasmine remained relaxed, even with Jubal's touch.

I saw her in his memories, Dax told Riley. *She didn't even like to be around men after what happened to her, but both he and Gary made a point of building a friendship with her. Jubal has two sisters, and he hated that she was so alone all the time. He's really made an effort to spend time with her.*

He's a good man, Riley said. *I don't know what I would have done without the two of them, Gary and Jubal.*

"I didn't have a chance to tell you how sorry I am about your mother," Juliette said. "A terrible loss. Gary and Jubal told us what happened."

Meaning they knew the truth. Riley's fingers curled in Dax's hand. She was glad he was there beside her giving her comfort. Without being surrounded by plants and the soil, Riley felt her mother's loss acutely. Dax slipped his arm around her, pulling her beneath his shoulder.

"Sometimes I feel like our world has been turned into a killing ground," Jasmine said. "I dread going back there with my baby, but I don't like the city."

"Why don't you recoup in the Carpathian Mountains?" Jubal suggested. "Solange is there right now with Dominic. We could take good care of you there. And your cousin would be thrilled to see the new baby."

Juliette stirred, scowling at Jubal, obviously not caring for the idea.

Jasmine's face lit up. "That's a good idea. I never thought about going somewhere altogether different, but I'd love to visit that area. It looks so beautiful, and it's remote enough that I think I could breathe there."

"Riordan won't be able to get away from here for a while," Juliette cautioned. "Months maybe. We'll take you as soon as we can though, if that's what you want."

Jasmine reached out her hand to her sister. "I'm quite capable of going by myself, Juliette. You can't spend your entire life worried about me. You've already spent far too many years doing just that. I'm all grown up."

"You're my family, Jasmine," Juliette said. "I like being close to you. It's important to me. If you think for one moment you're a burden, you're not and never have been. I'd hoped you and Luiz . . ." Her voice trailed off.

Jubal scowled darkly, sitting up straight, all that languid cool dissipating. "Luiz? Who the hell is Luiz?"

Uh oh. I think Jubal has a thing for little Miss Jasmine, Riley confided, amusement spilling into Dax's mind. *Mr. Calm, Cool and Collected has been hiding a secret, biding his time and getting ready to swoop in and get the girl when she isn't looking.*

"Luiz is just a friend," Jasmine said. "He and Manolito are friends," she added in explanation to Jubal. "He was jaguar, like Juliette and me. He did his best to help us, and the other males had turned on him. He's Carpathian now."

"You could be Carpathian," Juliette insisted. "Anytime you want . . ."

Jasmine was already shaking her head. "I just want to be me for a little while. So much has happened and I'd just like to have a little peace and enjoy my baby."

"Luiz would be so perfect," Juliette said. "Are you certain? He understands the jaguar in you and he knows our past. He'd be good to you."

"I don't love him," Jasmine returned gently. Firmly. "I'm sorry, Juliette. I know I must frustrate you, but when I settle down with a man, I want what you have. Real love. Real commitment."

"Then you need a Carpathian."

"Are you saying human males aren't capable of real love for their women? Because I'm going to tell you right now, that isn't so," Jubal demanded, an edge to his voice. "My father is totally devoted to my mother and he always has been."

"I have to admit," Riley chimed in, "my father was devoted to my mother as well. We knew several couples who had been together well over fifty years. That should count for something."

"I'm sorry," Juliette apologized immediately. "I know that sounded very wrong. I didn't mean it that way. It's just that the idea of me outliving Jasmine is upsetting to me." She ducked her head, looking down at her hands. "We both have lost so much. There's only Solange and Jasmine on my side of the family."

Jasmine held out her hand to her sister. "It's always been the three of us. Now we'll be four. I haven't ruled out converting yet, but I want to know if my baby is capable of converting before I even consider it."

Jubal sank back in his chair, looking for all the world as if he hadn't a care. Jasmine glanced at him and then down at her hands.

There's trouble right there, Dax predicted. *He doesn't like the idea of her converting.*

Both of his sisters have, Riley pointed out. *Couldn't he? He must have the same ability. Can't a male be converted?*

I would assume so. Obviously this Luiz was. I caught impressions of him as a jaguar. Dax turned his head just as Juliette did. Riley felt him frown. *Riordan is back and he is very unhappy. He's asking Gary to get Jasmine inside.*

Riley glanced at Juliette. She blinked back tears and kept her face carefully averted from her sister. Definitely something was wrong.

Gary emerged from the house. "Jasmine," he called, waving at the others. "I've been without a worthy chess opponent for a long time. Come put me out of my misery."

"Hey!" Jubal objected.

Jasmine smirked at Jubal. "You haven't been holding up your end of the chess matches?"

"Watch yourself, woman," Jubal cautioned. "Don't be throwing out challenges you aren't going to be able to win."

"Any time, any place," Jasmine offered. She laughed and held out her hand to him. "Stop being lazy and help me up. I'm a beached whale."

"You're beautiful and you know it. Stop fishing for compliments," Jubal said, lazily coming to his feet. He drew her up, not moving back so that when she stood, her body was up against his. He rested his palm on her swollen belly. "You're not even very big."

"I'm big." She didn't move, just looked up at him, nor did she remove his hand.

Jubal smiled and stepped back, giving her the space to go around him. "Go practice. You'll need it."

"You're going to eat those words," Jasmine warned.

"Any time, any place." Jubal threw her words back at her.

Her laughter floated back to them. The strain and tension were gone from her, and she sounded young and happy again.

"Thank you," Juliette said to Jubal. "I haven't heard her sound like that since . . . the last time you were here."

Riordan appeared on the terrace and Juliette went to him immediately. He put his arms around her, holding her close to him.

"I take it there wasn't good news," Jubal said.

Riordan shook his head. "No. I think Jasmine is right. Someone has been following her, and they're after the baby."

Jubal swore. "Damn it. Jaguars?"

"Probably. They would be the most likely suspects."

"Maybe not," Dax said. "We didn't have time to tell you. Your pilot asked us to check on Juliette's friend."

Juliette turned her head to look at Dax, but Riley could see by her face, she already knew what he was going to tell them.

"I'm sorry, Juliette," Dax said formally. "She was dead. Murdered."

"Her baby?"

Riley tightened her fingers around Dax's.

Dax shook his head, his tone as stoic as ever, his face carved from stone. Only she felt that blast of emotion, the volcano going off deep inside him. "Mitro killed the child as well as the mother. I need to know everything going on here. Everything."

18

"Jasmine is going to give birth any minute," Riordan explained. "Juliette feared complications, so we've been bringing her to a doctor they know here in the city. She's jaguar and takes care of many of their women. A couple of days ago, she began to feel as if someone was following her. I wasn't with her, but some of our people were and they saw nothing to make them suspicious. Juliette and I went out when we rose and we couldn't find a hint of anyone watching her. Still, she was so uneasy, I didn't dismiss it."

"Thank God," Juliette said.

"This evening, I received a call, first from a friend in the police department and then from Jasmine's doctor. The police made a grisly find when they busted a warehouse filled with drugs. A bunch of Goth kids belonging to some underground cult were making their home under the warehouse and they had the bodies of six infants dipped in gold. They claimed the babies had been stillborn, and they were selling them on the black market."

Horrified, Riley stepped back and bumped into Dax. He dropped his hands onto her shoulders to steady her. Instantly, she felt comforted. His hands were large and strong, but his touch was very gentle. He didn't say much, but he didn't need to.

"That's disgusting," Jubal said. "I hope they throw away the key."

“There are some cultures that believe having the body of a child dipped in gold in their home brings luck,” Riordan said.

“Who in their right mind would think that an infant’s body covered in gold would bring them luck?” Jubal demanded. “That’s sick.”

“Nevertheless,” Riordan said. “It happens. It’s just that Dr. Silva, Jasmine’s doctor, thinks all six babies came from women going to her clinic. All jaguar women. She said that six of her patients in various stages of pregnancy had suddenly stopped coming to her; they’d just disappeared. She tried contacting them, but no one called her back. Jaguar women can be very elusive . . .”

“They have to be,” Juliette defended. “But they wouldn’t stop going to their doctor before giving birth.” She stepped away from him and paced in agitation some feet away.

Riordan reached out to her. Juliette immediately put her hand in his. “I know you’re worried about her, but nothing will happen to Jasmine. She’s got all of us to look out for her.”

“She’s been through so much,” Juliette said. “To add this is just wrong. If she really knew they were after her again, she’d be devastated.”

“Her doctor warned her to be careful. She had a bad feeling about the other women and had even gone so far as to go to the police, but no one seemed alarmed. Dr. Silva said two of the women had acted uneasy and one said she thought someone had been outside her house the night before,” Riordan continued. “Most of the jaguar men are scattered, but many have gone to the cities. We were afraid they would begin stalking the women here.”

“That’s what Dr. Silva thought,” Juliette said. “That the men had found them. All of those targeted were carrying jaguar babies, so we assumed it was the males looking to take them back.”

“Juliette and I went to the women’s homes, believing we could pick up the trail and get the women back,” Riordan added. He shook his head and glanced at his lifemate.

“It wasn’t jaguar men,” Juliette assured. “There was no evidence of any of them anywhere near the women’s homes or properties. I would have been able to scent them.”

“You believe a vampire has something to do with these disappearances?” Riordan asked Dax, cutting to the chase.

"You're uneasy. Juliette is uneasy. Jasmine is."

Riordan frowned as he nodded slowly. "I felt the presence of evil but I couldn't track it. It was very strange. We hunt the forest and cities all up and down South America. This felt different to me. I couldn't quite catch the scent, but I knew it was there. Very evil and yet so faint that I couldn't follow the trail. I hunt vampires and yet this was . . . *different* is the only word I can think of. I couldn't identify it as the undead."

"We tracked Mitro here to this city," Dax said. "It would not surprise me if he was behind this. He is unlike any vampire you have ever faced, and it is not easy to track him, not even for me and I've followed him for hundreds of years. He is . . . different."

Juliette shuddered and moved closer to Riordan. "Jasmine can't know this, and she has to be guarded around the clock."

"Gary and I can stay with her during the day," Jubal volunteered.

"And thanks to Juliette's cousin, Solange, we're able to be up longer during the day, so if there's need we can come to your aid," Riordan said.

Dax felt the familiar leap in his brain connecting dots. "Solange?" He needed more information. He had no idea what he was onto, but he'd been following Mitro for so long that he knew the way the vampire thought and acted. His brain had jumped at the casual conversation, his instincts suddenly kicking in.

"Solange is my cousin," Juliette said. "Lifemate to Dominic."

"Of the Dragonseekers? He still lives?" Dax asked.

Riordan nodded.

Dax crossed to the railing. He was unused to being so close to so many people, and looking out at the lights of the city made him feel less closed in. "What is different about Solange's blood that allows you to stay in sunlight?"

"She's jaguar royalty," Riordan explained. "She's exchanged blood with us, and that's allowed us to handle the sun for longer periods of time, but there is a cost. The weakness is severe and comes on unexpectedly and very rapidly. We try not to use that ability too often because you can find yourself in danger very quickly, but it does give us some advantages we didn't have before."

"Does all jaguar blood allow Carpathians to stay longer hours in the sun?" Dax asked, staring straight ahead at the dazzling display of lights.

"If that was the case, I would have been the first to discover it," Riordan said. "Juliette was jaguar. I would have been able to spend more hours awake."

"How do you know that you couldn't? Did you try?" Dax asked.

Riordan and Juliette looked at one another, clearly shocked. Riordan eventually shook his head. "I didn't think to try, why would I? Still, I don't think Juliette's blood could have done what Solange's blood does, and of course now, Juliette's wholly Carpathian so it's a moot point."

Dax turned to face the Carpathian. He was a hunter first, and he knew his prey almost as well as he knew himself. If Mitro was behind killing pregnant women and taking their babies, it wasn't all for his amusement. He had targeted each victim deliberately. If he had found a way to prolong his time in the early morning or evening hours, he could do even more harm than he already was doing. He made a formidable enemy already. By adding daylight hours, he would have more time to recruit his army and more time to kill or make puppets.

Riordan shook his head. "No vampire could ever go out in the sun. It isn't possible."

"Mitro is no ordinary vampire," Dax cautioned. "I took his heart and threw it in the magma pool and still he lives."

Riordan went very still. Juliette's gasp was audible.

Dax had no way of knowing, but the morbid, depraved taking of unborn infants from their mothers *felt* like Mitro. He looked at Riley. Obviously, she was thinking along the same lines as he was. She looked horrified. Truly horrified. He wanted to put his arms around her and shelter her close to his heart, keep her from twisted, depraved monsters.

Her eyes met his. She sent him a small, reluctant smile and his heart turned over. *I'm all right. We've seen how bad he is. And we came here for this.*

Arabejila's blood as well as her gifts—and those of her ancestors—ran deep in Riley's veins. If there was one person who could track Mitro, it was Riley, and she understood that.

"Take us there, to one of these houses where you felt a presence," Dax ordered. "Tonight. We have no time to lose." He didn't give the others time to refuse, turning on his heel, holding out his hand to Riley and gliding toward the door.

There was relief in leaving the inside of the house. He could see how the Carpathians had designed it to suit them, but they were used to the modern world and civilization. He was not. The air didn't feel the same. *Nothing* felt the same to him inside four walls. Riley's presence helped, but he preferred the outdoors and the mountains.

Riordan hesitated. "Juliette?"

"I'll stay with Gary and Jubal. We can watch over Jasmine. With safeguards, if the vampire has targeted her, his puppets won't be able to get in here if you don't return before the sun comes up. We'll be safe as long as we're inside."

Riordan nodded and then followed Dax out. Both hunters inhaled deeply, scenting the air, seeking information. Riley crouched low as both worked on the safeguards for the house, sinking her hands into the soil. Dax linked with her to gain knowledge the earth might provide to them.

There was always that first little resistance to his push into her mind. She hadn't quite figured out how to be open mind-to-mind at all times, but she couldn't resist the way he poured warmth into her once he touched her. His half of their soul cried out for hers, and hers answered. There was no more being alone, every shadow gone, and each time they shared minds, they both found it difficult to break apart.

His blood surged hotly the moment they shared their intimate connection. He waited until the first rush passed and watched his heart, that he didn't change the rhythm of hers. Deep in her veins, a pulse thrummed, keeping time to her heartbeat. She seemed to be concentrating on what should have been her own pulse.

He stepped closer to her, dropped his hand on the back of her neck, and moved deeper into her mind. She was following something she understood, but he hadn't quite grasped yet. He stayed still, waiting. He was a hunter and he had learned patience. Whatever was eluding him surely would come to him, there was no doubt in his mind.

There it was. A tiny irregular beat *inside* her pulse. He listened intently.

It's not right, Riley said. *This is strange. Something is very wrong here. Feel the way my blood moves in my veins. It's very faint, but there is something pulling me toward the edge of the cliffs, over to the left. I think he was there . . .*

She broke off, shaking her head, and turned to look around her. A small grove of trees was off to the left, branches swaying slightly.

I would know if he was here.

You're right. It wasn't him, but his blood was here. A distance so as not to disturb the occupants, but someone or something is watching.

Dax pushed a brushing of air that would feel like a touch on Riordan's shoulder to warn him. He switched to the common Carpathian mind link. *We are not alone.*

The watcher was no doubt following the movement of Riordan's hands as he set the safeguards over his home in the city, rendering those inside vulnerable.

You are certain of this? Riordan didn't stop the motion of his hands, but he set the weaves in odd patterns.

Riley is certain of it, and that's good enough for me. I catch a faint trail, but it isn't Mitro. Riley says his blood is here, Dax informed the other Carpathian.

He had taken both Jubal's and Gary's memories, but he had not done so with Riordan. Memories were sacred to each Carpathian male. Sometimes honor was kept only with memories. He felt handicapped by his lack of knowledge of what had transpired in the history of his people. Gary had the most knowledge, but he was human and didn't have the data required for centuries of fighting vampires or what information the hunters had on them or the tricks they used.

Riley trembled beneath his fingers, and Dax started a slow massage. *Just continue what you're doing,* sivamet. *We will find it, this watcher. Can you track the blood without the watcher?*

Her mind moved against his and once again he experienced that strange weakness in the vicinity of his heart. She didn't protest, or fall apart, but kept her hands deep in the soil, her head down as if listening intently.

Yes, I think there have been others, back in the same grove of trees. More than one, but a few days ago. The trail is very faint, but if I listen to my blood, the call is there.

Dax continued massaging her neck with one hand, the other down at his side, hand open, subtly moving, shifting the wind just slightly, bringing it rushing up from the ravine, swirling around the grove of trees and gusting straight to him.

Second tree from the left. High up in the branches. A rodent. Mitro's using him the way the mages used familiars, he informed Riordan.

I've got him now, Riordan acknowledged, dropping his hands as if he had finished and thought his home safe.

You'll have to come with us, Dax whispered softly into Riley's mind. *If you don't, he'll know we're onto him.* He had to keep reminding himself she wasn't Carpathian, but she didn't flinch, although she didn't attempt to hide her silent reluctance.

She took the hand he extended to her and got up, taking her time dusting off her jeans. He knew she was giving herself time to compose and steel herself for whatever was to come.

"I'm ready," she said aloud, flashing a smile to him and then to Riordan. "Let's go. I'll do the shopping. Those boys are starving, and I doubt the two of you know much about grocery shopping." She even managed a small laugh at her own joke.

He tangled his fingers with hers, amazed at her playful tone, not overly loud; in fact, he wasn't certain the watcher could hear her, but it didn't matter. She acted perfectly natural. He quickened his pace without seemingly doing so. Riley fell a step behind, but he appeared not to notice, leaning toward Riordan to say something in a low voice as they walked down the winding path to get to the vehicle parked in the left-side garage nearest that small grove of trees. She tucked in behind him in that way he was coming to love, her hand slipping into his back pocket as she matched his pace, using his body as a shield.

It's tracking your lifemate, Riordan warned. *It isn't looking at either of us, just her.*

Dax was careful not to look at the creature directly, but he'd already seen the beady eyes glowing bright through the foliage and the stare was directed solely at Riley. *Mitro believes she is someone else and he fears her. He rejected his lifemate Arabejila and he intended to kill her, but he couldn't force himself to finish the job. She is the one person he can't kill, so he'll send every minion he has to do the job for him,* Dax explained.

That thing is looking at me, Riley hissed in his mind.

She sounded scared. Her hand transferred from his back pocket to the small of his back. She bunched his shirt tightly in her fist.

It will be all right.

That's easy enough for you to say. It isn't looking at you.

He suppressed a smile. *Stop looking at it.*

It has big teeth.

Of course it does. It is meant to kill you. I'm certain the claws are of equal size. They were in striking distance now.

She thumped him hard on his back. *Do you think you'll ever get the concept of watering down the danger level?*

I don't understand what that means. He was genuinely puzzled. She was half serious, half joking, but he didn't like the idea that he might be failing her on some level. How did one "water down"—whatever that was—*danger*? Any creature a vampire used to do his bidding was extremely dangerous, especially one that wanted to kill his lifemate.

Of course you don't.

There was a hint of laughter in her voice. Arabejila had a gift allowing a Carpathian male who had lost all color and emotion to feel some faint sensation, but the times he managed to feel something, the reaction had been so faint and distant, he'd never been entirely certain whether or not the sentiment had been merely a long-ago memory, or if he'd really experienced feeling. Certainly not humor. Arabejila had always had a sense of humor, but he hadn't always understood her laughter.

Now, with Riley, humor had become fun. He liked teasing her. And he liked that she teased him. He was coming to understand humor, and hers always showed itself at unexpected times.

It's getting ready to attack.

Dax could tell Riordan's voice in her head startled Riley, but the only sign was the way she bunched the back of his shirt tighter in her fist and pressed her forehead against his back, making herself smaller. All the while, she stayed in step with him.

When I say, let go and crouch low.

He was in her head and heard her silent protest, but she nodded several times indicating she heard him. She was afraid. Really afraid. He was used to Arabejila, who always followed his orders without question. Like him, she didn't fear death. Both had lost all hope of a lifemate, and knew death was now a matter of honor. Now, he had everything to live for, but fear was something he wasn't familiar with.

I would not allow you to come to harm, Riley. It was a simple truth. He *couldn't* allow such a thing. She was his lifemate, his world, light to his darkness and there was no possible way he would let anything hurt her. Arabejila understood that . . .

If you compare me to that woman one more time, I'm going to hit you over the head with a very large object. I'm not Arabejila, and I'm not wild about the comparisons.

He swore her teeth snapped together just shy of his skin. She might have torn his shirt.

I think the dragon would be a good thing right now. Maybe you ought to call him out. He's big and he's got teeth, too.

She was royally angry at him, but again, he didn't really understand why. Lifemates were much more difficult than he'd ever considered. And the dragon? She wanted the Old One to protect her? He felt a faint stirring of an emotion he couldn't quite catch or identify.

All the while he tried to puzzle out her illogical reasoning, he kept most of his attention centered on the rodent. Small flames had begun to burn in the beady, glowing eyes. Muscles bunched as it gathered itself in wait for its prey to get close enough.

Now. He gave the command as the watcher leapt from the branches, bursting into the open, hurtling itself through the air straight at Riley.

She dropped low, releasing his shirt as scales slipped over his skin, that hard armor protecting him, and he swung at the creature with a hammerlike fist. He connected with the long snout, smashing through razor-sharp barred teeth, and driving the fangs back down the rodent's throat.

The rodent flew backward, right into Riordan's hands. He caught the watcher around the neck and held tight, staring into the flame-filled eyes. Deep inside those red flames burned black hatred. Riordan only caught the briefest of glimpses in the midst of the swirling, leaping towers of fire raging inside the eyes of the beast.

He's shadowed, Dax, you were right.

The creature snarled and ripped at Riordan.

Now, but watch for the sliver to try to save itself.

Before the shadowed rodent could sink its claws into Riordan's skin, the hunter hurled it into the air. Dax summoned dragon fire, opened his mouth and breathed a torrent of flames to engulf the watcher, burning it fast. The smell was terrible, noxious, even poisonous. The snarling turned to a terrible scream. Riley put her hands over her ears and held her breath.

Both hunters didn't take their eyes off the burning rodent as it fell to the ground. Shockingly, it got to its feet and staggered toward Riley. Dax sent another sweeping torrent of flames at the creature, the force so strong the watcher rolled over and over away from Riley. Burning fast, squealing, the rodent opened its mouth and coughed out a small sliver of darkness, a mere shadow. The shadow fell to the ground and began burrowing deep. Without the shadow of Mitro keeping it alive, the hapless creature burned hot and bright, turning to nothing but ash.

"Stop it, Riley," Dax commanded the moment the sliver landed on the ground. "Don't let it use the soil to get away. Drive it back to the surface."

She plunged her hands into the soil without hesitation, although her fear was tangible. He didn't need their mind bond to feel it. Her murmured chant was low but strong and firm without hesitation. Mother Earth answered her child.

At once the ground rippled, rolled and then shuddered. Dirt burst into the air, a geyser spewing high as the sliver of evil was rejected. The wind shifted away from the Carpathians. Dax and Riordan both leapt through the spray of soil, eyes trained on the single dark shadow as it was taken in the direction of the trees.

Once more Dax called the fire, inhaling deeply, drawing on the reserve in his belly, and sending the stream of flames directly into that sliver of darkness. Screams of rage and pain rent the air. Dogs howled throughout the neighborhood, the alarm spreading throughout the city. Car alarms went off. Sirens sounded. Windows shattered in some homes and businesses. The promise of retaliation—of vengeance—came as the unholy noise faded away.

Riley knelt with her hands over her ears, head down. Riordan checked to make certain both the sliver of evil and the creature were dead.

"It's over," Dax said, hurrying to Riley's side. He reached down and lifted her to her feet, pulling her into the shelter of his body.

Riley leaned into him for a brief moment, taking the comfort he offered. He wrapped his arm around her, nearly crushing her to him, inhaling, drawing her deep into his lungs. Her scent wiped out the repulsive, offensive stench permeating the air around them.

"What was that?" She rested her head on his chest, betraying nerves by the nervous little strokes of one hand over his heart.

"Mitro created a watcher by putting a small sliver of himself into the creature so he could see what it did. That way he could send it where he wanted, have total command, and obtain information at very little risk to himself," Dax explained, bringing one hand up to the nape of her neck to gently ease the tension from her.

She turned her face up to his. "You live in a very scary world. What did he hope to gain?"

"Clearly he was having someone watch either the Carpathian hunters or Jasmine."

Over her head he could see Riordan once again weaving new safeguards around his home. This time there would be no watcher able to report back to Mitro the exact patterns of the wards, knowledge of which would have essentially given his minions free entrance into Riordan's house. Now, it would be nearly impossible for anyone wishing harm to gain admittance.

"You believe he's after Jasmine." Riley made it a statement.

"Don't you?"

Riley stepped back, her eyes meeting his. "Absolutely. He's after her child for some reason and we're going to have to find out why, Dax, and stop him. He's a serial killer. You can call him anything you want, but in the end, he seems to take great pleasure in torturing and murdering innocent people. He's ritualistic in his killings."

"He wants others to think that, Riley. The rituals are put in place to impress his followers. He wants them to worship him and to do that, he demands his sacrifices."

Riley sighed. "If there is a faction of young, lost Goth kids that he's impressed, then he's building an army, a cult, young people looking for answers and strengths, somewhere to belong when they don't fit in. Believe me, Dax, there are so many runaways and throwaways looking for a home, and they'll do anything for the right charismatic leader. They're lost souls, and he's collecting them."

"But the killing of these jaguar women, that has nothing to do with his followers, other than they bring the women to him," Dax said. "At least that's my suspicion. I need you to confirm that for me and see if you can follow the trail."

Riley nodded. "I said I would and I meant it." She gestured toward the burnt ashes. "That changes nothing, but it was after me, wasn't it?"

Dax nodded. "Mitro will do anything to destroy you. You have to understand, his ego, his vanity is enormous. He believes himself superior to all beings, all species. Remember the village in the Amazon?"

She shuddered, giving him one look of reprimand. "It's impossible to forget."

He stroked a caress down her long hair. "He *needs* to be worshipped. That need drives him all the time. He fears nothing on this earth but Arabejila—his lifemate—and her blood is strong in you."

Riley made a little face at him. "When I'm dead and in the ground, I've got a few things I want to say to that woman. I longed for adventure when I was teaching at the university, but I have to tell you, thanks to Arabejila, normal seems really, really perfect."

Dax found his mouth actually curving into a smile at the little bite in her voice. He hastily tried to hide it, knowing it wasn't the smartest move on his part, smiling when she was a little annoyed. He took her hand and urged her gently toward Riordan.

"Take us to the home of the woman who disappeared most recently."

Riley shook her head. "Not there. The doctor's office. Her clinic. Let's go there first."

Riordan frowned. "There're too many people in and out. You'll never get a clear trail."

"If you see a pregnant woman walking down the street, can you tell she's a jaguar woman? I was introduced to Jasmine, and I couldn't tell by look or scent that she was any different than a human woman. Can you? By scent maybe?" Riley asked.

Dax had to concede she had a point. "No, the jaguar is usually well hidden, especially in a pregnant woman."

"So the common thread has to be the doctor they choose to see. *She* has to be how they target the women. They can't just randomly pick a woman walking down the street, not if your theory that Mitro wants jaguar babies for some nefarious purpose is correct. If this Dr. Silva is the only doctor jaguar women trust, then once Mitro knows that, he can figure out that the majority of the women who go to her are probably jaguar. That takes the guess factor out of the game."

Riordan nodded. "Do you think you can catch the trail even with the number of people in and out of that place?"

"Mitro can't be getting the information himself. He wouldn't use a watcher," Dax said. "He can't risk weakening himself. He has to have a human aiding him. And whoever it is wouldn't just be hanging around outside. Someone would notice eventually."

"You think his puppet actually works at the clinic?" Riordan asked.

"That would make sense," Riley said. A small shiver went through her body. "Whoever is helping Mitro sees these women, talks to them and probably has access to their medical histories. They work there and might even deliberately befriend these women. The women would be unsuspecting if they ran into one another somewhere else. Not every one of Dr. Silva's patients is jaguar. How could they be? Does she turn everyone else away?"

"No, of course not. She sees many human patients as well," Riordan said. "No one will be there at this time of night."

Riley shrugged. "I'm perfectly okay with that. I thought we were just going to pick up a trail. I don't want to run into anything that vampire has created."

Riordan flashed a grin. "Where's the fun in that, ma'am?"

Riley sent him a look from under her lashes, her mouth curving slightly, but she didn't answer as she followed Riordan to the car.

Dax found the idea of traveling in a vehicle silly when they could just fly and get there much faster. "Why?"

"We need to fit in," Riordan explained. "With the new technology, we have to be more careful than ever and appear human."

"No one is around. Your home is secluded. Let's just get this done," Dax said.

Riley raised her hand. "I don't fly. I just thought you might like to know that before you make a decision. I have feet, not wings."

Dax caught the little flutter of excitement as the image of the dragon came into her head. He was grateful she didn't mention the dragon to

Riordan, although the Carpathian hunter would assume he simply had shifted into the mythical creature, using the illusion for flight. The Old One was not friendly. He accepted Dax and Dax's woman, but the rest of them—he might consider barbecuing them.

It wouldn't do to have a giant dragon breathing fire over a major city. It would end up on YouTube. There was laughter in Riley's voice.

I am unfamiliar with YouTube.

She sent him images, but he still couldn't quite grasp the concept. Computers and television had to be seen first before he fully understood it. Nevertheless, she was right, it wouldn't do to have the Old One in the skies where airplanes thought it was their space. As far as the red dragon was concerned, the skies were his dominion.

Dax wrapped his arms around Riley and took to the sky, masking his presence from any who might be out. He didn't want to argue about fitting in or using a vehicle. He didn't like that method of travel.

Riordan's laughter echoed in his mind. *I suppose it would be difficult to get used to modern ways after all this time. We were lucky to have seen history unfold. Cars and planes are necessary to us.*

Dax took the time to enjoy holding Riley in his arms. She clutched him tightly, her face, rather than being buried against his shoulder, was turned toward the wind as usual, her long hair streaming around them, brushing his face and shoulders like silken threads.

You love this, don't you?

Her laughter filled his mind. *You know I do. I can't help it. Isn't this the most incredible experience? The stars above us, the lights below, the wind in our faces? Doesn't it make you feel alive?*

He took flying for granted. He'd been doing it for centuries, but now that he was no longer in the volcano, he could appreciate the freedom it gave him. Riley gave him so much more. He was seeing through fresh eyes, experiencing flying for the first time all over again and like Riley—because of Riley—he felt exhilarated. Each time they took to the air, he found joy spilling into him. Hers, his—it didn't matter who felt it first. It was there.

His emotions had returned, but because he wasn't used to feeling, he reverted to using logic, not trusting the intensity around anyone but Riley.

She was at ease in the modern world, yet she managed to function in his world with grace and intelligence even when she was afraid.

She had a way of slipping inside him—into his soul. He knew the Old One felt it as well. As much as the dragon didn't want to feel affection, he was far too emotional not to make those connections. He was fiercely loyal and Riley and Dax were his only family now. He had been protector of a large family unit. The Old One was not a solitary creature as many might think, and Riley had gotten into the dragon's soul as well.

Dax found he was still shaken by the knowledge that she existed—that in his darkest hour, he'd found his lifemate. He had long ago given up any hope of such a thing. He had no idea the intensity of emotion a man could feel for a woman. At times his growing love for Riley was a storm inside of him, a whirling tornado that threatened his stability. He'd always been stoic and calm, yet she shook the entire foundation of his carefully controlled world.

She made him feel vulnerable, exposed to the world whenever he looked at her. He knew it showed, the way she made him feel. He hadn't expected that she could do that to him, make him feel so much that the solitary man he'd become would do anything to keep her.

He found himself fascinated with her smile, watching for it—needing it the way his kind needed the soil. He loved the way her eyes lit up and her face changed the moment her lips curved. He wanted to be the one to bring that smile to her face. There was serenity in her and yet, she had a sense of fun about her which made him think of the possibilities.

Her inevitable mourning for the loss of her mother was so deep even the Old One tried to comfort her. That told Dax she loved without reservation, with her entire heart and soul. He had never considered that she would feel that same intensity, that deeply about him. He felt he'd been handed a miracle.

Dax rubbed his chin on the top of her head, feeling the silky waterfall of thick black hair against his skin. He found it astonishing how quickly a man could adapt to being with a woman. She seemed like a part of him already. He was aware of her every breath, her very heartbeat. He could see why lifemated males rarely hunted. They had too much to lose, and they could so easily be distracted at that crucial moment.

It was necessary to have Riley track Mitro; she was the only one who could do it so fast. And the vampire needed to be stopped, but Dax didn't have to like it.

As if sensing his thoughts, Riley turned her face up to his. *I'm afraid at times, Dax, but I've never felt so alive, and I wouldn't want to be anywhere else but here with you.*

Their minds weren't connected, yet she was so tuned to him she had to be catching part of his concerns, the lifemate bond at work. It was nearly impossible to hide anything from a lifemate, nor would he want to.

I chose a profession I thought I'd love because I have such a love of languages, but I find the students come in and they don't love all the various languages in the same way. I've always longed for adventure. I thought my abilities would carry me into interesting situations, but instead, I became bogged down in the same dull routine.

Riley held her arms out as if she was hugging the night sky, her face turned up toward the stars as they flew over the city. Her soft laughter teased his senses.

If I forget to tell you thank you for these experiences later, I'm saying it now.

He didn't know how to tell her she turned him inside out sometimes, so he tightened his hold on her, drawing her closer to the warmth and shelter of his body. He was keeping her in danger—worse, subjecting her to the depraved cruelty of a monster—yet she was thanking him.

I'll keep you safe. It was the best he could do.

She turned her face up against his chest and rubbed like a cat. *I know you will. Still, I can't help being afraid when some horrible ratlike creature as big as a dog is staring at me with red eyes and strings of saliva dripping from its mouth.*

I don't like to feel your fear. It is a new experience for me, this emotion and yours is intense. Especially fear.

She rubbed her body against him again, much like a cat, sending fingers of arousal crawling down his spine and up his thighs. A fire started in his belly and spread down to settle in his groin.

Behave yourself, päläfertiilam, *we have work to do.*

19

The clinic was small, but very neat. It was dark inside, but with her acute vision, Riley had no trouble seeing inside to the dark, wide-planked floor and the cool, mint-green walls. The rooms, even the lobby, smelled of disinfectant. The three of them each spread out to take one room at a time on their own, hoping to detect the taint of Mitro.

If Riordan hadn't managed to do so by now, Riley feared it would only be the call of blood that would lead them to him—and although Dax had taken Arabejila's blood many times over the centuries, his blood had mingled with hers. The tie was there, but very faint. No, Riley knew if anyone was going to feel that feeble trace, it would be her.

After seeing Dax's memories, those terrible images in his head about Katalina and her unborn child as well as Juliette's friend and her unborn child, and feeling unable to comfort him, she was determined to do this for him. She would lead him to Mitro, and he would destroy the vampire once and for all. *I'm counting on you, Old One.* She whispered it in her mind like a mantra. *To keep him safe for me.*

She let the two hunters go through the examining rooms and even back to Dr. Silva's office. She headed for the reception desk and the files. Whoever chose the victims for Mitro had to have access to the medical records—and she was banking on whoever filed them. Mitro would want to know which women were jaguar, where they lived and everything else about them. Their records would have each patient's address. And whoever was doing the filing was touching each and every record and leaving that tiny invisible trace behind.

Her mother and grandmother and all the women who had held gifts before her had given those gifts to her for one purpose. This was her moment, her time. She was the one who had to point the hunters in the direction of the prey.

At first, as she casually opened drawers and touched each file, she felt nothing at all—and she should have, right? She took a deep breath and let it out, stilling her mind, reaching not only with the gifts the earth had given her, but also with the enhanced senses her blood exchanges with Dax had given her. Still, nothing.

She stood for a moment looking up and down the stacks of files, the endless shelves of them and the cabinet set near the doctor's office. This had to be the right place. She knew she was right. What was she really looking for? Not the clerk. The shadow. The one directing the clerk. The slice of a shadow would be inside that human puppet, and Arabejila had left her one more priceless gift—her bloodline. Her blood called to Mitro's. If there was a sliver, even a small shadow in the clerk and Mitro had put it there, her blood would know.

The idea of any connection to him was so repugnant she actually stood there for a moment with her stomach twisting into knots. Riley set her shoulders and closed her eyes briefly before she reached out and touched the chart on top of the stack waiting to be put away. Her veins pulsed. Throbbed. There it was, the tiniest of threads, but she could track it now that she had it. It was so faint, barely there, but her blood knew him. He couldn't hide from her.

Elation swept through her. "I've got him, Dax. I can find him now. Or at least the one who can lead you to him."

Dax and Riordan joined her immediately. Dax put his arm around her and swept her close. He leaned down to brush a comforting kiss on her forehead. "I knew you'd find him."

"The touch is feminine to me," Riley corrected. "I have no idea who it is, though, but I think I can follow the trail."

Even with Dax standing close, she felt the throbbing in her veins, a drumbeat that lingered in the touch of the clerk. Riley turned and walked past the doctor's office to the back door. "She goes this way to leave."

"Let's go find her," Riordan said. "I'd like to know where she lives."

"If Riley has correctly identified this clerk as the puppet, you have to know that means Mitro is directing her in every one of her actions," Dax pointed out. "She'll be as dangerous as any one of his ghouls." He stated the caution aloud, wanting Riley to understand they weren't dealing with a person anymore. Whoever she had been was long gone. She belonged to Mitro now.

"Keep in mind always," Riordan added, "that this person is responsible for the deaths of at least six babies and their mothers."

Riley moistened her lips. She knew what they were doing—preparing her should they find the woman and have to destroy her. They didn't want her to feel guilty. She'd seen what Mitro had turned villagers into—she really didn't need the warning—but she appreciated it all the same. She knew both men were looking out for her, and that was a comfort.

Dax and Riordan dropped back to allow her to take the lead. Dax scanned outside the clinic and deeming it safe, waved his hand to open the back door. Riley found the spot where the woman kept her small scooter. It was still early enough that there were people on the street. Dax caught Riley's shoulder to halt her, taking another long look around.

"You catch anything?" he asked Riordan.

Riordan shook his head. "I don't feel any danger. I think she's safe, and we'll both protect her. I'll keep everyone from seeing us. Let her track the undead's puppet."

"Are you up for this?" Dax asked. "You don't have to."

"I do," she corrected. "We're going to stop him and this is the first step."

Dax took to the air, holding Riley in front of him, Riordan flanking them, ensuring they were shielded from the evening crowd.

"To the right. Stay to the right." Riley couldn't be caught up in the beauty of the night, or flying. Holding on to that weak link between her blood and that almost nonexistent trace of Mitro was difficult and took every ounce of concentration and discipline she'd developed over the years.

The scooter had turned off the street to follow a narrow alley, through a parking garage and then down through another series of alleys, two so narrow they were more like footpaths between buildings. The buildings seemed old and worn, paint peeling, windows broken. Garbage cluttered the ground and the elderly, mentally ill and addicts shuffled along the alleys or lay under cardboard tents. Prostitutes trolled the corners of every block, some sporting black eyes and most looking hopeless. This part of the city was scarred and ugly, a hidden underbelly beneath the dazzling lights.

There was a short stop at a small store. And then the faint trail was back, the clerk making her way through a maze of back alleys until she came to what looked like an abandoned factory. The high chain-link fence was damaged in multiple areas and the scooter slipped through one of the many tears. The fence was held back with large barrels, just enough for a person or a small vehicle such as a scooter to slip through.

Dax scanned the building. "There are several men and women here."

"Underground," Riordan added. "This seems to be their residence."

"They're making their way out here to the parking lot," Dax added. "Riley, we'll keep them from seeing you. Can you pick her out of a crowd?"

"We'll see. I think so. In any case, we have to follow them just in case she leads us to someone else. She might be one link in a long chain," Riley said.

"Maybe," Dax said, "but given Mitro's personality, if this woman can function in the world working as a clerk, she's probably one of those closest to him. He wants worshippers. He needs a few priests and priestesses. He'll want them to go out and collect others. If he deems them worthy, he'll keep them as followers, otherwise, he'll sacrifice them, and each time he does, he'll make certain his flock is watching him."

"If you believe this woman gathering the names of pregnant jaguar women is a high-ranking member of his inner circle," Riordan said, "then I'm with Riley. Let's get as far on this trail as we can tonight."

They watched the group emerge. Three men and two girls came out of the warehouse. All five were dressed in black. One of the men the others referred to as Davi wore leather pants and a vest. His hair was grungy and long. His arms and chest were covered in tattoos depicting very graphic violent scenes, mainly involving naked women. He shoved his dark glasses on his nose and wrapped his arm around one of the women. He seemed to be in charge, the others agreeing with everything he said as they pushed their way through the chain-link fence and started down the uneven road.

Riley studied the two women. Both were about the same height. Both were covered in piercings and wore the same short black skirts, net stockings, corsets and high heels. The woman with the bright, dyed red hair had her breasts nearly exposed by the grungy male groping her as they walked along the dirty road. Davi called her Ana. Riley dismissed her almost immediately. She was too submissive, too easily controlled and enthralled by her male partner. Riley couldn't see Mitro willingly sharing loyalties. She turned her attention to the other woman.

Riley's pulse jumped when she concentrated on the one the others in the group called Pietra. She walked a little apart from the others, her eyes overbright as if she was on some drug. Her fingers continually twitched against her thigh as she walked, those long, painted black nails tapping out a rhythm only she heard. She carried herself slightly aloof from her companions. She walked a little faster than the others as if she was eager to reach her destination.

Riley closed herself off from everything, trusting Dax to keep her safe. She listened to that tiny throbbing drumbeat in her veins. It was deep, a nagging thump nearly drowned out by the sound of her own racing pulse.

Pietra. The one they call Pietra, she identified.

Pietra suddenly began muttering, her body jerking around her, those bright eyes going dark, almost demonic. Her face pulled into a mask of rage. She looked around her, a careful, thorough sweep of rooftops, the air above her and the buildings surrounding her.

Riley held her breath. Dax tightened his grip on her, drawing her close to him. *Mitro is strong in her. He's looking through her eyes. Don't speak, not even to me.*

She wasn't about to make a sound. She could see the difference in Pietra. Her beautiful face had been the mask covering evil. The woman looking around her, lips pulled back in a snarl of hatred—that was the true character behind that sweet, almost childish face. Riley realized that Mitro had chosen this woman to be in his inner circle because she was easily corrupted. She already had the seeds of cruelty and depravity in her.

Mitro appeals to her. She finds him sexy and dangerous. When he kills others in front of her it turns her on. She bathes in the blood of his victims just as she believes the countess Elizabeth Bathory did. Dax pushed the information into her mind. *She has killed before. Her mother. A sister. A woman she thought was making a move on a man she liked. She was ripe for Mitro.*

What in the world was she doing working in Dr. Silva's clinic around all those pregnant women? Riordan demanded.

I'm afraid your doctor isn't able to read minds in the way we can, Dax pointed out. *She doesn't have that advantage. I imagine this woman is quite cunning and can appear innocent and sweet. That would also appeal to Mitro. He loves deception. The thought that he could send a killer into a place where life is brought into the world would be especially gratifying to him.*

Riley wanted to weep for those lost women, victims of such atrocities, mothers to be, looking forward to the birth of their children, only to meet a woman like Pietra. Beautiful on the outside but cold and rotten on the inside. The women had trusted her, just as the doctor had.

She waited until the small group had gotten a distance in front of them and Pietra had resumed moving steadily toward her destination, no longer suspicious.

They have to be stopped, Dax. Whatever it takes, we have to stop them. She understood the drive Dax had to destroy evil now.

Dax had devoted his life to the purpose of ridding the world of creatures such as Mitro. His life had seemed filled with honor, but terribly bleak and depressing, a stark, ugly world of vile criminals. She felt the need to be right beside him, no matter how terrifying it was. People such as Pietra had to be stopped. And malicious, evil creatures such as Mitro had to be destroyed.

She felt she understood and loved Dax all the more for the insight. How could she not? He might look at his life as one of duty, but she knew just how much looking at those dead people, their lives taken from them in such brutal ways, had affected him. He lived with the memories every day.

She felt the brush of his mouth over the top of her head. *I have you to take the memories away, Riley. Don't feel bad for me. I don't. My life just . . . is. It was my choice.*

She was well aware he had made his choices, just as she was making hers. Whatever it took, being with Dax was worth it. On some level, from the moment she'd laid eyes on the warrior, so badly wounded, she'd known he was meant to be with her.

She poured warmth and love into his mind. They might be surrounded by evil, but they could sustain one another through it.

She began to hear the muffled sounds of music and voices as they approached another set of abandoned warehouses. They followed Pietra and the others through a splintered door hanging on broken hinges. Inside the room were old mattresses, trash, needles and cigarette butts. They went through the large room without hesitation to a narrow opening that led to a staircase.

The music grew louder as did the voices as they descended. Davi pulled open a heavy door, and music blasted out. Riley clapped her hands over her ears.

Turn down the volume, Dax instructed.

It took a couple of minutes to figure out how to consciously control her ability to hear. There were hundreds of conversations going on. She could actually hear individual ones at the same time. Between that and the melancholy music, she felt a little insane. Everyone was dressed in the same dark clothing, with multiple piercings over their faces. Many wore dark glasses even in the dark of the warehouse.

Riordan nudged Dax and lifted his chin toward a man moving among the dancing crowd. Clearly he was selling drugs. Riley looked over the room and noted several dealers in the throng.

Pietra and her friends didn't deign to speak to anyone on that level, but swept across the room to the other side. The crowd parted for them immediately, never hindering their progress, which told Riley a lot about Pietra's status in the underground club. A door on the far side of the room led to another staircase leading down. As far as Riley could tell, the place was a firetrap. There were too few exits and too many people, most of them bored, drunk and high, a bad combination.

Riley felt as though she was descending into hell as they followed Pietra down the stairs to the next level. They came to a doorway with two men guarding it closely. Pietra didn't say a word, but lifted her chin, and one of the guards hastily opened the door. Dax went through fast with Riley. Riordan had to slip beneath the door when the guard shut it just as fast.

Riley nearly gagged. There was a revolting, foul feel to the air. Every breath she took felt as if she was drawing something oily and vile into her lungs. Her heart jumped in alarm. The stench of evil permeated this level. The music jangled her nerves. There were no melancholy strains, but pounding, beating chaotic notes with the crowd mindlessly freak dancing in the space much smaller than the one above them.

The smell of sweat and drugs mixed with soil and blood. The walls of the "club" were dirt, as was the floor. They weren't in a dance club. They were in Mitro's lair, surrounded by his human puppets. Great twisted vines rippled across the walls with obscene life. Riley noticed that everyone stayed well away from them.

Again the crowd parted to allow Pietra through. Davi, Ana and the others followed her, winding their way to the front of the room.

He isn't here yet, but can you feel the anticipation in this room? They're all waiting for him, Dax said.

The drug consumption here is appalling, Riordan said, looking around at the frantic, moving bodies.

There are bloodstains on the floor, the walls and up there on that dais. Dax indicated the platform at the front of the room where Pietra had draped herself casually over a chair, her elegant legs crossed, her foot tapping a rhythm to the pounding beat.

Riley studied her face. Her eyes were nearly glazed, her mouth twisted into a grotesque parody of a smile. The whites of her eyes were nearly gone. A sick black spread like a disease, nearly covering all of her eyes. Riley shuddered. A small sliver of the most evil creature on earth dwelled inside of Pietra, binding itself to the woman's own revolting, malevolent nature.

I need to feel the soil, Dax. She could feel the pain, hear it just underneath the beat of the music.

That's not going to happen. If you put your hands into the soil and his resting place is anywhere beneath us, and he's there, he'll know exactly where you are.

Riley shook her head. She couldn't explain, but she already knew Mitro wasn't in the ground. He was out hunting. The soil was calling to her. Begging her. The mutations he'd created were in pain. Their eagerness for blood was not natural. The human sacrifices fed to them burned like acid, but they had no choice.

The vines stirred restlessly, the wooden liana clacking against one another, leaves lifting as if they might reach for her. Each time the plant moved, it released a gaseous stench of evil into the room, threatening to choke her.

Dax, I can turn the very soil against him. I hear it crying out against an abomination. Nature has an order, and he goes against everything nature stands for. This might be our edge.

And he might kill you, Riley. I don't want to take that chance.

There is no living without you. You're here fighting him. I have to fight him in my own way. I look at that horrible woman sitting up there all smug, knowing she marked six women to be murdered, their babies sacrificed before they were even born, and it sickens me. She's marked Jasmine now, too.

Riley was passionate about her argument. She was angry and determined this was going to end. She might not be a warrior, but she was a child of the earth. She could heal the soil and plants before Mitro returned if Dax would just give her the chance. If Mitro tried to escape Dax and Riordan through the earth, he would be in for a huge shock. She just needed the chance to stop him, and he'd provided the perfect situation without realizing it.

Dax leaned down and put his mouth against her ear, but spoke directly into her mind. *You're certain you want to do this?*

More certain than anything in my life other than I love you with all my heart, she assured him. *Let me do this, Dax.*

First and foremost, she wanted this nightmare to end for him, but the simple truth was Mitro couldn't be allowed to continue with his revolting depravity. Arabejila and every one of her ancestors who had come after her had poured their strength, their gifts into her, making her a vessel for them.

She looked around the room. It was more of a basement, only much deeper beneath the earth. Mitro could bring the high walls down on his followers in seconds should he choose. He could open the earth and dump them into the very pit of hell should he want—and she was certain he probably had constructed this room with that idea in mind. His worshippers would all perish here, in this living tomb while he rose again and again somewhere else once he was bored, or the hunters got too close.

He thinks he's safe for now, Dax conceded. *He has no idea we're even in the city.*

And he obviously doesn't have a clue who I am, Riordan added.

Let's do it then. Riley will need to be at the opposite end of the room, shielded from Pietra. If Mitro uses her eyes to check the room before he arrives, we can't have him spotting her, Dax cautioned.

We have to look like everyone else so we don't draw attention, Riordan suggested. *Everyone is dressed the same way. Black seems to be the color of the day. Change her features as well as your own. Appear younger. Blur your features. If she happens to spot us, and she might, at a glance, she might not really notice us.*

The soil and the plants surrounding them moaned continually. The vines wept poisonous gas. The wooden stalks rattled continuously. They were ravenous, their hunger insatiable. Each plant waited like a bloated spider for prey to come to it. A fight broke out at the far end of the room, up near Pietra. She stood on the dais and watched with glowing eyes as a much larger man shoved a thin, drunken male back toward the wall.

The crowd gave a collective, eager gasp. Instantly, the entire atmosphere of the room changed. All conversation ceased, but the group began to chant, a low sound at first, but quickly swelling to a frenzied volume as one vine snaked out and shackled the boy's wrist, dragging him into the plant. Instantly vines came alive, wrapping around the struggling body.

"Eat! Eat! Eat!" the crowd shouted over and over.

The hapless victim screamed as more and more vines surrounded him, much like giant snakes, wrapping him up and squeezing.

"Eat! Eat! Eat!" The sound swelled in volume.

They sounded as if they were summoning some creature from the very depths of hell. Taproots sprang from the ground, great cables of liana, twisted and gnarled, writhing like snakes across the ground toward the terrified boy.

The sense of anticipation heightened. The crowd watched with glazed eyes and shocking smiles, urging the taproots to gorge on the blood of the victim. The taproots found him in seconds, rearing back and stabbing deep in multiple places. The boy screamed. The crowd roared. Blood ran into the roots so that they swelled and turned deep red black.

Horrified, Riley turned her face into Dax's chest.

I'm taking you out of here. Riordan and I can return and . . .

No! I see what he's doing. Don't you? He really does believe I'm Arabejila. Riley understood Mitro now. *Arabejila was all good. She couldn't conceive of this kind of twisted evil. He knew that. He counts on that.* Determination stiffened her spine. Mitro had made one huge error.

I don't see how knowing that is going to help. Mitro can't possibly know we're here.

No, not yet, but he created this for Arabejila. To shock her. To hurt her. He believes she couldn't face such an abomination of nature. He wanted to use the very thing that is such a part of her to hurt her. This is his slap in the face to her, and at the same time, he believes she would be unable to function in the face of such an atrocity.

She probably couldn't. Not right away. But she'd recover.

Riley's head went up. She turned to face the twisted vines. *His mistake is, Dax, I'm not Arabejila. I'm not all good. Arabejila and the others gave me a gift and a power he has no concept of. I can take back this ground. Consecrate it. He won't be able to penetrate below this room or use the walls. He'll have only the ceiling, and you and Riordan can keep him from that.*

Dax studied her upturned face, the orange and red flames burning bright. His skin was hot against hers as if the volcano in him was very close to the surface. He slowly nodded his head.

Riley had never been more relieved—or more scared. She knew this was her purpose, her moment. The women in her family had prepared her for this and she felt ready, but confronted with such evil, she had to admit, the prospect was daunting if not downright terrifying.

Dax set her on the floor of the club. The crowd was already going back to their mindless dancing or drinking and doing drugs. No one paid attention to three more people dressed the same. Riordan and Dax didn't use a shield, which might attract the attention of the shadow of Mitro in Pietra, rather they simply blurred their images a bit, and looked much younger to blend in.

If Mitro returns, Riley, he'll know you're here. Hurry and do whatever you're going to do right now if you've made up your mind.

Riley sank to the floor and, refusing to let her nerves get the better of her, plunged her hands into the soil. There was an edge to Dax now. He'd gone from lover to warrior and she had no doubt that at the first sign of Mitro returning, if she wasn't ready, he'd take her out of there without consulting her. He was lethal, capable of exploding into violence instantly.

The soil cried out to her for aid, thick with the oily sludge of the abomination of the undead. Riley summoned every healing skill given to her by the women who had gone before. They were there, whispering to her, guiding her through the cleansing ceremony. The ground was leeched of every mineral and nutrient. The only way for the plants to survive was the twisted feeding of the mutated taproots Mitro had provided. Even the insects had fled.

Riley closed her eyes and blocked out the chaotic music and the strange buzz as the crowd danced, marionettes performing for the puppet master pulling their strings, living and dying at his whim. She went deep, searching, calling, drawing . . . Past the terrible stench of the undead's resting place. The ground was soaked in blood and rotting corpses. Human bones were scattered throughout layers of soil.

For a moment her stomach lurched and she nearly pulled her hands from the soil. This job was impossible. The ground had been turned into a bed of evil. The heartbeat of the earth had been silenced, as if Mitro had managed to reach into the very core and destroy that as well.

I'm right here with you, Dax whispered into her mind. *You can do this. Think of it as a cemetery and these people need to be properly laid to rest.*

I am with you, the Old One added. *Their souls cry out for aid.*

My beloved child, Annabel murmured softly. *They are caught between. Only you can bring them peace.*

The voices of the women who had gone before her added their assurances.

Strength poured into her. It wasn't an impossible task to heal the earth. She was born for that purpose. She couldn't allow those Mitro had killed in such a barbaric way to never find rest because of the oily, slimy, disgusting ooze he'd created there in the soil.

Riley had to destroy the malevolent taproots, mutated and rotting with evil. She reached downward, toward the very core of the earth. *I call on the power of the molten light, lend me your might for that which needs to be done, I draw forth your energy to wield and destroy that which is evil and is used as a ploy.*

Riley stretched her hand downward toward the oldest taproot, channeling the molten light she had drawn from the heart of the earth, using it as she would a laser to cut into the root. *Mother Earth I call to you. I seek a gift deep from within your womb. Gift me a stone that I may use it to destroy that which is evil while also releasing these souls, sending them back into a place of peaceful rest.*

Riley sank her free hand deep within the rotting, soil bringing forth a jade-green stone that the earth had harvested for her to use in her fight. Chrysoprase, green in color, cool and smooth, a strong stone used to make conscious what is unconscious while lending Riley its vibrational qualities to tranquilize the evil that was fighting her to live. Riley infused the energy of the light deep into the chrysoprase, channeling it into each taproot. *I combine thee light and jade-green stone destroy these roots that hold to bone, release these spirits so they may rest, give them peace and clear that which is left.*

Riley's hands began to weave a pattern using the remaining healthy roots one knot at a time. A pattern began to emerge. The pattern had to be tight, unable to be penetrated or broken. *Hands that hold divine light twist these vines hold them tight.* Riley worked the vines into an intricate series of woven knots and then sank them deep down into the soil. *Mother Earth hold this tight. I weave these vines to sustain your might. I gift you back what you have born to hold your shape, to sustain your form. Mother who bore us, mother of might, I weave this gift to sustain your life.*

The roots responded to her commands, shooting out hundreds, no thousands of long, thin, very strong secondary roots. From those secondary roots a third and fourth system burst forth. The individual strands began to twist into braids, over and over, spreading through the ground until the mat was a foot thick, two feet thick and building fast, growing in depth, always growing. Fed by the rich loam, driven by Riley's command, the roots kept spreading, weaving themselves together, an impenetrable jungle of fibrous growth just below the surface and going down hundreds of feet.

Exhausted, Riley swayed. She was dizzy, disoriented and she still had to do the same thing to the walls of the room. She felt Dax's arms, so strong, offering her shelter. His skin was so hot, burning against her cheek. She turned her head and nuzzled the heat and fire and defined muscles that were so synonymous with him. His fingers massaging her scalp and neck eased some of the tension.

Take what I offer, sivamet. His voice was pure temptation.

She had been unable to eat anything. The most she'd done was drink water. There was that small part of her that was still human enough to hesitate, but she was so far into his world, it didn't take more than his hand bunching in her hair, turning her mouth to his chest, to those beading drops he'd supplied with one stroke of his fingernail across his muscle.

Every cell in her body reached for sustenance. Craved Dax. Needed him. Burned for him. Dax poured into her, all heat and fire. Power and strength. He filled her. Sustained her.

Riley used her own tongue to try to seal that thin line, unwilling for Mitro to catch the scent of powerful Carpathian blood. *Thank you. That helps.*

He helped. The way he held her. The way he believed in her enough to let her try to heal the earth when everything male in him insisted he protect her no matter the cost. She was in his mind, she knew how difficult it was for him to allow her to be in such danger.

Riley plunged her hands into the soil once more. She could feel the heart beating in the soil again where before there was a deathly silence, like a withered organ a vampire might have. Now, the soil teemed with life. Insects burrowed deep. The roots were quiet now, settled, hundreds of feet deep, woven so tightly together nothing could possibly slip through a crack, not even mist.

She turned her attention to the vines surrounding the wall. This would be much trickier. The first weave had to be subtle, so subtle that it would not draw the attention of Pietra, but would still set in motion the building of thick impenetrable walls around the room the moment Mitro stepped in.

Dax dropped his head on her shoulder. Her heart jumped. Deep in her veins, that terrible throb beat harder. The temperature in the room dropped so that every breath released was a steady stream of white. The leaves on the vines recoiled. Rats climbed along the few supporting beams overhead.

In the midst of so many hearts pounding came the sound of another, stronger, the rhythm different. The beat boomed loud and then softened, only to swell in volume again. The drumming beat pounded at Dax, beat at Riley. Their hearts jumped, almost in recognition. The throb deep in Riley's veins pulsed rapidly.

A hush of anticipation swept through the room. Tension mounted. The crowd swayed back and forth, a mass hysteria, worshipping, eyes opaque. Pietra climbed up on the dais, her face glowing. She looked out over the crowd, arms wide, presenting her offering to her master.

Dax and Riordan closed ranks in front of Riley, making certain there was a group of worshippers in front of them. The music changed, the notes a heralding of evil. Lights flashed on and off, a strobe adding to the hypnotic effect Mitro had on his followers. Mist moved through the crowd, a dense stream of foul air, weaving through the swaying group.

Gasps. Faint cries. The scent of blood rose in the air. Red droplets splattered into the crowd. As the mist trailed through, a hand with long, sharp talons emerged from the vapor and sliced into flesh. Breasts. Chests. Necks. Throats. Most were shallow cuts, but a few unlucky ones had deep cuts. One had arterial spray but didn't seem to notice as he leapt up and down and spun with the others in a frenzy of worship.

Each time the hand materialized from that cold gray cloud, Mitro's congregation went wild. The mist continued its slow procession through the crowd until it was at the dais. The vapor stacked dramatically in the shape of a man, but when it wavered, and went transparent, there were rats piled upon one another forming that man. As they dropped away, unable to hold position, Mitro emerged.

Hands outstretched, wearing a black, hooded robe lined in crimson, he opened his arms to the worshippers. Their yells shook the building. Hands caught at the man with the torn throat, shoving him forward, many dipping their hands in the blood and painting themselves with it. The boy stumbled to the platform, gazing up at Mitro in awe and terror. He made no attempt to cover his torn flesh.

Mitro pointed to the floor of the dais. The boy crawled up onto it. He scuttled across the floor on all fours, groveling, reaching Mitro and wrapping his arms around the vampire's leg. Horrible gurgling sounds came from his torn throat as he begged and exposed the wound to the undead.

The crowd went wild. "Eat! Eat! Eat!" The chant swelled in volume.

Mitro reached down and caught his victim by his hair, dragging him to his feet. The boy had blood running down his neck, into his shirt and dripping on the floor now. Mitro jerked his head back hard, exposing the deep wound.

A cheer went up and the chant grew louder. "Eat! Eat! Eat!"

Mitro opened his mouth wide, exposing his fangs, those blackened, sharp points, pausing for dramatic effect, waiting for his followers to roar again before he sank his teeth deep into the wound.

Mitro would be consumed with the blood thrall, gulping and tearing messily, showing off, feeding on the terror of his victim as the boy became aware he would not be vampire, but was truly fodder for a predator.

Now, Dax ordered.

All three acted simultaneously. Dax rose to the ceiling, positioning himself above Mitro, his scales sliding up and over his body for protection while the red-gold scale dust rained down on the vampire. The dust settled over the vampire like a sticky silken net, holding him in, acting like a glue, so there would be no chance of shapeshifting.

Riley plunged her hands into the soil and gave her command to the vines. The vines instantly complied, weaving tight braids back and forth, up and down, floor to ceiling, closing off every entrance and every inch of dirt that could possibly be used to slip through.

Riordan slammed a bolt over the heads of the crowd, forcing them all to the floor, where they lay dazed, unable to move. He had to trust Dax to kill the undead while he controlled the puppets.

Pietra fell half on, half off the dais, upside down, arms outstretched toward Mitro. The vampire flung the dying boy from him. The body hit the wall of vines and fell to the floor. Mitro drew back his thin lips to snarl a challenge. Fresh blood smeared his chin and dripped from his fangs. His head slowly swiveled from side to side, a cold reptilian motion that made Riley shudder.

Mitro opened his arms. "Welcome, Danutdaxton. Meet my chosen ones. They are always hungry. Rise! Rise, my army, it is your time. Feast on these intruders. Their blood will bring you into my world. You will be powerful and immortal. Eat! Feast! Rise now!"

He's given them his blood. He truly has created an army, Dax warned.

A collective growl rose as the followers of the undead struggled to rise at his command. With Mitro's blood burning and scarring, prodding so many on, Riordan dropped back to protect Riley. Several of the strongest managed to get to their feet and stumble toward him, eyes burning with the need to kill.

Riley fought down panic, plunging her hands into the soil in order to communicate with the vines. She might not be a warrior, capable of helping Riordan with the rabid followers of a vile vampire, but she could at least enlist the plants to help where they could. The vines snaked out along the floor, reaching for the ankles and legs of those struggling to reach Riordan.

In the ensuing chaos, Mitro tried to shift, just as Dax had known he would. The sticky scale dust clung to his cells, refusing to allow him to change to another form. In a fit of rage, he kicked Pietra off the dais and then rocketed into the walls and hit the woven vines so thick they were impossible to penetrate.

He whirled around just as Dax dropped on him from above, his heavy body driving him to the ground. Mitro stabbed at the hunter's eyes, even as he rolled, burrowing into the ground to get away. That escape was closed to him as well, the roots too thick to allow passage. Rolling over and over into the crowd, he slashed and tore at Dax, trying desperately to get through the scales to the flesh and blood.

He opened his mouth and expelled a noxious gas cloud along with death beetles, directly into Dax's face. Dax countered with a blast of fire, incinerating the bugs and lighting the gas cloud. The explosion rocked the ground and building above. The walls expanded and contracted trying to contain the blast. Mitro shrieked in rage and pain as a wall of fire raced over him, blanketing both Dax and the vampire as well as the human puppets closest to them.

Pietra, her clothes on fire, scuttled across the floor like a crab, shrieking, raising a ceremonial knife high and stabbing down repeatedly at Dax's exposed back as he straddled Mitro. Flames rose around all three. Pietra's arm rose and fell one last time and then she crumpled to the floor, rolling, spreading the flames everywhere. The dark sliver of Mitro burst from her body, seeking another host. It shot across the distance back to Mitro, sealing itself to him, adding to his strength.

Dax shut out the sounds of Riordan's battle, his fear for Riley and the smell of burning flesh. He barely felt the flames. He was a fire dragon. He barely felt Mitro tearing at him. He was a Carpathian hunter with one purpose. To destroy evil. He listened to the strange rhythm of the offbeat heart. Mitro had created the heart for the water dragon. The fire dragon's remains had been smashed open.

Call to your heart. Dax was certain he was correct.

The Old One's heart had been left behind in the volcano. Even as he instructed the dragon, he realized, he and the dragon had slowly merged. He used his own heart, just as with the water dragon, strengthening the beat, drawing the other to him.

Mitro shrieked his fury and clawed and spit acid, trying to stop Dax's diamond-hard nails from slicing through his chest. This time, Dax followed the sound, low and to the left. Mitro grew frantic. He sliced at Dax's throat, and tried gulping the ancient blood. Dax concentrated on burrowing deeper into the rotten carcass. Around him Riordan battled the undead's army, keeping them off of the hunter. Around him the flames leapt higher, but Dax was of a single-minded purpose.

His fist closed around the hard gem. He dragged it from the body, opened his hand flat and thrust it into the flames to bathe it in fire. Mitro sprang toward the heart, his hand outstretched. Dax opened his own chest and thrust the brilliant gem inside. The moment his body swallowed the dragon's heart, he closed the wound and watched Mitro.

The vampire's mouth stretched wide in protest. No sound emerged. Insects poured out, maggots fell around him, the flames instantly incinerating them. Mitro shook his head, unable to believe he'd been defeated. He turned his head toward Riley, hatred in his eyes. He lifted his hand, bent on revenge. The fire engulfed him entirely. Without the fire dragon's heart, with no heart of his own, his body rotted, going up in flames.

Dax stepped back away from the noxious-smelling remains. Riordan caught up Riley and they took to the air, rising toward the ceiling as the flames spread throughout the room. Riley coughed and choked, reaching for Dax. He was covered in blood, but she didn't care, wrapping her arms around him, grateful he was alive. He looked tired, the lines in his face etched deep. Beneath them, Mitro's worshippers had succumbed to smoke and flame without their master's blood to sustain them.

Dax and Riordan exited through the ceiling, leaving nothing but ashes behind. "Mitro had been searching for centuries in volcanos," Dax told Riordan and Riley. "Somewhere he must have acquired the knowledge that when dragons die, their hearts remain behind and become petrified. They turn to gemstones. The heart kept him alive until I restored it to its rightful owner."

"I want to go home," Riley said. "Take me home, Dax."

20

Dax set Riley down on the mountain that had been home to him for the last few centuries. The Old One had been born here, as had his children. They had all died here. Riley had been born here. Her mother had died here. The heat fed him, the earth called to him. This volcano was as close to home as he had to give her.

The ruins of the Cloud People stood valiantly, undeterred by the volcano or the passage of time, the stone guardians staring out over the edge of the cliffs, daring anyone to come close. He was surprised that he was the one tense, even trembling a little inside. Riley was as steady as a rock, absolutely resolute, while he was wavering, afraid if something went wrong, he would lose her.

He slipped his arm around her waist as they looked up into what remained of the cloudy forest. "It truly is beautiful here."

"Isn't it?" Riley smiled up at him. "When I was a little girl and my mother would bring me here, I'd pretend I was climbing up a ladder of stars and when we reached the clouds, I would be in heaven."

Dax wrapped a length of her thick braid around his fist and brought her hair to his face. He would never tire of the feel of all that blue-black silk. "Nothing can happen to you."

She looked up at him from under her feathery lashes, her generous mouth curving into a smile of pure love. His heart actually hurt in his chest. Sometimes, like right at that moment, when she was so certain of her love for him, he couldn't find words to express the way he felt about her. There were no words adequate enough for the truth.

He knew she had changed everything for him. She had something about her he couldn't resist. She moved inside of him, wrapped herself deep, and there was no way he could get her out even if he wanted her gone. There was no hiding from her. No running from her. She turned him inside out with just one look from under those long, feminine lashes. She lit up his world with her smile, with her soft, contagious laughter. Her smile took away every bad moment in his life, replacing them with—her.

He was a warrior from centuries past, from a species on the brink of extinction. A predator who survived on the blood of others. There was a wildness in him, and she saw that clearly. She looked into him and saw everything he was, every part of him, and still she stood with him. Calm. Serene. Standing side by side in the face of utter evil, no matter how afraid she was. Her courage was terrifying. Absolutely terrifying.

He turned her to him and she came to him without hesitation, circling his neck with her slender arms, leaning her soft body into his. Her eyes and soft skin held the coolness of the earth. He was flames and heat, the very core of the earth. The moment he touched her she caught fire.

He didn't wait, but lifted her, cradling her in his arms against his chest. He took her into the maze of chambers deep in the mountain. The magma chamber had collapsed in on itself, but he was heading for a special chamber he'd found, located a mile from where the magma pool had formed. He regulated her temperature for her, knowing some of the hallways were far too hot for her tender skin to tolerate. Her lungs wouldn't find enough air.

The opening to the gem-studded chamber was small. He had to set her down to allow her to slip through. He actually had to shift enough to fit, but the interior was well worth the effort. He waved his hand to light the chamber. He heard Riley's gasp of awe and surprise. His heart stuttered in answer. She was pleased.

The walls glittered with rough, uncut diamonds of all sizes. Dark rubies blazed fire across the ceiling. The small natural mineral spring bubbled, steam rising in the cooler air he'd provided. The soil was almost black with richness, good healing soil for her once the conversion had taken place.

"It's so beautiful," she whispered, turning in a circle to take in everything.

He crossed the small distance to her. It would be easy enough to rid her of clothes with a single thought, but he wanted the pleasure of opening her garments and uncovering her glorious skin like the gift she was. His hands went to her blouse. Very slowly, his eyes holding hers, he began to unbutton those tiny covered buttons. His knuckles brushed the swell of her creamy breasts, his fingers skimmed over soft skin.

He parted the material, pulling it back away from her before he dropped his gaze. Her lacy bra pushed up her breasts and the tops of areola and nipples. His breath caught in his throat. He pulled the blouse free of her arms and allowed it to float to the side of the chamber.

He knelt and untied her hiking boots. "Put your hands on my shoulders," he instructed.

When Riley complied, he tugged her boots free, removed her socks, massaging each foot as he did so. Remaining on his knees in front of her, he reached up to the waistband of her cargo pants. His fingers brushed her bare skin and his body tightened, a savage ache only she could assuage. He tugged on her trousers and pulled them over the curve of her hips, encouraging her to step out of them.

She stood in her lacy bra and scrap of panties, the glittering rubies making her glow there in the center of the chamber.

"Take your hair out of its restraints."

She smiled at his choice of words, but said nothing. She pulled the tie from her hair and let it fall free the way he liked it. She shook her head, allowing her hair to settle around her like a living cape. He caught her hips and pulled her to him, pressing a kiss into her intriguing little belly button.

The conversion might ultimately be painful, but he wanted so much more for her. She had given him trust from the beginning, putting herself into his hands, into his keeping, and he intended to cherish and protect her, love her and keep her happy for all their days. He wanted to start out right.

Dax got to his feet, still holding her hips, keeping her anchored to him. "They didn't have undergarments such as these when I was a young man growing up. I'm fairly certain of that." With a wave of his hand, the bra and panties found their way to her blouse and cargo pants. Once again he lifted her, shedding his clothes at the same time.

Riley laughed softly and buried her face against his neck. "That is one handy ability."

"Stripping off your clothes?" he teased, carrying her to the bubbling spring. "I think so."

He stepped into the hot springs. The water came up to his thighs. "The rocks are smooth, like a seat," he told her. "It's shaped like a bowl beneath the water. There's a natural seat and, like a bed . . ." He frowned, searching for the right word. It eluded him completely. He sent her a mental picture.

"Lounge?" she asked.

He nodded. "You can stretch out and the water will barely flow over you, keeping you a little cooler." He lowered her feet slowly into the heated water, watching for discomfort, keeping her close to him. His arm snaked around her, holding her to him as he walked her into the middle of the pool.

Riley gasped as heat enveloped her, as millions of tiny bubbles burst against her sensitive skin. His fist wrapped in her hair, bunching it tight, hauling her head back to give him access to her mouth. His mouth came down on hers, brushing, teasing, coaxing. The moment she opened to him, he took control, kissing her over and over, a fierce claiming. He got lost in her mouth for a few minutes—or maybe much longer; time slipped away.

His cock was aching, painfully swollen with anticipation. He trailed burning kisses from her mouth to her throat, his teeth nipping, tiny little bites that excited him even more. Her taste burst onto his tongue, spreading through his body like a lightning bolt. His mouth wandered across her shoulder, along her collarbone, down lower to her breast.

She arched her back, cradling his head as he tugged and rolled her nipples. She gave a little cry when his sharp teeth nipped her. His tongue instantly took the sting away. She moaned and pressed closer to his mouth. He suckled strongly and then went back to her sensitive nipples, pulling them taut, teasing them into tight peaks. Her hips moved restlessly.

Dax slipped one hand down the soft curvy contours of her body, over her narrow waist to her flat belly and lower still to her flared hips. His palm cupped her mound, his thumb moving in slow circles. She was wet, hot, as hungry for his body as he was for hers. His mouth wandered up her breast to the creamy slope while his fingers slipped inside the heat of her body. He lapped at the soft temptation with his tongue, his teeth scraping back and forth. Each time his teeth nipped, her sheath tightened around his fingers and bathed him with a fresh flood of liquid.

His teeth lengthened. His mouth watered. He sank his fangs into that pounding pulse and the taste of her burst through him like the eruption of a volcano. Her body reacted to the flash of pain, clamping down hard, and as pleasure raced through her, he felt her muscles ripple in need. She tasted exquisite, perfect, addicting. He took more than his fill, enough for a blood exchange. The third blood exchange. It took discipline to run his tongue across those pinpricks and seal them.

Dax turned her in his arms as he ran one sharp fingernail across the pounding pulse in his chest. He needed her mouth on him drinking his essence, his ancient blood bringing her fully into his world. Her lips moved against his chest, her tongue sliding over the tiny beads bubbling through the thin cut. He held his breath, cradling her head, everything in him going still. Waiting. Needing. Her mouth moving against his chest was the most erotic thing he had ever felt. Her body was naturally sensual, moving against his in restless hunger even as she accepted the invitation into his world.

He could barely make himself stop her, but his body was making its own urgent demands. He murmured softly to her. "Enough, *päläfertiilam*, ancient blood is rich."

Her tongue lapped at his offering once before she lifted her head, her eyes slumberous, sexy, dark with desire. "I want you right now. I have to have you right now."

Dax wasn't prepared to argue with that demand. He urged her toward the side sweeping lounge. He pressed one hand on her back to force her to bend, to place her hands on the rock for balance. Her hair hung down around her body, her breasts swinging free. Her buttocks were rounded, and he rubbed and massaged the firm flesh before sliding his hand between her legs once again.

He pressed his aching, swollen flesh against the heat of her slick entrance. She moved her hips back, trying to force him to enter faster. His fingers flexed on her hips and then he dragged her body hard over his, at the same time, surging forward. She wailed, a low keening cry of pleasure, filling the chamber with her music as he buried himself over and over in her. Her sheath was alive with silken fingers gripping and squeezing, surrounding him with scorching heat. She was tight, so tight she strangled him, the friction exquisite. He took them both up hard and fast, a piston driving into her over and over. She gasped for breath, her body moving in perfect rhythm with his. He heard the change in her breathing, felt the rush of hot liquid and then her tight sheath clamped down on him, demanding, milking, as around him all that silky heat rippled with one powerful orgasm after another, taking him with her.

She chanted his name, a soft lilting cry that wrapped coils of emotion around his heart. Dax pulled her into his arms, dropping his head over hers, holding them both up while he calmed their hearts and pushed air into burning lungs. He sank back into the water, pulling her with him until he was seated on the natural rock and water swirled around his shoulders. Riley swept her hair up, wrung it out and knotted it on top of her head. She settled back beside him, stretching out her legs and looking around the cavern.

"It's beautiful here, Dax. Really exceptional. I won't forget it, ever." Her voice trembled. She slipped her hand into his. "I'm not afraid. It's just . . . unknown. What happens next?"

His fingers closed around hers. "We wait. Your body will fight the conversion, believing you're dying. Try not to resist, just let yourself go. I'll be with you every step of the way. Gary indicated there were things I couldn't help you with." He detested that. He would take on every bit of her pain if he could, but Gary had made it clear that it was impossible.

"Where do you want to live, Dax? We never talked about it."

He drank her in, his gaze moving over her, studying her body for any signs of discomfort. "I would like to make our way back to the Carpathian Mountains and see the new prince." He laughed softly at himself. "I guess he's not really new. He's been the prince for some time, but he's new to me."

"That sounds like fun. I've always wanted to travel to other places."

"I'd like to see where you grew up," he added. He brought her hand to his mouth and nibbled on her knuckles. He hoped the hot water would take some of the pain from her body when the time came. "After we've traveled the world, you can choose a place you want to make our home base."

A look of alarm crossed Riley's face. She tried to let go of his hand, but

Dax tightened his grip. The Old One stirred. Dax pushed gently into her mind, and she pushed back hard to keep him out, vigorously shaking her head.

"I don't want you to feel this with me, Dax." Again, Riley tugged on her hand, her body hunching. "I can't worry about how distressed you are." She took a breath, pressed her hand to her stomach and turned her face away. "I should do this alone, in privacy."

And she would. That was one of the things about her that turned him inside out. Dax waved his hand toward the rich, dark earth. The soil peeled back to provide a deep bed.

"I'm going to be sick." Riley turned, leaning over the side of the pool, and wretched over and over.

When Dax put his hand on her back, her outside shell was cold while inside she was on fire, her organs twisting and reshaping. Her body convulsed and would have slipped beneath the water had he not caught her and laid her down on the natural lounge, so that the water covered her skin. Her muscles were hard knots, great lumps all over her body, rigid with tension. The springwater, fed by the volcano, was hot and helped to ease the knots from her body.

The pain came in great waves that sometimes lifted her up and slammed her down. Dax cushioned the fall while her body twisted and writhed. Her eyes were wide open, but she didn't look at him. With glazed eyes she looked up at the gem-studded ceiling, the glittering rubies that flowed over their heads. She breathed through the pain, and Dax found himself breathing with her, trying to stay on top of the waves rather than succumb to them.

In one of the brief moments of reprieve, she touched his face, frowning as her hand came away with beads of blood. "I'm alright, Dax. I can do this," she assured.

"I know you can," Dax replied, his stomach in hard knots as well. The conversion was brutal and there was little he could do to help her. He'd ignored her command to stay out of her head. He tried to take her pain on himself, but it was impossible. Trying not to show his growing alarm, he brushed kisses over her eyes until the next big wave.

The Old One began to struggle for supremacy, needing to stop the terrible pain taking Riley. Dax had never experienced panic, but it was setting in fast. The hot water was no longer doing any good. Nothing could stop the violent convulsions, and it was dangerous with so much rock around. She was sick constantly, her body fighting to rid itself of toxins.

He lifted her into his arms. *I've got her, Old One. She isn't dying.*

She is, you fool. We're going to lose her.

Riley's hand moved. Smoothed his hair. Soft amusement spilled into his mind despite the pain and fever raging in her body. *Men are definitely the weaker sex. I'm getting through it. Stop fighting you two.*

That fast the amusement was gone as the next brutal wave took her, robbing her of breath, nearly tearing her out of his arms as her body locked rigid, nearly breaking her bones.

She was a child of the earth and he was counting heavily on that. He carried her to the open soil and floated them both down, placing her body in the cool dirt. Instantly the whispers started, female voices, soothing, reaching.

The Old One subsided, but Dax felt him reaching, touching the only thing he could—Riley's soul. The threads binding Riley to Dax stretched to include the soul of the Old One.

Be certain, Dax cautioned, shocked at the generosity of the old dragon. His time had passed, yet he had given his soul to Dax to aid in destroying evil. Now he was including Riley in that decision, offering his soul to her as well to get her through her journey into the Carpathian world.

I am certain. She is worthy of you. She can call me forth when she needs me. The fire dragon was fierce about it. Dax and Riley were his. He would defend them with everything he was.

Binding Riley's soul to his, the Old One wrapped himself in her, trying to do what Dax couldn't—help to heal her faster. The soft whispers in the earth grew in volume. Dax noted Riley became calmer, the lines etched into her face easing as the voices soothed and the Old One pushed her organs to greater speed.

With one horrible wheezing gasp, one death rattle in her throat, one last wave of excruciating pain, the convulsions subsided. Riley was very still for a moment, and then she turned to him, her eyes wide, haunted. Exhaustion was on her face, a fine sheen of sweat dampening her body. Tiny droplets of blood beaded on her forehead and trickled down her body.

"Childbirth better not be this hard," she whispered. "Or you're doing it."

He forced a smile. His mouth felt stiff. Even his jaw hurt. He kissed her hand, afraid of touching anything else. "That's a deal. I'm sending you to sleep now. It's safe. I'll be with you every moment."

As will I, the Old One assured.

I'm holding you in my arms, Annabel whispered.

You are safe, the female voices added.

"I love you, Dax," she whispered. "Thank you, Old One. You've given me a great gift." She managed a small smile. Incredibly, her eyes were lit up with love when she looked at him. "I'm tired."

For a moment, his throat was so clogged he could barely speak. He swallowed the lump. "When you wake, you'll be fully in my world."

Dax curled his body around Riley's as he sent her into a deep sleep, his arms wrapped tight around her as the rich, healing soil poured over them. The safeguards were in place, and the Old One was on the watch. Mitro was dead and Arabejila could be at peace. He buried his face in the wealth of blue-black silk and inhaled her scent one last time before he succumbed to the sleep of his people. Life was good.

Appendix I

Carpathian Healing Chants

To rightly understand Carpathian healing chants, background is required in several areas:

1. The Carpathian view on healing
2. The Lesser Healing Chant of the Carpathians
3. The Great Healing Chant of the Carpathians
4. Carpathian musical aesthetics
5. Lullaby
6. Song to Heal the Earth
7. Carpathian chanting technique

1. THE CARPATHIAN VIEW ON HEALING

The Carpathians are a nomadic people whose geographic origins can be traced back to at least as far as the Southern Ural Mountains (near the steppes of modern-day Kazakhstan), on the border between Europe and Asia. (For this reason, modern-day linguists call their language "proto-Uralic," without knowing that this is the language of the Carpathians.) Unlike most nomadic peoples, the wandering of the Carpathians was not due to the need to find new grazing lands as the seasons and climate shifted, or the search for better trade. Instead, the Carpathians' movements were driven by a great purpose: to find a land that would have the right earth, a soil with the kind of richness that would greatly enhance their rejuvenative powers.

Over the centuries, they migrated westward (some six thousand years ago), until they at last found their perfect homeland—their *susu*—in the Carpathian Mountains, whose long arc cradled the lush plains of the kingdom of Hungary. (The kingdom of Hungary flourished for over a millennium—making Hungarian the dominant language of the Carpathian Basin—until the kingdom's lands were split among several countries after World War I: Austria, Czechoslovakia, Romania, Yugoslavia and modern Hungary.)

Other peoples from the Southern Urals (who shared the Carpathian language, but were not Carpathians) migrated in different directions. Some ended up in Finland, which accounts for why the modern Hungarian and Finnish languages are among the contemporary descendents of the ancient Carpathian language. Even though they are tied forever to their chosen Carpathian homeland, the wandering of the Carpathians

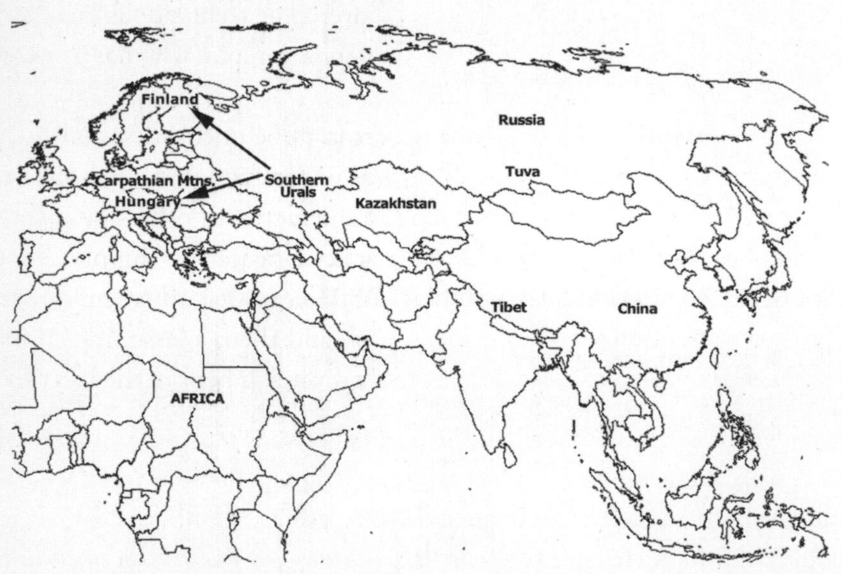

continues as they search the world for the answers that will enable them to bear and raise their offspring without difficulty.

Because of their geographic origins, the Carpathian views on healing share much with the larger Eurasian shamanistic tradition. Probably the closest modern representative of that tradition is based in Tuva (and is referred to as "Tuvinian Shamanism")—see the map on the previous page.

The Eurasian shamanistic tradition—from the Carpathians to the Siberian shamans—held that illness originated in the human soul, and only later manifested as various physical conditions. Therefore, shamanistic healing, while not neglecting the body, focused on the soul and its healing. The most profound illnesses were understood to be caused by "soul departure," where all or some part of the sick person's soul has wandered away from the body (into the nether realms), or has been captured or possessed by an evil spirit, or both.

The Carpathians belong to this greater Eurasian shamanistic tradition and share its viewpoints. While the Carpathians themselves did not succumb to illness, Carpathian healers understood that the most profound wounds were also accompanied by a similar "soul departure."

Upon reaching the diagnosis of "soul departure," the healer-shaman is then required to make a spiritual journey into the netherworlds to recover the soul. The shaman may have to overcome tremendous challenges along the way, particularly fighting the demon or vampire who has possessed his friend's soul.

"Soul departure" doesn't require a person to be unconscious (although that certainly can be the case as well). It was understood that a person could still appear to be conscious, even talk and interact with others, and yet be missing a part of their soul. The experienced healer or shaman would instantly see the problem nonetheless, in subtle signs that others might miss: the person's attention wandering every now and then, a lessening in their enthusiasm about life, chronic depression, a diminishment in the brightness of their "aura," and the like.

2. THE LESSER HEALING CHANT OF THE CARPATHIANS

***Kepä Sarna Pus* (The Lesser Healing Chant)** is used for wounds that are merely physical in nature. The Carpathian healer leaves his body and enters the wounded Carpathian's body to heal great mortal wounds from the inside out using pure energy. He proclaims, "I offer freely my life for your life," as he gives his blood to the injured Carpathian. Because the Carpathians are of the earth and bound to the soil, they are healed by the soil of their homeland. Their saliva is also often used for its rejuvenative powers.

It is also very common for the Carpathian chants (both the Lesser and the Great) to be accompanied by the use of healing herbs, aromas from Carpathian candles and crystals. The crystals (when combined with the Carpathians' empathic, psychic connection to the entire universe) are used to gather positive energy from their surroundings, which then is used to accelerate the healing. Caves are sometimes used as the setting for the healing.

The Lesser Healing Chant was used by Vikirnoff Von Shrieder and Colby Jansen to heal Rafael De La Cruz, whose heart had been ripped out by a vampire as described in *Dark Secret.*

Kepä Sarna Pus (The Lesser Healing Chant)

The same chant is used for all physical wounds. "Sívadaba" ["into your heart"] would be changed to refer to whatever part of the body is wounded.

Kuńasz, nélkül sivdobbanás, nélkül fesztelen löyly.
You lie as if asleep, without beat of heart, without airy breath.

Ot élidamet andam szabadon élidadért.
I offer freely my life for your life.

O jelä sielam jõrem ot ainamet és soŋe ot élidadet.
My spirit of light forgets my body and enters your body.

O jelä sielam pukta kinn minden szelemeket belső.
My spirit of light sends all the dark spirits within fleeing without.

Pajńak o susu hanyet és o nyelv nyálamet sívadaba.
I press the earth of our homeland and the spit of my tongue into your heart.

Vii, o verim soŋe o verid andam.
At last, I give you my blood for your blood.

To hear this chant, visit: http://www.christinefeehan.com/members/.

3. THE GREAT HEALING CHANT OF THE CARPATHIANS

The most well-known—and most dramatic—of the Carpathian healing chants was ***En Sarna Pus*** **(The Great Healing Chant)**. This chant was reserved for recovering the wounded or unconscious Carpathian's soul.

Typically a group of men would form a circle around the sick Carpathian (to "encircle him with our care and compassion") and begin the chant. The shaman or healer or leader is the prime actor in this healing ceremony. It is he who will actually make the spiritual journey into the netherworld, aided by his clanspeople. Their purpose is to ecstatically dance, sing, drum and chant, all the while visualizing (through the words of the chant) the journey itself—every step of it, over and over again—to the point where the shaman, in trance, leaves his body, and makes that very journey. (Indeed, the word "ecstasy" is from the Latin *ex statis*, which literally means "out of the body.")

One advantage that the Carpathian healer has over many other shamans is his telepathic link to his lost brother. Most shamans must wander in the dark of the nether realms in search of their lost brother. But the Carpathian healer directly "hears" in his mind the voice of his lost brother calling to him, and can thus "zero in" on his soul like a homing beacon. For this reason, Carpathian healing tends to have a higher success rate than most other traditions of this sort.

Something of the geography of the "other world" is useful for us to examine, in order to fully understand the words of the Great Carpathian Healing Chant. A reference is made to the "Great Tree" (in Carpathian: *En*

Puwe). Many ancient traditions, including the Carpathian tradition, understood the worlds—the heaven worlds, our world and the nether realms—to be "hung" upon a great pole, or axis, or tree. Here on earth, we are positioned halfway up this tree, on one of its branches. Hence many ancient texts often referred to the material world as "middle earth": midway between heaven and hell. Climbing the tree would lead one to the heaven worlds. Descending the tree to its roots would lead to the nether realms. The shaman was necessarily a master of movement up and down the Great Tree, sometimes moving unaided, and sometimes assisted by (or even mounted upon the back of) an animal spirit guide. In various traditions, this Great Tree was known variously as the *axis mundi* (the "axis of the worlds"), Ygddrasil (in Norse mythology), Mount Meru (the sacred world mountain of Tibetan tradition), etc. The Christian cosmos, with its heaven, purgatory/earth and hell, is also worth comparing. It is even given a similar topography in Dante's *Divine Comedy*: Dante is led on a journey first to hell, at the center of the earth; then upward to Mount Purgatory, which sits on the earth's surface directly opposite Jerusalem; then farther upward first to Eden, the earthly paradise, at the summit of Mount Purgatory; and then upward at last to heaven.

In the shamanistic tradition, it was understood that the small always reflects the large; the personal always reflects the cosmic. A movement in the greater dimensions of the cosmos also coincides with an internal movement. For example, the *axis mundi* of the cosmos also corresponds to the spinal column of the individual. Journeys up and down the *axis mundi* often coincided with the movement of natural and spiritual energies (sometimes called *kundalini* or *shakti*) in the spinal column of the shaman or mystic.

En Sarna Pus (The Great Healing Chant)

In this chant, ekä ("brother") would be replaced by "sister," "father," "mother," depending on the person to be healed.

Ot ekäm ainajanak hany, jama.
My brother's body is a lump of earth, close to death.

Me, ot eküm kuntajanak, pirädak eküm, gond és irgalom türe.
We, the clan of my brother, encircle him with our care and compassion.

O pus wäkenkek, ot oma śarnank, és ot pus fünk, álnak ekäm ainajanak, pitänak ekäm ainajanak elävä.
Our healing energies, ancient words of magic and healing herbs bless my brother's body, keep it alive.

Ot ekäm sielanak pälä. Ot omboće päläja juta alatt o jüti, kinta, és szelemek lamtijaknak.
But my brother's soul is only half. His other half wanders in the netherworld.

Ot en mekem ŋamaŋ: kulkedak otti ot ekäm omboće päläjanak.
My great deed is this: I travel to find my brother's other half.

Rekatüre, saradak, tappadak, odam, kaŋa o numa waram, és avaa owe o lewl mahoz.
We dance, we chant, we dream ecstatically, to call my spirit bird, and to open the door to the other world.

Ntak o numa waram, és mozdulak, jomadak.
I mount my spirit bird and we begin to move, we are under way.

Piwtädak ot En Puwe tyvinak, ećidak alatt o jüti, kinta, és szelemek lamtijaknak.
Following the trunk of the Great Tree, we fall into the netherworld.

Fázak, fázak nó o śaro.
It is cold, very cold.

Juttadak ot ekäm o akarataban, o sívaban és o sielaban.
My brother and I are linked in mind, heart and soul.

Ot ekäm sielanak kaŋa engem.
My brother's soul calls to me.

Kuledak és piwtädak ot ekäm.
I hear and follow his track.

Saγedak és tuledak ot ekäm kulyanak.
Encounter I the demon who is devouring my brother's soul.

Nenäm ćoro, o kuly torodak.
In anger, I fight the demon.

O kuly pél engem.
He is afraid of me.

Lejkkadak o kaŋka salamaval.
I strike his throat with a lightning bolt.

Molodak ot ainaja komakamal.
I break his body with my bare hands.

Toja és molanâ.
He is bent over, and falls apart.

Hän ćaδa.
He runs away.

Manedak ot ekäm sielanak.
I rescue my brother's soul.

Alədak ot ekam sielanak o komamban.
I lift my brother's soul in the hollow of my hand.

Alədam ot ekam numa waramra.
I lift him onto my spirit bird.

Piwtädak ot En Puwe tyvijanak és saɣedak jälleen ot elävä ainak majaknak.
Following up the Great Tree, we return to the land of the living.

Ot ekäm elä jälleen.
My brother lives again.

Ot ekäm weńća jälleen.
He is complete again.

To hear this chant, visit: http://www.christinefeehan.com/members/.

4. CARPATHIAN MUSICAL AESTHETICS

In the sung Carpathian pieces (such as the "Lullaby" and the "Song to Heal the Earth"), you'll hear elements that are shared by many of the musical traditions in the Uralic geographical region, some of which still exist—from Eastern European (Bulgarian, Romanian, Hungarian, Croatian, etc.) to Romany ("gypsy"). Some of these elements include:

- the rapid alternation between major and minor modalities, including a sudden switch (called a "Picardy third") from minor to major to end a piece or section (as at the end of the "Lullaby")
- the use of close (tight) harmonies
- the use of *ritardi* (slowing down the piece) and *crescendi* (swelling in volume) for brief periods
- the use of *glissandi* (slides) in the singing tradition
- the use of trills in the singing tradition (as in the final invocation of the "Song to Heal the Earth")—similar to Celtic, a singing tradition more familiar to many of us
- the use of parallel fifths (as in the final invocation of the "Song to Heal the Earth")
- controlled use of dissonance
- "call and response" chanting (typical of many of the world's chanting traditions)

- extending the length of a musical line (by adding a couple of bars) to heighten dramatic effect
- and many more

"Lullaby" and "Song to Heal the Earth" illustrate two rather different forms of Carpathian music (a quiet, intimate piece and an energetic ensemble piece)—but whatever the form, Carpathian music is full of feeling.

5. LULLABY

This song is sung by women while the child is still in the womb or when the threat of a miscarriage is apparent. The baby can hear the song while inside the mother, and the mother can connect with the child telepathically as well. The lullaby is meant to reassure the child, to encourage the baby to hold on, to stay—to reassure the child that he or she will be protected by love even from inside until birth. The last line literally means that the mother's love will protect her child until the child is born ("rise").

Musically, the Carpathian "Lullaby" is in three-quarter time ("waltz time"), as are a significant portion of the world's various traditional lullabies (perhaps the most famous of which is "Brahms' Lullaby"). The arrangement for solo voice is the original context: a mother singing to her child, unaccompanied. The arrangement for chorus and violin ensemble illustrates how musical even the simplest Carpathian pieces often are, and how easily they lend themselves to contemporary instrumental or orchestral arrangements. (A wide range of contemporary composers, including Dvořák and Smetana, have taken advantage of a similar discovery, working other traditional Eastern European music into their symphonic poems.)

Odam-Sarna Kondak (Lullaby)

Tumtesz o wäke ku pitasz belső.
Feel the strength you hold inside.

Hiszasz sívadet. Én olenam gæidnod.
Trust your heart. I'll be your guide.

Sas csecsemõm, kuńasz.
Hush my baby, close your eyes.

Rauho joŋe ted.
Peace will come to you.

Tumtesz o sívdobbanás ku olen lamt3ad belső.
Feel the rhythm deep inside.

Gond-kumpadek ku kim te.
Waves of love that cover you.

Pesänak te, asti o jüti, kidüsz.
Protect, until the night you rise.

To hear this song, visit: http://www.christinefeehan.com/members/.

6. SONG TO HEAL THE EARTH

This is the earth-healing song that is used by the Carpathian women to heal soil filled with various toxins. The women take a position on four sides and call to the universe to draw on the healing energy with love and respect. The soil of the earth is their resting place, the place where they rejuvenate, and they must make it safe not only for themselves but for their unborn children as well as their men and living children. This is a beautiful ritual performed by the women together, raising their voices in harmony and calling on the earth's minerals and healing properties to come forth and help them save their children. They literally dance and sing to heal the earth in a ceremony as old as their species. The dance and notes of the song are adjusted according to the toxins felt through the healer's bare feet. The feet are placed in a certain pattern and the hands gracefully weave a healing spell while the dance is performed. They must be especially careful when the soil is prepared for babies. This is a ceremony of love and healing.

Musically, the ritual is divided into several sections:

- **First verse**: A "call and response" section, where the chant leader sings the "call" solo, and then some or all of the women sing the "response" in the close harmony style typical of the Carpathian musical tradition. The repeated response—*Ai Emä Maγe*—is an invocation of the source of power for the healing ritual: "Oh, Mother Nature."
- **First chorus**: This section is filled with clapping, dancing, ancient horns and other means used to invoke and heighten the energies upon which the ritual is drawing.
- **Second verse**
- **Second chorus**
- **Closing invocation:** In this closing part, two song leaders, in close harmony, take all the energy gathered by the earlier portions of the song/ritual and focus it entirely on the healing purpose.

What you will be listening to are brief tastes of what would typically be a significantly longer ritual, in which the verse and chorus parts are developed and repeated many times, to be closed by a single rendition of the final invocation.

Sarna Pusm O Maγet (Song to Heal the Earth)

First verse
Ai Emä Maγe,
Oh, Mother Nature,

Me sívadbin lańaak.
We are your beloved daughters.

Me tappadak, me pusmak o maγet.
We dance to heal the earth.

Me sarnadak, me pusmak o hanyet.
We sing to heal the earth.

Sielanket jutta tedet it,
We join with you now,

Sívank és akaratank és sielank juttanak.
Our hearts and minds and spirits become one.

Second verse
Ai Emä maγe,
Oh, Mother Nature,

Me sívadbin lańaak.
We are your beloved daughters.

Me andak arwadet emänked és me kaŋank o
We pay homage to our mother and call upon the

Põhi és Lõuna, Ida és Lääs.
North and South, East and West.

Pide és aldyn és myös belső.
Above and below and within as well.

Gondank o maγenak pusm hän ku olen jama.
Our love of the land heals that which is in need.

Juttanak teval it,
We join with you now,

Maγe maγeval.
Earth to earth.

O pirä elidak weńća.
The circle of life is complete.

To hear this chant, visit: http://www.christinefeehan.com/members/.

7. CARPATHIAN CHANTING TECHNIQUE

As with their healing techniques, the actual "chanting technique" of the Carpathians has much in common with the other shamanistic traditions of the Central Asian steppes. The primary mode of chanting was throat chanting using overtones. Modern examples of this manner of singing can still be found in the Mongolian, Tuvan and Tibetan traditions. You can find an audio example of the Gyuto Tibetan Buddhist monks engaged in throat chanting at: http://www.christinefeehan.com/carpathian_chanting/.

As with Tuva, note on the map the geographical proximity of Tibet to Kazakhstan and the Southern Urals.

The beginning part of the Tibetan chant emphasizes synchronizing all the voices around a single tone, aimed at healing a particular "chakra" of the body. This is fairly typical of the Gyuto throat-chanting tradition, but it is not a significant part of the Carpathian tradition. Nonetheless, it serves as an interesting contrast.

The part of the Gyuto chanting example that is most similar to the Carpathian style of chanting is the midsection, where the men are chanting the words together with great force. The purpose here is not to generate a "healing tone" that will affect a particular "chakra," but rather to generate as much power as possible for initiating the "out of body" travel, and for fighting the demonic forces that the healer/traveler must face and overcome.

The songs of the Carpathian women (illustrated by their "Lullaby" and their "Song to Heal the Earth") are part of the same ancient musical and healing tradition as the Lesser and Great Healing Chants of the warrior males. You can hear some of the same instruments in both the male warriors' healing chants and the women's "Song to Heal the Earth." Also, they share the common purpose of generating and directing power. However, the women's songs are distinctively feminine in character. One immediately noticeable difference is that, while the men speak their words in the manner of a chant, the women sing songs with melodies and harmonies, softening the overall performance. A feminine, nurturing quality is especially evident in the "Lullaby."

APPENDIX 2

The Carpathian Language

Like all human languages, the language of the Carpathians contains the richness and nuance that can only come from a long history of use. At best we can only touch on some of the main features of the language in this brief appendix:

1. The history of the Carpathian language
2. Carpathian grammar and other characteristics of the language
3. Examples of the Carpathian language (including The Ritual Words and The Warrior's Chant)
4. A much-abridged Carpathian dictionary

1. THE HISTORY OF THE CARPATHIAN LANGUAGE

The Carpathian language of today is essentially identical to the Carpathian language of thousands of years ago. A "dead" language like the Latin of two thousand years ago has evolved into a significantly different modern language (Italian) because of countless generations of speakers and great historical fluctuations. In contrast, many of the speakers of Carpathian from thousands of years ago are still alive. Their presence—

coupled with the deliberate isolation of the Carpathians from the other major forces of change in the world—has acted (and continues to act) as a stabilizing force that has preserved the integrity of the language over the centuries. Carpathian culture has also acted as a stabilizing force. For instance, the Ritual Words, the various healing chants (see Appendix 1), and other cultural artifacts have been passed down through the centuries with great fidelity.

One small exception should be noted: the splintering of the Carpathians into separate geographic regions has led to some minor dialectization. However the telepathic link among all Carpathians (as well as each Carpathian's regular return to his or her homeland) has ensured that the differences among dialects are relatively superficial (e.g., small numbers of new words, minor differences in pronunciation, etc.), since the deeper, internal language of mind-forms has remained the same because of continuous use across space and time.

The Carpathian language was (and still is) the proto-language for the Uralic (or Finno-Ugrian) family of languages. Today, the Uralic languages are spoken in northern, eastern and central Europe and in Siberia. More than twenty-three million people in the world speak languages that can trace their ancestry to Carpathian. Magyar or Hungarian (about fourteen million speakers), Finnish (about five million speakers) and Estonian (about one million speakers) are the three major contemporary descendents of this proto-language. The only factor that unites the more than twenty languages in the Uralic family is that their ancestry can be traced back to a common proto-language—Carpathian—that split (starting some six thousand years ago) into the various languages in the Uralic family. In the same way, European languages such as English and French belong to the better-known Indo-European family and also evolved from a common proto-language ancestor (a different one from Carpathian).

The following table provides a sense for some of the similarities in the language family.

Note: The Finnic/Carpathian "k" shows up often as Hungarian "h." Similarly, the Finnic/Carpathian "p" often corresponds to the Hungarian "f."

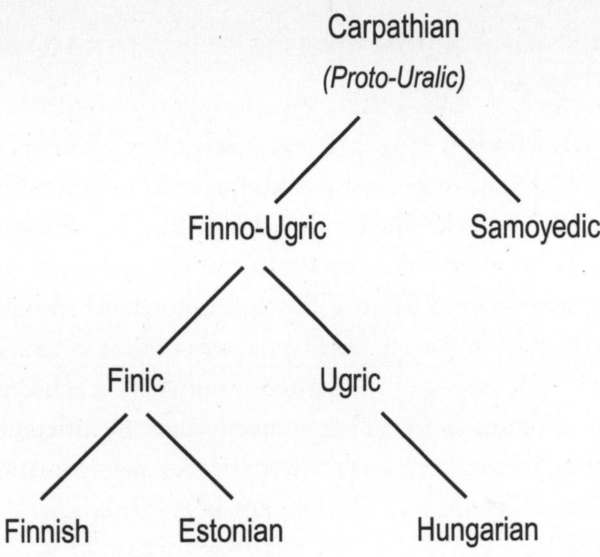

Carpathian *(proto-Uralic)*	**Finnish** *(Suomi)*	**Hungarian** *(Magyar)*
elä—live	*elä*—live	*él*—live
elid—life	*elinikä*—life	*élet*—life
pesä—nest	*pesä*—nest	*fészek*—nest
kola—die	*kuole*—die	*hal*—die
pälä—half, side	*pieltä*—tilt, tip to the side	*fél, fele*—fellow human, friend (half; one side of two) *feleség*—wife
and—give	*anta, antaa*—give	*ad*—give
koje—husband, man	*koira*—dog, the male (of animals)	*here*—drone, testicle
wäke—power	*väki*—folks, people, men; force	*vall-vel*—with (instrumental suffix)
	väkevä—powerful, strong	*vele*—with him/her/it
wete—water	*vesi*—water	*viz*—water

2. CARPATHIAN GRAMMAR AND OTHER CHARACTERISTICS OF THE LANGUAGE

Idioms. As both an ancient language and a language of an earth people, Carpathian is more inclined toward use of idioms constructed from concrete, "earthy" terms, rather than abstractions. For instance, our modern abstraction "to cherish" is expressed more concretely in Carpathian as "to hold in one's heart"; the "netherworld" is, in Carpathian, "the land of night, fog and ghosts"; etc.

Word order. The order of words in a sentence is determined not by syntactic roles (like subject, verb and object) but rather by pragmatic, discourse-driven factors. Examples: *"Tied vagyok."* ("Yours am I."); *"Sivamet andam."* ("My heart I give you.")

Agglutination. The Carpathian language is agglutinative; that is, longer words are constructed from smaller components. An agglutinating language uses suffixes or prefixes whose meaning is generally unique, and which are concatenated one after another without overlap. In Carpathian, words typically consist of a stem that is followed by one or more suffixes. For example, *"sívambam"* derives from the stem *"sív"* ("heart") followed by *"am"* ("my," making it "my heart"), followed by *"bam"* ("in," making it "in my heart"). As you might imagine, agglutination in Carpathian can sometimes produce very long words, or words that are very difficult to pronounce. Vowels often get inserted between suffixes to prevent too many consonants from appearing in a row (which can make the word unpronounceable).

Noun cases. Like all languages, Carpathian has many noun cases; the same noun will be "spelled" differently depending on its role in the sentence. Some of the noun cases include: nominative (when the noun is the subject of the sentence), accusative (when the noun is a direct object of the verb), dative (indirect object), genitive (or possessive), instrumental, final, supressive, inessive, elative, terminative and delative.

We will use the possessive (or genitive) case as an example, to illustrate how all noun cases in Carpathian involve adding standard suffixes to the noun stems. Thus expressing possession in Carpathian—"my lifemate," "your lifemate," "his lifemate," "her lifemate," etc.—involves adding a particular suffix (such as "*-am*") to the noun stem ("*päläfertiil*"), to produce the possessive ("*päläfertiilam*"—"my lifemate"). Which suffix to use depends upon which person ("my," "your," "his," etc.) and whether the noun ends in a consonant or a vowel. The table below shows the suffixes for singular nouns only (not plural), and also shows the similarity to the suffixes used in contemporary Hungarian. (Hungarian is actually a little more complex, in that it also requires "vowel rhyming": which suffix to use also depends on the last vowel in the noun; hence the multiple choices in the cells below, where Carpathian only has a single choice.)

	Carpathian (proto-Uralic)		Contemporary Hungarian	
person	**noun ends in vowel**	**noun ends in consonant**	**noun ends in vowel**	**noun ends in consonant**
1st singular (my)	-m	-am	-m	-om, -em, -öm
2nd singular (your)	-d	-ad	-d	-od, -ed, -öd
3rd singular (his, her, its)	-ja	-a	-ja/-je	-a, -e
1st plural (our)	-nk	-ank	-nk	-unk, -ünk
2nd plural (your)	-tak	-atak	-tok, -tek, -tök	-otok, -etek, -ötök
3rd plural (their)	-jak	-ak	-juk, -jük	-uk, -ük

Note: As mentioned earlier, vowels often get inserted between the word and its suffix so as to prevent too many consonants from appearing in a row (which would produce unpronounceable words). For example, in the table on the previous page, all nouns that end in a consonant are followed by suffixes beginning with "a."

Verb conjugation. Like its modern descendents (such as Finnish and Hungarian), Carpathian has many verb tenses, far too many to describe here. We will just focus on the conjugation of the present tense. Again, we will place contemporary Hungarian side by side with the Carpathian, because of the marked similarity of the two.

As with the possessive case for nouns, the conjugation of verbs is done by adding a suffix onto the verb stem:

Person	Carpathian (proto-Uralic)	Contemporary Hungarian
1st (I give)	-am (andam), -ak	-ok, -ek, -ök
2nd singular (you give)	-sz (andsz)	-sz
3rd singular (he/she/it gives)	— (and)	—
1st plural (we give)	-ak (andak)	-unk, -ünk
2nd plural (you give)	-tak (andtak)	-tok, -tek, -tök
3rd plural (they give)	-nak (andnak)	-nak, -nek

As with all languages, there are many "irregular verbs" in Carpathian that don't exactly fit this pattern. But the above table is still a useful guideline for most verbs.

3. EXAMPLES OF THE CARPATHIAN LANGUAGE

Here are some brief examples of conversational Carpathian, used in the Dark books. We include the literal translation in square brackets. It is interestingly different from the most appropriate English translation.

Susu.
I am home.
["home/birthplace." "I am" is understood, as is often the case in Carpathian.]

Möért?
What for?

csitri
little one
["little slip of a thing," "little slip of a girl"]

ainaak enyém
forever mine

ainaak sívamet jutta
forever mine (another form)
["forever to-my-heart connected/fixed"]

sívamet
my love
["of-my-heart," "to-my-heart"]

Tet vigyázam.
I love you.
["you-love-I"]

***Sarna Rituaali* (The Ritual Words)** is a longer example, and an example of chanted rather than conversational Carpathian. Note the recurring use of *"andam"* ("I give"), to give the chant musicality and force through repetition.

***Sarna Rituaali* (The Ritual Words)**

Te avio päläfertiilam.
You are my lifemate.

Éntölam kuulua, avio päläfertiilam.
I claim you as my lifemate.

Ted kuuluak, kacad, kojed.
I belong to you.

Élidamet andam.
I offer my life for you.

Pesämet andam.
I give you my protection.

Uskolfertiilamet andam.
I give you my allegiance.

Sívamet andam.
I give you my heart.

Sielamet andam.
I give you my soul.

Ainamet andam.
I give you my body.

Sívamet kuuluak kaik että a ted.
I take into my keeping the same that is yours.

Ainaak olenszal sívambin.
Your life will be cherished by me for all my time.

Te élidet ainaak pide minan.
Your life will be placed above my own for all time.

Te avio päläfertiilam.
You are my lifemate.

Ainaak sívamet jutta oleny.
You are bound to me for all eternity.

Ainaak terád vigyázak.
You are always in my care.

To hear these words pronounced (and for more about Carpathian pronunciation altogether), please visit: http://www.christinefeehan.com/members/.

Sarna Kontakawk **(The Warriors' Chant)** is another longer example of the Carpathian language. The warriors' council takes place deep beneath the earth in a chamber of crystals with magma far below that, so the steam is natural and the wisdom of their ancestors is clear and focused. This is a sacred place where they bloodswear to their prince and people and affirm their code of honor as warriors and brothers. It is also where battle strategies are born and all dissension is discussed as well as any concerns the warriors have that they wish to bring to the Council and open for discussion.

Sarna Kontakawk (The Warriors' Chant)

Veri isäakank—veri ekäakank.
Blood of our fathers—blood of our brothers.

Veri olen elid.
Blood is life.

Andak veri-elidet Karpatiiakank, és wäke-sarna ku meke arwa-arvo, irgalom, hän ku agba, és wäke kutni, ku manaak verival.
We offer that life to our people with a bloodsworn vow of honor, mercy, integrity and endurance.

Verink sokta; verink kaŋa terád.
Our blood mingles and calls to you.

Akasz énak ku kaŋa és juttasz kuntatak it.
Heed our summons and join with us now.

To hear these words pronounced (and for more about Carpathian pronunciation altogether), please visit: http://www.christinefeehan.com/members/.

See **Appendix 1** for Carpathian healing chants, including the *Kepä Sarna Pus* (The Lesser Healing Chant), the *En Sarna Pus* (The Great Healing Chant), the *Odam-Sarna Kondak* (Lullaby) and the *Sarna Pusm O Maγ et* (Song to Heal the Earth).

4. A MUCH-ABRIDGED CARPATHIAN DICTIONARY

This very much abridged Carpathian dictionary contains most of the Carpathian words used in these Dark books. Of course, a full Carpathian dictionary would be as large as the usual dictionary for an entire language (typically more than a hundred thousand words).

Note: The Carpathian nouns and verbs below are word stems. They generally do not appear in their isolated, "stem" form, as below. Instead, they usually appear with suffixes (e.g., "*andam*"—"*I give*," rather than just the root, "*and*").

a—verb negation (*prefix*); not (*adverb*).
agba—to be seemly or proper.
ai—oh.
aina—body.
ainaak—forever.
O ainaak jelä peje emnimet ŋamaŋ—Sun scorch that woman forever (*Carpathian swear words*).
ainaakfél—old friend.
ak—suffix added after a noun ending in a consonant to make it plural.
aka—to give heed; to hearken; to listen.
akarat—mind; will.
ál—to bless; to attach to.

alatt—through.
aldyn—under; underneath.
alə—to lift; to raise.
alte—to bless; to curse.
and—to give.
and sielet, arwa-arvomet, és jelämet, kuulua huvémet ku feaj és ködet ainaak—to trade soul, honor and salvation, for momentary pleasure and endless damnation.
andasz éntölem irgalomet!—have mercy!
arvo—value; price (*noun*).
arwa—praise (*noun*).
arwa-arvo—honor (*noun*).
arwa-arvod mäne me ködak—may your honor hold back the dark (*greeting*).
arwa-arvo olen gæidnod, ekäm—honor guide you, my brother (*greeting*).
arwa-arvo olen isäntä, ekäm—honor keep you, my brother (*greeting*).
arwa-arvo pile sívadet—may honor light your heart (*greeting*).
aššaa—no (*before a noun*); not (*with a verb that is not in the imperative*); not (*with an adjective*).
aššatotello—disobedient.
asti—until.
avaa—to open.
avio—wedded.
avio päläfertiil—lifemate.
avoi—uncover; show; reveal.
belső—within; inside.
bur—good; well.
bur tule ekämet kuntamak—well met brother-kin (*greeting*).
ćaδa—to flee; to run; to escape.
ćoro—to flow; to run like rain.
csecsemõ—baby (*noun*).
csitri—little one (*female*).
diutal—triumph; victory.
export—to fall.
ek—suffix added after a noun ending in a consonant to make it plural.

ekä—brother.
ekäm—my brother.
elä—to live.
eläsz arwa-arvoval—may you live with honor (*greeting*).
eläsz jeläbam ainaak—long may you live in the light (*greeting*).
elävä—alive.
elävä ainak majaknak—land of the living.
elid—life.
emä—mother (*noun*).
Emä Maγe—Mother Nature.
emäen—grandmother.
embε—if, when.
embε karmasz—please.
emni—wife; woman.
emnim—my wife; my woman.
emni hän ku köd alte—cursed woman.
emni kuŋenak ku aššatotello—disobedient lunatic.
én—I.
en—great, many, big.
én jutta félet és ekämet—I greet a friend and brother (*greeting*).
én maγenak—I am of the earth.
én oma maγeka—I am as old as time *(literally: as old as the earth).*
En Puwe—The Great Tree. Related to the legends of Ygddrasil, the axis mundi, Mount Meru, heaven and hell, etc.
engem—of me.
és—and.
ete—before; in front.
että—that.
fáz—to feel cold or chilly.
fél—fellow, friend.
fél ku kuuluaak sívam belső—beloved.
fél ku vigyázak—dear one.
feldolgaz—prepare.
fertiil—fertile one.
fesztelen—airy.

fü—herbs; grass.
gæidno—road, way.
gond—care; worry; love (*noun*).
hän—he; she; it.
hän agba—it is so.
hän ku—prefix: one who; that which.
hän ku agba—truth.
hän ku kaśwa o numamet—sky-owner.
hän ku kuulua sívamet—keeper of my heart.
hän ku lejkka wäke-sarnat—traitor.
hän ku meke pirämet—defender.
hän ku pesä—protector.
hän ku piwtä—predator; hunter; tracker.
hän ku vie elidet—vampire (*literally: thief of life*).
hän ku vigyáz sielamet—keeper of my soul.
hän ku vigyáz sívamet és sielamet—keeper of my heart and soul.
hän ku saa kuć3aket—star-reacher.
hän ku tappa—killer; violent person (*noun*). deadly; violent (*adj.*).
hän ku tuulmahl elidet—vampire (*literally: life-stealer*).
Hän sívamak—Beloved.
hany—clod; lump of earth.
hisz—to believe; to trust.
ho—how.
ida—east.
igazág—justice.
irgalom—compassion; pity; mercy.
isä—father (*noun*).
isäntä—master of the house.
it—now.
jälleen—again.
jama—to be sick, infected, wounded, or dying; to be near death.
jelä—sunlight; day, sun; light.
jelä keje terád—light sear you (*Carpathian swear words*).
o jelä peje terád—sun scorch you (*Carpathian swear words*).
o jelä peje emnimet—sun scorch the woman. (*Carpathian swear words*).

o jelä peje terád, emni—sun scorch you, woman. (*Carpathian swear words*).
o jelä peje kaik hänkanak—sun scorch them all. (*Carpathian swear words*).
o jelä sielamak—light of my soul.
joma—to be under way; to go.
joŋe—to come; to return.
joŋesz arwa-arvoval—return with honor (*greeting*).
jŏrem—to forget; to lose one's way; to make a mistake.
juo—to drink.
juosz és eläsz—drink and live (*greeting*).
juosz és olen ainaak sielamet jutta—drink and become one with me (*greeting*).
juta—to go; to wander.
jüti—night; evening.
jutta—connected; fixed (*adj.*). to connect; to fix; to bind (*verb*).
k—suffix added after a noun ending in a vowel to make it plural.
kaca—male lover.
kadi—judge.
kaik—all.
kaŋa—to call; to invite; to request; to beg.
kaŋk—windpipe; Adam's apple; throat.
kać3—gift.
kaδa—to abandon; to leave; to remain.
kaδa wäkeva óv o köd—stand fast against the dark (*greeting*).
kalma—corpse; death; grave.
karma—want.
Karpatii—Carpathian.
Karpatii ku köd—liar.
käsi—hand (*noun*).
kaśwa—to own.
keje—to cook; to burn; to sear.
kepä—lesser, small, easy, few.
kessa—cat.
kessa ku toro—wildcat.

kessake—little cat.
kidü—to wake up; to arise (*intransitive verb*).
kim—to cover an entire object with some sort of covering.
kinn—out; outdoors; outside; without.
kinta—fog, mist, smoke.
kislány—little girl.
kislány kuŋenak—little lunatic.
kislány kuŋenak minan—my little lunatic.
köd—fog; mist; darkness; evil (*noun*); foggy, dark; evil (*adj.*).
köd elävä és köd nime kutni nimet—evil lives and has a name.
köd alte hän—darkness curse it (*Carpathian swear words*).
o köd belső—darkness take it (*Carpathian swear words*).
köd jutasz belső—shadow take you (*Carpathian swear words*).
koje—man; husband; drone.
kola—to die.
kolasz arwa-arvoval—may you die with honor (*greeting*).
koma—empty hand; bare hand; palm of the hand; hollow of the hand.
kond—all of a family's or clan's children.
kont—warrior.
kont o sívanak—strong heart (*literally: heart of the warrior*).
ku—who; which; that.
kuć3—star.
kuć3ak!—stars! (*exclamation*).
kuja—day, sun.
kuŋe—moon; month.
kule—to hear.
kuly—intestinal worm; tapeworm; demon who possesses and devours souls.
kulke—to go or to travel (on land or water).
kulkesz arwa-arvoval, ekäm—walk with honor, my brother (*greeting*).
kulkesz arwaval—joŋesz arwa arvoval—go with glory—return with honor (*greeting*).
kumpa—wave (*noun*).
kuńa—to lie as if asleep; to close or cover the eyes in a game of hide-and-seek; to die.

kunta—band, clan, tribe, family.
kutenken—however.
kuras—sword; large knife.
kure—bind; tie.
kutni—to be able to bear, carry, endure, stand, or take.
kutnisz ainaak—long may you endure (*greeting*).
kuulua—to belong; to hold.
lääs—west.
lamti (*or* **lamt3)**—lowland; meadow; deep; depth.
lamti ból jüti, kinta, ja szelem—the netherworld (*literally: the meadow of night, mists, and ghosts*).
lańa—daughter.
lejkka—crack, fissure, split (*noun*). To cut; to hit; to strike forcefully (*verb*).
lewl—spirit (*noun*).
lewl ma—the other world (*literally: spirit land*). *Lewl ma* includes *lamti ból jüti, kinta, ja szelem*: the netherworld, but also includes the worlds higher up *En Puwe*, the Great Tree.
liha—flesh.
lõuna—south.
löyly—breath; steam (*related to lewl: spirit*).
ma—land; forest.
magköszun—thank.
mana—to abuse; to curse; to ruin.
mäne—to rescue; to save.
maγe—land; earth; territory; place; nature.
me—we.
meke—deed; work (*noun*). To do; to make; to work (*verb*).
mića—beautiful.
mića emni kuŋenak minan—my beautiful lunatic.
minan—mine; my own (*endearment*).
minden—every, all (*adj.*).
möért?—what for? (*exclamation*).
molo—to crush; to break into bits.
molanâ—to crumble; to fall apart.
mozdul—to begin to move, to enter into movement.

muonì—appoint; order; prescribe; command.
muonìak te avoisz te—I command you to reveal yourself.
musta—memory.
myös—also.
nä—for.
nâbbŏ—so, then.
nautish—to enjoy.
nélkül—without.
nenä—anger.
nó—like; in the same way as; as.
numa—god; sky; top; upper part; highest (*related to the English word: numinous*).
numatorkuld—thunder (literally: sky struggle).
nyelv—tongue.
nyál—saliva; spit (*related to nyelv: tongue*).
ŋamaŋ—this; this one here; that; that one there.
ńiŋ3—worm; maggot.
odam—to dream; to sleep.
odam-sarna kondak—lullaby (*literally: sleep-song of children*).
olen—to be.
oma—old; ancient; last; previous.
omas—stand.
omboće—other; second (*adj.*).
o—the (*used before a noun beginning with a consonant*).
ot—the (*used before a noun beginning with a vowel*).
otti—to look; to see; to find.
óv—to protect against.
owe—door.
päämoro—aim; target.
pajna—to press.
pälä—half; side.
päläfertiil—mate or wife.
palj3—more.
peje—to burn.
peje terád—get burned (*Carpathian swear words*).

pél—to be afraid; to be scared of.
pesä (n.)—nest (*literal*); protection (*figurative*).
pesä (v.)—nest (*literal*); protect (*figurative*).
pesäd te engemal—you are safe with me.
pesäsz jeläbam ainaak—long may you stay in the light (*greeting*).
pide—above.
pile—to ignite; to light up.
pirä—circle; ring (*noun*). to surround; to enclose (*verb*).
piros—red.
pitä—to keep; to hold; to have; to possess.
pitäam mustaakad sielpesäambam—I hold your memories safe in my soul.
pitäsz baszú, piwtäsz igazáget—no vengeance, only justice.
piwtä—to follow; to follow the track of game; to hunt; to prey upon.
poår—bit; piece.
põhi—north.
pukta—to drive away; to persecute; to put to flight.
pusm—to be restored to health.
pus—healthy; healing.
puwe—tree; wood.
rambsolg—slave.
rauho—peace.
reka—ecstasy; trance.
rituaali—ritual.
sa—sinew; tendon; cord.
sa4—to call; to name.
saa—arrive, come; become; get, receive.
saasz hän ku andam szabadon—take what I freely offer.
salama—lightning; lightning bolt.
sarna—words; speech; magic incantation (*noun*). To chant; to sing; to celebrate (*verb*).
sarna kontakawk—warriors' chant.
śaro—frozen snow.
sas—shoosh (*to a child or baby*).
saγe—to arrive; to come; to reach.

siel—soul.
sieljelä isäntä—purity of soul triumphs.
sisar—sister.
sív—heart.
sív pide köd—love transcends evil.
sívad olen wäkeva, hän ku piwtä—may your heart stay strong, hunter (*greeting*).
sívamet—my heart.
sívam és sielam—my heart and soul.
sívdobbanás—heartbeat (*literal*); rhythm (*figurative*).
sokta—to mix; to stir around.
soŋe—to enter; to penetrate; to compensate; to replace.
susu—home; birthplace (*noun*). At home (*adv.*).
szabadon—freely.
szelem—ghost.
taka—behind; beyond.
tappa—to dance; to stamp with the feet; to kill.
te—you.
Te kalma, te jama ńiŋ3kval, te apitäsz arwa-arvo—You are nothing but a walking maggot-infected corpse, without honor.
Te magköszunam nä ŋamaŋ kać3 taka arvo—Thank you for this gift beyond price.
ted—yours.
terád keje—get scorched (*Carpathian swear words*).
tõd—to know.
Tõdak pitäsz wäke bekimet mekesz kaiket—I know you have the courage to face anything.
tõdhän—knowledge.
tõdhän lõ kuraset agbapäämoroam—knowledge flies the sword true to its aim.
toja—to bend; to bow; to break.
toro—to fight; to quarrel.
torosz wäkeval—fight fiercely (*greeting*).
totello—obey.
tsak—only.

tuhanos—thousand.
tuhanos löylyak türelamak saγe diutalet—a thousand patient breaths bring victory.
tule—to meet; to come.
tumte—to feel; to touch; to touch upon.
türe—full, satiated, accomplished.
türelam—patience.
türelam agba kontsalamaval—patience is the warrior's true weapon.
tyvi—stem; base; trunk.
uskol—faithful.
uskolfertiil—allegiance; loyalty.
varolind—dangerous.
veri—blood.
veri-elidet—blood-life.
veri ekäakank—blood of our brothers.
veri isäakank—blood of our fathers.
veri olen piros, ekäm—literally: blood be red, my brother; figuratively: find your lifemate (*greeting*).
veriak ot en Karpatiiak—by the blood of the Prince (*literally: by the blood of the great Carpathian; Carpathian swear words*).
veridet peje—may your blood burn (*Carpathian swear words*).
vigyáz—to love; to care for; to take care of.
vii—last; at last; finally.
wäke—power; strength.
wäke beki—strength; courage.
wäke kaδa—steadfastness.
wäke kutni—endurance.
wäke-sarna—vow; curse; blessing (*literally: power words*).
wäkeva—powerful.
wara—bird; crow.
weńća—complete; whole.
wete—water (*noun*).